Nathaniel's Call

Nathaniel's Call

Robert John Andrews

For My Children

Prologue

Farewell mother you may never
Press me to your heart again,
But, oh, you'll not forget me mother;
Off I'm numbered with the slaine.
"Just Before the Battle Mother," by George Root

Her son was dead. Some said she should be proud. She didn't feel proud. Just vacant. And useless. And tired. So very tired. The tightness sometimes made it hard to breathe. Not a second went by without her thinking about him or picturing his face or seeing him in her mind working alongside his father, although the memory of his voice seemed to be melting away, like a dream you try to remember when you wake up or like sugar spooned into tea.

Her son was dead. This evening's service was the first she had attended since the letter had arrived. It felt better to stay away from others. They had no right to share her grief. Yet they tried. She hated that. When she did visit town, a few would step across the dirt road to avoid talking with her, and that pained her. Worse were those who would rush up to her to try to embrace her unyielding shoulders and sympathize with her. That pained her even more. Especially, she wanted to stay away from him. The last thing she wanted was him talking to her.

Going out in public also meant looking at herself in the mirror and she refused to look into the mirror anymore. The anger had creased age into her young face.

Did she return because she thought she should? But she was not a woman easily governed by shoulds. Maybe she wanted them to see what it really felt like. Let them now boast about the nobility of the cause. Look at me and see. Let him see what it really means.

Perhaps deep inside in that place where her son still lived she felt there was nowhere else to go, even if it meant listening to him preach. That she could try to tolerate. His voice she could try to ignore while listening instead for the words within. They still mattered. Those words she still needed to hear, even if she could not sing anymore. The hymns stabbed her like cold steel. Is that how her Philip died? Cold steel? The letter never said. The letter said so little even as it told her everything. Her son was dead.

Nor could she sit in the familiar pew. There was that notch cut in the bench when she caught Philip trying to carve his initials with his penknife during a particularly long sermon. There was that page in the Psalter, torn by clumsy little hands when he stood on the pew trying to hold the book for his father. Nobody, she noticed, sat in that pew tonight.

Why she allowed him to drive her home tonight, she couldn't really say. She simply obliged her pastor without a word, letting him sit on the bench seat beside her. She let him hold the reins even though her horse knew the way home by habit.

Chapter One

Lost and Found

How dull it is to pause, to make an end,
To rust unburnished, not to shine in use!
As though to breathe were life.
"Ulysses," Alfred, Lord Tennyson

He heard the camp before he saw it. Boisterous. Raucous. Men shouting. Some singing. Others laughing. Sounds of cheering. Sounds of fist fights. Plenty of curses. Wagon wheels creaking. The rattle of pots and pans. Mules braying. Horses galloping. Dogs barking. Gunfire echoing in succession off in the distance. The commotion of thousands of men thrust into each other's company in a confined space with little to keep them occupied except each other's noisy company.

Before he heard the camp he smelled it. Mud, wet wool, and excrement.

They rolled through the crossroads of a small village, which once boasted a tavern, church, and several homes, all now abandoned by their original inhabitants and occupied by the army. Each structure had been converted to other purposes, excepting the tavern. From there they entered the Division encampment where tedious acts of apparent routine achieved a frenzy of obsession. A caisson buzzed around the slower wagons, forcing his wagon into the ditch by the side of the

1

pike. Nathaniel clung onto the bench with both hands, terrified about being jerked into the muck. "Pog mo thoin," his driver swore after them, more out of habit than Irish anger. With a 'fhluck,' the driver spat an impressive stream of tobacco juice before withdrawing again into silence. The rain dropped from the brim of Nathaniel's hat onto his knees. Stubbled trunks of felled trees covered vast areas of brown ground. Across the meadows, veined with wheel ruts and worn footpaths, spread hundreds upon hundreds of shelter tents, resembling flocks of seagulls floating on a brown sea. Marked by Regimental flags, wall tents bunched together beneath the few remaining shade trees. An entire group of conical tents sat huddled to the far left, near the edge of the woods. Tents of varied fashion spread out toward the horizon.

Farmhouses and barns, similar to the design of the house and barn near the entrance to the camp, could be spotted in the distance, tucked up near the woods beyond the meadows. Far off, he noticed a block of a thousand men, drawn up into companies, drilling on the worn incline of a hill. They marched in columns of four, moving in a mass at the echoing sounds of bugle and drum. The mass formed attacking lines, two ranks deep. It reminded him when, as a boy, he use to toy with his mother's pearl necklace on her marble top dresser. How, with a simple push, he could adjust the string of pearls to form a new shape. "What is the string," Nathaniel quizzed aloud, "that holds these men in formation?" The driver next to him spat, the spittle dribbling into his beard.

Nathaniel's nose wrenched him to a new direction.

Hundreds of men flowed to and from the line of trench latrines on the far right, those exiting were adjusting their trouser suspenders. Next to the latrines stood a large tent. A yellow flag bearing a green 'H' waved outside the entrance.

Deeper into the congestion of camp the wagons creaked until the rambling wagon train halted in front a small log house. The agent from the first wagon slid from his bench onto the ground with a squish and slurp of mud, and entered the building. He came out several minutes later accompanied by a Captain who proceeded to inspect the wagon train. The first agent, after mumbling something through his beard to the agent in the second wagon, stepped back up onto his seat. The Captain returned to the door of the log house and waved them on. They lurched forward, the trailing wagons creaking each in turn.

The agent in the second wagon turned around, took off his hat, shook the water from it, and called back to Nathaniel, pointing toward a stone farm house at the upper side of the meadow. "We're heading there. Storage in the barn. Your unit should be on the way there." Nathaniel waved back in appreciation.

"By the way pastor," the agent turned around and called again: "Welcome to the Army of the Potomac." Nathaniel's driver leaned over the side of the wagon and spat a cheekfull of tobacco juice, Honey Dew fine cut, with a velocity that splattered the wagon wheel.

Everywhere he looked there were clumps of men seated around pots hung by bent bayonets over fires. A wet mutt curled up against a soldier palming a mug, the brim of his kepi shielding his face. The campfires struggled vainly to keep aflame despite the cold drizzle. Beneath arbors of dripping evergreen men sat on wobbly boxes and played dominoes. One soldier rested against his tent pole and plucked the strings of a miniature guitar. Each clump of soldiers sported an array of dress: homespun or blue blouses, brown trousers or red pantaloons, straw hats or dark blue kepis. Other soldiers busied themselves sewing patches onto their uniforms or trying to repair the holed soles of their heavy brogans. Beyond the tents Nathaniel saw and heard a group of men in a circle cheering loudly as two half-naked men wrestled by what appeared to be very few rules of sportsmanship. Far more puzzling were the variety of women sauntering about camp, hoisting their skirts above the mud.

Wiping the drizzle from his eyes, Nathaniel spotted the Regimental flag of the First Reserves flapping limply from a drizzling gust of wind. The wagon train rolled into this section of tents. Nathaniel began eagerly looking about for familiar faces. But, unlike the Regiments they passed through on their way through the encampment, very few men in this unit were visible. The place seemed deserted. Few men lounged about, and none of them in uniform.

The wagons jostled into an open area toward the center of the section. There Nathaniel spotted a large assembly of soldiers. They stood in formation, attentive to some kind of activity in front of them. The men were silent. A strange sound of slapping and grunting came from the area, similar to the sound of reins smacking a mule's rump. Nathaniel rose from the wagon bench and looked over the collection of the formed Companies. A man, his head shaved, stripped to his trousers, his muslin blouse hanging from his belt, was tied by the wrists facing a wagon wheel. A bayonet had been tied crosswise in his mouth as a gag. A burly Sergeant flogged him with heavy strokes, the sergeant's belly heaving with each swing. The Sergeant, with a bored expression, wielded a short handled

4

whip, rhythmically flogging the man's back in three quarter time. A waltz of whipping. The leather straps tore into the man's flesh. Blood splattered and oozed. The silent teamster stayed seated and 'fhlucked' another ounce of black liquid.

◎◎◎

A man dressed in dark blue trousers and a brown stained blue jacket relaxed against a small tree on the fringe of the crowd. A knapsack was slung over his shoulder. A sagging red plume stuck out from the band of his wide brimmed blue hat. He turned away from the spectacle and noticed a man dressed in black standing on a wagon bench behind the crowd. The man tossed the twig he had been twisting in his hands to the ground and angled his way through the ranks and files toward the wagon train. He approached the wagon from the side and clutched one of the spokes of the muddy wheel. "Well, hell, it's about time. Nice of you to arrive when we are at our best." Reaching up to slap Nathaniel's shiny boots, he smiled at his best friend. "Nice boots."

"A gift from my congregation. They had a feeling I'd be doing a lot of walking." Leaping to the muddy ground, Nathaniel embraced him. Valentine O'Rourke smelled of mildew and whisky. They pounded each other hard on their backs with open hands. Several soldiers in the rear rank turned around, only to get ordered to face front by their Sergeant. Valentine caught the attention of the nearest Sergeant and called him over. "Hunt, come here." The huge man shook his head and muttered a curse, though his words were muffled by his full black beard. After getting his orders from Valentine, the Provost Sergeant returned to the rank and selected five men by

5

jabbing them in their backs with the butt of his Sharps carbine and nodding toward the wagon. "Shift your ass," was all he said. Valentine elbowed Nathaniel. "Better than watching a flogging." Nathaniel pointed out his baggage to the five men.

"Now where do you think you're going to put all that gear?" Valentine complained with feigned annoyance. "This ain't the University, Nate. Good God, I thought the scriptures said something about how you fellows were supposed to travel light."

With sheepish grin, Nathaniel tried to justify himself: "Well, you know Alice. Also the congregation was quite generous. Some of this is...well, actually a lot of this is for their boys. Besides, there's a few things in there for you."

"Fine, fine, for now," Valentine groaned. "We'll sort it all out later." Valentine looked at the five waiting soldiers. "You fellows," he commanded, "try if you can to cart this damn mercantile store to my tent. And don't drop it in the mud." They moved to the rear of the wagon. "This is why God invented Privates," Valentine said. The teamster slid Nathaniel's trunks into the soldier's hands.

Nathaniel looked up at the teamster. "Much thanks for all the help. God bless."

The mute teamster finally spoke: "Luck, preacher. You'll need it." With another 'fhluck,' the wagon lurched to catch up with the rest of the train.

Nathaniel screwed up his face as he waved toward the punishment. "Is this usual?"

"Poor, stupid sot. Got caught pinching some tobacco and a few dollars from a tent mate." Valentine stroked his trimmed goatee. "You have your work cut out for you. A lot of damned souls need saving around here." Valentine grinned as he

6

nodded toward the Company forced to watch the man lashed to the wheel. "You have your work, and," he paused dramatically, "so do I." Valentine tapped his medical knapsack. "I get to clean the bastard up. Or at least I have to make sure my Steward bandages him up. Then I'll catch you up. Wait for me, please; there's a few things we need to go over. My tent is over there. That'a way." Valentine pointed down the row of wall tents. "Follow those good fellows. Nobody else wanted to share a tent with a preacher, so you're once again stuck with me. Or is it once again I'm stuck with you?" Valentine shoved Nathaniel in the direction of the tent. "Hurry now, get out of the drizzle. Around here, you learn fast to value dry clothes."

Nathaniel copied where the soldiers stepped and followed them to the wall tent where he began to sort out his luggage. About a half hour later the tent flap opened. Valentine jumped inside and collapsed onto his cot, his muddy boots hanging over the edge. Grinning like a school-boy, Nathaniel pushed the smallest of his trunks under his cot with the heel of his boot and sat facing his friend.

"Well, it's sure busier here with these bucks than treating all the gout of my father's stately and plump friends back in West Chester," Valentine smiled. "Of course, mostly here it's chronic diarrhea and I am damn near out of Ipecacuania. You wouldn't have brought any with you, would you?"

"Don't even know what it is. I did, however, bring this. . ."

Valentine, smelling a present, swung his legs around the cot and sat with his knees almost touching Nathaniel's knees. "It may be a bit cramped, 'specially now, but we'll do fine."

"A little gift from Alice," Nathaniel explained as he reached under his cot. "She told me to tell you it is a bribe to treat me right." He pulled out his trunk, lifted the lid, and removed a small wooden case, which he handed to Valentine. Recognizing the familiar box, Valentine eagerly unlatched the lid and opened it. From the sawdust he pulled out two bottles of Kentucky Bourbon Whisky.

"What a woman you got there, Nate. Valentine fondled the bottles, kissing the labels. "Mind if I toast the lady."

"She'd insist."

Valentine cut the wax seal with a knife pulled from his coat pocket and unplugged the cork. "God, I love women," Valentine gushed. Then, saluting Nathaniel by raising the bottle, he tilted the neck toward his lips for a deep, slow draught. The amber liquid pooled in his mouth. He kept his head tilted back as he savored the glow draining into his chest. With a deep, exquisite sigh of pleasure he slammed the cork back into the bottle. "Must save for a rainier day." He teased the bottle toward Nathaniel. "Unless you'd like a taste, my abstemious friend."

"I'll have you know I have brought my own stock of intoxicants." Nathaniel rummaged through his bag and pulled out a rolled woolen shawl. He flipped it across his cot, letting the brown bottle of sherry roll toward the end of the mattress.

"You're joking, right?"

Nathaniel amiably rewrapped the bottle of sherry in the shawl and stored it back in his bag, which he pushed back under his cot with his heel.

Valentine jumped up and walked over to his writing desk. He pulled out from under a pile of papers a package wrapped in linen and handed it to Nathaniel. "Well, here, I've got something for you. An early Christmas present for your wee lasses back home."

Unwrapping the linen in his lap, Nathaniel held up two small oak carvings: one of a dove at flight, the other of a sleeping cat. "These are marvelous. Beautiful."

"Got to keep the men busy at hospital. Some have quite a talent for these things."

"The girls will treasure them. Thank you."

"No, I thank you," Valentine replied, patting the box next to his leg.

Nathaniel waited. He checked his silver watch. "Here, you haven't seen them for some time. My beauties." Nathaniel, opening the lid with a flick, held his watch out toward his friend.

He took it, paused, and gazed at the painting of the girls. "You are a lucky man."

◎◎◎

Only three weeks ago Nathaniel had stood with them at the train station at Penningtonville. Two men from the freight station dashed over in the rain to help them unload his three trunks, one box, and two bags onto the covered platform. The congregation, with an intuitive consensus, respected the family's privacy. Nor were there any bugles. No banners. No speeches. The heavy rainfall further encouraged the privacy of the good-byes. Their morning featured none of the drums nor waving flags that heralded the embarkation of the boys turned soldiers of Company C.

It was a soggy, dreary autumn morning. The fat raindrops fell from gray clouds, crowning on the wooden platform beyond the protection of the overhanging roof of the station. No fanfare of farewell. Simply a wife, daughters, a grandfather,

9

and a border collie gathered inside the station house bidding love and tears. Margaret chased Jenny, who pranced and yelped and, crouching, tried to herd Margaret back to the bench. Penelope, clutching her mother's hand, steadied herself, then toddled toward the low windows to look for the locomotive.

The station master had hesitated before he intruded. "Reverend McKenna. Would you be kind enough to speak with me for a moment. Alone please."

Nathaniel followed the stationmaster outside onto the wet platform. The station master glanced around the platform cautiously, afraid of prying eyes. "Pastor," he confided, "just before dawn one of the Smallwood boys ran over and gave me this package. He said that he was told to tell me to be sure to deliver it to you privately before the train arrived. She'll be along soon. The boy said that all I am able to tell you is that it simply is a gift from a friend."

Nathaniel took the soft package from the station master, who immediately returned inside and headed toward his office. Nathaniel opened the package, and, untying the paper, discovered it contained a linen money belt and an envelope. He opened the envelope first. The note inside contained a carefully printed list of seven names complete with descriptions of their locations. Three in Maryland, the rest in Virginia, one even located in Richmond. A message was written at the bottom of the note: *'You may find these Friends a blessing.'*

Shoving the note and envelope into his waistcoat pocket, he looked up through the rain at the stone farmhouse on the hill above the railroad station. Nathaniel was among those few in town who knew about the tunnel that led from the farmhouse toward the quarry located on the east side of Mount Zion Hill.

On seven occasions, Nathaniel had played his part. A faint light glowed from the second floor windows. Nathaniel squeezed the money belt. Each of the three compartments of the belt bulged. Nathaniel unfastened one of the buttons and gasped. He quickly counted at least fifty dollars in small bills. Nathaniel glanced around. He buttoned up the pocket. Nathaniel guessed the money was intended for uses other than his own, for some better use. But for what? he wondered. He re-wrapped the belt in the paper and carried the package back inside the station house. Father and wife avoided inquiring. Nathaniel joined the station master inside his small office. "Please now, with your permission, if I may..." The man exited and Nathaniel pulled off his suspenders, loosed his waistcoat and shirt, and wrapped the money belt about his waist, tightening it snug so as for it not to be too visible under his waistcoat.

Alice cocked her head to the side as he returned to the waiting room: "You look as if you've gained a few pounds."

"All is well," he said, silencing her with a kiss on her lips. He next walked over to his father who was seated in the corner of the station house. Nathaniel confided to him that there were some letters in an envelope in the top drawer of his desk; they were to be opened only if necessary. His father understood.

"Well, if all the mystery and surprises are over, I have one more," Alice announced. "Let our gift be the last." She beckoned to Margaret, who skipped eagerly to the satchel her grandfather had set down at his feet. Margaret pulled out a small box and rushed over to her Poppa, who rested on one knee in front of his daughter.

"And what is this?"

"Open it, Poppa. Open it. Quick, before the train arrives." Margaret spun her body in a circle, her dress twirling. "I think I hear it. Trains scare me. Quick, Poppa, o' quick, please."

Penelope teetered over to help her Poppa open the special box. He let her tear away at the white tissue paper with her small, chubby, clumsy fingers.

Inside, wrapped in a square of linen, he found a silver pocket watch attached by a silver chain to a blue cameo.

Alice leaned down over him. "It is from all of us, my darling."

"It's beautiful."

"Your father purchased the watch in Princeton." Alice wrapped her arms around him. "You never did own a decent timepiece."

Nathaniel, still kneeling level with his babies, held the watch in his palm, letting the chain and the cameo dangle. With his other hand he lifted up the blue cameo. He peered around and up at his wife, his eyes wide and moist. "This is yours, Alice. I gave this to you when we married. Why?"

Alice knelt also and pressed against him, their heads touching. "I had a jeweler in Lancaster make it into a fob. I didn't have a picture of me to give you. I thought some remembrance would be nice. Now open the watch. Open it, Nathan."

Nathaniel pressed the release with his thumb. The smooth silver cover sprang open. The glass glistened, the hour and minute hands pointed at the elegant Roman numerals. The second hand moved in its smaller orbit. Inside the lid of the watch case was inserted a minute portrait of Margaret and Penelope. Nathaniel pressed his eyes tight to capture his tears. He held the watch out to his daughters, showing them the picture, "Look at the two most beautiful girls in the world. Do you see them?"

Margaret barged in front of her little sister, "Yes, Poppa, it's us. It's us. We are so pretty, aren't we?"

"The most beautiful. The most beautiful in the world."

Penelope tried to grab the watch in her chubby hands so she could see too. Her Poppa held it in front of her face so she could look at the painting. She kept trying to grab it. Poppa diverted her. "Here, listen. Quiet now, and listen. You can't hear when you're busy talking." He cupped the ticking watch against Penelope's ear. Penelope giggled and bounced. Jenny pushed her nose between them and sniffed the watch.

Margaret touched her father's arm. "Me too. My turn. My turn."

"Of course. Listen now, sweetheart." Nathaniel pressed it against her ear. Margaret, ever intent, listened to the ticking watch. He lowered it and showed the watch face to her. "Can you tell me what time it is?"

Another sound startled them, this one painful, as the whistle of the steam engine announced itself west of the village. Penelope jumped in a panic and fell into her mother's arms. Two more long, warning whistles followed. His father put his hand on his son's shoulder. Nathaniel wrapped his arms around his daughters, telling them to be good to their mother, kissed them again, then stood to hold his Alice for as many seconds as time allowed.

Her lips touched his ear as she whispered: "Write as often as you can."

Those last kisses were the most difficult.

◎◎◎

"Alice keeps waiting for you to settle down, you know," said Nathaniel.

"You, my friend, stole the last good one available," Valentine said with a silent twinge of regret, quickly followed by a wink. "Which leaves, I suppose, the rest for me." Valentine paused a little bit longer, admiring the small painting. He again stroked his goatee, followed by a flash of a grin. "Good thing they take after their mother." He handed the open watch back to his friend. Valentine drummed both hands against the wooden frame of his cot.

Nathaniel caught his eye. "All right, Val, what's the matter?"

Valentine grunted. "Get yourself comfortable before I throw you to the wolves. You do remember what I tried to teach you back at University, don't you? That there are only two types of people in the world: them that skin and them that get skinned. It's all a skin game. Anyhow, I know you want to meet your boys and I'd like to introduce you around the Regiment, but," he paused, "we got a wee problem." Valentine scratched his chin, distractedly inspecting himself for lice. "Roberts ain't here no more."

"Nobody told me that in Washington City," Nathaniel said with annoyance, blowing air through his mustache. "For that matter, nobody told me anything. That's why I arrived with the Christian Commission. It took my father's friend, Pastor Gurley to arrange that."

"Say, how is your father?" Valentine side-stepped.

"He's fine. Misses mom. Covering for me in the pulpit will be good for him—Princeton Seminary let him take this as a sabbatical—plus being around his grand-daughters. Well, Alice will fatten him up. It's good that he's feeling useful again. It's his way of contributing. I am grateful for him and all his

14

connections. I tell you, if it weren't for Gurley I would have been lost. I had to stay with him for two weeks trying to get my papers in orders. He pulled a few strings for me. Back in Washington nobody seems to know anything. The Christian Commission seems to be the only ones aware of what to do."

"No surprise to us. Nobody sees the big picture. Nobody knows what's going on. A bloody circus. There have been so many changes up there in Washington City, what would they know about who's in command down here? The last word was that we belong to something called the Left Grand Division, under Franklin. First Corps."

"Maybe I should have asked Lincoln when I had the chance. Gurley introduced me to him after church two Sunday's ago."

Valentine abruptly bent toward Nathaniel. His voice lowered as he continued. "Listen, you got skinned. I tried to reach you before you left, that is, when I could, but by then I figured you were already on your way. I hoped Alice might get word to you. But hell, you should have read about his resignation in the papers back home anyway. Roberts got called back to Harrisburg by Governor Curtin early this month."

"We heard nothing," Nathaniel sputtered.

"Must of been in the works for the last couple of months," he added. "Back into politics. He's taken up duties at the Executive Military Department. Bless him, he'd be safer here. At least Bobby Lee shoots you when facing you. So God bless the good Colonel. I'd rather be here." He poked Nathaniel in the chest with his finger. "But you are neither here nor there. Here's the rub: you simply don't have a commission anymore."

"But I have my papers with me," protested Nathaniel, reaching into the inside pocket of his frock coat and pulling out a folded envelope. "My appointment from Roberts and the Governor came in the mail just before I left."

"Let me repeat: even if Governor Curtin did sign it, your papers mean nothing anymore. You can put the paper to better advantage in the latrine, because your commission means nothing. At least not until Bill Talley meets you and approves you. Talley's a solid man, trusty, but far too military."

"But I'm already here. I've come all this way."

Valentine reclined on his cot, his boots again hanging over the edge, his heels tapping his footlocker. "The Colonel, you see, doesn't approve of the need for fellows of your persuasion in our midst. He thinks you chaplains are a waste of good government money that could be better spent on more musket-toting Privates who get shot for me to patch up." Valentine tossed a book at Nathaniel, hitting him on the shoulder. "You fellows, you see, can lose the war for us surely, teaching too much charity of neighbor and all that crap. Hard to go out and club your neighbor to a bloody pulp after listening to the gospel, don't you think?" Abruptly, Valentine swung his legs around. "I'll take you to the Colonel's tent, but then I got to leave you there alone and check on our thief and a roomful of dysentery."

"I'll take the Colonel instead."

"Good choice."

16

Chapter Two

The First Reserves

If amid the din of battle,
Nobly you should fall,
Far away from those who love you,
None to hear your call.
Who would whisper words of comfort,
Who would soothe your pain?
Ah! the many cruel fancies,
Ever in my brain.
"When This Cruel War is Over," Charles Carroll Sawyer

Within the half hour, Nathaniel found himself standing in front of the Colonel's table rubbing the front of his muddy boots against the back of his trousers. Should I stand at attention? he asked himself. Nathaniel held the wide brim of his black felt hat between his thumbs and fingers, nervously turning the hat in circles. Colonel William Talley tossed the commission documents aside and frowned at the chaplain-candidate. The last time Nathaniel felt this exposed, this awkward, this inadequate, was the day he sought his Presbytery's approval for ordination, when the veteran pastors spent forty five minutes examining him from the floor, dissecting his theological viewpoints, strutting their scholarship in front of their colleagues.

"Reverend McKenna." The Colonel's voice turned caustic. "You're not one of those 'one cent by God' chaplains are you? Goddamn misfits. Ran the one out in the Regiment next to us. Thought he was entitled to profit off the men's mail with his personal surcharge. Goddamn hypocrites. His 'handling fee' he said. I swear he fancied his spirits more than the Holy Spirit." Talley glanced up to see if Nathaniel's eyes betrayed offense.

"No sir. I've heard of them. My own character speaks for itself," he said with a dogged earnestness. Nathaniel immediately regretted what he had said. A little less proud, please, a little less defensive, he reminded himself silently.

"Does it now?" Talley replied with squared jaw.

Nathaniel coughed. "What I mean, sir, is that I'm prepared to do my duty, Colonel. I've read *The Military Handbook and Soldier's Manual*. Cost me 25 cents. I've also developed some fortunate contacts with the Christian Commission. Plus, with the support back home, I hope to obtain some necessary goods for the men, sir." Nathaniel, unthinking, set his hat on Talley's desk. "I'll do my job, sir."

The Colonel held up the palm of his hand, choosing to ignore the black hat covering his stack of reports. Nathaniel stopped talking. Nathaniel was unaccustomed to following orders. Roles had been reversed. The Colonel leaned forward on his elbows. "Why exactly are you here, Reverend?"

Nathaniel suddenly wanted to burst out in laughter and tell the Colonel to go ask Alice for the answer, but instead he rubbed his forehead with his palm, then nervously jerked on the ends of his moustache. Hmmp. Why indeed? His face reddened. Alice, his mind recalled in an instant, telescoping time, told me it was because I was bored. That I hated missing out. Worse, because I was jealous. That stung. But she had a way of recognizing when I had made up my mind even before I knew I had. What did she say to me? That I had been restless for years? I tried to tell her it was because of a sense of duty. She never did like me patronizing her. She had read the letter Valentine sent me and she said I envied him. That I always had.

Perhaps.

But Nathaniel also knew there was another reason, for he never did tell Alice what Jane said to him that night she let him visit with her. That night weeks ago.

◎◎◎

He was glad Jane Reynolds had returned to church. After her two months absence it was a positive sign that she was healing and accepting God's will. It wasn't the Sunday morning service, but still it showed progress. His prayers and pithy words of comfort must have helped draw her back to God. God is good.

They rode home from church together after services that night. It was awkward but he was pleased she allowed him to comfort her. He handed the reins of the carriage over to her handyman. He followed her into her house. Nathaniel stood for a minute waiting to be invited to sit at the table, then, with no invitation offered, decided to squat on a child's stool near the fireplace. The bottom of his frock coat bunched on the floor.

He lifted the palms of his hands to the warmth of her hearth. The flames melted away the ache in his knuckles caused by the chilly October night. A pile of cut wood from an old apple tree was stacked to right of the fireplace. He tossed a damp twig into the fire. Out of habit, he slipped his fingers into his waistcoat pocket searching for his pocket watch, but immediately removed them. He patted the empty pocket twice, muttering: "Got to get it fixed someday." The clock on the mantle chimed the hour. The last strike faded, leaving him listening to the rhythm of the pendulum and mechanical click of the gears. The damp twig popped in the flames, shooting a small spark near his foot. With the toe of his old shoe he wiped out the spark. He watched the flames flicker, their light shifting the shadows in the stonework of the hearth. Absentmindedly, he plucked a straw from a small broom hanging at the edge of the fireplace next to the poker and traced the crevices between the stones.

Jane Reynolds carried a tray from the kitchen and placed it on an oval cherry table beside her rocking chair. She poured and handed Nathaniel a cup of tea. The steam rose in a swirl. He thanked her with a benevolent, paternal smile. She nodded and then settled into her rocking chair. They sipped their tea for while in silence, listening to the crackle of the small fire, the tick of the clock, and the creak of her rocker on wooden floorboards.

Jane Reynolds slowed her rocking. She silently pursed her lips to the teacup and sipped a teaspoon of tea, then said over the lip of the tea cup: "I suppose, Pastor McKenna, you want to see the letter they sent."

Before he answered, Jane Reynolds set the cup heavily on the tray. The china cup rattled against the saucer. Standing, she reached over to the mantle. The letter leaned against the clock. She took the letter, removed it from the envelope, unfolded it, and handed it to her pastor. She sat down again and resumed rocking.

Weighing the letter in his hands, he could guess what the official letter reported about her Philip. Colleagues had shared their tales of reading similar letters from their parishioners. They all sounded alike. Now it had become his turn. It was such a burden that he and his colleagues bore. Nathaniel tossed the straw into the fire, stood up from the stool, and turned the elegant script toward the light of fireplace.

Nathaniel held the letter up to the light glowing from the fireplace. Nathaniel tried to see beyond the words of the formal script: *fiercely contested fight... mortally wounded...with honor...deepest condolences.*

He noted the handsome signature. R. Biddle Roberts. Nathaniel lowered the letter. Pastor McKenna offered a casual remark, feeling the need for words: "You may remember, my best friend from University is the Surgeon in that Regiment." He regretted his remark immediately. "At least your son," he said in an attempt to correct himself, "never knew of his father's death. There must be some comfort in that Philip never received your letter about your husband John. He was a fine man."

Jane Reynolds offered no response except for a slight tightening of her upper lip, which Nathaniel might have noticed had he been paying attention to her.

He tried a different tack to invite her to unburden her sorrow. "You must know that the whole town is keeping you in prayer," he offered generously. "With John's death and now Philip's, it must be terribly painful. So soon," he continued, trusting in his words. "Yes, it must be difficult." Nathaniel always believed it healing for him to mention the names of the

21

deceased. Had he been looking at her face rather than at his shoes he might have seen that her tight lip relaxed into a wry smile.

Jane Reynolds raised her hands as if to say something, then lowered them into her lap. She closed her eyes and breathed several heavy breaths. The rocking chair creaked. Nathaniel sat down again and waited for her to speak. She didn't.

He reached toward her, reaching to fold her hands between his. She kept her hands in her lap. Nathaniel clasped his hands together pretending that that is what he wanted to do anyway. Then gesturing as he spoke, he raised his right hand. "Jane, we must hold fast to the Lord's promises." His emphatic, preaching voice crept into his quiet counsel. "You know how necessary it is, especially now, for you to believe with all your heart and soul. He is our Good Shepherd. Our Rock and our Salvation. It is not for us to comprehend the purposes and mysteries of God. What is done is done. Let us accept what God ordains. We must trust in the will of God, especially in these dark hours and dreadful days."

The rocker stopped rocking. "Oh, I have faith, Pastor McKenna," she said as she rose and walked toward the lowered drop-leaf of the walnut secretary upon which a thick Bible sat open. "I have faith, pastor. You wish me to understand so I will believe." She touched the Bible with her fingertips before she turned to face him. "How dare you," she accused.

Startled, he looked up.

She saw that she had surprised him. That felt good. It also felt freeing for her to finally speak. "Every night I read John's favorite Psalms from our family Bible. Oh yes, I have faith, pastor." Jane Reynolds turned a page and traced the verses with her finger. "We three would sit at the table after supper and read passages. On Sunday we often discussed your sermon. Philip learned so much from you. I daresay you have no idea how intently he listened to everything you said. He was so impressed by you." She stroked a page of the Bible with the back of her fingers. "And John...," her voice trembled and faded for a moment, then, tapping into her anger, found a renewed vigor. "You saw him that day after worship—John felt so proud signing his son's enlistment consent." Jane turned another page of the Bible. "Yes, pastor, you need not fear about me or my faith. I still believe in God. I trust God."

Nathaniel felt three foot tall, like a school-boy sitting on a stool in the corner of a classroom.

With indignation mixed with pity, she looked down at Nathaniel. "Forgive me for saying this, pastor, but I now have my only son buried in some grave far away. I don't even know where he was buried..."

Nathaniel interrupted: "Would you like us to plan some ceremony for him?"

She ignored him. "...and I don't know what words were said over him." Her voice smoothed into an indictment. "Don't you dare tell me about how I should believe in God. I believe in God." Her eyes were ice cold. "It is you I no longer trust." She turned her back to him. "Please leave my home." She spoke no more. Her son was dead.

Nathaniel swallowed the last drops of his tea in silence, listening only to the sputter of the fire and the fluting of wind across the lip of the chimney. He tasted tea leaves in his mouth. He rose to leave. She didn't move. Her hand remained resting on her Bible. As he walked by her he began to reach his palm out toward her shoulder, but hesitated and returned his hand to fumble with his coat buttons. He bundled himself against the cold, let himself out the front door without a good-bye, and prepared for the long walk home over Mount Zion, taking Newport Pike back to town.

Nathaniel paused on Jane Reynolds' porch. He breathed steadily through his nostrils. His mind told him to go back into her house, defend himself, and help her deal with her grief, but a deeper pity for her displaced his annoyance at her misdirected anger. Better would be for him to forgive her. Yes, he would forgive her.

After turning his collar up against the wind, he thrust both hands into his pockets. Through the ripped lining and torn pockets of the old coat his left hand held onto his right wrist, tightening the coat around his body. The cold air made him blink several times. Through his nostrils he drew deeply the crisp, night air and the aroma of the fruitwood from the fireplace inside. His nostrils cleared themselves of the mustiness of indoors. The wide aroma of autumn was welcome. His eyes adjusted to the dark and starlight. According to the Almanac, the full Harvest moon would shine in two weeks. Growing up in Princeton his father often took him for long strolls at night through the University grounds. His father would point out the various constellations and tell their story.

Looking east across the farming valley toward the cluster of homes in the tiny hamlet the locals called Little Boston, he watched the white smoke rise a few feet from the top of the stone chimneys, then, suddenly, with every erratic gust, the smoke was smeared across the sky, the way a rag sweeps away chalk on a worn blackboard. The edges of his great coat whipped against his knees. The bones of his hands begin to ache again. Nathaniel urged himself: "I better hurry. Supper will be waiting." He stared back at Jane Reynolds's darkened door, half expecting her to rush out and apologize, half dreading it were the door to open.

◎◎◎

Nathaniel's eyes turned away from staring over the top of Colonel Talley's hair. Talley still waited for his answer. "Answer me man," Talley repeated. "Why exactly are you here, Reverend?"

"I'm not sure," he mumbled.

Talley's jaw loosened into a hidden smile before he leaned back and sighed. "An honest man. Well, sometimes none of us are. Sure, that is." Talley refolded the commission papers, slid them back into the envelope, and handed them back to Nathaniel. "I trust you will learn." Talley stood and reached across the desk to shake his hand. "You will find no tabernacle tent here for you. You'll have to make the best of things, the same as everyone else. The Catholics in the ranks can either go worship with the Bucktails or not. Or with you. That is up to them. Doesn't matter to me either way. Understand me, Reverend, unlike some commanders, I will not command attendance at worship." Talley blew his nose into his handkerchief as he walked around the side of his desk. "In addition to your spiritual duties you'll manage the mail as well as notifying the families of the men killed and wounded. Your rumored felicity with words may be better suited for offering expressions of solace and condolence than mine own. Besides, I hate writing the damn things. Other tasks may emerge as necessary. Just do not get in any one's way. Funerals, I may add, are not uncommon. Oh, yes, you have a final duty.

25

Colonel Roberts was fond of invocations and benedictions at dress parades. Out of respect for him, I shall continue the tradition. Do you follow me, Reverend?"

"Yes, Colonel. Quite. I did not expect it to be easy." Nathaniel reached out and gripped Talley's extended hand firmly a second time. "But I hope it will be worthwhile." Nathaniel retrieved his slouch hat from Talley's desk.

Talley escorted him to the door of his tent. "That it won't be easy is guaranteed, I assure you, Reverend. The rest? We'll see. You'll eat with the staff officers." At the door flap, Talley hesitated. "I understand Surgeon O'Rourke is an acquaintance of yours."

"Indeed," he replied eagerly, grateful to have the chance to mention his personal connection with O'Rourke. "We attended the University of Pennsylvania together. He stayed on at Medical School there while I returned home to Princeton Seminary. He stood with me at my wedding. Yes, he is a very fine friend."

"Reverend, it is with some reluctance that I entrust you to his tutoring. I am not sure if knowing him vouches for your character or not. I'll trust the works not the word." The flap of the tent seemed to open on its own from the outside. Talley walked Nathaniel outside into the rain which fell on their bare heads. "General Order Number 91 gives me thirty days to see if you will meet our expectations. May God help you if you prove unfit—I'll have you drummed out of camp so fast you'll feel like a cannonball. Harvey," he yelled, "where are you?"

Captain Harvey appeared from around the corner of the tent.

"My Adjutant will deliver you to Quartermaster Waggoner, then to the sutler. Get yourself fitted out with whatever necessary kit you require for remaining with the Regiment." Talley inspected Nathaniel's clothes. "Some chaplains of our Volunteer Regiments tend to think their honorary rank entitles them to a Captain's uniform and a Captain's shoulder bars. I find such actions presumptuous and pretentious, if not damn silly and damn confusing. At times it is downright dangerous. For the men, I mean. Remember, sir, you are not a combatant. I stand with the opinion of the regular Army: black dress is fine with me. No ornamentation permitted."

"Yes, sir. Thank you, Colonel."

Adjutant Harvey signaled Nathaniel to follow him. Nathaniel breathed a sigh of relief. Lifting his face into the rain, Nathaniel exhaled a deep breath again. Harvey smiled. Side-by-side, Harvey and he walked down the lane between a row of tents.

◎◎◎

Nathaniel sniffed the air the instant he and Valentine entered the officer's mess later that evening. The aroma was familiar. He traced the source to a young Lieutenant puffing a pipe.

Nathaniel sniffed again as he approached the officer. "Black Cavendish?"

"From Demuths," the Lieutenant replied, rising from his bench and turning around. "My compliments." His longish, black hair was slicked back. He sported long sideburns, a trim mustache turned up slightly at the ends, and a tuft of hair beneath his lower lip. The buttons on the Lieutenant's uniform shone. The blue of his jacket and trousers still was bright. "East King Street, Reverend. A splendid tobacconist."

"That's where I get mine, when I can. I'm particularly fond of that blend myself. Not too sweet, none of that cherry flavor, with a slight kick, almost tangy." Nathaniel said as he admired the Lieutenant's pipe, a white pipe carved into the shape of a bear. "That looks like a very fine meerschaum."

"A gift from my father when I mustered into the Regiment."

Valentine intruded: "Nate, permit me to introduce to you Lieutenant William Bear of Lancaster. First Lieutenant Bear of Company B, please meet my one and only respectable friend in the world, the Reverend Nathaniel McKenna. And you thought I was joking. I promised you men that I could deliver someone who could raise the level of our little society." Valentine added with emphasis: "He's not yet the Reverend Doctor McKenna, Th.D., but give him time."

"We must share a bowl full or two, Lieutenant Bear," Nathaniel promised with a warm handshake. He bent toward Bear and hinted: "I've got two tins stored amongst my baggage."

"We shall be friends, indeed. Please, call me Bill," Bear said. Bear then elbowed Valentine. "Thank you, O'Rourke, you just made me win my bet against Talley. Our Colonel bet me an Eagle that you didn't have any respectable friends."

"Well, this group hasn't improved my reputation."

Bear put his hand on Valentine's shoulder. "With your permission, let me introduce our new chaplain to our band of the disreputable, starting with my Captain: Captain Thomas Barton," said Bear, signaling at the man seated across the table. Barton laid his spoon across his plate, stood, and bowed. As they were named, each of the officers at mess rose to greet him. Nathaniel strained to sink in his memory their names and faces. Joseph Drew, Company F, from Delaware County.

Tobias Kauffman, Company I, Cumberland County. Captain Warren Stewart, Company K, from Adams County, along with his friend and Second Lieutenant, Henry Minnigh. Dobson from Phoenixville. Wasson of Company D. Jacob Diffenderfer, the principal musician of the Regimental band. Harvey he recognized.

One First Lieutenant, a short, stout, and muscular man, moved from around the other side of the table to greet Nathaniel personally. He was clean shaven, slightly balding, and older than most of the other officers. Before Bear got the chance, the man introduced himself: "My name's Coates. Joseph Coates. I'm a pipe man myself, 'cept mine's more Missouri meerschaum." Coates chuckled as he pulled from his pocket an old, scorched corn-cob pipe. "We've met before, Reverend. When Presbytery met at my church in Coatesville. There's a few of us Christians here who hold fast to the infallible truth as found in the Westminster Standards."

O'Rourke, leaning against the tent pole, his arms folded, groaned. "God save us."

Seeing Nathaniel dismiss Valentine with a patronizing wave, Coates huffed a a second though cautious chuckle. He then continued: "I've commanded Company C since Sam Dyer got himself promoted and took over the 175th. We've been shy a Captain for a month now." Coates offered his hand. "I do believe you know many of the men in my Company."

Nathaniel pumped Coates's hand eagerly. "I'm very pleased to meet you, Lieutenant. The boys have mentioned your name in their letters home. Yes, I'm very eager to visit my boys. I've brought a few items for them from their folks."

"They'll be pleased. Call me Joe, Reverend. I know many of my men have been looking forward to you joining us. The

29

word has been out for weeks." Coates continued, tugging Nathaniel's elbow. "If I may impose—Corporal Wentz thought you might be persuaded to close the day with a short service of worship. The name of God has been used frequently by the men of late, but, regrettably, not frequently enough in the context of praise." Coates, still clutching Nathaniel's elbow, pulled him toward his spot at the table, "Please dine next to me. I'll fill you in on the men."

Nathaniel looked back at Valentine, who shrugged.

Bear tapped Nathaniel on the shoulder. "We'll have time to share a bowl or two later."

◎◎◎

The bonfire burned and crackled. As First Lieutenant Coates escorted Nathaniel toward the circle, with Valentine trailing, Nathaniel started recognizing familiar faces beneath the bummers and kepis, their faces illuminated by the firelight. Some faces still appeared young, ruddy, boyish. Most faces, however, betrayed a tightness, a weathering about their eyes that had aged them since he had last seen them. Their youthful chubbiness had turned taut, angular. The young boys they sent off one hot day in July with bugle and banner, a year and a half ago, now stood around this circle with flint-like, stoic features. Theirs was a warm greeting, yet a greeting made melancholy when they remembered the missing among them.

"Isaac, good to see you, my boy," Nathaniel called out. "Your mother misses you. You too, Edward! I've a special message for you from your Rebecca, Charles Townsend! How you've filled out. You'll be glad to know your brother's arm is fully healed. He's hoping to enlist his next birthday."

Then Nathaniel spotted Joe Wentz bouncing at the center of the crowd, eagerly waiting to greet his pastor. Nathaniel strolled up to him and placed his hand on his shoulder. "So good to see you." They shook hands. "You've really, grown, Joe—your parents would be so proud. I have so much to tell you." Joe grinned broadly.

Nathaniel dangled the satchel that he had been carrying. "Lots of letters from home," he announced. "And, Joe, I want you to be sure to find time to stop by my tent tomorrow. Your father took me aside before I left and gave me something special he wanted you to have, but he made sure you can only have them on the condition that you promise that you won't let your mother know. You know your father. I guess he thinks you're old enough now. In my trunk are three boxes of very fine cheroots. Good cigars for his boy turned soldier. You know how your mother would not approve.

Coates touched Nathaniel's elbow. "Corporal Wentz, why don't you introduce Chaplain McKenna around to the men." Coates stepped aside.

"That'd be fine, sir. Thank you. But first, with your permission, I've practiced a song for Pastor McKenna. May I?"

"Of course, Corporal," Coates replied. "Let's hear it. Sing out, son."

Joe Wentz stepped closer to the fire. "In your honor, pastor," he said to Nathaniel with a slight bow. He cleared his throat. But Joe didn't sing a hymn from the church hymnbook back home but a song drawn from the campfires.

Joe's tenor—a doleful tenor, rounder and purer than Nathaniel recalled from the choir at church—drew several more soldiers toward the circle. At the end of the song, a voice asked Chaplain McKenna if he would say a few words. Another voice protested. "More singin' less talkin'!"

Nathaniel set the satchel down on the ground. "Well, sorry friend, but I'm a better talker than I am at leading hymns. I'm sure we can get Joe to sing a few more songs. But bide with me for a moment, because I would like the chance to say a few words, especially now that I see how these boys have changed from when we sent them off." Nathaniel traced his fob with his fingertips, trying to recite from an article he once wrote. "Joe and these others already know my beliefs about this war. You others in this Company who don't know me deserve to know also. For me, it's always a matter of right belief. Right convictions. Knowing the difference very clearly about right and wrong. From the very beginning I supported these necessary steps toward war." Nathaniel moved to the center of the circle, nearer the bonfire. He picked up a stick and toyed with it, poking it at the flames. "But you should also be aware that I do not support war." The men of Company C glanced at one another.

Colonel Talley strolled by unnoticed in the shadows.

"Who here does?" Nathaniel continued. "My church hates war but confesses we must practice war, for we see with clarity the moral failure if we neglect this terrible responsibility. It is all very clear." Nathaniel stood at the edge of the flames and looked around at the circle of faces. "Your Colonel asked me earlier this day in his tent, 'Why was I here?' I confess I had to answer him that I didn't know."

The men chuckled lightly. But not all of them.

"But the more I look into your faces, Joe's face—Isaac's, and Charlie's, and you others—the more I am sure why." Nathaniel squatted and played with a branch. "I am here because I am trying not to imagine what would happen were we to allow the South to secede and destroy us all, this Union, this hope and promise God has invested in this young nation. I am here because I trust in the destiny God has willed for our land and people."

Several more faces joined the circle surrounding the fire.

"I suppose I should have told the Colonel I am here because I am trying not to imagine what would happen if we were to ignore it and allow the Rebels to extend that empire of slavery into the future. I am trying not to imagine what sorrows—we here, by you men here, and by your blood which you have already shed—yes, I am trying not to imagine what horrors you are preventing for your children and all children yet born." Nathaniel peered into the fire. The men waited for him to continue. Nathaniel resumed, beginning to choke up as he spoke. "One night almost two months ago, after I heard about the death of Philip, Philip Reynolds, I realized I could no longer bear the alternative of inaction. One of you, now gone, taught me that. I trust the Almighty will show us all the way."

Valentine O'Rourke stood beneath a tall tree beyond the crowd. "I do admire his certainty," he said to himself with a cluck of his tongue. Valentine drifted off alone back toward his tent. Another taste or two of Alice's gift called him.

Late into the night, even after the tattoo beat, Nathaniel huddled near the bonfire, sharing the fire with the young men from his village. Lieutenant Coates allowed the infraction. Nathaniel distributed the letters he had carried in his trunk from home. After devouring them, they talked of home till midnight.

Eventually all but two retired to their tents. The last two left sitting near the dying flames were Joe and Nathaniel. After a long quiet, Nathaniel placed a thick branch back onto the embers and watched the bark begin to kindle.

"It's time, Joe," Nathaniel finally said. "Please tell me how Philip died at South Mountain. I have to know."

Joe listened to the crackling of the fire. Inside his brain, he heard again the gunfire.

Philip never made it to the stone wall.

Joe and Philip had stood next to each other, shoulder to shoulder, when the Colonel barked the order: "Forward." At the command, the bugles blared, drumbeats resounded, the Regiment formed the line of battle, flags were unfurled, and the men themselves formed a massive, moving wall of blue wool and white flesh. The Reserves were to advance against the Rebel position defending the heights and capture the gap. General Seymour wanted the gap. Turner's Gap. One of the men in line quipped: "How the hell do you capture a gap?"

As they marched forward, packed together, shoulder pressing shoulder, the Rebel skirmishers posted behind the stone wall were joined by the sharpshooters. They opened up with a killing fire. The blue wall of men staggered, halted, then replied with their own fire.

Philip's eyes were blackened from the powder, his eyes red and burning from the smoke. The side of his mouth was smudged dark from tearing cartridges with his teeth, his skin chilled from rising panic. The provosts and file closers screamed and cursed from behind the line of battle, warning, threatening, hitting men in the back with the flat part of their swords. Joe shivered. He wanted to turn and run but the thick bearded Provost Sergeant behind him terrified him more than the gunfire in front of him.

The minie ball screamed through the air, striking Philip to the right of the temple, the slug bursting into shards inside his brain.

Joe instinctively wiped his face, smearing the sprinkle of tissue and blood that splattered his cheek. Trembling, uncertain, he stepped over his dear friend, propelled by the press of the file.

With a yell, the Reserves drove the enemy from the wall. There simply were more of them than the Rebel muskets had time to repel. The wall of wool and flesh became the mob, the officers vainly trying to keep formed the battle line. Companies got mixed up, the result of the varied paces of resolve or hesitation. Still they moved forward, following Colonel R. Biddle Roberts and banner. Some men halted to crouch and reload, ramming cartridge, slipping on percussion cap. Some reloaded while trotting. Most presented empty barrels tipped by bayonet.

Abandoning the stone wall the surviving Rebels dashed toward cover, hunched over, racing up hill, their rifles clenched tight in their hands. Their Companies above them laid down covering fire, the leaden bullets thudding into the blue disarray, finding their marks. They didn't shoot at men, just at motion.

The Reserves, swelled by their success, surged upwards toward the guns and smoke. A push, a pull, ebb and flow, then a trickle of momentum as the Rebels evaporated before them, retreating, leaving them the gap gained and summit won.

That was Sunday. On Monday Joe watched from a distance the General and his staff. He and several of the others from Company C, all from the same town, all boyhood friends, had come back to find and bury Philip. Their eyes, empty, dry, and bloodless, betrayed numb confusion. This was not what they had expected. Yes, others had been killed before. Eleven at New Market. But never one of their own.

Joe knelt beside the rigid body of his friend. No more lazy days along the wandering Octorara creek to fish for brown trout or hunt eels. No more climbing the rock outcroppings above the creek. No more singing together in the choir back home. No more contesting over who was going to return home a hero and marry Marian Landis. No more anything. The corpses had begun to bloat by the late time of their collection. For Philip, it was a shallow grave and the disgusting chaplain's abrupt and drunken benediction.

Nathaniel repeated his question. "Joe, please tell me. I promised his mother."

Joe sniffled and wiped his nose with his sleeve. "It just were his time, pastor. It weren't real nice." Joe began humming, then sang softly to himself one more song before he said goodnight to his pastor.

Chapter Three

First March

Aura Lea! The bird may flee, the willows golden hair
Swing through winter fitfully, on the stormy air
Yet of thy blue eyes I see gloom will soon depart,
For to me, Sweet Aura Lea, is sunshine through the heart.
"Aura Lea," by W.W. Fosdick

"Wake up, Nate! Nap time is over!" Valentine shook his arm so roughly that Alice's letter fluttered from his chest toward the timber flooring of the tent. In the distance he thought he heard the rhythm of a drum rattle. Nathaniel failed to snare the letter mid-air.

...yes darling, there were five puppies. You just had to let her out for a run before you left, didn't you? For as smart as you are, you can be such a fool. Only one failed to survive the night. When Margaret discovered him not nursing, she sobbed all morning. Jenny is a very proud mother. I am most sorry to report that we shall have to work further on the matter of your son as soon as you return home. What chance of furlough, darling?...

"I guessed it!" Valentine bragged as if he had won a contest. "I predicted something big was up, bright lad that I am. Medical supplies arriving in plenty. Orders to ship out the invalid sick north to the general hospitals. Even sending the

37

wives, surplus luggage, and sutlers away yesterday, Sunday or not. And the whores. Well, most of them. You know there's going to be a battle when they chase the whores out of camp. Yes indeed, when the Colonel's foot lockers get loaded on wagons, start packing your haversack and knapsack."

"You know, you're a pain. You ruined a great dream." He swung his legs off the cot. "How do you keep track of the days here?" Nathaniel asked groggily as he ran his fingers through his oily hair. "If I write now, they'd get my letter by Christmas, shouldn't they? I've got the package with your carvings ready for the girls."

"No time now. You should have mailed them before the weekend, my tardy and lazy friend. Watch, therefore, for you know neither the hour nor the day." Valentine stuffed his toilet kit into his haversack. "Who knows when we'll get the chance? Who knows what the day will bring? Listen, we're moving. Orders from Division."

Nathaniel reached down and retrieved his wife's letter. "Why, I do not know, but my Alice sends you her love again."

"Of course she does. You know, Nate, she's madly in love with me."

"That's because," Nathaniel said as his tossed his pillow at Valentine, "she hasn't seen you in three years."

The Regimental drum again rata-tat-tated. Drums echoed throughout the valley and across meadows. The call to routine made Nathaniel feel like a small child again. He looked around the tent trying to figure out what he should pack first.

"Time to go, recruit. Let me show you."

An encamped Army is notoriously indolent, rousing slowly like an old family hound getting ready for a hunt when master calls. There's the stretch and the shiver of the overweight pet.

Tents struck, cookery supplies stored, the stroll to the paddock and livery for the harnessing of the mules and horses, the practiced allocation of baggage stored in the rear wagons for the indefinite journey, differentiated from the baggage needed for the next encampment or the coming engagement.

Each soldier prepared the Regiment as a body for the march toward its unknown new home, followed by each soldier preparing his solitary self. Haversack and knapsack. Cartridge box and cap box. Musket. Unplug the tampion from the muzzle. Fill canteen. Pull the bayonet from the ground and unstick the candle from the bayonet, scrape off the wax, and slide the bayonet back where it belongs. Check rations. Double-check cartridges.

An entire Army was on the march, and only the barest few had the faintest notion as to where. Fewer understand why. But they all knew they would soon learn. How was easy. By wagon, by horse, by foot. Fall in line by Company. Adjutants and pioneers to the fore. The Regimental band competed with the musicians of the other Regiments. Talley and staff rode proud on horseback. Captains, on foot, led by Company, soldiers four abreast.

Nathaniel, confused as to where he fitted into the machinery of this enormous martial engine, followed a veteran Valentine and guessed his place was walking with the medical staff. It was as good as any other place. Two miles outside camp, Valentine, along with his two assistant Surgeons, Samuel Chapin and Stephen Chilson, took advantage of their train of hospital wagons and ambulances and hopped on board. Nathaniel waved them off and soon hastened his pace and marched among the various Companies. None of the soldiers felt as if they needed him to talk to them, especially after the seventh mile, but they did notice how their chaplain marched on foot with them. Tread and tramp. A few of the soldiers, he later heard from Joe, thought him trying to prove himself too much. Hell, they would ride if they could. Valentine thought it inspiringly democratic of him to join the march, and told him so after they arrived and set up temporary camp at White Oak Church.

Two days were spent at White Oak Church waiting for orders, which finally arrived on the third day, a cold and frosty Thursday. The ruts in the muddy road had begun to freeze. Cat ice replaced puddles. Nathaniel watched as the artillery was hauled to the front of the line of march to set up the advance batteries. The wheels of the field artillery deepened the ruts. He shivered from the cold. He shivered from the thrill of it all. His feet, despite his new boots, were cold and wet.

A new drum roll sounded. He studied the veterans for cues. He did his best to imitate them. Light marching order. They left the tents behind and settled on the north side of the river close enough to observe events in the pretty town opposite their position. Three pontoon bridges, manufactured during the night by the engineers, each one only a little wider than a wagon, lay below them, crossing the river less than a mile downstream from the center of town. What appeared to be a wooden planked floor, or a larger version of his tabour checkerboard, had been rolled out by the engineers from bank to bank across horizontally placed boats. Two days ago, he had seen these huge canvas boats pulled by teams of mules. He then thought them ridiculous: canvas feeding troughs on wagon wheels.

The guns that had careened through camp an hour earlier, smoothbore 12 pounders as well as both 10 and 20 pound

Parrotts, now, amidst smoke and sulfur, thundered and screamed over them from the heights behind. The explosions startled Nathaniel. General Burnside, Commander of the Army of the Potomac, had begun his battle. General Lee, Commanding the Army of Northern Virginia, defended the ground and town across the river. Nathaniel at first crouched with each roar. Eventually he learnt he didn't have to duck with every barrage, though the sound unnerved him throughout the entire day. He shivered from a cold chill that he couldn't blame on just the weather.

The absurd turned normal. The artillery hammered the handsome town. A stone mill, its water wheel braked, fronted the river. Three stone pilings stood like wrecked sentries in the middle of the river, the railroad bridge burnt, the rails sunk, the blackened ties having floated downstream, some snagged along the riverbank. The heights behind the white-washed town provided a backdrop to the tall steeples and spires sprouting from the downtown churches. Nathaniel tried to guess their denomination from their architecture. The Episcopal Church must be the one nearest center of town.

Nathaniel peered closer and saw puffs of smoke from the windows of the houses located along the river. He saw the smoke before he heard the report of the sniper gunfire. He observed, as if peering through a long tunnel, men rushing, jumping, crawling along two pontoon bridges that reached only two thirds across the river as they stretched toward the city's center. Ice had begun to collect around the upstream edges of the pontoons.

One engineer dropped the anchor for one of the pontoons. The man suddenly bolted straight up and then slowly, gradually, bent over and gently dove head first into the river.

41

"Why would he do that?" Nathaniel wondered. The man's body reemerged on the other side of the bridge, floating, his arms and legs trolling in the water.

He had seen men die. As a pastor, he had been with them when they died. Held their hands. Felt the clammy sensation and smelled the smell. Felt and matched the tightening of their hands, and then the gentle release when the fiber that binds the flesh finally yields and relents. He had comforted them as they died. Looked into their fogging eyes. He had shared with them the final moment and the last exhalation of borrowed breath. Then he would speak the words, read from scripture, offer the blessing. He had seen in death both a peace unimaginable as well as in some faces a confused panic. Not all deaths were peaceable deaths. Yes, he had seen men, women, even children die. But never before had he seen anyone killed. One anonymous man on the river killed by another anonymous man from the other side of the river. So casual. The man simply stood upright and calmly slid into the icy waters, his body floating downstream. Nobody seemed to notice let alone care. How detached it all seemed. Perhaps it was not the catastrophic, deliberate evil we should fear the most, but the casual evil, the innocent, ordinary, anonymous malevolence.

The bombardment from the guns behind him intensified. Fires erupted throughout the town following each blast, only to be snuffed out by succeeding explosions, the way you blow out a candle. One explosion ignited a new fire, itself to be extinguished by the next bombardment. Smoke and dust from collapsing buildings billowed in dark, filthy columns, as when burning wet leaves or rubbish smudges the sky.

Fires burned through the night until the smoldering embers died out in the dampness of the morning mist.

Thursday's noise yielded to the eerie quiet of Friday morning. Christmas was in thirteen days. On both sides of the river there was the hush of anticipation as before a theater's curtain opens, a hush interrupted only by the occasional shell from the Rebel lines or as snipers attempted to fell the brash. Behind it all remained the constant, churning sound of the river's current. Later, throughout Friday afternoon, the sounds of combat gained a new accompaniment: the muffled clang, rumble, and trudge of modest men crossing the river and spilling into the town. From the town, men marched over to the left flank to face the woods of Prospect Hill.

Valentine, who had been searching for Nathaniel, spotted him returning from the latrine buttoning his waistcoat.

"Nate! Come on, we're soon to move across. Tonight we get to bivouac on the other side of the river. Lee and Jackson are waiting just for you. Heard that direct from Division." Valentine slapped Nathaniel on the back. "Don't take too much. Forget the personal kit. I need you to carry what medical supplies you can. Stuff every pocket. I have a terrible feeling. Terrible feeling." Valentine hurried with a practiced efficiency. Pannier, medical knapsack, saddlebags—all were checked.

"Steward, put those damn musicians to work. I want the ambulances lined with evergreen boughs. Find some, hurry!" Valentine rapped the side of the wagon. "Should have done it sooner."

Nathaniel admired the experience of his friend.

"What fun, 'eh Nate? I get the advance dressing station, which means plenty of whisky and opium pills. I'm leaving both Chapin and Chilson to work at the Division hospital. They'll need them there as dressing Surgeons." Hands on hips, he surveyed his small command. "We, friend, get to cross over. Stick with me. You, you stay with me."

Valentine crossed the Rappahannock by riding the hospital wagon which preceded the ambulances. The Steward leaned over and spat into the river. Nathaniel, walking ahead of the wagon, marched with Company C across the swaying, bouncing pontoon bridge. He peered over into the flow of frigid water as he crossed. The force of the river bent the pontoon bridge into a curious curve, a perverse and broad grin. Stepping from the planks of the bridge they stepped onto a shore churned into slick and slippery mud by the shoes and boots of hundreds who had gone on before.

The Reserves assembled among dozens other Regiments of the Division, taking position on the extreme left, bivouacking upon the open field south of town. Despite the previous battles, despite depletions due to dysentery and pneumonia, and despite the lack of replacement volunteers, the Reserves remained an ably manned Regiment. The Regiment's ten companies averaged forty-five men each. Forty-five Springfields times ten. And tomorrow, as they all had heard from the rampant rumors, they would face Jackson. Jackson himself. Small campfires gave large comfort as they wrapped themselves up for the night in blankets and song.

Nathaniel listened as the men sang. It was a night of soft song on this meadow east of town. Some songs sounded cheerful, the flippancy of bravado; many of the tunes sung by these campfire choirs were doleful and melancholy. Concertina and banjo had been left behind. Sometimes the men only hummed. Sometimes harmonica or Jews-harp accompanied homely lyrics. Sometimes, when the wind blew from the south, Nathaniel believed he could discern the sound of other men singing, their songs faint, wafting from the woods and heights beyond.

An anxious Valentine double-counted his supplies and twice repacked his knapsack. Twice he shuffled the supplies bulging in the pockets of his frock coat before he hung it from the wagon's brake handle. Nathaniel, inventing some way to be useful, made a point of touring among each of the ten companies in the Regiment, inviting the men to join him for a short prayer and shorter conversation around their campfires.

The nearly full Frost moon illuminated the clouds, whirling and gray. A rare star defiantly filled a window of blackness and shone brightly before the dulling clouds swept across and obscured it. Two owls hooted in conversation with each other.

That night they slept under thickening clouds, Valentine and Nathaniel rolled in their blankets, their voices talking over a campfire kindled by twigs and crackling pine needles. The bulky shadow of the medical wagon loomed above them. The canvas top flapped in the wind. A leather saddlebag leaned up against the wagon wheel. Valentine rested his head against the saddlebag. Valentine was tempted to raid the medical trunk for a taste of whisky, but dismissed the thought; it'll be needed more tomorrow. Nathaniel used his haversack as a pillow. Both men stared up at the hidden sky.

"You're not saying much," observed Valentine.

"I've just been thinking," said Nathaniel.

"There's a surprise."

Nathaniel rolled over onto his side. "You know, Valentine, I've been thinking about all that talk back home about heroes. Here, I've noticed, it is the small things these fellows talk about. Irrelevant things. The way pine tar burns or who makes better coffee at mess." Nathaniel rolled himself closer toward the small fire, the flames more orange than yellow. He picked up a twig and held it in the flames till the end caught fire. Then he removed it and held it up, watching the fire at the end of the stick burn itself out. "Remember all our readings with Professor Lawvere in classic literature? The Aeneid and the Iliad, Chaucer, and all the rest."

Valentine rolled what was left of his cigar between his fingers and inhaled a deliberate draught of the tobacco smoke. The red end brightened before it ashened. He raised his chin, rounded his lips, and blew the smoke in abrupt huffing puffs from the back of his mouth, trying to blow smoke rings. The intermittent wind erased the rings, the air far from calm enough. He gave up after several attempts. Yes, Valentine smiled to himself, I damn well remember those tedious recitations. "I appreciated your gift with languages. Saved my sorry ass."

"You know, Valentine, I'd like to go back now to our Professor and debate the difference between pathos and tragedy." Valentine rolled his eyes. "I've come to the conclusion that Roland at Roncesvals was an idiot." Nathaniel recited:

Count Roland's mouth is filling up with blood;
the temple has been ruptured in his brain.
In grief and pain he sounds the Oliphant…

"A beautiful story, but, really, what a waste. Roland may have been terribly brave but he also was terribly stupid. I think I'm coming to the conclusion that this whole business is pathetic." Nathaniel tightened the blanket around him. "I don't know about you, but I've given up my plans on being a hero tomorrow. I'm no man of action. Give me words." Nathaniel whistled. "Me? I just plan on surviving."

"It's a deal," Valentine said as he flicked the wet stub of his cigar into the fire, then screwed up his face, pulling the corner of the blanket over him. "But wait till you hear the horns blow. Wait till you hear the bugles."

Neither man truly slept. The noisy whippoorwills chattered all night, accompanied by the click-clacking of the katydids. Both men remained restless in their minds, their brains too preoccupied and heartbeats too accelerated to gentle their bodies, until, two hours from dawn, fatigue finally subdued their raging thoughts and demanded an hour of oblivion.

Chapter Four

The Dressing Station

We shall meet, but we shall miss him,
There will be one vacant chair
We shall linger to caress him,
When we breathe our evening prayer.
"The Vacant Chair," by George Root

They awakened to a dead fire, frozen ground, and thick fog.
A soft rustle near his face invited Nathaniel to open his eyes without stirring his body. A shrew nosed about for worms, its senses tingling, sniffing blindly for some muddy softness in the frozen soil. Nathaniel watched him for several peaceful minutes. The shrew, focused on his hunt for food, hadn't smelled the man. A piggish snort from Valentine's blanket startled it. The shrew lowered his trembling body to the ground, poised for the escape on his short legs, its fast heartbeat betraying its attempt at stillness. The tip of the long, pointed snout of its narrowed skull twitched. Nathaniel finally puffed a mist of breath at the shrew and it vanished into the taller grass beneath the wagon.

Nathaniel, beginning to feel the ache of his bones and muscles, kept his head reclined on the haversack, his eyes trained at the spot where the shrew had hunted. He wished for the shrew's return but the shrew stayed hidden. Other men were already stirring or up. Nathaniel finally relented to dawn and duty, and, as he sat up, opened his eyes wider, blinking and rubbing them. But he could not wipe away from them sleep's fuzziness. But it was not his eyes. The haze came from the thick fog which had settled along both shores of the river, smothering the length of the valley, a deep mist clamped between the heights on both sides of the river. The cold ground and colder water met warm air. But the air was windless. Nathaniel twisted around and saw the sun beginning to crest over the horizon of the heights on the other side of the river, glowing as through a veil.

After rummaging through his knapsack, he pulled out his silver timepiece and fob, along with his pocket Bible and prayer book. Before opening the testament to read a chapter from the Gospel of John as part of his morning devotions, he thumbed open the watch case and bid good morning to his daughters, gently rubbing the blue cameo fob. He pressed the fob to his lips. He wound the watch slowly, deliberately, as if as long as he kept winding the watch time itself remained under his control.

The thickening fog and quelled breeze made it hard to see beyond the wagons. The hospital Steward, bending over a cook fire shielded by the ambulances, poked bacon slabs and fried hardtack in hot grease. The bacon splattered and sizzled.

Cursing from the dampness and chill, Valentine, awake and stomping, grabbed a tin cup of hot coffee from the Steward.

"God bless you, Penningtonville," Nathaniel muttered while scrolling up his woolen blanket inside his rubber blanket. The rubber blanket had been one of the several gifts given him by his congregation before he enlisted. He tied the bedroll tight and stored his kit in a corner of the medical wagon.

"Here," Valentine grunted as he handed Nathaniel a tin cup of coffee. "Can't see a damn thing. Let's hope it stays like this for a while. Not that you see anything anyway." They leaned against the wagon, Nathaniel pursing the cup in his palm like a monk at prayer.

"How long do you think it will shroud us," Nathaniel asked?

Valentine noisily gulped the bitter coffee, the grinds gritting his gums. He stomped his feet. "You probably won't see much either after it starts. All you know is that you have joined this gigantic spectacle of bloody fools and it is being played out with thousands involved—you hear it all around you. Trust me, we'll soon make our own fog. If we see more than twenty yards around us, we're doing well." He flung the dregs of the cup onto the tall grass under the wagon, tossed the mug on the ground next to his Steward, and turned toward Nathaniel, poking his finger in his chest. "So, listen, hero, don't go getting yourself lost chasing the noises. Ain't no Oliphant here. Stay near the dressing station. That's where you can do the most good right now."

The camp's bizarre pretense of nonchalance and normalcy, soldiers occupied with the homely activities of toilet and meal, jumped at the sound of bugle and drum into a flurry of excitement. At a different sound of bugle and drum roll, the invisible hand guided, and the pearls which were men merged into a column four abreast. The men moved in a single mass. The sound altered again and they formed attacking lines, two ranks deep. The ends of the line faded into the fog. From the noise of marching and rattling sounding across the hidden field of battle, Nathaniel surmised their actions were mirrored by thousands of other invisible men.

There the Reserves stood in formation for over an hour. Soldiers fingered the wide trigger guard of their older, 1842 model muskets, .69 caliber Springfields. Originally smoothbores, the muskets were rifled and modernized a few years prior to the Rebel assault on Fort Sumter. Nathaniel checked his watch again. The Captains made sure the lines remained dressed. The file closers slapped the men with their stubby swords. The provosts patrolled to the rear. Except for the occasional cough or sneeze, the men stood in silence. From both coffee and apprehension, several released their bladders and urinated in their trousers as they stood in formation. Nathaniel watched the dull orb shining behind the haze creep higher. It grew brighter and clearer as it ascended. A touch of warmth penetrated the chill and dampness. As the fog began to lift from the river, small tufts of clouds drifted off into the bluing sky. The shroud began to dissipate, thinning off from the field of men, rolling off the land to concentrate its last thin puffs of misty breath over the length of the river itself.

Beams of sunlight broke through the evaporating fog. White light gleamed off the polished metal of the bayonets held aloft by the revealed thousands of soldiers. Nathaniel gasped at the unveiling of the troops and flags in all their martial splendor. As if a burden had lifted, the men stood taller, readier. Excitement pulsed from Regiment to Regiment. Horses snorted and whinnied as earnest officers galloped past. Blue and brass. The previously quelled wind rose and the unfurled flags twitched, flapped, then waved. It was a gallantry intoxicating, ethereal, resplendent. Legends were come alive.

Behind the assembled Federal army flowed the river. Residual mist lingered above the Rappahannock in cottony streaks. To the far right, Nathaniel heard the distant commotion of shouting and marching as men attacked through the streets of the town clearing out the Rebel snipers and skirmishers. Nathaniel strained his eyes to see toward the heights southwest of the town. Flickers of sunlight glinted from barricades built along the top of the hill. The town was cleared, but, at the top of the hill, commanding the high ground, there Lee waited. Shielding his eyes, Nathaniel scanned back toward the large plain that his Regiment faced. Beyond the plain was a small hillock thick with trees. A little more than midway between the hill they faced and their position, ran a length of railroad tracks from the town, the tracks curving due south. Staring, he believed he saw gray men and black cannon shifting amongst the woods, fading in and out of the light and shadows.

Jackson.

Bugles sounded, followed by roll of drum. The musicians at the rear began to play. Colonel Talley dismounted and stood beside the Regimental flag as he offered a few sparse words of exhortation, his sword brandished. The men cheered.

"Chaplain McKenna," Colonel Talley commanded, surprising him with the mention of his name. "If you would honor us." He beckoned him with his polished sword and pointed its tip to a spot in the grass.

Nathaniel fumbled with his coat buttons until he grasped the Colonel's instruction. He gulped and paced toward the Colonel. The eyes of the entire Regiment watched him. How do you properly bless a battle? he asked himself silently. He reached inside his coat pocket for his prayer book. The ends of his open frock coat rustled in the breeze. His hand hesitated, but only for the barest of moments. He took his book from his pocket. He joined Talley near the flag and bowed respectfully at the Colonel. The flag flapped across the face of the standard bearer. The Adjutant stepped forward and shook Nathaniel's hand. Nathaniel turned to face hundreds of men. Never before had he faced such a large congregation. Some spit tobacco juice. Some looked upon him intently. Some fidgeted with the leather strap of their musket. Some stared with bored uninterest beyond him toward the woods. He spotted Joe in the front rank. Joe grinned at his pastor. That helped. Never talk to the crowd. Talk to the boy. These are words they need to hear. Words Joe needs. Nathaniel raised his trembling right hand and extended his arm toward the Regiment, summoning them to accompany him in prayer. His left hand held the open prayer book in front of him, trying to hold it still, his thumb and pinkie holding down the pages. The red page marker fluttered. He read loudly from the section entitled, 'On the Eve of Battle.'

At the prayer's conclusion, half of the soldiers echoed his closing "Amen." He closed the prayer book and returned it to his coat pocket. He patted it.

"Thank you, Reverend," the Colonel said courteously as he turned toward the hillock. "You may retire now." With his thoughts elsewhere, he didn't hear the Colonel. Nathaniel remained standing beside the flag. A rider galloped and whirled to a stop immediately in front of Colonel Talley. The eager messenger shouted words Nathaniel didn't pick up. Talley returned the salute. Commands were echoed down the line. Skirmishers broke rank and went forward. Then the men, as a body, stepped to the assault. Nathaniel faced them. They stepped forward in formation following their flag, following Talley and his upraised sword. Nathaniel remained fixed to his spot as the Regiment proceeded, his legs unable to move. The files of men parted around him as they advanced, like brookwater around rock. As the men passed him by, some grinned at him, some gruffly asked him to pray for them, several touched him for luck, him a talisman of a divine preservation.

Their advance triggered artillery fire from the hillock beyond the plain. Quickly Nathaniel found his legs. While jogging back to the dressing station he turned and saw that the Regiment held a steady blue line across the open plain. More fire erupted from the hill. Heavy fire. Blasts that deafened. Nathaniel trotted faster toward the dressing station. A new fog born of sulfur smothered the field. The resplendent gleaming faded into a gunpowder mist of an obscured and unseen battle. Cheers became screams as shrapnel shredded the formed lines. Men stepped over wriggling bodies and reformed the line. Commands became desperate shouts for the men to close ranks. Artillery fire alternated with the crackle of musketry. A frightening, feral yell rose from the distant end of the field, silenced almost immediately by a sudden, stunning fusillade. Amidst the claustrophobia of battle, bullets whizzed and shrieked, then thudded.

Soon the stretcher bearers arrived at the dressing station. The yellow flag with its green 'H' drew dazed and bloodied men from other Regiments. Soldiers arrived dragging a wounded cousin or carrying a tentmate on boards torn from fences. At first Nathaniel tried to assign them their location at the dressing station: the seriously wounded by the wagon, the walking wounded to gather nearby the fire. But soon, overwhelmed by the sheer number of caualties, all categories merged.

Valentine, his linen apron tied over his uniform, circulated beneath the rude canopy of tents and evergreen bowers extended from the medical wagon. "Not too bad, not too bad." So far he judged there were few serious wounds, mostly in the limbs. A few necks seared. Uniforms, neat, crisp, and blue merely hours before in formation, arrived torn and muddied, crusty with caking blood.

"Here take this," the Steward offered as he wandered among the lightly wounded, handing them opium pills. Nathaniel followed and offered them a gulp from a canteen filled with whisky. The pills were swallowed with a burning glug. The lightly wounded men, bandaged by Surgeon or Steward, watched and learned to nurse each other as more wounded arrived, freeing the Steward to assist Valentine with the critical wounds.

One solider writhed on the ground clutching his belly. The Steward forced a pill into the man's mouth, shoved his jaw up with the palm of his hand, and pinched his nose so he would swallow it, then he grasped the man's wrists and pinned his arms down to the ground as Valentine removed the torn fabric from the bloody mass and scrubbed it. Valentine pulled bandages from his coat pocket, trying to pack the wound with persulphate of iron.

"Watch for hemorrhage on that one. Pulse is still strong. By God, he's gonna' leak bad."

Men lay near the medical wagon, their skin cold and clammy, surrendering to the pallor of shock and weak pulse as their blood dripped into the earth. Into casks of water Nathaniel plunged canteens and refilled them. He moved among the wounded offering fresh water. Men, in their delirium, muttered and moaned.

"Steward," Valentine casually and calmly reminded above the groans of the wounded and the continuous sound of musket fire, "please make sure you fill the ambulance before you send it back to Division."

Another soldier squirmed and groaned as Valentine stuck his finger into the fleshy wound in his thigh, probing for the misshapen bullet. Valentine looked over at Nathaniel standing nearby ready with a tourniquet. "More bandages Nate, would you please." Valentine dug a cold probe deep inside the man's thigh. "Ah, got it; extractor please. Damn, would someone get me more bandages!"

"Yes, I'll do it." Nathaniel stopped staring, and, tossing the Steward the tourniquet, he rushed around toward the back side of the medical wagon to find the wicker supply chest. Turning the corner of the wagon he nearly tripped over a young man, clean faced, who was squatting near the rear wheel. Nathaniel noticed the uniform was perfect except that the boy wore only one shoe. The woolen sock was damp and muddy. Nathaniel knelt down beside him.

"Where is your musket, son?"

The boy looked up at Nathaniel with pleading eyes. "You're the preacher? Can't I stay? Let me stay. I can help."

Nathaniel knelt down and placed his hand on the young boy's shoulder. The boy started sobbing. "No one will blame you, son. Sure you can help me here. We have enough to do."

Abruptly, Nathaniel was shoved aside. Nathaniel tumbled sideways, his shoulder colliding against the spokes of the wagon wheel. A voice growled: "Damn preachers. He doesn't need a mother right now." The Provost Sergeant stood where

Nathaniel had knelt. The huge Sergeant stared down at the cowering young boy.

"You heard the preacher, boy. Where's your musket, soldier?" the Provost Sergeant demanded, not yelling, but with a stern voice, a voice not to be ignored.

The boy refused to look up at the Sergeant. His eyes searched for Nathaniel's and found them.

The Provost Sergeant stepped between them. The Provost Sergeant hammered the boy on the shoulder with the butt of his Sharps, smashing him to the ground. He yelled through his thick black beard: "Answer me! Where is your musket?"

The boy sprawled, clutching his shoulder.

"Stand up. Damn you, Private, stand up!"

The boy, trembling, staggered to his feet. The Provost Sergeant slung his carbine. With flat palms he struck the boy fully square on his chest, pushing the boy backwards against the wagon. The boy stumbled. He hit him again. The Provost Sergeant swung his large hand and cuffed the boy hard across the side of his face. The boy staggered sidewise, his nose bleeding. The boy tried to wipe his nose with his sleeve as the Sergeant grabbed him by the upper arm and half dragged, half pushed him forward, toward the fury of musket fire and screech of cannon.

"Damn you, soldier! Back you go. We'll find you a weapon."

Nathaniel felt irrelevant. Humiliated. Ashamed even. He watched the two of them disappear. A bloodied hand touched Nathaniel's shoulder. He turned to face Valentine.

"They'll run sometime. Lots of times. Hell, I would. Hell, I have. Didn't like the prospect of no more kisses from pretty girls. Hell, we all have run." Valentine wiped his hands with a bloody rag. "Right now the boy is bloodied by the panic.

58

Comfort him and he's wounded for life." Valentine patted Nathaniel's shoulder. "If you're smart, you'll stay out of Sergeant Hunt's way." Valentine pivoted Nathaniel back toward the wagon. "Come on, I need you. I need those bandages."

Nathaniel glanced over his shoulder at the spot in the woods where the boy and the Provost Sergeant had entered. Biting his lip, he walked over to the wagon to rummage through the wicker basket.

Cannon fire erupted from behind them, joined by the barrage from the nearer batteries hauled earlier in the morning across to the southern side of the river. The din of cannon overwhelmed the terrible rumble of a thousand men shrieking, cursing, shouting, yelling. The scattered few trickling past the dressing station became a stream of retreating soldiers. The commotion surrounding the station escalated as the line of battle, once concentrated on the hill beyond the railroad bed, had shifted back near the morning's line of formation. Musket fire drew closer. Handfuls of retreating solders became squadrons.

Nathaniel noticed Valentine pausing every few minutes, turning his ear toward the sound of battle. Valentine began rushing to stack the wounded onto the ambulances and ship them back to Division as fast as possible. Nathaniel assisted the musicians as they carried the men by stretcher and hoisted them into the wagons. Nathaniel noticed Valentine looking around and measuring the increase in soldiers arriving at the dressing station and those rushing past it.

"Not good?" Nathaniel guessed aloud, trying to read the signs. Nathaniel began to pack up what supplies he could save should they be forced to retreat.

"Not yet, Nate, not yet," Valentine counseled, seeing what Nathaniel was doing. "They might hold it yet."

Valentine guessed right. Division held the line and the surviving men lay on their arms at the same spot where they began their advance that morning.

On a return trip from the Division hospital, the ambulance driver reported to Valentine that his skills were required there. He had been ordered back. Without a good-bye, Valentine gathered up his knapsack and surgical kit and rode the next ambulance with its final shipment of their seriously wounded back across the pontoon bridge.

By a courier sent to the dressing station, Talley ordered Nathaniel to attend to him. A sweaty and tired Nathaniel jogged as best as he could after the boy. They wound their way through Companies of spent men. Talley sat on a rock, surrounded by his officers underneath the branches of an old, barren maple. Talley's hands shook, making it difficult for him to insert ball and powder into the chamber of his Colt revolver. Finally he noticed the chaplain standing in front of him. Concentrating on his revolver, Talley said: "Chaplain, it has been a long day for all of us, but I have a request of you. Reverend, as the rest of us have other duties, if you would be so kind…we've accounted for most of our men but still seem to be missing a dozen or more. Please look to your flock, sir."

As Nathaniel left the copse of trees, he heard the skidding thud as Talley threw his revolver down on the ground. Talley's voice raged before the assembled staff officers: "Where was the damn support! Dammit, we almost had Jackson himself. We had the breakthrough! We had the breach!"

Nathaniel searched the various Regimental dressing stations hunting for any who belonged to the 30th. The sights at several of the other stations, worse than his own, sickened him. Stopping to rest against a wagon, he overheard three men talking about how the troops who faced the heights above town were now entrenched, trapped, shielding themselves from enemy fire with the bodies of their own dead. Some Regiments, they reported, had suffered over half their number in casualties.

It took him searching through seven different stations, but eventually he accounted for eight men from the Reserves. His heart chilled as he thought about where he had to search for the few still lost, for he knew he must search the battlefield.

Guided by the twilight Nathaniel stumbled across a tree root. He thought he heard a sound of whimpering nearby. Was there also a rustling and a slight splashing? He slipped down a small bank, his left foot sinking into the mud of a tiny creek. With a slurp he pulled his boot from the mud and steadied himself, his hand reaching for the trunk of a small tree. In the water, at a bend upstream, he believed he spotted movement, so he headed in that direction, crossing first to the flatter side of the creek bank.

What was left of a man was lying in the stream. His face was hidden beneath the bent brim of his kepi. The man reached out with a weak arm, trying to cup his hand and draw water from the creek toward his mouth. He failed twice before Nathaniel could reach him and kneel beside him in the cold water.

"Here, take this," Nathaniel said as he pulled the cork from his own canteen and held it toward the soldier's face. The soldier flopped his head back to receive the water. As he did his cap fell into the creek. Nathaniel brushed the soldier's hair from his forehead. It was the face of the young boy without a shoe. Nathaniel looked down. The boy's leg was shredded, his blood draining into the creek water.

The boy pursed his lips to the water. Most dribbled out of his mouth. He looked up into Nathaniel's face with a slow, dawning recognition. He gurgled: "Thank ya'."

Nathaniel reached under his arms and tried to lift him into a sitting position. The young boy grimaced. He again looked at Nathaniel. He squeaked: "I'm dead, ain't I?"

"Don't you worry, son. We'll get you fixed. Our Surgeon's the best. We'll get you fixed." Nathaniel looked around hoping to spot a stretcher team. He stared at the boy's leg and began to remove his own belt for a tourniquet.

The boy, with cold and muddy hands, reached out to stop him. His eyes widened in panic. "I went back. I did go back. But I'm scared, preacher. I'm scared. More scared now."

Nathaniel held the boy's hand in his. His left hand stroked the boy's forehead. "I've got you. You're not alone. You're not alone," Nathaniel repeated.

"I ain't never been baptized, preacher," the boy gulped with a dry throat. The boy tilted sidewise. "I'm scared of hell."

Nathaniel's eyes misted. He didn't feel the coldness of the water in which he was kneeling. "No need to be afraid…" Nathaniel paused. "…not any longer." He put his hand under the boy's chin to help him focus on his own eyes. Their eyes met. "You believe in Jesus, don't you, son?"

"Yes sir, I do."

"Then in Jesus' name I baptize you." Nathaniel cupped his palm and dipped it into the bloody water flowing between their legs. He poured the water from his palm onto the top of the boy's head. The dark water dripped down across the boy's eyes and down the bridge of his nose. "In the name of the

Father, and of the Son, and of the Holy Ghost." Nathaniel instinctively intoned a familiar hymn, brushing the boy's wet hair back from his forehead.

Let the water and the blood,
From Thy riven side which flowed,
Be of sin the double cure,
Cleanse me from its guilt and power.

Before the last ember of the boy's eyes dimmed, he lifted his face up at Nathaniel. His eyes were soft, yet puzzled, and he tried to say something, words which Nathaniel could not make out. The words merely bubbled from his mouth. The boy relaxed against the bank of the creek.

Nathaniel stood up in the middle of the creek, refastened his belt, and looked down at the young boy. No more words did Nathaniel speak. What words could he speak? A dark figure loomed above him. On the rise of the creek bank stood the Provost Sergeant, his carbine cradled in his left arm. "It will keep us both busy," he said, extending Nathaniel his right hand.

Later that night, before he rolled himself up in his blankets, Nathaniel lit a twig from the camp fire and held it over the bowl of his pipe. He drew a deep draught and held the black Cavendish flavor of the tobacco in his mouth. Releasing the draught, he watched the smoke dissipate into the night sky.

Sunday morning was spent at the dressing station, tending to the few soldiers not injured enough to warrant being transported back to Division. Worship that Sabbath afternoon consisted only of funeral services. Nathaniel learned the boy's name from two of his mates: Abraham Tinsely. Around noon they buried the young Tinsely alongside another soldier from the Regiment, Alfred Webb from Company C. Thirty-four were wounded but only these two killed. Jackson had been gentle with them. Friends sawed a plank in half for two tombstones, names scratched by knife into the tough, weathered wood. Nathaniel helped cover the shrouded bodies with several shovelfuls of dirt. Later that afternoon Valentine returned exhausted from surgery. More amputations than he could remember. They kept bringing them. That evening, as they lay bivouacked in the same spot as the night before, an Aurora Borealis shimmered in the clear sky for over an hour.

The next day the beaten Federal army withdrew back across the river.

Chapter Five

Blood and Ink

Love rules the court, the camp, the grove,
And men below, and saints above;
For love is of heaven, and heaven is love.
"The Lay of the Last Minstrel," Sir Walter Scott

The army, mauled, slunk away from Fredericksburg and hid near Belle Plain.

The once grand Confederate earthworks that were built up along the Potomac, dug during the days of a defiant optimism, now formed the foundation for a Union supply base. Here the retreating Union Army had returned for safety, for support, for recuperation – the hungry giant stretching itself out across this little valley of rolling inclines worn barren by wartime traffic and winter weather. Plucked patches of shrubs edged the paths. The hills and valley were stripped of trees. Stumps dotted the landscape, save for a few larger elms and black walnut left for the benefit of their promise of shade and nut come summertime.

From the crest of one of the surrounding rolling hills, Nathaniel, on his way to the Regimental hospital, gazed down upon the wide river, itself vast enough to be called a lake at this juncture. Gulls darted and pestered. An upper wharf and a lower wharf slid out into the waters. Steamers, barges, and transport paddle-wheels had moored their bows snug into the slips of these makeshift wharves, looking like so many hungry piglets swarming at the sow's teats. From these wharves, muddy veins of roads led along the river, then up over the hillsides. Along these roads pulsed the ant-like procession of men and horse, cattle and wagon.

Inland bound wagons were laden with arms, ammunition, food, dry goods, supplies. Outward bound ambulance wagons rumbled to these wharves, delivering a parade of litters bearing wounded, broken, and diseased men dressed in new clean linen shirts. These men were destined to be stacked and shipped to the general hospitals upstream which were scattered throughout the capital city. Tent hospitals had been erected farther inland at Brook's Station and Aquia Creek, with each Corps grouped according to Division, the source for this flow of maimed sons sent home. Or at least closer to home. The wounded returning. The dead stayed.

Nathaniel spent most of his days at the Regimental hospital writing letters home for the wounded men who were too weak or too illiterate to do anything but dictate. Pencils replaced the pen, the nib flattened, spreading and smearing the ink from writing what must have been a hundred and fifty letters. The knuckles in his right hand ached. He pulled on his fingers and tried to rub away the cramping soreness. Between letters, he sent one of the medical orderlies out to the sutler to barter for more ink and extra nibs.

For a man of letters, to discover here in hospital and camp the visceral power of words surprised and fascinated him. Here words meant something intimate, the measure and means of relationships. The letters he handed out when he distributed the mail seemed as steak and eggs for a man fed only hardtack. They were even better than food. The letters were folded and re-folded, re-read, they were savored. A link. A hint. A hope. The anger or sullen melancholy to which the letters would give rise were worth the reminder of loved ones at home. A worthy pain. Nathaniel would read to the patients their letters from home and he would see in their eyes how they could visualize home and wife and daughter. Why not? Alice's letters he reread every night.

The number of men in the Regiment who could not read or write, who needed him because he could, baffled him.

"Bill, what do think of this idea?" he eagerly quizzed Lieutenant Bear that night at mess. They ate their Christmas dinner of rice, salt pork, and turnip. "If we stay encamped here, what do you think about me holding some kind of school? I could teach them to read and write. It's a scandal how many can't. I'm sure I could get my hands on all sorts of books, chalk, tablets, even some primers."

Bear chewed on his pipe stem. "Forget it."

"Huh," replied Nathaniel. "I thought you'd support the idea."

Oh dear, thought Bear to himself. "Well, okay, I see you mean well, Nate," Bear said. "But come on," he added with a soft chuckle, "I really think these fine fellows are past the point of McGuffey Readers. Think about it." Bear started laughing to himself at the image of these veterans squeezed into school chairs with slates poised on their laps. *Here is John. There is Ann and Jane. Ann has a new book. It is the first book. Ann must keep it nice and clean.* "Besides, how many do you think will come forward and admit it?"

"Some might."

"Sometimes it's best, friend, just to let things be. You don't always have to meddle. In some ways, Nate, I envy them. I think they're a whole lot better off than you or me, maybe even happier than we are. Let them be."

"But...," Nathaniel stammered, wanting to explain himself.

Bear continued. "By now, I'd suspect, most who can't read have found a mate to help them, if they want help. Then, you know, there's those who don't bother to write much anyway. They got nobody at home anyway who can read the letters they might send."

"I don't know, I still might ask around." Nathaniel clung to his good intentions. "Maybe I could hold classes right after worship."

"Always worth a try," Bear conceded. "But you're forgetting one last point: when are you going to find time?"

◎◎◎

The Regiment rested and healed itself, occupying itself with the mundane normalcy of chores, tending to the boring necessities of camp life. Always the mud and the routine. The smell of an Army. All commands reported that they had been assured by higher command that these indeed were to be the Regiment's permanent winter quarters. Talley twice assured his staff this was where they would stay. He got the word from Corps headquarters itself. The men, ranging deeper into the woods beyond the expanding perimeter of the camp, hauled back what timber they could find, constructing log stockade huts or setting about readying their tents for winter.

The men at camp, assigned to rows according to Company, spent their days bored and equally content with being bored.

Boredom was far saner than marching into battle. Far better was the familiar routine than the anxious worry over what the next hour of stark terror would bring you. But William Bear, Nathaniel hated to admit, was right about one thing: he had enough work to do. There was precious little time for him to enjoy being bored.

There was so much these men lacked. There was so much they needed. More ink, for a start. Stamps and paper. Some decent vegetables wouldn't hurt. He had begged for his Regiment's share of blankets and canned fruit from the Christian Commission. He had handed out enough Bibles and tracts. If they used the tracts for personal necessities, he could understand it, but he did hope they would respect the Bibles. What bothered Nathaniel the most was that with Washington less than fifty miles away, why couldn't they obtain better provisions from the Quartermaster? Six men went down with scurvy just last week. Valentine was livid at the incompetence of the supply lines. Val was fortunate his Surgeon's skill forced them to tolerate his temper. There was so much the men deserved.

Yet they kept on doing what soldiers do. Settling in and making a home of it. Unlike the officers, the men were used to doing without. A veteran soldier's talent at adaptation. Make a home of it. Suitable. Serviceable. Spend your energy making life as tolerable as you can make it for yourself and your mates. Scavenging for sardine cans to make slush lamps. Stealing hardtack boxes for tables. Digging a furnace hole into the ground below the hut or planked floor of the tent, and tunneling it outside for the smoke to escape. Creating these earth and rock chimneys to cut the edge of these chilly three dog nights. Instead of the family dog to keep them warm, they had to rely on their small fireplaces plus the body heat from their tent mates. Side by side by side.

The men medicated the sting of retreat by blaming their officers along with their own homespun remedies of mischief. The tonic of homespun adaptability. A Fresh Fish assigned to the Company quickly found himself welcomed by fifty men hollering and hooting, grabbing him by arms and legs and vaulting him helplessly onto a blanket held taut by a square of his new comrades. The trick was to see how many times and how high they could toss the recruit before his flailing bounce caused him to plummet outside the square of the blanket. They then picked him up, dusted him off, and laughed. The smart recruit laughed with them. "Welcome kid. Here, have a cup of hot coffee. What news of home?"

Then there was the mock dress parade, often held during the free time after the noon meal, with the fancy dressed Regimental musicians replaced by washtub drummers and platoons of off-key harmonicas, irregularly dressed soldiers shouldering mops and brooms in place of muskets. Sergeants with odd accents and officers with glaring eccentricities needed to be good sports, Nathaniel observed, as the men would target them and caricature them cruelly. It was all just blowing off a little steam lest resentment build and explode. No harm. Nothing personal. It was the necessary license of tease and ridicule from the ranks, especially if the mocked officer or Sergeant wanted their respect and obedience later.

The men amused themselves as they could, for they didn't get the chances for refreshment as the officers did. A lucky few officers, especially those who could cough convincingly enough, received much envied furloughs, winning the prize to travel north by steamer or rail or wagon train and spend a few recovering weeks through the holidays and into the new year with their wives or lovers or both.

On his way back from the hospital listening to the banter and song, Nathaniel gradually accepted that Bear was right. He too began to envy the men for their adolescent spats over checkers or whose turn was it to go out into the woods and gather more firewood. They enjoyed the freedom of simply thinking about themselves and their few buddies. Theirs was the indolence of being told what to do. Their hours got marked by the tedium of the day, from roll call to parade ground inspection. Days defined by meals and drills. Theirs was the mindless tidiness of reveille, tattoo, and taps.

Routine defined their days. Chaos defined Valentine and Nathaniel's. The common soldier adapted to the vermin and filth, even befriended it. Valentine and Nathaniel spent their days and nights fighting the grim and virulent Mr. Mortis. The common solider called the Rebels their enemy. Surgeon and chaplain strove against their own more elusive, elastic, and evasive foes. They spent their hours preoccupied with cleaning up the mess and gore of battle, which the other men of the Regiment, including the officers, were able to shove behind them and ignore.

Later, alone in his tent, Nathaniel relaxed with a smoke and a dram of the last of the sherry that he had been saving. A toast and a prayer. He wanted something warm to help him sleep. It was difficult sleeping alone. He missed her. He missed her smell. He missed slipping under the covers and pretending to doze with his eyelids partially closed. She'd undress in the flickering candlelight then tie the bow on her nightgown. He cherished how Alice secretly enjoyed him watching her seated at the vanity, where she released her long auburn hair and slowly brushed her hair.

She is so beautiful. She had her pick. Including him. But she chose me. Yes, I am a lucky man. More than I deserve.

Holding her finger in front of the flame she'd puff out the candle, then, in the dark, she'd open the curtains of the bedroom windows so she could welcome the morning light when it arrived. Alice enjoyed sleeping with the curtains open, the moonlight offering a gentle light into her favorite room of the house. She loved lying in bed at night with her sleeping husband, close under the comforter, watching the branches of the dogwood wave outside the window. The shadows and movements that once frightened her as a little girl, when she was the age of her own daughters, now pleased her, comforted her. He missed brushing her hair from her eyes with a sweep of his fingers, him untying the bow. He missed the sweet sleep that followed sweeter intimacy…

"Whew," he puffed. He exhaled into his sweat stained pillow: "Well, this sure doesn't help." With his eyes forced closed he next imagined Alice far away tucking their daughters to sleep. Bedtime stories, prayers, the night-night song. Penelope loved Alice singing 'Beautiful Dreamer.' She called it 'boo-ful deamer.' Then it was a pouting Margaret demanding 'kiss me too, poppa.' How scared they'd get if momma and poppa forgot to leave the door ajar. Neither girl liked sleeping in the dark.

Despite the dram of sherry, he slept a lousy night.

◎◎◎

Words kept Nathaniel busy. Flesh was Valentine's work. Valentine spent his days and nights temporarily detached to the Corps tent hospital where his growing surgical reputation was recognized and his equally increasing ferocity was required. Which worked just fine for him. He much preferred cutting to having to administrate sick call or write out those annoying Surgeon Certificates. He was a fast cutter when it came to the major limbs. During the Mechanicsville and Gaines Mill days it took him nearly eight rookie minutes for a leg. By Antietam he cut the time in half. He relished the race. Valentine hated to lose.

One night, only days after Fredericksburg, neither Valentine nor Nathaniel, despite their exhaustion, could sleep. Nathaniel, his hands behind the back of his head, spoke first. "Of course you can't sleep, Valentine. You're cursed."

"I've known that for years."

"No really. Your curse is that you think you can fix them. You think you can cure them all. You hate it when you can't."

"Isn't that your problem also?" Valentine replied as he rolled over. "Ain't we the pair."

To avoid blood poisoning Valentine preferred the circular amputation. When allowed time, he performed this technique. The mark of the finer Surgeon. But the flap proved faster. Faster proved kinder. Faster was usually all the time he had. Plus, it used less chloroform. Easier for the patient to endure. The excruciating pain was intense but brief, at least until the ache and throb began. Thank God for chloroform. With all the chances the Generals had given him to practice, Valentine could perform most amputations in less than two minutes.

Valentine preferred it when his orderlies gripped the meat of the bleeding limb with their bare hands. Tighten and go to work, relying on the flexibility and accuracy of strong fingers. Hands were suited for compressing the bleeding vessels. Thumbs that could plug. The assistant would finger back the soft tissue, leaving a large flap of tissue for later covering the stump. Then Valentine could reach in and get at the exposed bone, sawing away like a carpenter or filleting it like a butcher. He had nicked a few of his assistants' fingers in the process, which, according to Valentine, was their own stupid fault for not staying out of his way or that of his Liston knife. They should have figured out by now where his knife was going to slice. After the cut, slice, and saw, it was tie tight the arteries. Snare, hook, and pull. Curved needles closed the cuff of skin. Pack the wound.

Valentine relished a precise, clean amputation, even when a stump had turned gangrenous and required a secondary amputation. Unlike some other Surgeons, his patients rarely bled to death. A clean amputation gave him a fair chance to ease the pain. What he hated was the damned body flux. "Dammit," he swore, "you can't cut away dysentery."

Christmas dinner for Val included a small plate of pickled beef with a boiled potato eaten in between treating several cases of dysentery. "Give them ipecac and a diet of oysters," he told the Stewards. "See if there's any Blue Mass left." He already had diagnosed several cases of typhoid. One case of measles. Disease scared him to death. "Let's try cupping the blisters and spoon small doses of turpentine. Got any gunpowder? Bring me some. That's an old-fashioned remedy my father taught me. We can spoon them an elixir from gunpowder and hot water."

Dining on his Christmas dinner Valentine didn't bother removing his coat, stiff and crusty from blood and pus. He did

74

sit to eat, his swollen feet elevated on a nearby cot, the tin plate balanced on his lap.

After dinner, it was one more secondary resection of a gangrenous arm, requiring further amputation higher up toward the shoulder. "Just a little more chloroform, please. Keep him still." Bromine was trickled on the floor to reduce the vapors. The wound was daubed with swabs of treated lint. More bromine was sprayed in the air lest the foul vapors spread to the other patient's nearby. A rhythm of warm and wet dressings followed, removed and rinsed and re-used. Then began the real fight, the desperate battle against the poisoning, this persistent, elusive, and unrelenting opponent, this his real foe. When gangrene required the reluctant secondary surgery you didn't even need to bother informing the patient. He was already delirious.

☉☉☉

The next day, Friday, the day after Christmas Day, Nathaniel walked the distance to the Corps hospital to visit the few wounded men from the First Reserves who had been transferred there. He sought out Valentine and pulled him aside. They shared a cup of bitter coffee outside the hospital. Nathaniel pulled his pocket Bible from his coat pocket and removed from its pages a folded letter. Valentine drooped his head and listened as Nathaniel traced her delicate script with his fingertips and read the letter aloud:

...you write that you think of us, of me, every moment. May thoughts of home bring some grace to the dreadful sights that you must be seeing these days. We too think of you always, not a moment passing without us expecting to see you walking through the door

with Jenny at your feet. Margaret cannot pass by a window without looking for you coming home. Penelope jumps every time the train whistles. The nights are long, my beloved. We long to see you, but are glad you and our Valentine face these days together. He is our dearest friend. Penelope has yet to let go of the dear carving he sent. She carries her kitten everywhere. Margaret keeps her dove on the table near the bed. I and the girls have many kisses for him also when he returns with you. May it be soon...

Nathaniel refolded her letter and placed it back into the Bible, then pocketed it. He checked his timepiece. "Well, Jacob's waiting for me. It's time to visit the wards and write more letters."

"What you really mean," an exhausted and jaundiced Valentine frowned, "is that it is time for you to find out how many of the other kind of letters you have to write." Valentine touched Nathaniel's arm. "Sorry we can't do them better for you. God, I need a drink."

"Lots of sorry to go around," Nathaniel responded.

They both walked away toward their duties, saddened at how the other looked awfully sunken and gaunt.

⊚⊚⊚

"Go ahead, Jacob, tell them what you want to say. Your words don't have to be fancy." Nathaniel warmed his aching joints by cupping his hands and huffing his breath on folded fingers. "Imagine you're back home at the kitchen table and you're talking with them," Nathaniel coached the lethargic young man. A fly bothered Jacob's face by trying to land on the sores around his mouth. Nathaniel flicked his hand at it. Some ink from the pen flung onto his frock coat. A tiny splatter landed on Jacob's cheek.

Jacob, with pursed, dry lips, muttered a few words, barely audible. Nathaniel leaned closer to his mouth, foul breath puffing against his ear. He was getting better at figuring out what they were saying when they were like this. Nathaniel leaned closer as Jacob drifted farther away, toward someplace interior. Nathaniel, his head bent sidewise, failed to see the smallest crease of a smile on Jacob's face as he slid into a memory.

Death by pneumonia can be a gentle death. The winter fever. The drenching sweat and paroxysms and deliriums yield to the pervasive lethargy as the poison increases the metabolic demand. Soon follows the shallow breathing and the rattling cough from the welling phlegm. Eventually you become too weak, too ineffective to even cough. The poisoned blood spreads into the bloodstream. Simply not enough oxygen. So tired. Too tired. Drifting. So sleepy. Yet sleepless. You are bone tired. Your muscles ache for rest, but the body is denied its own rescuing, this deep restfulness. That is, until. Until your lungs finally are too lethargic to even bother trying to breathe anymore, so shallow that you finally stop. You stop. You end. Only then does your true rest finally arrive, when the chaplain says his prayer over the cold and damp body that remains. Then the chaplain pulls out pen and ink bottle and prepares to write home your parents.

Death by pneumonia can be a gentle death. It is what leads up to the pneumonia that is not so gentle.

In the letter home that Nathaniel had to finish for Jacob, he chose a Lutheran epitaph, quoting Psalm 46, Martin Luther's favorite Psalm: "*Be still and know that I am God.*" The letter he packed along with Jacob's few remaining personal affects.

Finally walking back to camp an hour before dusk, Nathaniel found himself returning to a camp roused and anxious. Immediately he was summoned to join the officers already gathered in Talley's tent. Evidently, shortly after he had left to visit the Corps hospital, orders had arrived for the men to cook rations, pack wagons, make ready general movement. None was happy about these orders. Surely none of the command staff was happy. Throughout the day Talley had been sending messengers to Division Headquarters demanding verification of these orders. March where? For what? There's been no advance word. No word at all.

Rumors flew among the men that their Cavalry already was on the move toward Kelly's Ford. Rumors circulated of another major offensive, of flying feints to distract Southern eyes from the general movement. Talley glared around at his staff with frustration smoldering in his eyes. He spoke too plainly, but the officers remained silent in a brotherly bond of agreement. "Fredericksburg area again? God, no. He can't try there again. No one is ready. Our shoes and uniforms are still damp. Nearly a quarter of the men are on sick call. We are still busy burying our dead. What the hell is that fool Burnside thinking of?"

Just as suddenly as the orders arrived, orders were rushed down by courier from Division informing Talley and his Regiment to stand down. There would be no general movement of the Army. Plans were abandoned as precipitously as announced. More disarray. More confusion. More resentment. More rumors spread of furious correspondence between Washington and headquarters. Rumors spread among the ranks of subordinates protesting, warning the contacts in Washington in clandestine communications.

Discontent and disquiet disturbed Lincoln's Army.

On Sunday morning, they awakened to discover Burnside had been summoned to Washington.

Boredom no longer was agreeable. The earlier, playful mischief of a week ago soured and stank like rotted beef, fostering maggots of mean-spiritedness. In several of the Companies the Captains had to act harshly to discipline an escalating unruliness. Some of the fights between the troops turned ugly. One man was beaten into permanent disability by a gang from his own unit. His skull was cracked open. They accused him of cheating at cards. Three of the most brutal offenders were tied to tree limbs with their bayonets gagged in their mouths. The fever of frustration, lethargy, and despair rapidly festered and infected the body of the Army of the Potomac. Nobody knew how to cut out this sickness.

Late one evening, following mess, Colonel Talley summoned Nathaniel into his tent. Talley invited Nathaniel to sit on the folding chair beside his desk. He strummed his fingers against a small ledger, then, shaking his head, looked up at Nathaniel.

Nathaniel's tongue explored a space between two of his molars. His eyes trained themselves on the articles on Talley's desk. He pulled on his mustache. He waited.

Talley leaned back in his chair and rocked precariously on its back legs. "Your work is appreciated, chaplain. And I will be honest with you. Despite my initial reservations, I would not want to lose you..." Talley lingered for effect. "...for the moment." Talley tilted his chair back farther and crossed his leg. "I judge my officers by how the men respect them. You have gained influence among the ranks during these difficult weeks with us." Talley then tilted forward and rested his forearms across his desk. "Chaplain McKenna, I'm not certain if this will help the troops or not, but we have just received orders that we are to proclaim this document throughout the entire Army. You are the first, after myself, to see this. It is a circular fresh from Washington. I have decided to give you the privilege of reading it to the men tomorrow." He pulled a folded sheet of paper from underneath his forearm and presented it to Nathaniel. "This proclamation is, as we speak, being printed in every newspaper."

Nathaniel read the document, his eyes racing across the typeface:

And by virtue of the power and for the purpose aforesaid, I do order and declare that all persons held as slaves within said designated States and parts of States are and henceforth shall be free; and that the Executive Government of the United States, including the military and naval authorities thereof, will recognize and maintain the freedom of said persons.

Smoothing the circular out on his lap, Nathaniel looked calmly at the Colonel. Inside his heart pounded. "Nobody should be surprised," he observed. "It's been in the works for months. Since Antietam. Our man said he would do this. He's a man of his word. For all that our men have endured, it is about time we were reminded of the moral urgency. It's about time. It's about time someone told us why we've gotten ourselves into this mess."

"I agree, chaplain." Talley replied. "Although I'm a soldier, which means I refuse to confuse myself by being a moralist, I agree that it is high time someone tells us why we are here."

"I've only been here among you for weeks, but my guess is that the men will be proud, maybe even relieved." Nathaniel looked back down at the document in his lap, shaking his head, "Lincoln did it. He really did it. Thought for sure they'd stop him."

Talley signaled Nathaniel's attention with a tap of his finger. "I'm not sure you have read all of it. Oh no. Open it. Read on, chaplain, read on."

Nathaniel picked up the document again.

And I further declare and make known that such persons of suitable condition will be received into the armed service of the United States to garrison forts, positions, stations, and other places, and to man vessels of all sorts in said service...

Talley stood and reached to retrieve the circular. Nathaniel stood also. "You see, chaplain, our troops may be surprised by this twist. This possibility has been debated for the last year. Lincoln has tipped the scale. You watch them now." Talley refolded the document and suddenly slapped it against the edge of his desk. "They finally did it, Nathaniel," he called out. "They finally did it," he shouted. "After all the debating and threats and conniving, I didn't think he'd go through with this final proclamation. Didn't think he'd really sign it. I really didn't. I thought they'd get to him too." Talley gripped the document. "We're now not just an Army of preservation but of liberation. Finally we have a real Commander-in-chief!"

Nathaniel was uncertain as to what surprised him more: the Emancipation Proclamation or Talley's glee. Nathaniel nodded his head and smiled broadly. "My God, it's true, Colonel. Colored troops. Imagine it. The ante is upped."

"They can do more than serve as our burial details. Now how do you think the men will respond?" Talley asked, as he gazed beyond the tent flap. He reached his hand toward Nathaniel's. "By the way, Reverend, I may be a day late, but happy New Year."

Chapter Six

Mosby's Confederacy

We've been fighting today on the old camp ground
Many are lying near;
Some are dead, and some are dying
Many are in tears
"Tenting Tonight," Walter Kittredge

"We's in Mosby's Confederacy now, boys."
The Sergeant's face twisted into a wry, menacing grin while his molars tore at a Honeydew chew. The Company relaxed around the covered well on the grounds of the stately, red bricked Fairfax Courthouse. Several of the newer men of the Reserves glanced nervously over their shoulders, suspicious of every civilian who could be possibly watching them from the nearby windows or from behind every porch or picket fence. One soldier seated himself comfortably on the low bench that surrounded the well, resting his back against his heavy field pack as he read a yellowed and torn copy of *Harpers Weekly*. Canteens were replenished from the bucket drawn from the deep well. Pipes also were filled and smoked. A dry cigar was lit. For others, it was time to steal a quick nap against a tree. Nathaniel tilted his head back and gazed up from his seat on the ambulance toward the Courthouse cupola.

Lieutenant Bear stood on the ledge outside the cupola surveying the horizon. With one hand clinging to the rail, his other hand shielded his eyes with his right hand from the noonday sun.

Somewhere out amongst those pine woods and farms lurked Mosby. Every lightning raid against the Federal wagon trains was blamed on Mosby. The Army sent our numerous patrols these last months in the vain attempt to capture him. But it was like trying to catch a terrier that had slipped its leash, complete with bites and scratches to show for it. Somewhere out in the countryside Mosby and his mounted guerrillas were galloping quick and clever as they scurried around the Regiment to harass and plunder. In small squadrons of twenty to eighty men he slipped between picket and outpost, at once attacking your front, then flanking you on both flanks, swiftly whirling around to take a bite out of your backside. This terrier had sharp teeth.

The Reserves' job? To stop him. If they could. To deploy themselves along the Orange and Alexandria railroad and protect the telegraph wires, the signal stations, and the rail itself. To run guard patrol for the rumbling caravans of mule drawn trucks that Mosby and his partisans nipped with a frequency and an efficiency that unnerved and frightened the War Department to its spine. Orders came down from Headquarters for heavier guard. Stop him. Stop Mosby.

Mosby. John Singleton Mosby. A former lawyer who commanded men who had abandoned the saber and the carbine in favor of revolver and violent surprise. The saber clanked in its sheath too noisily, sounding too tell-tale an advance alarm. Stealth and dash was preferred over brawn and armament. The breechloading carbine served well for the quick dismount and skirmish, but when Mosby's rangers dashed from hiding among the pine trees to pounce upon the wagon train, their fighting always turned close quarter. Revolvers served them best. Shoot your enemy in the face. Blind him. Hit and run. Light cavalry. Bushwhack and ambush, then vanish into the countryside, along with prisoners, horses, hinnies, mules, and the even more prized Union supplies. Eight captured mules per truck could feed a whole Regiment of hungry Confederates.

The Reserve's duty, even if it meant defending against this phantom Mosby and his rangers, was far better work than what they endured two weeks ago. Two weeks ago was Burnsides blunder. It also was his farewell performance as Commanding General of the Army of the Potomac.

Two weeks ago, precisely at 10 PM, the Army set out on Burnside's grand scheme to flank Lee under the cover of night. A snowfall, mixed with driving sleet, followed by pouring rain, bogged an entire Army in thick muck. The weather conspired with the clay of Virginia to retard their advance. Wagons, limbers, caissons, and cannons sank to their axles, requiring men to be detailed to grasp the wooden wheels and crank them, inch by inch, through the glue which once were highways, cranking them across the fields become marsh and mire.

The artillery finally had to be left behind as simply impossible to haul through such glue. The Mud March, they called it with curse and derision. Mules slid sidewise, kicking and flailing, struggling to raise themselves. Timbers had to be felled and laid sidewise in certain impassable sections to construct a corduroy roadway. Men slogged through the mixture, churned deep by the march of a thousand other men, each man sinking up to his knees. Their boots gained double their weight with every step, till they were so covered with muck that you saw no shoes, just balls of gluey red clay at the base of your legs.

Forced to slog throughout the cold and wet night, the Army's advance was retarded so severely that the scheme of surprise became a ridiculous fantasy. Come daylight, the Rebel army, encamped snugly across the Rappahannock, watched not in alarm but in embarrassment. They were too astonished to mock the Federal forces. The Rebels went through the motion of marshaling their forces at the fords, prepared to repulse an Army, but they knew the assault would never come. The Union troops had already been vanquished by Virginia.

Two days later the Army of the Potomac plodded home to where they had begun, only wetter, dirtier, colder, and far more demoralized. Three days ago, the foolish soldiers had burnt their stockade huts to the ground in a bold confidence in this valiant advance. They had boasted that they would warm themselves instead in Richmond. Instead, they had returned to where they had begun and had to pitch their dog tents on the ground and sleep on damp ashes of ruined comfort.

Burnside was promptly recalled to Washington. Few among the Regiments grieved his departure.

Confronting the spectre of Mosby was worth the price of exiting this camp of filthy, angry, exasperated comrades-in-arms. Mosby's unpredictability was, at least, far more appealing than the predictability of many more months of soggy boredom of winter encampment. Better doing something than waiting for Washington to figure out how to run this damned Army. To a man, the entire Regiment looked forward to arriving at Fairfax Station, east of Fairfax Courthouse, and begin guarding the rail from Union Mills to Alexandria. To a man, the Reserves agreed that they'd rather take a revolver's bullet or face the risk of capture than suffer the almost certain bout of chronic dysentery raging throughout the encampment of the Army of the Potomac. Rather than suffer another epidemic of measles, they preferred Mosby.

Capture was a possibility Nathaniel hadn't seriously pondered until the alert sounded throughout the Reserves following Jeb Stuart's raid on Dumfries, where his Cavalry captured twenty five wagons and over two hundred prisoners. A teasing Nathaniel quizzed Valentine one night: "Do you think Headquarters would bother exchanging a captured chaplain?"

"Depends on the denomination, I suppose," quipped Valentine. "How many Protestants for one good Catholic priest?"

The next day, Fitz Hugh Lee crossed the Rappahannock near Falmouth and surprised an encampment there, his Cavalry seizing one hundred fifty Union prisoners.

"They'd probably keep you though," said Nathaniel. "Chain you to the ambulance. Or, you sot, they'd just bribe you with some of that Kentucky bourbon you can't get anymore."

That spies lurked everywhere none doubted. Only last week two Quaker farmers suspected of spying for Mosby were shipped by Talley under armed escort to Washington for interrogation and tribunal. Neither prisoner arrived, their guards themselves mysteriously becoming prisoners, surfacing in a later exchange.

The Rebels relished living up to the legend. Theirs was the luxury of being able to ride wherever and whenever they wished, vanishing like vapors through the picket lines, spiriting through the gaps between the loose chain of outposts. Twice Nathaniel, touring on borrowed horse while checking in on the Companies posted along the line, arrived minutes after such a raid. The telegraph line had been yanked down moments before his arrival. Unchallenged by absent sentries, he cantered into camp to find the soldiers circling in a frenzy, officers rushing to send out horsed pursuit and ordering Sergeants to take roll call and count the number of their ranks missing.

Talley didn't like the idea of his chaplain turning into such a freebooter, but if the men couldn't come to him the chaplain was resolved go to the men. With Regimental headquarters set up at Fairfax Station and the Companies posted along the railroad for miles, Nathaniel combined delivering the mail with the chance to deliver a sermon. He soon began to feel like one of the Methodist circuit riders back home, as well as learning to admire a Methodist's callused rump in the saddle. Except they usually rode mules. He got to ride a magnificent bay Morgan.

"I need her again, Rupert. That is, my friend, if you don't mind lending her for the work of the Lord," he asked the newly promoted Adjutant. "You should understand, Alfred, that Harvey was always pleased to loan me his horse. He considered it an honor. It's part of the privilege of being Adjutant."

"Yeah, Nate, I talked to him before he left. He warned me about you," replied First Lieutenant Alfred Rupert. "When are you going to get your own horse?" Rupert asked each time, making a ritual of his weekly complaint. "Jesus rode a donkey, as I recall, so stop making it sound as if God personally requires my Morgan."

"Ah, but He does, but He does, my son. I am quite sure Jesus would have preferred a Morgan, had he had a choice. The work of the Lord must go on," Nathaniel preached. "You see, I had a vision: God prefers to ride the finest. Would you deny your Lord that?" Nathaniel asked with upraised arm. "Besides, Rupert, I will purchase my own horse as soon as our government bothers to pass that bill and pay me the same as any Regimental staff officer." Nathaniel continued with a wink: "Being a servant of the Lord doesn't mean I had to take a vow of poverty." With a click of his watch cover, he'd quote the newly popular hymn: "Time to ride on, ride on in majesty!'"

"That man is either terribly religious or terribly blasphemous. I haven't quite made up my mind," Rupert would comment to his aides with a resigned shrug. "I fear he's been hanging around our Surgeon far too long now."

Ten Companies—A to I and K—were to be visited in rotation along the line. During the first week he found he could visit three Companies every day. Sometimes he'd ride alongside the dispatch riders, but, because they rode too fast for him, himself still a novice on horseback, he usually rode alone, to the grudging discomfort of Colonel Talley. Valentine thought him a plain fool. Valentine himself was busy taking advantage of the relaxed duty, letting Assistant Surgeon Barber and his Steward manage sick call, bunions, moldy feet, and the ever-persistent diarrhea.

With a friendly, "Howdy, parson," the triads of soldiers assigned picket duty would greet the familiar frock coat coming down the turnpike. Despite being wrapped in their light blue colored great coats, they were always frozen and frostbit from the prohibition of fires while on sentinel. Some Captains allowed him to sort through the mail he carried and hand out any letters or packages the men on picket duty were meant to receive. Most Captains, however, preferred that these men were not so distracted, a lesson Nathaniel discovered after a few polite yet official reprimands.

After greeting the men on picket, Nathaniel would ride into camp. There was usually a man or two who missed a favorite horse back home along with the feel of curry comb in his hands, so he'd gladly tend to the Morgan. The appearance of the chaplain was sufficient announcement that it was time for worship. The men who were so inclined, along with the others looking for something to do, would heap a few more logs on the fire and gather in a circle. With seared fronts and frozen backsides, with the smoke bothering eyes, it was time for a few songs sung from memory or lined by a volunteer deacon in their midst. Then scripture was read and a few words of reflection offered, followed by time for prayers, which Nathaniel always opened up to the men to share, if they wished. He had long ago given up praying his long, formal prayers. He had weeks ago stopped relying on the prayer book.

It amazed Nathaniel how his liturgical practices had changed these few months in the field. He even performed several baptisms in camp for men who felt the call. He wondered if his Professors back at Princeton would approve. After all, he may be acting decently, but it sure was out of order.

These months on campaign had taught him a few tricks to this chaplain trade. For one, Nathaniel had learnt it best to hand out their mail and collect their letters home following services. Before he trotted to the next unit, the men would surround him and he'd gather and stuff in his saddlebag what letters they wished to post homeward. During one solitary ride between camps he began to understand how insignificant his role really was. "You know, partner," he mused aloud, scratching the ears of the Morgan, "it really isn't that I do much of anything. I'm simply a link. Not much to that, is there?" The Morgan shoved its head closer into the scratch. "Funny," he added, "how everybody at first thinks their job is the dirtiest."

One late March night, clip-clopping on his return to Fairfax Station, having recently finished a hot meal and friendly talk with his boys in Company C, Nathaniel admired the clear winter sky. He had stayed later than usual helping celebrate the three new promotions of John Thompson from Sergeant to Second Lieutenant, Edward Larkin from First Sergeant to First Lieutenant, and Joseph Coates from First Lieutenant to the newly gazetted Captain of the Company. Nathaniel looked into the southwest sky and admired Orion shining bright. A shooting star crossed the belt. "Yep, not much to it." Lowering his eyes, he noticed the glint of the dangling telegraph wire swaying in the wind.

His horse, pricking its ears, heard the hooves and the rustle of branches before he did. He strained forward over the neck of the Morgan and thought he saw a collection of shadows emerging from the pines at the bend in the turnpike ahead. Surprises were unwelcome at this hour. That was military knowledge enough for Nathaniel.

Stark fear and shameless prudence combine to form admirable and wise companions. Before several of the shadows could spring out from the treeline onto the open road, Nathaniel wheeled his Morgan around. He slammed the heels of his black boots into the horse's ribs and galloped back toward Company C.

"Rangers! Mosby! Partisans!" he shriekd to the out-lying pickets as he galloped past, unable to pull back the reins firmly enough to slow the racing horse. Musket fire erupted behind him as he continued galloping into the camp, where he finally was able to twist his horse to a near stop, aided by the firmer hand of Lieutenant Thompson, who jumped toward the withers of the horse, and, with both hands, snared the bridle. The horse sidestepped with his hind legs and knocked over a tripod of three Springfield muskets, sending a leather cartridge box skidding.

"Rangers!" Nathaniel again shouted, his alarm punctuated by more popping of muskets and a returning volley of pistol fire. The men stumbled for their weapons and hastily formed a defensive line. Coates, sword drawn, the blade circling above his bald head, his colt waving in his other hand, dashed near the edge of camp to mark where he wanted his men to form the repulse. Dark horsemen broke into the clearing.

The rangers meant to escape by a brazen charge right through the middle of camp.

"Fire!" Coates shouted as he leveled his pistol toward the charge. A flashing fusillade of fire ripped through the night. Through the smoke, Nathaniel saw several figures tumble from their saddles. The riders galloping behind them vaulted over their fallen friends. Nathaniel watched as one rider, slight of build, whirled around to help hoist a wounded comrade onto his horse.

"Fire!" Thompson shouted to the second rank. The horsemen sped on, whooping as they poured through the files of the standing blue coats. Their revolvers, with hot barrels and warm chambers, blasted at the infantryman face high to prevent them from trying to club them from their saddle. Soldiers staggered, others were shoved to the ground by the sudden collision with the shoulders and chest of galloping horse, these falling men struck and bruised, their bones broken, by iron hooves.

Nathaniel leapt behind a large tree to avoid the crush. The slender horseman who rescued his comrade galloped down toward him. In the campfire light he noticed that the skilled horseman bore the rank of a Confederate Captain. The Captain whirled his horse between Nathaniel and Nathaniel's Morgan. With bright eyes and a broad smile highlighted by a trim mustache, this young Captain doffed his feathered hat and saluted the chaplain, then leaned over and seized the reins of Nathaniel's borrowed Morgan, inviting his prize of war, along with Nathaniel's gear, to join the stampede south.

Loose clumps of Company C pivoted and fired erratic volleys as forty horsemen raced into the darkness at the far side of camp.

"It's Mosby himself," Nathaniel guessed, pulling on the ends of his mustache.

A panting Coates rushed up to Nathaniel. Similar to the rest of the men, Nathaniel simply stared into the dust and shadows. Coates slapped him on the back. "Nice friends you brought back with you. Wasn't one good-bye enough."

Nathaniel pointed toward the woods. "They took my horse." He then patted his coat pocket. His pocket Bible was there but he must have stored his prayer book in the saddlebag. "Mosby took my prayer book." The men gathered around him, joining Coates in laughing. Nathaniel also laughed as he turned around to face them. "Actually, they took Rupert's horse." The men laughed louder. "And your letters," he realized. The men started swearing.

Coates surveyed the damage. It was a fortunate few seconds for the Company. None killed. It was too swift an assault for serious damage. Mosby rarely let himself get caught in any prolonged engagement. They were fortunate that all he wanted was escape. Three of Mosby's rangers fell in the attack though. One survived, bruised from the fall. This was the real prize as far as Coates was concerned. Worth the price. Worth being caught unawares. The Colonel would judge it a victory. For few of Mosby's men ever had been captured. Usually it was the other way around. Headquarters would be eager to interrogate the prisoner.

Through the remainder of the night Nathaniel helped substitute for the lack of dressing Steward and Surgeon. Schooled by his initiation from these recent months on campaign, he dressed many of the facial and shoulder wounds, as well as mending the broken arms. Horses can be nasty brutes in a collision. Two wounds however exceeded his novice skills. One of the boys was shot in the gut, another in the upper thigh. Both required probing and extraction of the bullet. Both wounds ran risk of hemorrhage.

Before dawn he started out toward headquarters seated on the two-wheeled 'avalanche' drafted into ambulance service. The two men groaned and ached with each jostling bump. The driver tried to avoid the ruts, yet speed was the more urgent necessity. Nathaniel signaled the driver to hurry the pace back to Fairfax Station, back to the Regimental field hospital set up in the school house. By the time they arrived, Nathaniel's back ached from the jostling and the two casualties were nearly unconscious from pain.

Valentine was waiting for them. "Heard you had a little excitement last night, Nate." Valentine signaled for the injured men to be unloaded, then he helped his friend down from the 'avalanche's bench. Valentine led him into the school house. "You weren't the only one busy last night, as you can see." Two days ago the field hospital was empty except for sick call. Now a dozen casualties convalesced on cots around the room.

"Yesterday and last night our friends coordinated several attacks throughout Fairfax and Loudoun counties," Valentine explained. "They tore down telegraph lines at several sites. One railroad bridge burnt."

The teacher's desk in front of the blackboard had become the operating table. At the top left of blackboard, smudged but not erased, Nathaniel read what remained of a multiplication table. The orderlies picked up the litter of the man wounded in the gut and they placed him on the desk. The movement roused him. He moaned. Assistant Surgeon Barber tended to the thigh wound at another table set up in the corner. Chasing the flies away from the gore and odor of the wounded belly, Valentine peeled away the dressings. "You do this?" He asked, looking over at Nathaniel.

Nathaniel shrugged and tilted his head.

"Adequate for a first year preceptor."

Nathaniel leaned up against the wall.

"Get out of here and get some sleep."

Nathaniel ignored him. Something in him refused to leave. He needed to see it through. Pride perhaps. Stubbornness more likely.

Valentine knew why he refused to leave. "Listen, they'll be okay," he said to him. "They'll both make it. You did good. Now get out of here and let me finish." Valentine fingered for remnants of the woolen uniform stuck inside the wound. Blood started oozing from the man's belly onto the table, leaking onto

Valentine's boots. "Goddamn it. Steward! Give me the damn forceps! Then more packing!" The soldier screamed as Valentine explored the insides of his intestines. Valentine spread the wound apart and reached the forceps inside. "Look at the pus already. Laudable." He twisted the dripping forceps with his bloodied hand. "Got it! Got the bastard. Quick, I can sew a bit here." Valentine twisted around, anxious for the Steward to bring him needle and silk surgical thread.

The Steward held out his hands and looked at his shoes, refusing to look back at Surgeon O'Rourke. "We're out."

"What the hell do you mean, 'We're out?'"

"I've been trying to get some the last couple of days. All we got is the spools from the sewing kit my mom sent me, my 'housewife.'"

"Goddamn it. Give it here." Valentine reached inside the man with the needle and began stitching. "What the hell am I, a surgeon or a goddamn seamstress? How the hell do they expect me to fix these men without the right sutures? Unacceptable. Unacceptable. Pack it, pack it. More lint! Where's the damn nitrate? Got any perchlorate? Pack it, pack it. No obits today! I don't have time for it. I will not allow it! Give me that nitrate!"

The Steward again looked down at his shoes. "Ain't none. All gone this morning."

"Dammit—if he dies all hell's going to break lose. Goddamn useless Army." Valentine hurled a soggy bandage against the blackboard. The blood splattered and the bandage smeared a red trail as it slid to the wooden chalk gutter. "Give me anything. I'll take anything for a styptic. Whatever you have, whatever you have…"

Valentine tightened the final bandage around the wound and, with a toss of his head, signaled for the orderlies to carry the man to his cot. Rinsing his hands in a porcelain bowl, he walked over to the Steward. As he dried his hands against his apron, he asked in a controlled, precise tone: "Steward, where is everything? I thought I saw the supply wagon arrive two days ago."

The Steward turned and looked out the window. Barber, Chilson, and Chapin circled around to listen. The Steward faced Valentine. "It did. Plenty of food on it. Even a few more cots and blankets. Some new sheets and bed shirts for the men. But no medical supplies. I checked. I really did. I double-checked. It's a mystery to me. I'm sorry, sir. We're low on everything: lint, bandages, silk, iodine, styptics. We're down to our last box of opium pills. Until last night, I thought we'd sneak by."

"Obviously," Barber chimed in, "we didn't. Guess I used the last of the nitrate on the thigh. The perchlorate is long gone."

"Is he okay?" Valentine questioned.

"He'll be fine. Painful, but clean," Barber reported.

Valentine scanned his patients, then tightened his lips and pulled on his goatee. "Husband everything, you hear me. Holy Mother of God. Conserve it all. Use what we have for the worst cases. In the meantime, I'm going to talk to the Colonel. Maybe Resser first." Valentine's eyes narrowed as his voice chilled. "Yes, Resser. He's first." Valentine paused at the door. His shoulders slumped, finally surrendering to the weariness. He turned. "Barber? John? Please keep on eye on that belly. Will you be so good to do that, Doctor?" he asked in a flat iron voice. Valentine looked over and noticed Nathaniel asleep against the wall. Valentine gestured toward him. "And get that man a cot."

Assistant Surgeon John Barber nodded and waved, then he turned to kneel beside one of the men brought in yesterday afternoon with a compound fracture of the leg.

"That's a good man, Barber." Valentine said as he threw shut the door to the school house behind him. "Let's hope Mosby decides it's time for a holiday."

Chapter Seven

Improper Channels

I think our song has lasted almost long enough
The subject's interesting, but the rhythms are mighty rough
I wish this war was over, when free from rags and fleas,
We'd kiss our wives and sweethearts and gobble goober peas!
"Goober Peas," by A Pender

"We're going on a little holiday," Valentine gaily announced as he tossed an empty carpet bag on a sleeping Nathaniel, half hidden beneath the bunched up blanket. "You've got two hours till the train comes backing up through our saintly corner of Christendom."

Nathaniel vaguely recalled the distant whistle of a train rumbling through the village several hours ago. It must have off-loaded then. It took two hours for the engine to back up from the burnt bridge in the next county over, forcing the train to chug backwards all the way into the city.

"Papers and passports signed and sealed. Get your gear and let's get kitted up." Valentine started tossing his gear into his leather satchel. "Took me some doing but I got you permission too. Had to nearly get on my knees and beg. You and your Commission friends might be of some influence. Our Colonel wasn't about to let you go...," O'Rourke paused and cast an evil grin. "...till I promised I personally would look after you."

"Hmmp. Why do I have the feeling," Nathaniel replied groggily, wiping the crust from his eyes, "that it is the other way around? If I don't go, you don't go."

"Come on, me darlin' duena. We've got a tough job to do. I'm looking forward to a fine brandy and a rare steak. I am damn near sick of all this salted beef and salted pork."

"But I'm, I'm supposed to check back on my boys down the line," Nathaniel stammered. "Young Joe had organized a Bible study. The book of Jonah, which scholars suggest is a riposte to Nahum's invective, and..."

"No time for your Bible today. After the other night, the Colonel has everybody jumping like jack rabbits. He's annoyed that his chaplain had to turn into his best scout. So for you, it's a holiday."

"From God?"

"Trust me. God'll appreciate it."

Valentine hunkered down on the edge of his bed and rounded his shoulders as he reached around and rubbed the back of his neck. He kicked a charred piece of wood toward the compact iron stove. "Listen, I want to know and the good Colonel wants to know. Division wants to know. Jesus Christ himself probably wants to know. We all want to know. We all want answers. Why aren't we getting what we need? Why aren't we getting what we should have?" Valentine plucked at his goatee. "I am sick of my men dying on me. I take it very personal. All Resser says, damn him, is 'Mosby.' Everything's Mosby. Nothing's getting through because of Mosby. Well, Mosby can't be everywhere they say he is. And the good Colonel and I want to know why. Even our tight-sphinctered

Colonel is fed up sending requisitions. Who knows? Maybe between my persuasive and tactful diplomacy and your pious connections we might be able to bring a few items back that my patients need. Maybe talk to that Gurley friend of your father's." Valentine's eyes twinkled. He placed his finger aside his nose. "Besides, you're right as rain. There's no way he would let me go alone. Can you believe it? He wanted Resser, that skinny Quartermaster, to go with me. Dear Lord, can you imagine Resser and myself on holiday together in the capital. Lordy no. I then came up with the absolutely brilliant notion of our trusty and worthy chaplain. Don't ask me why, but the good Colonel is beginning to become fond of you. You, friend, get to be my chaperone. You know my philosophy: when faced with adversity, dance! Come on, boy, time to go. We are authorized to rob, steal, bribe, or cuckold our way into bringing home whatever we need."

"Talley's orders, no doubt."

"Verbatim," Valentine insisted, pressing his palm against his heart.

Nathaniel folded his hands and closed his eyelids in mock prayer. Valentine swung and hit him with a leather pouch. Nathaniel rolled off the cot and soon found himself pleasuring in a warm shave from the water left in the basin overnight on top of the stove.

Standing in the middle of the tent, Valentine adjusted his uniform. "How do I look? Sword belt comfortably snug over green sash, gauntlets, and all the bright buttons. Time to look pretty." Valentine shook his head with exasperation at Nathaniel buttoning his black waistcoat. "Somebody around here has to appear gallant."

Steam billowed from the locomotive, the vapors swirling in the breeze. Nathaniel wound his pocket watch, his frock coat flapping like a sail about his legs. Though it was a double breasted coat, he rarely buttoned it, preferring to leave it open so he could stick his hands in his trouser pockets or, better, retrieve his brand new watch from his waistcoat. Buttoned, the coat made him feel trapped in a cocoon. The train, consisting of two flat cars, one box car, and one passenger coach, chugged to a crawl as it backed up to the Fairfax station house.

The depot was a whirl of smoke and steam, clanging bells, and the chugging rhythms of power and purpose. The incessant bell-clanging accompanied the 'fum fum fum' of the hasty heartbeat puffs of the locomotive's three turning, synchronized wheels. From the upside down funnel of a smokestack flowed fumes of soot. White steam hissed from valves atop and on either side of the huge black kettle of a boiler. A small patrol sat cross-legged on the flatcar. Two soldiers stood on either side of the locomotive cab located at the rear of the train. They clung to their carbines and stood shrouded in steam vapors. Another two Privates sat at the back edge of the hopper, the pile of timber half stoked. Their carbines lay across their knees, their faces vacuous and dusky from the dirty smoke.

Nathaniel followed Valentine as he leapt up the coach's two wooden steps onto the grilled platform outside the closed door of the coach. Valentine pushed open the door and stepped aside as he shoved Nathaniel into the coach ahead of him. Nathaniel entered and instantly was enveloped by an intoxicating wave of heady perfume. The man inside the black frock gulped, overwhelmed and aroused by this surprising and long absent feminine bath of siren sensuality. A dozen ladies, half likely in their young twenties, occupied the benches of the coach, their full dresses gathered up in bunches. Many of the women wore evening gowns. Draped shawls hid creamy breasts.

Valentine, tipping his hat as he processed toward two empty seats at the rear, leaned over and whispered into Nathaniel's ear: "Some actually might be wives." Nathaniel blushed, hoping none of the ladies had overheard.

"I'm in heaven," Valentine pronounced loudly. He relished this invitation of lace, silk, and perfume. Women refreshed him. Women animated him. Single, married, or widowed, to Valentine these women were all beautiful. Valentine treated them all as equals. Equally available. Equally delightful. And the ladies, Nathaniel noted, tingled to it. To him.

Nathaniel watched him with a bemusement mixed with grudging admiration. Valentine was cleverer than most. He always had been. He knew full well that these women, whether wives or otherwise, were use to brave heroes of rank and command regaling them with their martial exploits. Puffing on his pipe, he eavesdropped while Valentine coached Bear on the art of romance during one of those tedious nights after a particularly bad mess supper. "Well, of course, my naive apprentice, it's hardly the Privates and Sergeants who get to enjoy a woman's company while deployed in the field. Those sots have to pay for it. Now, if you're really clever, you'll let the ladies talk and you'll listen to them. You can't pretend to listen, trust me, because they'll catch on. You see, young William, they spend most of their lives listening to way too many bragging officers, husbands and paramours included. No, there is nothing more seductive than a man who listens."

Nathaniel had heard all this before. But Nathaniel had spent his career listening and, right now, he was sick of it. Listening to Professors. Listening to pompous colleagues who didn't know how to listen. Listening to complaining church elders. Listening to persons talk about their troubles expecting him to fix them. Listening to trolling women disappointed in their husbands. Alice long ago had warned him about the danger of being a good listener. It had led more than a few pastors down the garden path of trouble and defrocking. Yes, Nathaniel mused as he closed his eyes, I shall prefer rest over seduction. Valentine can handle them all.

Nathaniel chose to enjoy the upholstery instead. He reflected inwardly: for three months I have been sitting on rickety wooden folding chairs or perched on splintered wagon seats or on worn saddles. This is the first comfortable, cushioned, luxurious seat my sore backside has enjoyed since I left Washington three months ago and I am going to enjoy it. He shuffled deeper into the soft cushions. While Valentine began a conversation with one of the ladies sitting across from him, his speech betraying a hint of his father's brogue, Nathaniel pressed his head against the window pane and pulled his hat down over his face. I must be getting old, Nathaniel thought to himself as he tried to ignore everything and everyone around him, and let the train rock him to contented sleep.

The train rumbled past blockhouses and mansions, past jagged earthworks and rolling hills. Trees had begun to leaf out, the azaleas in bud. Gradually the number of clustered homes and civilians going about their afternoon business increased. The train rumbled backwards past earthen and stone fortifications thick with black iron cannons facing west and south. Nathaniel awakened in time to spot in the distance the unfinished Capitol dome. The wooden cranes, ropes, and steam driven derricks on top of the Capitol building made it look more like a ship than ship of state. Or else, Nathaniel fancied, with only two tiers erected of the hollow rotunda, it resembled a fancy wedding cake. Granite Ionic columns held aloft the fancy ornamentation decorating the front portico.

The train clattered across Long Bridge, headed toward the terminus, where, arriving, it jerked, jolted, staggered, and gushed to a stop. The men exited first and assisted the ladies down the steps onto the platform. A few of the ladies offered a view as they bent to receive their hands. Valentine paused to kiss the hands of several of his more recent intimates as he helped them into their awaiting carriages. A rustle of petticoats revealed appetizing ankles. With a dramatic sigh, Valentine latched their carriage doors. Nathaniel walked up to his friend, grasped him by the shoulders, pivoted him around, and together they entered the tedium that was Washington.

At their hotel, Valentine thanked Nathaniel. "You've always been helpful to me, my old comrade in arms. When I travel with you, the ladies actually suspect I am honorable. Ah, what a team we could make. And if you weren't so in love with your Alice, we could be truly devastating. Imagine the possibilities. We could give them the best of both: reputable you and dissolute me. You bait, I hook. We would be invincible."

◎◎◎

"What do you mean, 'there is no one to whom I can speak?'" O'Rourke roared. "I have my orders. I am here at my Colonel's behest. I have concerns here that I insist someone help resolve.

I want satisfaction." Valentine smacked the leather satchel of papers across the edge of the secretary's desk. "I don't care if I am not going through proper channels."

The secretary stood up, and, in a strained effort, extended his open hand. "May I please see those papers again? I'll check and see if someone on staff has the time to talk with you." Valentine pulled out a pile of papers from the satchel and slapped them into the man's palm. The secretary turned wearily and exited from the room through a door that led toward the rear of the building. The two men listened to the Grandfather clock as it clicked and began chiming four strokes. Nathaniel flicked out his pocket watch. "Their clock is five minutes off," he remarked to Valentine.

Except for a frail, elderly man waiting for an interview, his black medical case at his feet, the foyer was empty. Nathaniel paced while Valentine moved across the floor and leaned the side of his face against a doorway that led to an adjoining office. Pressing his ear against the crack, Valentine heard only a muffled conversation from the interior of the office. The conversation was punctuated by a puzzling tapping sound, then silence, followed by light laughter. Minutes afterwards the latch lowered and the door swung outward. Valentine pulled himself back from the doorway just in time and pretended to straighten his sash. Two men emerged. A distinguished looking gentleman, wearing a brown dress coat and cravat, his white hair matching his trimmed gray beard, had his left arm draped around the shoulders of man wearing a black dress coat with a fur collar. The man with the fur collar wore a bright red vest decorated with what appeared to be a design of golden dragons. A vast gold chain stretched across the expanse of the man's rotund stomach. He held in his left hand a beaver hat, white gloves, and his walking stick. The mahogany stick was decorated with a silver handle and silver tip. His black mustache, in contrast to Nathaniel's drooping walrus of a mustache, was trimmed and slick, turned up and waxed to a needle's point at the ends. He bore the signs and smells of frequent trips to the barber shop.

The distinguished older man shook the hand of the man with the cane. Speaking more to the room than to the man, he said: "We do appreciate your business. Come back anytime. You have always been able to provide what you promise. The prices may be dear but these are difficult times, and we cannot disappoint our valiant troops in the field."

The man with the cane twisted his upper lip into a half smile. "Our medicines are the finest possible." With the handle of the cane he tapped the elder gentleman on the arm. "We will fill this next order in the next couple of days, as soon as our shipment arrives from New York."

They shook hands again at the doorway leading to the avenue. The man with the cane pulled on his white gloves. With a tap of his cane on the wooden floor and a touch of his finger to his hat brim, he passed Nathaniel and exited.

O'Rourke confronted the older man before he got the chance to retreat into his office. "You're in charge of purchasing medical supplies?"

"I have that honor, Doctor." The gray haired man hesitated, studying Valentine's uniform, "or should I address you as Major?"

"Valentine O'Rourke, at your service. Surgeon." Valentine extended his upturned hand toward Nathaniel. "This is my friend and chaplain of our Regiment, Nathaniel McKenna."

McKenna nodded in greeting. The elderly man politely returned the nod but failed to introduce himself by name.

A more imperious than polite O'Rourke continued: "We are here for precisely the problem you may solve. I have papers from both Division and our Regiment appealing for an increase in our shipments. Several days ago, after a skirmish in the field, my hospital found its supplies inadequate. This is unacceptable. We must be supplied better."

The gray haired gentleman remained holding the inside latch of his office door, standing slightly behind the door. His face twitched.

"Dammit man, attend to me. Surgical thread. Gone. Perchlorate. Gone. Chloroform. Gone. My men are dying because of lack of adequate supplies. Are you in charge of supplies?"

"I suggest you speak with your Quartermaster."

"Dammit man, what am I, an idiot? My Colonel sent me here instead of the Quartermaster." Valentine swelled as he announced grandiosely: "I'm here speaking for Division."

"Then I would suggest you talk to the Headquarters of your Corps."

O'Rourke whirled and shouted at McKenna "Is he deaf or plain daft? Is he hearing me?"

With the advantage of the interior position, the man ducked farther behind his door. "Major O'Rourke, I appreciate your plight, but I'm afraid your concerns, even if legitimate, are beyond my jurisdiction. I simply procure the materials from such vendors as the other gentleman. I have no authority over its distribution. I suggest you speak with the secretary and make an appointment." He started to pull shut the space between the door and lintel. "I hazard to add, sir, that your request is highly irregular. Proper channels must be observed, Major. That I can recommend to you. Good day."

Before Valentine could respond, the man closed the remaining space and retreated behind the shut door.

It took the Grandfather clock chiming five strokes before the secretary returned from the back of the building to his polished desk. He remained standing as he handed the documents back to a Valentine who stood drumming his fingers on the man's desk. "I'm afraid the office is closing now for the weekend. I could find no one able to speak with you at the moment. I did try, sir. All I am at liberty to tell you is that shipments to the field leave the depot almost every night."

"Such as tonight?" Valentine challenged.

The secretary refused to answer. "Whether or not our shipments make it through is another matter altogether." His voice reached a higher pitch. "If our convoys had better protection, increased patrols, it might be another matter. Or if we could get priority transport on the trains. You have your complaints; well, sir, we have been complaining to the War Department for months. If they could only get rid of all these spies and partisans. There are no secrets in this town!" The secretary caught himself, smoothed his hair, and regained his composure and official monotone. "You are welcome to return Monday morning." The secretary moved toward the front door of the building, ushering both Valentine and Nathaniel outside.

The elderly man who had been sitting in the foyer reached down and picked up his medical bag and silently exited with them, descending the marble steps with a painful hobble. Before the secretary shut and locked the large front door behind them, he suggested to them: "Or you may wish to take up your concerns with the Quartermaster General in the War Department."

Valentine slumped down on the white marble steps, his chin in his hand. Two Captains cantering past stared at him. Nathaniel leaned down and lifted him by the armpit. "Come on, let's go back to the hotel and get dinner. I warned you, Valentine. I've been here before, remember? I'm used to not getting my way. You're not. I warned you. Nobody knows what they are doing here in this town. We'll try my contacts tomorrow morning. I promise we'll have better luck. Come on," he said, tugging at his friend's arm. "I'm tired and I'm hungry."

"And I could use a drink."

Dinner proved a pleasant compensation for the Sisyphus-like frustrations of government bureaucracy. "Hate these paper-pushers who think their paperwork, signed and notarized, stamped and counter-stamped, co-signed and sealed, is what causes the bloody sun to rise in the morning," Valentine complained boisterously. He ordered a steak and he soon got his steak, rare. He ordered his bourbon and got his bourbon in a tall glass. Neat, three fingers. He held the glass to his nose and inhaled deeply, then muttered: "God love the angel share, the angel share." Admiring the liquid, he pontificated: "That's what they call the smell of the evaporation when it's in its oak cask, Nate—'cause what makes bourbon a good bourbon is what is shared with the angels."

He ordered a second bourbon.

Nathaniel reached over and placed his hand on Valentine's wrist. "Don't you think that's enough, Val? This isn't as cute as it used to be."

Valentine flared at him for a hot instant then touched the tip of his nose with his finger. He looked straight at Nathaniel and downed the glass. Two more he ordered while Nathaniel stewed, shifting in his chair, looking around the room with embarrassment. He was ready to go upstairs to their room.

The glasses arrived in succession. Not magically but from competence, and Valentine reveled in the efficiency of the wait staff and bartender. Valentine spoke loudly and freely, suggesting that Lincoln should hire the bartender to be his Commanding General of the Army. He offered a robust toast to the bartender. "Here is somebody who can get the job done. Make him a General!"

Nathaniel raised his eyes and noticed a civilian seated at a nearby table drinking with a fat Captain whose uniform bore the insignia of the Quartermaster Corps. The civilian was learning forward talking discreetly to the Captain. It seemed he cocked his head in their direction and paused in his own conversation whenever Valentine resumed voicing his complaints about shortages. Through half closed eyelids Nathaniel watched as the Captain placed his hand on top of the civilian's arm and shook his head subtly, as if trying to dissuade him from some decision. The Captain then stood up, hastily clinked a few coins on the table, and departed. The civilian took teaspoon sips of his beer. Through his still half closed eyes, Nathaniel watched him slide back his chair, rise, and come toward them carrying his glass. He was a young man, clean shaven, with a pleasant, open, convivial face. He walked with a limp.

"Mind if I impose upon you gentlemen for a moment?" he asked, already pulling a chair from the adjoining table and setting his glass on their table.

"Looks like we don't have much choice," grumped Valentine, hunched over his plate, his two hands pawing his drink.

The young man sat and took another delicate, pensive sip. He wiped the froth from his lips. He then slid his palm onto Valentine's forearm. "You seem discouraged, friend." With his other hand, he took another sip. "It could be fortunate I happened to overhear you. I am in the business of helping others, helping those who may be, shall we say, discouraged."

Valentine pushed his hand off his arm and stared at him. "Don't need your help, friend," he snarled. "He's married and I treat too many syphilitics to become one. Can't get enough mercury anyway."

The young man smiled as he patted Valentine's arm. "No, heavens no. You mistake me, sir. Forgive me. Nothing so crude. Certainly not with our good shepherd here. Man of the cloth and all. Let me explain. I am not so much a procurer as I am...," the young man hesitated, then grinned, pleased by his own wit, "...a provider and a patriot. Mine is a nobler mission. Patriotic indeed."

"Listen, friend. Tonight I'd rather drink alone."

The young man tilted his glass and swished the remaining ounces of beer to a thin foam. "Allow me to explain myself. My colleagues and I expedite matters wherever or whenever the government, or, for that matter, the military, hinders." His words filtered over the dinner table with a beguiling patter. The youthful, open face assumed a sharper profile as he bent closer toward Valentine. "Forgive me again, but if I am not mistaken, you need medicines. Am I correct?"

Valentine rubbed his finger around the rim of his glass of bourbon. Nathaniel toyed with his fork.

The young man continued. "One can see from both of you that you are truly dedicated men. Truly interested in relieving suffering, yes?"

"We try," Valentine replied tersely. For some reason he wanted to continue the charade without the young man abruptly terminating the conversation. Curiosity? Devilment? Pushing the edge? A distraction? Pride? He was not sure why. Yet he wanted to persuade the young man that they were savvy men, and, even if they weren't themselves in the market, they would not be the type to turn him in to the authorities. He wanted, for some reason, the young man to think of them, at least himself, as men of expedient morality.

The young man, pleased with his approach and the subtle confidence, lowered his head closer to the table. "Morphine. Opium. Quinine. Perchlorate of Iron. Ipecac. Even Calomel. Mercury too. Such things as are proved difficult to obtain where needed most, on the field of battle, might we assume? Let us men of patriotic bent provide for our comrade in arms when the system fails them. It is our duty, don't you agree?" He glanced at the two friends who were looking coolly at each other. "I happen to know where such supplies can be obtained at a fair and equitable price. We all benefit by this...," he again hesitated, "...by this, shall we say, shortcut in the unfair burden of bureaucracy and self-serving politics."

Valentine finished the last finger of bourbon left in his glass with one deliberate swallow. He turned the empty glass upside down and slid it toward the young man's glass of beer. "I'm afraid," he offered, "we appreciate your, shall we say, noble offer, but sadly we lack the funds necessary for such a useful transaction. But thank you." Valentine guessed he had convinced him that they were the kind of men likely to let bygones be bygones.

The young man's voice betrayed no disappointment. He too drained his drink, residues of foam lingering on the inside of his glass. "Thank you, gentlemen, for the company," he said, rising. He turned to them before limping away. "My offer, by the way, applies for both personal habits as well as professional. Your servant, sirs." With an elegant bow he turned and limped toward the door, pausing to chat with one of the waiters. He again paused, appearing to stare out through the front window toward the street as if looking for someone. From the corner of his eye, Nathaniel saw him more interested in their reflection. Both Nathaniel and Valentine simply continued eating their apple pie as if the conversation never occurred.

"That man interests me," muttered Nathaniel, still watching him from the corner of his eye. "He's carrying around some of the answers we need, I just know it," he added, responding to a familiar nudge of intuition and instinct. He had learnt over the years to trust those nudges. "Finish eating. Let's get out of here," he said as he pulled on his mustache.

"Huh?" Valentine grunted in mid bite.

Nathaniel called over the waiter and settled the bill. Valentine, still chewing the last morsel of pie, grudgingly followed Nathaniel. They nodded to the young man, who had resumed talking to the waiter. The young man gestured in polite reply. Outside, the temperature having dropped, Nathaniel clutched his coat around himself tightly. Nathaniel and Valentine began strolling down the side of the avenue, when, beyond the lamplight, Nathaniel grabbed Valentine by the arm and dragged him around the corner of the hotel.

"Wha', what are we doing?" Valentine complained.

"Shssh," hushed Nathaniel.

"Ah, Nate, I want to go to bed." Valentine's voice trailed off. "Sadly, alone."

"Shssh," Nathaniel repeated. "Watch," he whispered, pointing toward the door of the hotel. The young man stepped out onto the cobblestone avenue, glanced up and down the street, then began walking in the opposite direction from where Nathaniel and Valentine hid.

"Listen Valentine, something's wrong. I know it. I sense it. You know people as objects—I know them by how they behave. While he was talking to you, I was studying him. He's more than he seems. Trust me, there's something we need to find out. There are some mysteries I just don't like. Come on, we're going to follow him."

"Nate, you really don't like me, do you?"

"Be quiet."

Keeping their distance proved easy. Keeping track of him proved difficult, given both his fast pace, despite the limp, and his familiarity with the avenues, side streets, and alleys. Turning a corner, they feared they had lost him for good, but hurrying past a raucous tavern Nathaniel caught a glimpse of him through the smoky window. Sidling up near the window, Nathaniel, less noticeable in his black clothes, spied on the young man. He was seated at a table sharing a drink with a man in uniform. Nathaniel squinted. This soldier, same as the Captain from the hotel tavern, bore the insignia of the Quartermaster Corps. A Sergeant. His features were flint-like, his nose thin and angular, his skin oily. You could almost have used his nose for a paper knife. His close cropped hair was thinning.

Nathaniel watched as the young man drained his glass. The Sergeant and he stepped outside the tavern together, the young man's limp more pronounced. The Sergeant swaggered. The young man and Sergeant began walking in their direction. Nathaniel pushed Valentine around the corner of the tavern into the adjoining alley, then pulled him beneath a wooden staircase. The Sergeant and the young man turned the corner of the tavern into the same alley only to stop and stand near the brick wall. The young man removed an envelope from his inside coat pocket and handed it to the Sergeant, who stuffed it inside his half buttoned campaign jacket. They said a few words, which Nathaniel couldn't make out, then left the alley and departed in opposite directions.

Valentine emerged first from the shadows, muttering: "I've got to get my head clear. Well, damn you, Nate, you got me curious too. You just have to poke the hornets nest, don't you?"

"Look who's talking."

"Well, we've gone this far." He looked up the avenue at the young man already a full block away. He looked down toward the sharp nosed Sergeant turning left at the next corner by the stables. "Which way, scout?"

"The Sergeant." Nathaniel pointed left. "Whatever it is, it has been passed to him. Follow the scent. The Sergeant."

Chapter Eight

Conspiracies

Your head may be thick as a block,
And empty as any foot-ball,
Oh, your eyes may be green as the grass
Your heart just as hard as a wall.
Yet take the advice that I give,
You'll soon gain affection and cash,
And will be all the rage with the girls,
If you've only got a moustache,
A moustache, a moustache,
If you've only got a moustache.
"If You've Only Got A Moustache," Cooper and Foster

They followed the sharp nosed Sergeant through a bleak row of shacks and sheds, past a livery which was busy and noisy even at this late hour, toward a brightly lanterned and bustling military depot. On their right were dozens of repair shops. Wagon wheels in various stages of disrepair littered the grounds. Stables for mule teams stretched for hundreds of yards. One entire field was filled with newly constructed wagons minus their canvas coverings, the hickory bows sticking up like rib cages.

They trailed him as he wound his way toward a block of warehouses. He signaled lazily to the two sentries as he entered one of the buildings. Valentine bent toward Nathaniel's face. "You stay here. You're not quite dressed for the part. Or better yet," said Valentine, animated by the excitement of the mischief, "I'm going inside. I'll meet you at the livery we passed. Not sure when. Soon I hope." Valentine pressed his hand on Nathaniel's shoulder. "I have a hunch, Nate."

"And I have a hunch we're going to do more traveling tonight," Nathaniel whispered. "I suspect we've done all the walking we can. I'll see if I can scare us up some decent mounts. Yup, we meet back at the livery." Before Valentine could question him, Nathaniel headed back. Valentine slipped behind a passing group of teamsters who were making their way toward the warehouse. Nathaniel turned around in time to see his friend returning the salute from the warehouse sentries.

It was nearly midnight before Valentine returned to the rendezvous. "It's amazing what a flask and a few dollars can get you. Not to mention what these shoulder straps can do. You find some horses?"

"Close enough. A little bartering of my own. The stableman was a bit grim, but the folding money sweetened his disposition. Come on, they're right inside. By the way, since I bought them I've chosen the liver chestnut."

"Where'd you get the money?"

"I'll tell you later."

"I think you'd better," Valentine replied as Nathaniel offered him the reins to his saddled horse. "This isn't some game, you know."

"No, but it sure is getting interesting," Nathaniel said.

"I'm still trying to figure out why we're doing this."

"Sometimes it just falls to you."

"Seems to me, though, we've made some choices along the way," said Valentine as he patted the withers of his short and stocky horse, an ugly blue roan. "But we're here now. Anyway, if they're on schedule, and if what I was told is accurate, we should be able to let them catch up with us along the Columbia turnpike west of Bailey's Crossroads."

"Catch up with whom?"

"Our friend, the Sergeant. I told you: a flask, two Quarter Eagles, and these bars. It seems he's leading a small wagon train, eight freight wagons. With paid teamsters. Promises them they'll pick up armed escort from Fort Runyon." Valentine labored to swing himself up on the saddle. "And guess what they're transporting?"

Nathaniel already guessed. He screwed his face up at the coming inconvenience.

"Yes, indeed. Medical supplies. Very official. They're supposed to be going down the line. Seems to be the theme of the day, 'eh, my friend."

Nathaniel vaulted himself onto his saddle. He reined in his mount as it backed up.

"Your horsemanship has improved these months."

"Got enough chances."

Valentine twisted around in his saddle. "Well, you started it. You like to follow so much. It seems we're going to follow a little farther. Still have your passport on you?"

Nathaniel patted his coat pocket.

"Good. We'll need our papers."

With all the eagerness of an adolescent exploit they rode out side-by-side toward Long Bridge. As they crossed the wooden bridge only the lonely clatter of the hooves echoed above the trickle and gurgle of the waters of the Potomac flowing below. The bored sentry stationed at the south side of the bridge barely lifted his eyes to challenge them. He decided to ignore them and let them pass by unchallenged.

The sentries at the checkpoint at Fort Runyon, however, inspected them with suspicion. It was unusual for two officers to be traveling at such a late hour. Scouts, yes. Couriers, yes. But rarely a Surgeon. Far more unusual for one dressed in clerical black. At Fort Albany, with one sentry keeping his rifle pointed in their direction, the second sentry took his time reading their papers.

"Come on, man, you can read faster than that," Valentine scolded while sitting on his horse high above the sentry, trying to speed him up. "Or maybe you don't know how to read." Nathaniel stiffened. Once again his friend's voice was assuming its haughty tone. "May I remind you that my men, real soldiers down the line, require my medical attention back with the Regiment."

Nathaniel sighed and murmured under his breath, "not now, Val, not now. Imperious only works on those who presume themselves superior." Authority defers to authority. The more you urge a subordinate who chaffs at his inferiority, the more resistance you will get. Guaranteed. A lesson in politics and pride, whether at church or in school, one he learnt the hard way with a few church elders. Please, O'Rourke, he prayed to himself, now is not the time be like this. Flatter him. He's the one wielding the power. Be nice, please. Don't insult them. Better is lots of grins and agreement. Grovel even. Hail fellow well met. Never, never, let yourself get trapped.

Valentine commanded: "Make it fast, man, or should I help you with the big words?"

To Valentine's exasperation, yet predictable to Nathaniel, the sentry read their documents even slower, tracing and mouthing the words. Twice he retreated to his guard house to join his comrades inside, double-check the lists, and take his time warming his hands over the coal fire.

Nathaniel glared over at Valentine. "Next time I do the talking, okay?" Valentine ignored him. By the light of the lantern, Nathaniel noticed how the remaining guard, who was still pointing his rifle in their direction, revealed a glimmer of a satisfied grin. Nathaniel figured he may as well dismount. Valentine remained perched on high.

Several times during this delay Nathaniel, while pretending to tidy up his saddlebags or tighten the belt, turned discreetly and scouted out their rear. Once he turned quickly, nearly panicking when he thought he spied the wagon train approaching them, but it only was a passing carriage turning the corner of the lane. He felt the eyes of the sentry burrowing into the back of his head. Was it obvious he was shaking and his heart pounding? The last time he felt like this was when he was a school-boy, and, for his first and only act of mischief, snuck out of his house at Princeton and ticky-tacked his pastor's house.

Nathaniel suddenly felt very worn out. He leaned his head against the leather saddle. His body began to feel the ache of the tense night, along with the sore thighs and sorer back. He looked up at Valentine. When did we become friends? he wondered. He could not remember. Long, long ago, Valentine, half drunk, confessed how lucky Nathaniel was to actually like his father, and his father him. Valentine was a frequent guest at their home in Princeton, even over holidays. Only once had Valentine ever invited Nathaniel to his house in West Chester. Envy perhaps? Alice, bitingly honest as ever, said as much several times. There it is, I suppose.

"Oh, lighten up, my boring friend," Valentine often urged him back in their University days. "You're way too serious." While Nathaniel thought himself daring by challenging a Professor's argument, Valentine's notions of daring included sneaking a young lady out the window of her parent's home. One friend gave the other vicarious atonement. The other gave daring. They each puzzled one another. It took grace to be whole.

Nathaniel shook away his school-boy memories and stared back from where they had ridden, toward the city, fearful that the wagon train might lumber into view. Nathaniel, still brooding, scratched his horse's ear. And now look where we are, Nathaniel chuckled to himself. Noise from a clattering wagon distracted both him and the sentry. His throat closed. He had little spit to swallow, his mouth dry and cottony. Once again he was the miscreant boy sneaking with kernels of corn in his pocket through the rhododendron around the corner of his pastor's house. No, it's not the wagon train, thank God. They'd be far clumsier. Just one empty wagon pulled by a pair of mules. Stop this, he chastised himself. He feared he was too nervous, too pale, too obvious. Valentine looked confident even if annoyed. Come on, let's go—let's hurry up! he screamed inside his skull. Their aim, and the luck of their task, required them to keep enough advance distance to remain inconspicuous. Good Lord, aren't we conspicuous enough?

The sentry emerged from the guardhouse smug, satisfied, and warm, and handed the passports back to the two shivering officers. His narrow eyes glinted with a gleam of contempt. O'Rourke reached down, snared his papers, and immediately cantered off. Nathaniel took his papers with a polite thank you, mounted, spurred his horse on, and quickly caught up with his friend who was already lost to the shadows beyond the fort. With the few flickering lights of the city and guard post slipping behind them, they let the horses walk along the gloomy turnpike. Only then did Nathaniel breathe a sigh of relief. They had been able to remain in advance of the train. Only the occasional cranky dog bothered barking at them.

Immediately after crossing a stream north of the Leesburg Turnpike, Valentine pointed for them to enter a grove of over-hanging trees. "This must be 4 Mile Run," Valentine said. "If my memory of Talley's maps is correct."

"When ever did you pay attention at the briefings?" Nathaniel asked.

"I didn't. I'd go in later. He really does have good taste in whisky."

"So we wait and let them pass. Is that what you have in mind?"

"Unless you can think of something better," Valentine replied. "I've about peaked being clever. That and the fact that I've got one devil of a headache."

Nathaniel dismounted. "We let them overtake us. So long as they travel where they're supposed to, right?"

"That's the idea," Valentine said as he too dismounted. "So how about telling me about this money."

Nathaniel ignored him. Nathaniel had studied the Cavalry troopers and observed how they kept the reins in their hands instead of tying them up. He did the same. With their horses on either side, the men themselves standing shoulder to shoulder, they waited for the wagon train to pass. The flanks of the horses twitched. Valentine's roan relieved itself. The men shivered from the damp, cool night, as well as from anticipation. All was quiet except for the trickling and lapping of the stream and the steady breathing of the horses. Vapors flowed from nostril of horse and mouth of man. Valentine straightened his green sash underneath his uncomfortable sword belt.

Nathaniel felt the urge to urinate. "Are you sure they couldn't pass another way?"

"I'm not sure of anything, Nate," Valentine admitted with a twinge of temper. Worry colored his voice. "Maybe they did. After all, we're making this up as we go along." As he rubbed the heel of his hand between his horse's ears, he offered a light chuckle. "What the hell are we doing here?"

Nathaniel suddenly cocked his head and placed his hand on Valentine's shoulder. "Shssh, Listen."

The lumbering labor of creaking wheels and snorting mules sounded from the dark, accompanied by the distant, obligatory yelp of a protective farmhouse dog. The two men pulled their horses back farther from the road and deeper into the shadows. From their hidden vantage, darkened further by the veil of yew and heavy branch of fir tree, they listened as the hooves and wheels splashed into the stream. They pinched their horses nostrils to keep them from making any noises, releasing their hold every so often to let the horses breathe.

Halfway across 4 Mile Run, the first wagon stopped. They listened as the teamsters up and down the line of single-file wagons grumbled and cursed.

One man shouted out: "Dammit, Boudeman, there should be more of a patrol."

"Shut up Walters, ya' bastard," cursed a coarse, guttural voice from the nearest wagon.

"Goddamn army," growled another man several wagons down the line.

"You shut up too!" the man with the coarse voice shouted at the growling man.

The growling man didn't shut up. "The way things are goin' these days between here and Fairfax Station, we should have a goddamn Regiment."

"Not my fault, so shut up, damn ya' all," the coarse voice in the first wagon yelled back, his craggy voice higher pitched "Don't blame me. I'm doing what I'm told to do."

"Yeah, well, we don't have to, Boudeman. We ain't Army."

"Damn ya' all if you don't do what I say," Boudeman cursed. "You want to get paid, then you do what I tell ya'. Bunch of bastards! Sons of bitches!"

A new voice spoke as a horseman splashed across the stream. The horseman shouted with authority: "Sergeant Boudeman, move them. You should know better than to let the mules drink. Move it, Boudeman! You're damned too slow. We should be halfway there by now."

Sergeant Boudeman's reluctant reply consisted only of the languid slap of leather on the rump of the mules.

Both O'Rourke and McKennna recognized Sergeant Boudeman as he drove past them driving the first wagon. It was the same Sergeant they had followed from the tavern to the warehouse. The oily one with the sharp nose. They counted eight freight wagons as they rolled in front of their hiding place. Three troopers escorted the freight wagons: the officer in front, two to the rear. Only the first trooper, the officer, bothered to inspect either side of the road.

"Thought so," breathed Valentine. "Damn, I hate being so smart." The two of them held their position, still pinching their horses nostrils. They waited until they could barely hear the last wagon and the clip-clop of the trailing cavalry troopers. Only then did they lead their horses back onto the dirt road of the turnpike. There they mounted. They now trailed the train.

Nathaniel looked at Valentine with a silly, childish grin. "It worked."

Valentine pointed in the direction of the wagon train. "Our turn now. Observe and report. That'a way, boy."

The attack came swift. Less than a mile west of the intersection of Columbia Turnpike and Little River Turnpike, in the dim light hinting of dawn, the attack came ruthlessly and brutally. At the first sound of gunfire Valentine and Nathaniel spurred their horses and galloped toward the bend. Coming into the clearing, they reared their mounts toward the shadows as they saw the wagon train surrounded by nearly twenty partisans, pistols leveled into the faces of the troopers and teamsters. One trooper, still on his saddle, clutched his listless, bloodied arm. The officer lay on the ground dead. The partisans kicked the two troopers from their saddles, their horses and weapons immediately confiscated. The teamsters were shoved off their wagon benches by partisans efficiently taking their places. All were shoved off, except for the Quartermaster Sergeant named Boudeman who remained seated in the first wagon.

The partisans rounded up the two surviving Cavalrymen and the seven cussing teamsters and shoved them to the side of the road.

One of the teamsters resisted but when threatened with a pistol in his face, let himself be pushed along with the rest. He then slapped the shoulder of one of his buddies. "Well, we're out of it tonight. Looks like a long walk back, 'eh, Walters?"

Sergeant Boudeman stood up from his wagon seat, wiped his face with a blue bandanna, and gestured to one of the partisans, a bent little man wearing a gray slouch hat braided in gold. Boudeman swept his thumb across his own neck. He spat. "Do it," he said.

Suddenly the prisoners understood. All but one looked at each other in panic. One teamster, silent up to this point, simply said, "Pog mo thoin," before spitting an impressive stream of tobacco juice with a loud 'fhluck' toward the feet of man in the slouch hat. Several of the men instinctively held up their hands in front of their faces. Pistols erupted. Nathaniel and Valentine jumped. The liver chestnut and the blue roan whinnied but none of the partisans heard them over the sound of gunfire and curses. The fire from the barrels of the revolvers singed the dead men's shirts and faces. Only the corpse of one of the troopers twitched in the dirt.

Sergeant Boudeman climbed down from his wagon and inspected the killings, kicking two of the bodies. He scowled to the partisan wearing the gray hat: "Make sure this time. Hide them good."

Nathaniel whispered to Valentine: "This isn't Mosby. This is murder."

The sun began to rise as the wagon train with its new drivers and escort entered the outskirts of Alexandria by way of Little River Turnpike. Still trailing, yet watching from a farther distance, Nathaniel and Valentine followed the wagons as they were driven to a warehouse south of town, down along the docks near the government wharves. Twin masted schooners, moored to docks or anchored farther out, rocked with the lazy waves and current of the Potomac River. The slight movement of hull from port to starboard accentuated the degree of the mast's sway. Cold water met warming air. The mists floated along the water as if they were ghosts and hugged the hulls of ship and boat. Steam-wheeled vessels lay snug against wharves, waiting to transport south stacks of cordwood, mounds of alfalfa, barrels of potatoes, boxes of hardtack, hillsides of coal hauled from the mines of central Pennsylvania.

Nathaniel slapped his reins into Valentine's hands. "My turn to reconnoiter," he said through tightened lips. He hadn't felt the cold for the last hour. His fists were clenched, knuckles white. Nathaniel muttered to Valentine: "Wish we had a gun of some kind."

Valentine stared as his friend's eyes narrowed in rage. He was angrier than he had ever seen him. He traced the movement of his friend's face as Nathaniel looked down at his black boots. The blood of the teamsters and troopers still was wet on his boots from when they checked to see if any were left alive. His eyes trailed after Nathaniel as he crept around the corner of the building, hiding behind a tower of barrels, finding a crack through which to observe. Four men stood outside the warehouse.

The limping young man from the hotel stood outside the sliding doors of the warehouse. Next to him was the fancy fellow they had seen yesterday afternoon at the Medical Headquarters, the man who wore the black dress coat with fur collar. He still wore his bright red dragon vest, the vast gold chain stretching across the expanse of his large waist. Both hands were gloved in white. He held in his left hand a beaver hat and walking stick. "A fop and a crook," Nathaniel muttered quietly. Nathaniel was close enough to see that the mahogany walking stick was decorated with a silver handle fashioned in the shape of a swan. Nathaniel whispered to himself: "Full circle."

The four men chatted casually for ten minutes. The young man laughed frequently. The fat fop lifted his cane and used it to point toward a schooner moored at the end of the wharf. The partisan in the gray hat, standing next to his horse, touched the brim of his hat. With his free right hand, the fop put his arm across the back of Sergeant Boudeman and escorted him inside the warehouse. The young man from the hotel limped toward the schooner.

Nathaniel started to turn back when his right boot stepped on a chunk of coal, crunching it into pieces and powder. Nathaniel froze. He looked back through the crack between the two barrels. The young man with the limp stopped. He pivoted and tried to determine where the sound came from. Nathaniel sank against the barrels. The young man cocked his ears. He slid his hand into his pocket, then stepped back towards the warehouse. He limped past the sliding door and stood directly beside the tower of barrels. Nathaniel, crouching in the shadows, held his breath as the young man methodically rapped his knuckles against one of the barrell's iron hoops. The young man tapped his knuckles twice more before he shrugged, turned, and resumed limping toward the schooner.

Nathaniel remained crouched and waited three minutes before he stole back to Valentine, who waited with the horses around the corner of the next building. "Better to retreat and tell." Nathaniel grabbed Valentine by the arm. "We're no heroes. I'll fill you in once we get some distance from here. But first, I really have to take a piss."

While the city stirred to begin the day, they rode back to downtown Washington directly to the War Department where they reported to the Provost Marshall's office what they had discovered. There they were advised not to inform the Medical Headquarters. The General explained: "We cannot know the extent of the conspiracy. We cannot predict how many are part of this profiteering ring."

They spent most of the afternoon repeating their discovery of murder and theft at five different offices to an equal number of Generals and their Adjutants. Each office recorded their testimony. Through an open door of one office they spotted the gray haired gentleman from yesterday seated in a chair, his hands folded in his lap, with two soldiers posted on either side of him. Later in the afternoon, after having waited for another hour on a return visit to the Provost's office, they finally received orders. They were to report tomorrow to General Stroughton, commanding in the field at Fairfax Courthouse before they returned to their Regiment. Couriers were being sent immediately with new directives from the War Department. Stroughton would be advised that Nathaniel and Valentine would be carrying dispatches complete with names of men under his command to arrest and interrogate. While waiting for these dispatches to be written, both men fell asleep on the divans in the foyer. The orderly had to awaken them.

It was early evening by the time they collected their mounts and rode back toward their hotel. They had to cross the grassy mall. Several flocks of sheep grazed on patches of grass. On a small knoll to their left stood a tall, smooth, marble tower. Its top was abruptly truncated, flat. The size of the blocks dwarfed them.

"This city is depressing," Nathaniel sighed as he tilted his head back to view the incomplete obelisk. "Similar to most things in this city. Big intentions, and all of them unfinished." Blocks of marble lay scattered around the base of the monument. Valentine watched as Nathaniel dismounted and paced the square base, his stride a yard long. 15 yards a side, he counted.

Looking southwest from the knoll, shielding his eyes with his hand, Nathaniel strained to peer across the busy Potomac. In a distant field, to the right of Long Bridge, thousands of small white objects were lined up in tidy rows. They mystified him. "What is that?" he asked, looking up at Valentine. Valentine shrugged, then remarked, "Ah, tents. Recruits." Tiny figures moved about the rows.

"Come on, I'm thirsty," said Valentine finally. Fifteen minutes later they arrived at their hotel where they enjoyed a full meal and a fuller night's sleep...

...Nathaniel once again is a boy. He is with his father and mother, walking between them, holding their hands. They are visiting Melrose Abbey in south of Edinburgh. The three of them spend their afternoon wandering about the ruins. They wander, waiting for the moonlight. The remnants of ancient stone walls, covered in lichen, long ago had collapsed to the ground with several portions still standing, buttressed. It was once a sanctuary of tall arches. One front section stands facing them, with its window frame intact. The Abbey, surrounded by the cemetery, all at once fills with the moonlight. Suddenly, his parents sink into the ground and disappear. He screams but no sound comes from his throat. He reaches for them. He shoves his hands into the loosened soil. His hand grabs something. The object throbs in his hand. He pulls his hand out from the soil and sees in the moonlight a bloody, beating heart. The bells from the Abbey start clanging, louder and louder they ring. The heart pulsates stronger in his hand. He screams again but again there is no sound except for the bells...

Washington City's church bells dragged Nathaniel from his dream. He awakened panting and sweaty. His eyes dashed about the room. In the light he noticed Valentine sleeping quietly. He listened to his own heavy breath. The bells from the city continued ringing, and Nathaniel realized it was late Sunday morning. It was the first time he could ever recall having forgotten it was Sunday. He wiped the sweat from his brow. Private devotions will have to do today, he supposed, still shaken by his dream. It took another half hour for Valentine to awaken. Neither felt like rushing.

Only after they enjoyed a decent lunch did they pack up the dispatches and ride out of the city.

By the time they rode the six leagues from Washington to Fairfax Courthouse at a walking gait, it was past nightfall. They were both saddle sore and stiff, their thighs and calves cramping. They had a few more miles to ride once they fulfilled this errand before they would return to the Regiment. The telegraph operator, keeping post in his tent on the square, directed them to Stroughton's headquarters, instructing them to look for the mansion with lights burning in every room. "You'll fit;" the telegraph operator said with a sardonic smile as he pointed at Valentine. Then he pointed his long finger at Nathaniel. "I'm just as certain you're not dressed for the occasion."

They walked their mounts past the hotel toward a handsome brick house on the Courthouse square, each window pouring light. They tied their tired horses to the iron post, which resembled a lion, and told the guards of their purpose. The guard led them up the brick steps to the door. He knocked. The only response was a high pitched giggle, followed by the running of fingers along the keyboard of a piano. The guard shrugged at Valentine and Nathaniel. He knocked again. No one bothered to open the door.

Valentine tugged on his sash, and, elbowing the guard aside, stepped forward. He pulled on the brass handle of the door. With Nathaniel following, he stepped into a roomful of music, candle-light, and laughter. On the curved stairway an officer in bright blue followed upstairs a lady in pink, both holding long stemmed champagne glasses. Her dress billowed over walnut steps. Their glasses were full. Another lady, her bosom ripe and overflowing within her tight bodice, sat at the edge of the piano bench. A Colonel greedily enjoyed standing behind her, leering at her, as she, giggling, attempted to play a sprightly dance tune. Another Colonel and his lady flirted with each other on the red velvet sofa, she tapping the officer's brass buttons with her lace fan. The festive table, covered with flowers and an assortment of treats, displayed several opened bottles of champagne. Two bottles lay on the table, empty.

The lady at the piano stopped playing. She looked up at their new guests who stood in the doorway. She again giggled. "My, is it already time for vespers?"

Nathaniel looked down at his boots and fiddled with his pockets.

Valentine strode inside the room toward the warm fireplace, smoothing his green sash and adjusting his sword. He stroked his goatee and beamed at the ladies. From the table he picked up a nearly full crystal glass of champagne. He savored the quality of the wine. The Colonel stood up from the sofa to confront him. Valentine announced to all in the room: "We're here for Stroughton," then drained his glass. Valentine waved the leather pouch in the air. "We've just arrived from Washington with important dispatches."

The Colonel reached for the pouch.

Valentine lowered the documents to his side. "Our orders are to give them to him in person."

"Good evening, gentlemen." All eyes in the room alighted toward the figure standing at the top of the curving steps. His palm pressed the banister. "I believe my name has been mentioned. I'm Stroughton." The General's jacket was unbuttoned and his blouse open. Nathaniel noticed a lady wearing a loose fitting night gown standing behind the General. Her long brown hair hung loose about her exposed shoulders. She leaned against a partially open bedroom door. Her right hand curled around the edge of the doorknob.

O'Rourke strolled across the rug toward the bottom of the steps, offering the pouch. The General held up his hand. "As you can see, we are somewhat preoccupied at the present. I'm sure you would not want us to inconvenience these lovely ladies.

McKenna, still standing near the doorway, interrupted. "Sir, 'er, I mean, General, this is important. We've ridden a long way. You should have received a courier about this matter earlier today."

The General pointed toward the Colonel who idled near the sofa. The Colonel smirked at them. "And fortunately I have just such officers for just such important business. The advantages of rank, Reverend." He released his hold of the banister, turned his back to them, and put his arm around the woman at the bedroom door. The bedroom door squeaked as it shut behind them.

Valentine set his champagne glass on the marble table next to the banister and said to Nathaniel: "Not worth trying now." He tossed the pouch to the smug Colonel, then returned to face Nathaniel. With his hands on his friend's shoulders, he pushed him toward the door. "Not the time nor place," he observed. He pushed open the front door for Nathaniel. "We'll let Talley worry about it tomorrow. We've done our share. Lord knows, we've done our share." Once outside, he said: "You know, Nate, these kind of people are really beginning to bore me."

It was minutes after 10 PM by the time they rode into their Regimental encampment and stabled their exhausted mounts. Talley had left orders to be awakened the minute his two prodigals returned. "We will discuss the rest in the morning," Talley said, curtly dismissing them after the interview. Before they left the tent, Talley called out: "Any success with our medicines?"

Valentine turned and shook his head. "Skinned again."

They fell asleep on their cots dressed in their clothes and muddy boots. Valentine didn't bother removing his sword.

Early the next morning Colonel Talley summoned them into his hut. "Reverend McKenna. Surgeon O'Rourke. Evidently we've again repaired the telegraph. Second time this week. We've just received an interesting bulletin," Talley said with a sigh. "Thought you'd both like to hear its contents, especially in light of your recent travels, not to mention, your party crashing." Talley read the transcription: "Brigadier General Edwin Stroughton captured. Presumed Mosby. Whereabouts unknown." Talley let the bulletin float down to the top of his desk. "My grapevine sources tell me it was early in the morning. Captured in his own headquarters. I am told he was not in a position to offer much resistance. Visiting the latrine, I've been told." Talley rubbed his left eyebrow. "Stroughton's probably already on his way to Libby Prison. Hope he had a pleasant night because it'll be his last for a long time. Poor bastard."

Three days later, following evening mess, Nathaniel sat at his portable desk studying for Friday's Bible study with Company C. He reached for his tobacco pouch. Valentine reclined on his cot reading the newspaper. "Hey Nate, would you care to hear yesterday's headline?" Valentine held out the pages of the *National Tribune* to catch the full candlelight. "Profiteering ring captured. Medical officials arrested. Treason in the Department of the Quartermaster. Quartermaster General Meigs declares full investigation." Valentine continued, snapping the newspaper so he could turn the page: "This is a very strange war."

"Worse part is," Nathaniel remarked, stuffing his pipe full of tobacco, "the cupboard is still bare."

Valentine snapped the newspaper again, turning the page.

Chapter Nine

Home Soil

Dearest love, do you remember,
When we last did meet,
How you told me that you loved me,
Kneeling at my feet?
Oh, how proud you stood before me
In your suit of blue,
When you vowed to me and country
Ever to be true.
Weeping, sad and lonely,
Hopes and fear how vain!
Yet praying, when this cruel war is over,
Praying that we meet again.
"When This Cruel War is Over," Charles Carroll Sawyer

Sporting the new blue Maltese cross of the Third Division of the Fifth Corps—red crosses for the first division, white for second—the Regiment took up the line of march, breaking camp at dawn on the 25th of June at Fairfax Station, crossing the Potomac at Edwards Ferry two days later, eventually encamping on the Monocacy. From there they commenced the long, dusty march to Frederick, where the Fifth Corps met up with the main body of the Army. The next day the Army of the Potomac pushed north toward Hanover. It proved to be an ugly march. An ominous march. The Cavalry skirmish days before had left behind the grisly tokens of fierce combat: bloated carcasses of horses, trampled grain, broken fences, bodies in shallow, mounded graves dug alongside the road, where arms had been dragged out from the freshly churned dirt and gnawed to the bone by curious and hungry dogs.

Talley trooped the Regiment and addressed them the instant they crossed the Maryland border into Pennsylvania. "Now the Army marches on our own soil," he declared to them plainly and without emotion. "We now fight invasion. Lee is on our ground, among our homes. Our families now are imperiled. War's come home."

Meade, appointed only two days before as the Commander of the Army of the Potomac, ordered his proclamation read throughout the Corps reminding them all of the duty of the hour.

The men of the First Reserves needed neither Meade's proclamation nor Talley's exhortation. The soil they marched upon was message enough. Each man already felt in his gut the twist of fortune and the disgrace of the hour. For every soul in the First Pennsylvania Reserves was indeed marching home. Home soil. Their land. This was their Pennsylvania. The war had turned upside down. Most of the men of the Reserves were returning nearer home than anyone else in the entire Army of the Potomac, Adams County boys among them. Company K came from Adams County. Half of the men of Company K had enlisted from a little town called Gettysburg.

Nathaniel detected a difference in the march these recent days. Each step was a step of resolution bent on erasing the disgrace, urging on the footstep ahead and behind, until the march became a rhythm of will measured out by them regarding Lee's invasion as a personal affront. The rumors of the road encouraged the quicker, heartier step. The Adams County boys set the tempo. It required the discipline of their officers, along with the stentorian shouts of the Provosts, to keep the Adams County boys from breaking rank and hurrying to make sure the folks at home were safe. The men, unbloodied for months, questioned themselves once again: "Will I pass the test, especially now?"

Six days of continuous march. Nathaniel marched with the men, having presented his liver chestnut to Rupert as a guilt offering. Five miles more they marched up the Baltimore Pike where they drew near Rock Creek, just east of Cemetery Ridge. The men let the locals know they were coming home. They sang boldly as they marched in column, singing confidently, full of the self-awareness of men that were expected to be cheerful and brave, despite fatigue and thirst, because neighbors and old friends, even boyhood friends who remained behind on the farm, now watched, hallooed, and saluted. They had come home to rescue them, to defend them. Lee had gone too far by invading their farms. They intended to let him know he was trespassing. They had come home.

The faces watching from the side of the road no longer were anonymous, no longer strangers, no longer the mulatto Negroes in torn trousers that populated Virginia. Here watching them march were neighbors and kin they could greet by name. Here were those familiar with them enough to call these neighborhood boys turned soldiers by their first names:

"Hey, you there, William McGren; what brings you home? Johnny Reb?"

"No, Uncle, I just came home to visit my best girl."

These faces on the other side of the fences were friends. They were family. The soldiers of the Reserves must be brave now. Braver than they had ever been. Little choice. They were being watched now. The women—girlfriends, grandmas, sisters, and mothers—waved their handkerchiefs and cried. Manhood was expected. Lee shouldn't be here, but here he was nonetheless and somebody was going to do something terribly foolish.

Nathaniel marched with the men of Company K. Reaching the summit of the hill east of town, the men of Company K gazed down on familiar village, farms, and homes, upon the tall steeples of their churches. The smoke and sounds of battle told them that their homes sat among enemy lines. Rage, like a foaming wave, surged through the ranks. Nathaniel could smell the men's restive anger. Some men can see details. Nathaniel could see emotion. These men had seen enough of Virginia devastated, Virginia's fat fields turned into wastes of chicory and weed. It angered them to think of the virgin bounty of Pennsylvania ravaged. This was wrong. They started this war; their farms should suffer because of it, not ours. Yet soon their thick wheat fields would be trampled by this crueler harvest, the stalks harvested by the scythes of sharp duty. Nathaniel looked up into the July sky. The sun hammered directly overhead.

Orders came down the line to stack arms and rest near Baltimore Pike, one mile east of Cemetery Ridge, near Meade's headquarters. They were too weary to make much fuss or gripe, too weary to think much of anything anymore except revenge. Elsewhere, to their left and to their right, the clamor of battle echoed, crashed, resounded. Few could nap. For two hours they witnessed the rush of frantic courier. Limbered cannons chased after by caissons careened past, pulled by overheated and lathering horses. For two hours they remained spectators to the thunderous percussion of cannon fire and the sharp whine of stray round. The men, sitting on the ground, counted and recounted their cartridges.

One young soldier tugged Nathaniel by the sleeve. "Chaplain, how 'bout putting in a good word with Meade. We're ready. Just let us at 'em and we'll send 'em running."

Nathaniel took off his hat and wiped his sweaty brow. He wrung out his bandanna. "Never you mind, Tobias. You'll get your turn soon enough."

"Well, chaplain, if you ain't gonna' go talk to Meade, would ya' mind asking God to turn down the heat a bit. It's getting mighty close."

"Makes the corn grow," he said while swatting a mosquito that landed on his neck. "You should know that. Don't you want your folks to take in a fat harvest? You mind yourself. God knows what God is doing even if we don't."

"Surely hope so."

"That, Tobias, you can count on."

Bandaged stragglers hobbled toward the field hospital that had been temporarily erected at the edge of the field. More men were carried there. The casualties all arrived thirsty. There was sufficient water but too few hands to hold the cup to parched, cracking lips. Some of the wounded crawled to the trough to soak cloth shreds in the dirty water and offer them to wounded friends, so that they, cradled, might suck on the rags. Ambulances sped back and forth, the pace increasing as the surrounding clamor of battle intensified. The wounded waited, many groaning, some shrieking, some already past the point of sensibility and pain, waiting until the Surgeon found time to cut or probe or bandage. Or until they fainted. Or until they died. Many died waiting. The Negro volunteers piled the dead in a swelling row to the side of the hospital. The hot sun moved from its stark position directly overhead to a quarter closer the horizon.

Somebody must know what is going on, Nathaniel hoped privately. He squinted up into the bright sky to notice far off, above a distant hill, a half dozen turkey vultures circling on the thermals, spiraling higher and higher. "What do they see from their heights?" Nathaniel asked aloud to no one in particular. It had been a long walk. He sat down on a small boulder. He pulled off his boots and rubbed his swollen feet. His hands absorbed the stench of the miles.

Some in the Regiment kindled small fires despite the heat and humidity. They ground coffee beans with musket butt. They filled the anxious waiting by brewing a welcome cup to sip and share. They had had no chance for coffee these six days of continuous march. Now they stole what time they might. The men talked little. With damp sleeves they wiped the sweat from their faces. Nathaniel decided to get up. He tugged his boots on over swollen feet and strolled through the Regiment, nodding, touching, shaking hands, offering the blessing and reciting snatches of Psalms when beckoned to join the group of men huddled together in prayer. They all sensed it. They would get their turn, unavoidably soon.

Soon finally arrived. With drum roll, it was sling knapsacks and double quick off to the left through several cultivated pastures and woods, over several rail fences, toward the crest of a small wooded hill. Lichen covered rocks protruded from the face of the incline. Smoke from musket fire and cannon fire shrouded the slope and top of the hill, the smoke of battle rising above the tree line.

Nathaniel stopped to view the fields below. His ears felt stuffed. He could barely hear. Everything sounded muffled and muted. The breeze picked up. It seemed the earth moved. After Nathaniel rubbed his eyes, he saw through the lifting haze that the undulations below belonged to the wriggling and straining bodies of men left behind from the day's earlier fighting. They wiggled like worms left in a bucket in the sun. One man crawled toward the small, listless creek that wove through the middle of the field between the rises of rock and earth. The man, capless, could have worn gray or blue. But now he wore a uniform of oxidized red, his woolen clothes brown from drying blood. He crawled to the edge of the creek, a solitary, sacred act among so much writhing. Like a crouching dog, he strained to drink from the bloodied water. But he lacked strength. His limbs trembled. Nathaniel watched the man slowly lower his face into the shallow water, too weak to drink, to weak to lap like a dog, too weak to raise his face from the stream. Suddenly the wind shifted and the black fog of battle returned and covered the field below. Nathaniel lay down on his back and peered into the turquoise sky. His fingers clawed at the grass. His hand drifted toward his watch chain and he caressed her fob. Sweat from his brow rolled down his neck and dripped into the earth.

The Regiment waited, bayonets fixed, late into the humid afternoon. The men rubbed their eyes burning from the sulfur and smoke. Some splashed water from their canteens onto their faces. After again swallowing several gulps, Nathaniel's ears opened. Swiftly the harsh noise of the chaos returned. The battle beyond the acrid smoke, filled with distant shrieks and shouts and wicked thuds, swept back across the little stream. The concussion of cannon fire made ears bleed. Retreating solders, many bereft of gun and kit, most wild-eyed, arms jerking, stampeded through their ranks. They didn't try to restrain them. A madness loosed is a difficult beast to leash.

Shouts from officers, the roll of drum, and blare of bugle distracted the tense Regiment from the scent of panic. Their turn had come. Gunlocks clicked. Nathaniel looked down into the field and watched as a Corporal bearing a flag rushed into the current of the retreating troops. The Corporal turned and faced the small rocky hill. Bodies writhed at his feet. With his back toward Confederate rifle fire, standing in the shadow of the larger hill to his right, he waved the standard. With a cheer, the men moved forward as one. The command was given. They fired their volley and pushed forward, reloading as they strode toward the enemy. Another man, and soon again another, claimed the fallen standard. Load in nine times. Fire by company. Fire by file. Fire by rank. Fire as best you can. Fire before you die. Then came the command to charge.

Like walking into a waterfall, so was their charge against the Rebel guns.

Sweeping down into the small, bouldered valley, tripping over bramble and brush, stumbling against granite rock and corpse, the men vaulted Plum Run and approached the slight hill and the tree line beyond. Up the side of the rise they charged, surging right. Rush and surge. They reached the exposed top. They pushed toward the gap and the field beyond. Screams of bullets and of men, equally incessant, surrounded them. Musket fire raked them. Bullets punched. The harsh clang of iron on iron. The cushioning thud of lead, wool, and muscle. Too few trees for cover. Only a few outcropping boulders. Run to kill. Run or die. Run and die. Over the stone wall. Scrambling. Through the narrow strip of woods, moving into the eastern edge of a trampled wheat field, a wheat field harvested by bayonet, rutted like veins, burdened by corpses. The dusk deepened, their way lit by muzzle fire and their lines defined by the flame pouring from roaring cannon.

The order to halt at the stone wall was more concession than command.

With his head resting against the lee of the stone wall, his lungs panting for breath, his mouth dry as ashes, his throat feeling like he had swallowed thorns, Nathaniel suddenly realized what he had done. Swept up by the madness, swept up by the mob, he had charged with the Regiment. A madness loosed. This time his madness. He charged unarmed. A personal madness. He charged into the maelstrom. He charged with them even though he was supposed to remain behind to care for and collect the fallen. Black frock amongst so much blue and blood. Panting, he felt sick. It scared him. He doubled over and threw up between his legs. He trembled from the chill of naked awareness. Heaving, he felt released. There was no will here, no decision. It was instinct. Primal instinct swelled and impelled. Reason became irrelevant before the sweeping surge of passions. It was best not to think for then one would easily become the coward. Then one could never act. Bravery is simple: stop thinking.

He threw up from the bile of a sick, bestial pride. Nathaniel had tasted an uncanny, exhilarating surrender to blood's passion, and it sickened him as he rested his sweaty head against the cool stone wall. He rolled over and vomited for a third time. If he had been armed, he would have killed. He would have plunged the steel deep into the enemy's chest and laughed, sporting in the squirting blood of his victim, his prey. He panted, catching his breath, resting his head against the stone wall. It frightened him. Yet, it thrilled him, aroused him. He felt sick for he enjoyed it. He had tasted it.

"Preacher, yer' bleedin'," observed the Private sitting beside him.

He reached for the moistness. The neck of his shirt was wet and warm, his neck seared. Now that he touched it, his neck began to sting from the wound. He pulled his handkerchief from his pocket. A minie ball fell from the handkerchief. He stared at the perfectly shaped bullet lying in the grass. It explained the ache he now felt at the top of his thigh. His finger probed the inside of his pocket, till it poked through the hole formed by the bullet as it sped into his coat: a spent round, cushioned by thick wool and Bible. He never noticed he had been shot. Twice shot. He reached and picked up the bullet. He rolled the bullet between thumb and fingers, then tossed the minie ball over the wall and began to daub his neck with his handkerchief. Killdeer swooped toward the bloody creek to dare a drink but abruptly fluttered away.

The soldier on the other side of him pressed his palm against his own shoulder; he was pierced, his collar bone broken.

The Reserves spent the night at the stone wall, lying low out of respect for the Rebel sharpshooters scanning for a neglectful mark. The madness of the afternoon surrendered to a morbid stillness as the full Thunder Moon of July rose and casted odd, phantom shadows about the field. Nathaniel, trusting providence, trusting the exhaustion of the enemy as well as their good-will, walked numerous trips, assisting the wounded toward the rear, returning with fresh water for the men remaining at the stone wall. It was a hot, windless night. For Nathaniel, it was a sleepless night. Too many trips with the stretcher bearers. Not enough water for anyone. It was a night busy searching by the stark moonlight for the living among the bodies littering the ground between the hillock to their rear and the stone wall the Regiment held. Fragments of bone and clumps of flesh lay scattered about the field. So also torsos and limbs shredded by canister, hacked by volley of musket fire or shell fragment. Other bodies appeared as if asleep, their cooling bodies unmolested save for a hidden, discreet wound.

Exhausted beyond will, Nathaniel returned and collapsed against the stone wall. He could only listen to the moaning of the dying. The moon, reappearing from behind gray cloud, laid closer to the horizon. "Did Alice look at the moon tonight?" he wondered aloud. He looked up and down his line of men as they crouched and slept against the stone wall. "We are so near home, so very near." The staccato of a Screech Owl called out from the distant woods. In the clearing sky above, Cygnus soared toward the eastern horizon. The Northern Cross looked down upon them all, Deneb brilliant. The gourd to the northwest poured its contents out.

Somewhere in the near darkness, far out in the field, a soldier began to feebly hum a familiar hymn. The hum became a whisper of a tenor solo in southern accent, the song rising like a mist above the sighing silence.

> *Jesus, Lover of my soul,*
> *Let me to thy bosom fly,*
> *While the nearer waters roll,*
> *While the tempest still is high;*
> *Hide me, O my savior, hide,*

Till the storm of life is past;
Safe into the haven guide,
O receive my soul at last...

A second weak voice from another part of the battlefield joined the gentle singing, and the solo became a doleful duet. The men lying on their arms on both sides listened. All they could do was listen. Another voice joined the anthem of this mortal choir, though this voice was hoarser, struggling to sing aloud the familiar verses. This was the hymn of the lost. Again joined another voice, until the battlefield of shadows and moonlight became a soft chorus as the chords of the hymn swirled into the night. Jesus, lover of my soul, they sang.

Slowly, as the voices had joined each other's, so they began to waver and drift off, until the final solo was sung, until, at last, the anthem ended.

One of the young men sitting at the wall swallowed and wept. "I use to hunt rabbits in these fields and hills," he said. He paused as he toyed with the ring on the trigger guard of his Springfield. "I don't think I'll hunt here again."

Chapter Ten

Stone Walls and Cannon

Sleeping, I dream'd love—dream'd love of thee;
O'er the bright waves, love floating were we;
Light is thy fair hair play'd the soft wind,
Gently thy white arms round me were twined,
And as thy song love swell'd o'er the sea,
Finally thy blue eyes beam'd love on me
"Sleeping I Dream Love," Hewitt and Hewitt

When Nathaniel was a boy he had sailed with his father and mother on the *Great Western* paddle steamer for a half year sojourn in Scotland. Reaching Bristol they took the train to London, then they traveled *The Night Scotsman* to Edinburgh. Father had been invited by New College to return to his alma mater and serve as visiting lecturer. There Nathaniel relished rummaging through the ancient library, exploring the tilted tombstones at the cemetery of Greyfriar's Kirk, or pretending to defend the black stone castle from English knights. For one of their holiday weekends they traveled by train from Edinburgh to St. Andrews. Father was to preach. That Saturday Nathaniel pleaded with father for permission to escape the innumerable cups of tea and soda bread. Allowed his freedom, he clambered among the forlorn ruins of the old cathedral. He played in the sand traps of the old golf course. He hiked the outline of the entire course, discovering it was shaped like a shepherd's crook. But he especially relished descending below the castle and darting about jagged black rocks, glacial draggings, which alternated with water-rounded rocks stretching like an apron all along the coastline. At high tide the North Sea floods with a vengeance. The waves, propelled by an icy wind, splash and crash against the craggy, fierce Scottish shoreline. The wind and waves, to a young boy climbing among the crags, cleanse and freshen. There is the thrill and threat of slipping and losing your footing. Low tide, he discovered, happens equally ferociously, as if all the water is sucked back toward the frigid deeps of the Norwegian Sea, leaving the shoals exposed. What is left behind is not a pretty sight.

During low tide he climbed down the cliff face below the ruins of the castle, down below among treacherous rocks. Only after he had climbed down, hopping the pools and eddies, did he notice the rats. A mob of rats. Hundreds of rats scampered from rock to crevasse. Some he scared off with a shout and jump. Most confronted him with bared teeth, for he was the intruder, requiring him to arm himself with stones and shells to chase the rats away from biting his ankles.

The ebb tide exposed what the North Sea deposited. The sea's retreat became the rats invitation to venture out and devour what they might find. Decaying fish. Debris and garbage from ship, boat, even from the homes above. It was more midden than tidal basin. The offal of sea and land.

☉☉☉

Nathaniel stood beside one of the six pieces in Hazlett's battery. Ten pounders. Its barrel radiated warmth from hot use. As he shielded his eyes from the glare of the rising sun to overlook the battlefield from the heights of Little Round Top, Nathaniel prayed silently for a divine tide to flood these fields and purge the debris of this bloody battle. The vermin had emerged, urged by the humidity and heat of this summer day, and the corpses littering the field had begun to blacken and swell.

"Not a pretty sight, is it Reverend?" The voice awakened Nathaniel from his private thoughts. The tall man stood slightly behind Nathaniel. He also was surveying the terrible field below. The officer stepped next to him. The tall figure twisted the ends of his full mustache which, longer than Nathaniel's, reached below his jaw. He wore a Colonel's bars.

"It takes me to another place," mused the chaplain.

"Where might that be, Reverend?"

"Far away. Another land. The coastline of Scotland. St. Andrews."

"Ah, yes," the Colonel said. "Not unlike where I call home." The sorrow in the Colonel's voice invited Nathaniel to draw closer. The stranger spoke again, offering more soliloquy than conversation: "I fear this will be the place by which we measure all others." He too shifted closer to Nathaniel. "My boys have been in the woods beyond." He waved his hand toward the left of the line, towards the wooded edge of Little Round Top. "The trees hid most of our fight." The Colonel blew a sigh through his thick mustache. "This is different. This is where you were?"

Remembering his madness yesterday, Nathaniel nodded.

"So open." The Colonel's deep set eyes scanned from valley to ridge. "So revealed."

"That secret thoughts of many hearts may be revealed," Nathaniel quoted with a forlorn smile.

The tall stranger paused before he heaved a long sigh. "Must get back to my men. They'll be grateful to hear we'll be relieved soon. Difficult day, yesterday. Yes, a difficult day."

"And I must get to mine."

Nathaniel and the tall Colonel turned toward each other. The Colonel clutched Nathaniel's wrist with his left hand as right hand clasped right hand. Nathaniel looked up at him: "Peace be with you, Colonel."

"And also with you, Reverend," he replied, familiar with the litany.

Nathaniel spent the remainder of the morning as he had spent much of the night: searching for the lost, gathering his sheep. The Confederate snipers ignored the searchers. They kept their aim toward the officers lurking behind the stone wall or neglectful gunners hiding behind the rocks and battery at Little Round Top. The snipers respected the battlefield armistice. The wounded had no uniform anymore. They knew their own wounded and dying would receive aid, perhaps a cup of water, perhaps a familiar prayer before they died. The lucky would survive long enough to be found, even if survival meant getting sent to prison camp, even to Elmira. At least then there'd be the chance for parole and exchange. Even Elmira gave them a chance. Left unfound on the field, they were left with no chance at all. The crows would have them. The snipers ignored the searchers and stretcher bearers, an act of civility for which Nathaniel was most grateful, as he and the others moved about as easy targets under the bright sun.

The searchers and stretcher bearers also served as a distraction for the soldiers on both sides who were still lying on their arms during the morning lull. It was to them a morbid kind of theatre. At the beginning the troops would even raise a slight cheer when one of the fallen was found to be alive, and they'd applaud as the chaplains would call for the stretcher bearers. As the morning wore on the cheers dwindled; fewer were found living. The men lying on their arms quit watching. By the end of the morning Nathaniel simply tried to account for the number of Regimental dead. Talley, hunkered behind the stone wall, was expecting Nathaniel's count so he could compare it with that of his Captains.

Nathaniel had nearly reached the wall when the cannonade erupted. He had paid no attention to the two signal shots fired moments earlier. Stunned by the wholesale eruption of cannon fire, he dove toward the security of the wall, tumbling against several of the men.

"Here we go again," shouted an animated Captain Coates. "Get ready, get ready. They're gonna' come back." The men of Company C double-checked hammers to confirm that caps were in place. Some unlatched cartridge box and counted their rounds. Most broke out canteens, uncorked them, and drank from what slack water remained.

Nathaniel rolled over and checked his watch. It was 1:10 in the afternoon. Thunder rolled successively from the Confederate positions far above them as well as from the northeast. The thunder never quit. The blasts of the bombardment rolled constant and persistent, growing louder and louder. The Union retort followed. At first the Union artillery fired a few single replies, finding range. Suddenly, it was the Union's turn to erupt into a volcanic bombardment.

Joseph Coates climbed over to lean next to Nathaniel, yelling over the explosions. "My God, what's happening? This isn't us. Over there. Bigger than us."

Nathaniel refused to compete with the bombardment. He just shook his head and clutched Coates forearm. Coates returned his revolver to its holster and secured it, fastening the leather thong onto the black button. Coates leaned closer. "Nate, you find him?"

"Nope," Nathaniel shouted back. "Not a word. Valentine is misplaced again." With his hand, Nathaniel imitated a sawing action. He followed this pantomime by pointing his finger to some unknown region behind their lines. Coates wiped his brow.

Joe Wentz, huddling against the wall over on Nathaniel's right, turned and tried to yell: "I wonder if they can hear this back home? We're just two counties away. Bet Mom and Dad can."

Minutes passed. The bombardment turned rhythmic, methodical, successive, ceaseless. On both sides. This was a polka in 2/4 time of deadly percussion.

Nathaniel checked his watch again. 1:30 PM. How long can this continue? he asked himself. He had a sinking feeling. He looked again at Coates. "Big indeed," he agreed. Coates looked back as Nathaniel slipped his haversack off his shoulder and pulled out his pipe and tobacco. Nathaniel looked over at Coates again and shrugged. He stuck his pipe into the pouch and stuffed the bowl full, packing it with his dirty thumb, then stuck the stem in his mouth. Rolling up the pouch, he put it back in his haversack. He rummaged for some matches but found none. Coates pulled a match box from his coat pocket and offered it to Nathaniel, who took it with a red eye wink.

Cupping the match, he lit his pipe, pulling the smoke deep, watching the tobacco burn red. With a long puff, cupping his left hand over the bowl, he exhaled. Coates took back his matches and admired the chaplain. Coates curled into the lee of the wall and tried to fall asleep.

Thunder followed thunder. The ground trembled. Thunder upon thunder. Soon the entire valley was choked by the thick, stagnant, sulphur cloud of cannon fire. There was no wind to disperse the stench of rotten eggs. There was only the heat and humidity to contain it, press it down. The earth itself shuddered.

"God, I'm thirsty," someone nearby shouted. "Can anybody spare some water?" The men tasted the acrid powder in their throats, the vile aftertaste of black powder and sulfur. Sulfur stung eyes and burnt their nostrils.

"Pastor! What's the time, pastor?"

"2:10."

"Say again!"

"I said, 2:10!"

Before Nathaniel could slip the pocket watch back into his waistcoat pocket, Coates reached out his open hand. Nathaniel lowered the watch into his palm by its chain. The silver case reflected a glimpse of sunlight that broke through the sulfur haze. It shone the light back into their eyes. "That's a beautiful watch," he yelled into Nathaniel's ear.

"Yes, thank you. Very special." Nathaniel shouted back. "Would you like to see?" he pantomimed as he yelled. He retrieved the watch from Coates and released the catch and held the watch cover open toward him. "It's my girls," he shouted.

"Yes, I know," Coates yelled. "You've shown me plenty times before."

Nathaniel stared at the inside of the watch cover. "As beautiful as their mother," he whispered. Instinctively, he stroked the blue cameo with his thumb. He grinned and again shouted at Coates: "Not the prettiest of places to bring them."

Coates called back: "You'll have to make it up to them." Coates squeezed Nathaniel's forearm.

Nathaniel's pointer finger touched the tiny painting of his children. Then he lifted the watch to his ear and tried vainly to listen to the sound of its ticking. Abruptly he closed and pocketed it. Nathaniel touched Coates on his shoulder, bent toward his ear, and pointed at the treeline toward the northeast. "My God. Imagine what it would be like over there."

Bleeding ears that had been staunched yesterday, bled again from the resonance. Some of the men stuffed lint into their ears. Others, up and down the stone wall, covered their ears, pressing kepis against the side of their heads. A few of the men, in defiant apathy, huddled together and tried playing a card game above the din.

"I hate cannon."

"I hate cannonballs."

"Canister's worse"

"Reckon you're right."

"It's those damn explodin' ones I hate. Hey, got a chew?"

"Once saw a guy lose his whole face."

A young man, covering his pale face with his kepi, began whimpering, crawling into the angle where stone wall met earth.

"Let him cry, let him cry," his friend said, putting his arm around the young man's convulsing shoulders.

More men along the line held back their own tears, though nobody cared if they did cry.

"Goddamn this, I can't stand this. Gotta' do something," shouted one Private as he began to thrash about. He pushed up and tried to stand but was wrestled back down by his Sergeant. A shot shrieked, chipping a shard of stone near his head.

"What time, preacher?"

"About twenty minutes from the last time you asked."

"It's slackening. Do you think? It sounds as if we've stopped firing back." Panic filled his voice. "What if they've taken out our artillery!"

"We must be getting slaughtered."

Joe pushed up against Nathaniel. "Wish I could see. Wish I were up there," Joe said as he pointed at Little Round Top. "I bet they know what's going on."

I bet they don't, thought Nathaniel.

Nathaniel, Coates, and Joe lifted up their eyes across the valley to the boulders and hills above them, toward the barren, rocky crest of Little Round Top. Hazlett's battery remained calm and mute, save the occasional attempt at a long distance shell. Several officers, making themselves easy targets in their dark blue coats, stood between the guns and peered through glinting binoculars northward beyond the patches of woods and fields, as if they were defending a castle upon this rock. Union signal men, garbed in their lighter blue coats, risked the gray sniper's accuracy because they had to.

"I doubt it, Joe," he yelled back. Nathaniel puffed a few smoke rings. "With all this smoke, what can they see?"

"Thought they might, pastor. Somebody should know. Gotta' be somebody."

"They do over there," Nathaniel said, waving his pipe stem toward the right of the line. "Or they soon will."

"Thank God we're here," Joe prayed.

Two of the men farther down along the stone wall started a spitting contest, trying to propel the jet of black juice farthest. Those huddling near them pulled out a few coins and some folding money and started taking bets.

Coates shouted: "What time…?" In mid yell, the Confederate cannons instantly ceased fire. Coates swallowed his question. The grand fusillade ended as abruptly as it began, except for a few distant rounds which shrieked, teasing to stake claim for having spoken the last word.

Nathaniel flicked open his watch. Nathaniel hesitated, cocking his ears, before announcing: "2:55." A few killdeers fluttered near Plum Run and dared chirp amidst the unexpected silence. An expectant hush filtered across the field.

"What next, I wonder?" Joe whispered reverently.

"I can guess," Nathaniel lamented, returning his watch to its pocket. "I don't know much about soldiering but you sure don't waste so much gunpowder without good reason. Where cannons fire, men must follow. Artillerists first, then infantry. It stands to reason."

"My God, after all this, can you imagine?" Coates said, unlatching his holster for the fifth time.

Men poked fingers into their ears trying to get rid of the ringing. Nathaniel thought he heard the sound of bugles and faint cheers echoing across the fields.

"What is going on over there?"

"We'll find out soon enough."

At precisely 3:20 PM, Hazlett's battery of 6 rifled, ten pound, bronze Parrotts opened up from Little Round Top, followed by the intermittent sharpshooter fire. The shells shrieked over their heads. "Time for rendering the butcher's bill."

"What is going on over there?"

They heard the fight but they never saw it. Bugle and drum. Muffled fusillade after muffled fusillade of musket and faint rifle fire. The savage sound of shrieking canister filled with grape shot. The distant Rebel yell matched by dim Federal hurrah. The continuous cascade from Hazlett's battery blasted, smoked, and shrieked over their position at the stone wall.

"Must be hand-to-hand."

"My God."

"God help us."

Joe clawed at Nathaniel's arm. "What's happening? Are we next?"

Chapter Eleven

Company C

Mid pleasures and palaces though we may roam
Be it ever so humble there's no place like home!
A charm for the skies seems to hallow us there,
Which, seek though the world, is ne're met with elsewhere
Home! Home! Sweet, sweet home!
There's no place like Home!
There's no place like Home.
"Home, Sweet Home," by John Howard Payne

By late afternoon the sniper fire and skirmishes slackened, hinting that Lee and Longstreet might actually be pulling back.

It took till mid evening for them to hear what really happened to their right, not until after the Reserves were brought into the fray as part of the final action of the day. Orders had arrived from Headquarters. Fifth Corps to Third Division to First Brigade to the Reserves. Talley sent word down along the stone wall by runner. The Regiment was to occupy the center of the Brigade's grand charge to clear out the woods in the front, moving against the rear-guard of Longstreet's two Divisions.

Captain Bear, puffing his handsome, yellowed Meerschaum pipe, carved in the shape of black bear, worked his way past the men of his Company. Company B had been his Company since March. His promotion, his command. He trotted, hunched over, toward Company C, where he eventually greeted Chaplain McKenna. Nathaniel breathed deep the favorite black Cavendish. "No time for a smoke with you, friend," he said as he tapped Nathaniel's shoulder with the hot bowl of his pipe. "Nate, Talley has orders for you. Especially for you. I am supposed to tell you this verbatim." Bear beamed like a schoolboy as he began his recitation: "'*Reverend, if you would be kind enough this time not to move with the Regiment. Please remember that you are a non-combatant. You will kindly stay behind.*'" Bear pulled a draught of smoke and released it in a slow stream. His face widened into a friendly smile, the corner of his mouth clenching the stem of the pipe.

Nathaniel looked around drowsily at the martial preparations. Flags were unfurled. The soldiers double-checked their rounds, nervously fastening and unfastening the double lids of cartridge box. They passed the tin cartridge boxes around to each other and stuffed handfuls of extra rounds into their pockets. Men again counted their percussion caps or pulled a quick chew or uncorked their canteen to swig a last drink. "Our turn," the men accepted, sucking their teeth.

Bear cupped the palm of his hand over the bowl, drew deep, removed the Meerschaum from his mouth, raised his chin, and exhaled the tobacco smoke high into the air. "I do not think it a request, Nate. He told me to tell you that should you object, you will consider yourself under arrest. He means it, Nate. He'll have the Provost Sergeant on you. These are your orders, chaplain: *'Please retire to the rear and assist the Surgeons.'*" Bear again tapped Nathaniel with his pipe. "He really means it."

"Your obedient servant, Bill," said Nathaniel as he smacked the dust off his hat. "I serve at my master's pleasure. Anyway, I don't like it much up here anyway. Too quiet. I'll leave it for you heroes." The lingering aroma smelled refreshing. Nathaniel's eyes drifted back toward Plum Run, the valley still littered with thousands dead and unburied. The black Cavendish was a far pleasanter smell than the smell of this charnel house. A sadness emptied his heart as he feared he may have missed finding and helping too many men. Dread thoughts invaded. How many of the wounded did we miss? How many did we overlook? How many did we fail to find in time? It's always a matter of time. There are just too many.

"This is almost my last bowl. I'm nearly out," Bear lamented as he packed the embers with his callused thumb. "What do you think, Nate? How about you getting Rupert to loan me his horse? You get me a good horse and I could gallop to Demuths and be back before midnight." William Bear looked longingly towards the pretty Pennsylvania village which had given its name to this battle, yet in his imagination he galloped the turnpike farther east. "Don't you find it peculiar, Nate? We're almost home."

"That's all I've been thinking about."

The drum roll snapped Bear back from rambling thoughts. "Must get back to my men. Luck to you," he said curtly, waving good-bye with his pipe as he turned and again trotted hunched over along the wall.

With an echoing bellow, Colonel William McCandless, a Regiment away, jumped over the stone wall, tripping over the contorted legs of a corpse of a Confederate boy, righted himself, and dressed their lines. Flags followed the Colonel. Skirmishers were deployed to front, right, and left. Bugles sounded, drums beated, and the grand charge commenced. The men jumped over the wall like bridegrooms over the broom.

Joe hesitated. Coates himself had to drag him over the wall by his collar.

Nathaniel swung his legs around and sat alone on top of the wall watching the men move into the wheat field. He checked his watch. 5 PM. Slipping the watch back into his waistcoat pocket, he slid his fingers along the chain and touched the raised relief on his wife's blue cameo. He swung his legs back around, stood up, rubbed his sore hip, and limped away in the opposite direction. As he threaded his way back toward the rear, stepping through the valley of the dead, he too looked eastward. "Yes, Bill, we are near. East to Hanover. To York. Cross the Susquehanna at Wrightsville. To Lancaster. Then home. How many miles? Less than a hundred? Seventy more likely. Home and Alice. I must write her. Haven't lately. It's been over a week. Over a week since I told her how much I love her and my girls."

A clump of orange daylilies opened in full bloom at the base of Little Round Top. Somehow they survived. He reached out instinctively to pluck a flower but recoiled at the thoughtless motion. "Leave it. Beautiful." All the more beautiful for the lily's brevity. He wished he had paid more attention to Alice and his girls. He turned back toward the wheat field and saw only waves of movement beneath the smoke and dust.

Beyond him, the Brigade moved in a dressed line of battle. Open column. Ranks and files arrayed, ready as dusk approached to draw shut the curtain of this day's fighting.

Little did they know then, but the Reserves were to play the final act to these three days of battle. Theirs was the postscript, the denouement, not just to the battle, but, as history would later reveal, also to the hopes of the entire Southern cause which had flared brightly merely hours earlier to their right, much the way a candle flame does before the wick is spent. Lee's failure to break through the Union center had settled an uncertain matter. The movement of McCandless' Brigade of Pennsylvania infantry, located to the left of the line, as it moved out from the stone wall, would close the book, ring the bell, blow out the candle. It would be Lee's final persuasion, the final act to convince Lee it was time for him to leave their homes. Time to be done with this. It would be worth the price to finish this.

Coates glanced over to William Bear who marched at the front of his Company. They nodded to each other as they drew swords and stepped forward in rhythm. The men followed. Bear, pocketing his Meerschaum, bit tight his lower lip. Coates felt a close bond with Bear. Company C and Company B. They've been yoked since the beginning. They both received their Captaincies the same day in March. Coates steeled himself from a confidence born from his knowledge that the Brigade marched in respectable strength, nearly half complete. Likely they had far more men bearing arms than the enemy facing them could boast. Yet still those men in butternut and gray, however many or however few, faced their Brigade.

From what Coates had seen lately of the Rebel prisoners—meager rations, the paucity of their scrounged and scavenged gear, the tattered blankets and torn trousers, not to mention the lack of decent shoes — he was amazed that they had persevered so far, so successfully, and with such ferocity of spirit. At times a frenzy. He supposed it took far more than a Trenton factory and reliable supply lines to fight well. "Ah," he said aloud with pride, "but my men got it now too. This ain't Fredericksburg. This ain't running picket against some partisans, protecting rails or telegraph wires. My men now have gained that spirit, tempered and forged, honed and steeled, by yesterday's anvil and hammer. We are different men today."

Coates took another step forward. He recalled the innocent May day when they all enlisted. When they mustered into the Army two years and a month ago, he boasted a full complement of seventy-nine enlistments. They mostly were boys from little villages, like the Wentz boy. There were a few farm boys still thick with their German accents, even a few lads smarmy from their boasts about coming from the big cities of Lancaster or West Chester or Coatesville. They belonged together now. He turned and swelled with pride at the pace of his Company as they followed him and the flag. His boys. His men. His Company.

He knew each man by name. They had fared better than most Companies in the Brigade, even better than most of the Companies in the Regiment. Seventy-nine enlistments they began with that bright, cheerful, back-slapping distant day at the end of that distant May. Promises of woolen blue uniforms and $11 a month. Side by side they recited in unison their oath of loyalty. Philip Reynolds, Joe Wentz, Charlie Townsend, Isaac Miller, all of them: "*And I do solemnly swear, I will bear true faith and allegiance to the United States of America, and that I will serve them honestly and faithfully against all their enemies or opposers whomsoever; and that I will observe and obey the orders of the*

President of the United States, and the orders of the officers appointed over me, according to the Rules and Articles of War."

Even Governor Curtin reviewed the Regiment the morning of July 4th when they and the Seventh Regiment paraded through the streets of West Chester, to be entertained afterwards by the citizens of their County seat at Everhart's Grove with lemonade, music, and pretty girls.

Seventy-nine men. That was before they started sending the letters home to the fathers who read the words with a farmer's stoicism and mothers who howled like injured wolves, then wept until their souls turned dry. They had been luckier than most. Since that May only five of his men had been killed in action. Philip their first blood at South Mountain, then next blood at Antietam, soon Fredericksburg with Alfred Webb. Two died of other causes. Two men got discharged for wounds received in battle. Thirteen men the Surgeon had certified as unfit or incompetent and had to be discharged, including Sammy Hinds. "Good Lord, he was only thirteen years old," Coates chuckled. Six men received promotions and transfers, including the man Coates himself replaced: Captain Sam Dyer. One man still sat in prison from his General Court Martial. Ten men simply never mustered in—they signed up but never showed up. What galled him the most were the twenty-six desertions. Damn them. One man a day deserted during those first days of August two years ago. Why? What was the problem with that month? Coates knew. That was when the war got serious. When the boys realized it wasn't going to be all fun and glory. One desertion a day after the men met their drill Sergeants and began the tough drills at camp. Curry and Lammy together ran off on Friday the ninth, releasing the floodgates. Nine men failed to show up for roll call that

Saturday morning. That August day was not a proud day for Company C. Thank God for the subsequent volunteers.

But yesterday rinsed the slate clean. Coates never had been prouder of his men. Forty-three men now stepping forward together following McCandless. Forty-three Springfields, plus his sword and his Colt revolver. Forty-three men of Company C at the ready. When it's only forty-three men it was easy to call each man by name. Stronger because of the intimacy. Bonds indissoluble. How can you disappoint your friend, your neighbor, when you stand and fight beside them? You're not fighting for yourself. You're not even fighting for home or country or cause anymore. You fight for him. You fight because he'll fight for you.

Coates poked the tip of his saber into the ground, then swept it like a school-boy at several pitiful stalks of wheat. He won't judge. He was past that. Those men who deserted that August may have had good cause. He won't begrudge them their reasons. Perhaps the corn was in or the cows back home needed more care than father could manage. Perhaps there was a longing for wife, girlfriend, mother. Perhaps they deserted because the drill Sergeants and camp life soiled their fantasies of glory and fame. Their illusions of war faded before the taxing boredom and hard labor of soldiering. Hell, most of them were boys. They may have had cause. He won't judge them. He pitied them. They must face being the lesser for their choice. Coates looked up at the reddening sky. We are simply men of choices. Coates recalled that touring actor who recited scenes from Shakespeare one night at the opera house back home in Coatesville. How did Shakespeare, he wondered, get it so right without having ever tasted battle? But he got it right. Dead right. They who deserted or failed to enlist never will be able to speak of this day. Curry and Lammy will be forced to be silent when others speak of this day. They will never be able to tell their stories to their grandchildren about how they stood before the guns and fought at Gettysburg. What is today? Yes, of course. July 3. Coates squinted toward the horizon. The day was almost done. But not yet. Not yet.

The guns from the opposite woods crackled at them.

"Hold your fire!" McCandless roared.

Erratic fire from the woods smacked into the ranks, hitting thigh, shoulder, limb. But with small effect. The enemy's independent fire, which yesterday was a hailstorm, seemed today more the chance summer shower. To Coates it didn't seem that their advance had surprised the enemy so much as the enemy simply was too dazed, too drained to comprehend and resist the flanking movement. It was more due to their exhaustion than our surprise. Whatever reason for the weak resistance, the advance succeeded. It succeeded due to both the Brigade's sheer determination as well as the evaporating muscle of their opponents. Coates watched in awe as McCandless led the entire Brigade forward. McCandless was seizing his moment.

The landscape of scattered granite boulders opened to fertile soil. The Brigade moved in one mass diagonally across the wheat field, facing the declining sun, moving toward the line of woods. Theirs was the open ground, plus the greater danger, for they advanced facing the puffs of smoke coming from these thick trees. Rifle fire cracked but fortunately did not pour from these woods. Men of the Brigade fell from the accuracy of the experienced Rebel marksmen. But there was no onslaught of lead raking their ranks. Individuals fell but not clumps of men. Coates glanced to his left in time to see Captain Bear stagger.

Bear stabbed his saber into the dirt, crumbled to one knee, only to rise unaided, shake himself like a Labrador Retriever emerging from a lake, and press on, his free hand wiping the blood from his arm which still held his sword. "Good for you, Bill, keep on," Coates muttered.

Bugles and drums sounded. The standards changed direction. It was a half-wheel to the right. Toward the rise. Hundreds of men heeded the choreography of the drill. Shoulder to shoulder. Linked by the invisible chain, they moved in mass. They moved toward the opening on the right where the slope leveled off. Houck's Height. Stoney Hill.

Sudden shouts and the flurry of horsed couriers spelled trouble. Coates cocked an ear along with the hammer of his revolver, and the sound of gunfire increased all along the Brigade's left flank. Bugles again blared. Drums beated. Suddenly the column wheeled direction by left flank and pressed forward again. A walking charge. Men stumbled, sweat salting and stinging their eyeballs. Down through the low-land they moved, then up through the woods. They stumbled into a ravine cluttered with toppled trees and shrubs. This was rough ground, where tree roots had clawed into the cracks of granite boulders. Brambles and branches forced the ranks into a chaotic scramble. The ground began to rise. The Confederate forces attempted only vain resistance. Pockets of Rebels, gathered about trees, stood their ground until they were either killed or captured. The rest joined the scattered retreat in the direction of the Peach Orchard. Pause, reload, and fire. Reload. Independent fire. Surges and minor retreats. Hold ground. Press forward. The pelting of Rebel bullets lessened. There at the edge of the Orchard, at the top of the hill, the Brigade drove back a stubborn Confederate battery.

They paused for breath and water. Their legs felt leaden. Then down again they plunged into the thinner woods toward their left, toward a distant gray stone farmhouse built on top of the next rise. A gentler descent this. Company C, among the first to emerge through the smoke out from the other side the woods, surprised members of a Rebel burial party, their British Enfields stacked. They held their shovels aloft in resigned surrender. Their gray comrades lay dead in the long row.

Coates barked: "Sergeant, gather them up, gather the prisoners up." Then tiredly he surveyed the long row, adding: "Let them finish first."

While the men rested, McCandless sent word down to Talley, along with his commendations. Talley relayed the word along to his Captains. The Brigade, McCandless commended, had captured one hundred prisoners and numerous small arms in this late afternoon's engagement, including one battle flag of the 15th Georgia Regiment. They also recovered one 12 pounder, three caissons, and, especially satisfying, hundreds of their own Union wounded left behind from yesterday's fight among these same woods, fields, and orchard. The Reserves' antique Springfields did good service today.

The Brigade settled in for the night in the gully near the creek at the edge of Rose's woods. They made camp between a squat two story stone farmhouse and treeline. Coates wiped his brow with a blackened, damp handkerchief. He looked up to see four men carrying a bloodied and dirty body by its four sagging limbs.

"Who?" Coates asked wearily.

"Young Charlie. Charlie Townsend."

Coates squeezed his handkerchief as he leaned over the body and stroked the boy's pallid forehead, crusty with dried blood. "How did it happen?" Coates asked softly, as if afraid of waking the boy. "We need to tell his parents how. Does anybody know?" He looked around at his men. Some shook their heads. Others simply hung their heads and closed their eyes.

No one spoke for none noticed.

Forty-two, Coates counted silently.

Chapter Twelve

Aftermath

I've been in the storm so long,
You know I've been in the storm so long,
Oh Lord, give me more time to pray,
I've been in the storm so long.
I am a motherless child,
Singin' I am a motherless child,
Singin' Oh, Lord give me more time to pray,
I've been in the storm so long.
Nineteenth Century Black Spiritual

The shouting sounded familiar. So too the temper. Valentine had been found.

Out from the barn door of the field hospital fled a distinguished, silver haired gentleman, his top coat missing. Valentine, wiping blood from his hands onto an already bloodied rag, chased him. He threw the rag at the man, hitting him with a squish and splat square in the back of his silk vest.

"Stay away from my patients!" Valentine hollered after him as the man stumbled toward the corner of the barn. The man tripped over a litter. Valentine seized the black bag carried by the orderly trailing him and tossed it at the man before he escaped around the corner. The man quickly darted back, retrieved his bag from the ground, then scampered off through the mass of wounded awaiting their turn to be treated.

Valentine noticed Nathaniel standing a few feet away. "Can you believe it? Goddamn butcher! He came here an hour ago offering his services. Called himself a Surgeon. Damn civilian. What he wanted was some interesting cases to experiment on. Damn him! I saw him. He actually undressed the wounds of one of my men, poked around, then moved off to the next man. He didn't even repack the wound, damn him! It wasn't interesting enough. It wasn't interesting enough! I'll show him interesting."

Valentine pulled a saw from the pocket of his apron and pointed it at the Steward. "Keep these locals away from me, hear me! Shoot them it you have to!"

"Good to see you too," Nathaniel greeted as he approached Valentine and rubbed his thumb against the stubble on his friend's cheek. "You look like you could use a shave."

"What I could use is a good sleep with a bad woman."

"Val, please."

Valentine scratched his cheek with the back of his hand, then extended his bloody hand to Nathaniel. "I gather you're still alive."

With a smile, Nathaniel slid his hands into his trouser pockets. "So far. Though I feel like I'm dead from having walked the length of this entire county. Twice."

Valentine noticed the bandage tied around Nathaniel's neck. "Speaking of blood..." Valentine fidgeted with the bandage. "What's with this neck?"

"It hurts a bit," Nathaniel said. "Not much to worry about though. Seems the bullet seared its own damage." Nathaniel blushed as he let his friend inspect the wound. "I hear some the locals have already balked at helping out with the burial details," said Nathaniel. They say it's none of their business. Whose business is it then?"

Valentine pulled Nathaniel toward a trough and dipped in a rag pulled from his apron pocket and wiped the wound.

Nathaniel flinched. "Careful, that hurts."

"Don't whine, the real soldiers are listening," Valentine chided while scrubbing at the neck.

"It's been a nightmare for everyone, believe me," Nathaniel continued. "It's been the same with some of my colleagues. You wouldn't believe what one local pastor did on my way here. Kicked out of headquarters, he spotted me walking to the rear here and asked me to intervene on their behalf with General Crawford. As if I know Crawford. Can you believe it? These citizens want reparations. Their curtains, it seems, suffered damage in the battle."

"Thank God for these all the more," Valentine said as he wagged his head toward a plump and bosomy woman who was ladling soup from a gigantic wheeled kettle. They both watched her as she whoosked about in her billowing, dark blue, taffeta gown, helping the men who were scattered about the grounds drink from the bowl she offered them, men too injured or too confused to feed themselves. She moved among these casualties, her dress brushing up against them, prompting among them the memory of the rustle of petticoats. Hundreds lay on the ground around her. Some leaned against each other. Those who could found relief beneath a hastily erected shelter tent or blanket strung into a lean-to. She attended to as many of the wounded as she could, offering the gift of warm soup and something fondly feminine. Amidst this all too masculine atrocity, she offered the tender gift of a woman's soft face looking back into yours. A woman's hand touching yours. A reminder of a long absent goodness.

"There's an angel for you. What an angel—she hasn't stopped for three days," Valentine gushed as he tied a fresh bandage around Nathaniel's neck. "Nate, I think I am in love." Valentine raised his voice. "I finally found me the woman of my dreams—right, Mrs. Sandra Lewis of Harrisburg?" His eyes admired after her. She ignored him, despite blushing visibly. "And, you know, Nate, at the beginning I really didn't think it fitting for women to see such things. Didn't think they had the stamina. Oh, forgive me, my darlin'," he shouted toward her. Blushing redder, she tried to help a soldier recline against a tree so he could sip from the bowl of soup.

"If it weren't for them," Valentine continued, lowering his voice and shaking his head, "I don't know how we could have fared. The Army can't deliver our supplies, but here these women arrive with wagons filled with blankets, bed-sacks, and bandages, even disinfectants and plenty of medicines. Bless them. Bless them, and your folks too. Finally found a use for your pious bunch." Valentine pointed at the flag of the Christian Commission suspended from a pole over a wagon at the edge of the hospital compound. "If it weren't for your people and the Sanitary Commission, frankly, Nate, many of these men wouldn't stand a chance. Bless them. You know, they even brought fruit around for my boys."

The orderly poked his head out the door. "Excuse me, sir, you're needed—it's the Lieutenant. He's ready."

"Damn. Yes, of course. In a moment." As Valentine retied the strings of his apron, he looked up at his friend. "Can you lend a hand?"

"Those were my orders. Talley didn't want me leading any more charges."

With a raised eyebrow, Valentine looked puzzled at Nathaniel. "Huh?" he grunted. "What trouble have you gotten yourself into now?"

"Tell you later," he said, lingering for a moment at the door. "Just promise never to tell Alice. Never. She'd kill me." At the doorway, Nathaniel turned to Valentine. "What can I do?"

"For this one I literally need you to lend a hand."

An acquiescence to an inevitable dread allowed Nathaniel to follow Valentine inside the barn. The Corps Hospital. They had commandeered the barn until they could organize enough men to set up the tents.

Entering, the stench of pus and ether mixed with the heady smell of the chloroform. One of the musicians, moving through the circles of light casted by the lanterns and from the shafts of waning sunlight streaking through the gaps in the walls, carried a large wooden bucket. Dust and straw floated in the rays. He was collecting from the floor of the barn pieces of flesh and bone, fingers, a hand, a foot, an arm. Another musician carried a complete leg warm and swaying at the knee. Nathaniel's eyes adjusted. Half of the wounded writhed on cots. The rest sat or rested on the planked floor in a daze, some blanketed. Aside from the mumbled groanings and slopping sounds, the barn was eerily serene. No screaming. No panic. No clamor. Just a quiet dread and the grinding of saws. Orderlies along with the attending musicians shuffled from man to man, bending, inspecting wounds, plucking out shreds of torn wool, linen, and cotton from the wounds. The Surgeons worked on tables set up at the far end of the barn. An orderly stood at one of the tables and signaled for O'Rourke. A second orderly had begun administering the chloroform to the Lieutenant, the cone already inserted over his beardless face.

Valentine grabbed Nathaniel by the elbow and steered him to the table. One man to their right, clutching his bloodied chest, gurgled, having been shot through the lungs. Another man, insensate, wore a binding of loosened bandages around his head, partially covering the missing chunk of skull and exposed brains. Yellow bones protruded, flesh sloughed off, the meat of limbs torn away, jaws shot away. Dozens of men sat together in a corner of the barn, dirty bandages covering blinded eyes.

One man was lying on a cot wearing only a shirt. More of a boy actually. Fuzz instead of stubble grew on his face. A small napkin covered his genitals. His upper thigh was wrapped in a large bandage. He appeared no older than seventeen years old. Nathaniel read aloud his name which was pinned to the front of his linen shirt: 'Joseph Andrews, 154th New York.' The boy awakened from his stupor to find this man in black staring at his wound. The boy smiled weakly at the chaplain. The smile turned into a wan smirk as he whispered: "Just glad it weren't any higher."

Nathaniel breathed a small laugh and patted the boy lightly on his shoulder. The boy drifted back asleep.

"Come, Nate," Valentine said, standing behind the table. "I need your help now."

Nathaniel joined them at the table and looked down at the drugged Lieutenant. Half of the calf from his left leg had been ripped away by canister. The bone mauled. His foot, still wearing its brown shoe, dangled severed from his ankle except for a thin stretch of muscle and ligament. "Tell me what you want me to do," Nathaniel said.

"Hold below the knee. I want the joint saved. Hold it tight. Tighten that tourniquet. Don't let it loosen. As I cut I need you to compress the vessels and try to pull back with your fingers as much of the tissue as you can, I need a good flap. Let's go. Come on, you've seen it before." Valentine sliced with his Liston knife into the leg below the knee. "And watch out, I move fast. The faster, the kinder."

It was a fishmouth incision. Surgeon O'Rourke cut into the leg at an angle to the bone. Nathaniel compressed and elevated the leg. "Pull the skin back," Valentine instructed. "Come on, Nate, you can do it." The knife flashed.

Nate swallowed his own vomit. Blood squirted onto his black coat.

"Squeeze it, Nate, squeeze it—trust me, you're not going to hurt him."

Nathaniel's fingers drew back the man's soft tissue, exposing the yellow bone. As often as he had seen amputations, he was always surprised how the bones never were white.

"Good, good, looks good." Without looking away from the wound, Valentine taunted: "Don't you just love the will of God?" Then he reached for the small chain saw left on top of the table and with both hands sawed away at the tibia. He paused only for a second to wipe his forehead and chase away the pestering flies, then finished sawing through. The fibula he divided with the bone cutter. "Love it when I can save the knee," Valentine congratulated himself. "He's lucky, he's lucky. Quick, now the tenaculum." The orderly handed him the instrument. With it the Surgeon hooked and pulled out the main artery, which he immediately tied off. Last, he ligated the vein.

"Nate, you can let go now." Nathaniel still clenched the leg. Valentine shouted again: "Nate, I said, 'you can let go.'"

Nathaniel released his hold and stepped back.

After sprinkling the wound with nitrate of silver, Valentine took the flaps of skin and folded them over the stump. With curved needles and silk thread he quickly sewed up a cuff of skin.

"Pretty as a Christmas present," he said. It took less than two minutes. The lower limb was kicked aside and the stump would be bandaged later. The orderly took the discarded portion of the Lieutenant's leg and dumped it onto the pile of other limbs in the stables behind the surgical tables.

"Listen," Valentine addressed Nathaniel as he dunked his bloodied hands into a bucket of pink water. "I want him to awaken quickly. Try fanning his face to purge his lungs of the chloroform. If that doesn't work splash some chloroform on his scrotum. Can you do that? It is important that he wakes up quickly. Got that?"

Nathaniel nodded feebly as he helped the orderlies cart the Lieutenant to one of the few remaining beds.

By the tenth amputation that he assisted, Nathaniel no longer felt the bile of his vomit rising. By the twentieth he helped knot the artery. Other Surgeons busied themselves with the broken bones not requiring amputation or probing for bullets. Most of Valentine's work was with those tagged as needing amputations. Only one of the twenty amputated that first hour died on the table. The patient's pulse sank and the liquor of ammonia failed to take effect.

"How many will survive the week remains to be seen," Valentine confided to Nathaniel between amputations. It was not the surgery that killed, though for some the cutting and sawing simply was too hard on the heart. Almost none died on the table from hemorrhage. "What kills is what sets in later. If we could only reduce the poisoning, the gangrene." He didn't comprehend why there was so much poisoning. After all, they washed the bandages and rinsed out the sponges before they used them on the next man.

Fevers did set in. Ague attacked more perniciously than Longstreet's Divisions. Men turned delirious, chilled, convulsing. So many arrived already suffering from asthenia, already weakened and sick from pneumonia or measles or lousy nutrition. "How do they expect them to survive such injuries when they already are sick, when they arrive weak?" Valentine complained, not expecting Nathaniel to answer. Nathaniel, for his part, gave up trying to give answers months ago. "Sorry, Nate," he said. "I'm getting tired." He looked to the orderly. "Who's next?"

While the Reserves enjoyed their bivouac at the edge of the Rose woods, grateful for their first real meal and first real rest in over a week—the men brewing coffee, cooking a few strips of bacon, chewing hardtack, wrapping themselves in blankets and falling into deep sleep—Valentine and Nathaniel continued working though the humid night.

At dawn, on orders from Colonel Talley, Adjutant Alfred Rupert rode to the rear, hunting for Nathaniel. Rupert found him collapsed against the wooden wheel of the kettle of soup, resting swollen feet.

"So there you are, lolly-gagging again," Rupert chided as he looked down at Nathaniel from the saddle of his liver chestnut. "Took me hours but I finally found this Fiscel farm."

Nathaniel squinted. "Nice horse." He began to rise, then, suddenly lightheaded and nauseated, staggered.

"Stay there. You don't look like you can move anyway."

"Thanks." Nathaniel again squinted at Rupert. "So how'd we make out yesterday?"

Rupert dismounted, keeping a hold on the reins. "We were lucky. A good day. We're still trying to sort out all the wounded. God, we were lucky. Only five killed yesterday." Rupert lifted his eyes, rubbed his chin, and recited the list from memory:

Company A - John Buchannan

Company B - Joseph Rutter

Company F - Harry Armstrong

Company G - Abel Force

Rupert lowered his eyes. "And, sorry Nate, Company C also lost one. Charlie Townsend. Real sorry, Nate."

Nathaniel grabbed at a clump of grass and threw it at his feet. "Townsend. Good kid. Good friend of Philip Reynolds," he mumbled. "Desperately poor folks back home. The Townsends are real poor. Guinea hens, a couple of pigs, and a shack by the Octorara. They eat a lot of eels."

Rupert continued reverently: "Eight men in all these last two days. Tolerable. Though I fear three others are awful bad. Real bad. Budd from F, Lusk from I, and Billy McGrenn from K Company. Are you remembering this, Nate? They're being treated south of here in a farmhouse along the Taneytown. McGrenn's mates tell me he was wounded near his girlfriend's farm. Hell of a way to celebrate Independence Day, 'eh?" Rupert caught himself. "Sorry preacher. Shouldn't swear."

Nathaniel plucked a long strand of grass and played it underneath his nose, stroking his moustache with it. "Pretty accurate though, Alfred."

Rupert walked up and tapped the bottom of Nathaniel's boot with his toe. "Sorry again, friend, but you're required. Talley sent me, and I quote our good Colonel: '*I require the chaplain's assistance in helping me finish my accounting of my Regiment.*' It seems a fair number of the men, especially those in Company K, appear to have gone home without proper leave."

Nathaniel whistled. "Wish we could go with them."

Valentine, eavesdropping from the barn door, intruded to quip: "They work, then we work, Nate." He walked toward the two men and extended his hand to Rupert. "Glad to see you."

Nathaniel pushed himself up from the ground and glanced at Valentine. "At least you get to save some. I just bury them." Nathaniel suddenly felt dizzy. He staggered, then regained his balance. "Rupert here has just told me we lost Charlie Townsend yesterday."

"He's in good company," Valentine said.

Rupert continued: "Joe Wentz and a few of the boys carried him back a little bit ago. By the way, the men were to move off. They should now be near Little Round Top." Rupert fiddled with the buttons on his uniform. "Take a look at Joe if you get the chance, O'Rourke. He doesn't seem right. I want a medical opinion."

Nathaniel absent-mindedly wound his watch and held it to his ear listening for the ticking. "Well, I must see to Charlie." Nathaniel removed his frock coat and slung it over his shoulder. "Lord, my clothes have been wet since we marched through Frederick."

Valentine rubbed his closed eyes with sore fingers. "Catch up with you later. Thanks for the hand."

The rains fell before Nathaniel returned to the Regiment. The rains turned heavy. Rivulets of red water flowed from the field toward the streams. Plum Run's trickle rose into a stream. Nathaniel took off his hat and looked into the sky. "Not enough of a cleansing," he said aloud to the gray clouds. "It would take Noah's flood to flush this battlefield."

Very few of the battlefield dead had yet been buried. Those that had, had been placed in rows according to the color of their uniform. Scores of corpses had been placed in attempted trenches, hundreds in hasty mound graves. Some bodies still hung contorted over fence rails. The swelling bodies had begun to burst out of their haggard clothes, finding weakness in the seams. Fluids leaked from wounds, eyes, nostrils, and mouths. The fetid air lingered like a fog. Maggots crawled. Nathaniel held his handkerchief over the lower half of his face. Among the bodies were scattered the other residue of battle: rifles broken in half, snapped bayonets, muddied pieces of paper, crushed cartridge boxes, torn haversacks, dented canteens, shattered shards of cannon balls, stumps and splinters of trees hewn by the incessant volley of rifle fire.

The crows had driven away the killdeer, for it was the season of carrion. The crows, ignoring both rain and chaplain, strolled well fed among the dead.

The rains fell harder. A distant shimmer of lightning drew his interest to the horizon. Soon followed the dull rumble of thunder. Nathaniel again removed his black hat, looked up into the gray, whirling sky, and let the rainfall drench his face.

Chapter Thirteen

Chasing the Badger

Open thy lattice, love listen to me!
In the voyage of life, love our pilot will be!
He will sit at the helm wherever we rove,
And steer by the load-star he kindled above;
his shell for a shallop will cut the bright spray,
Or skim like a bird o'er the waters away;
Then open thy lattice, love listen to me!
While the moon's in the sky and the breeze on the sea!
"Open Thy Lattice, Love," Morris and Foster

The Regiment awakened to a sullen, soggy dawn. The men were slow to stir despite the Provost Sergeant jostling them with the butt of his Sharps. Even he performed his duties with slow deliberation, as if it were sufficient for his men to open their eyes. The carbine stirred the men today rather than smack them. The Sergeant didn't have it in him today. There was none of his hoarse yell or harsh discipline.

The mists and clouds that remained from the night's torrential rain obscured the sun's slow efforts to shine upon the living. The soles of boots thickened with mud as they tended to chores and toilet, but even the dirt and damp made the men somber instead of surly. How could they complain today? For today they rose. Today they got the chance to witness the rising

185

of the sun, however veiled, as it ascended over Culp's Hill to claim the sky. All those troubles which in weeks before gave rise to bickering had been muted by the taste of life's ordinary presence. What once was urgent now seemed petty, trifling. Even burnt and bitter coffee in a tin cup tasted sweeter today than ever before.

Approaching Bear from the side, Nathaniel stopped and watched. Bear sat on a log at the edge of the campfire. Embers, smoking and popping from the wet wood, glowed red, inviting his dirty hands with their aching joints to reach out and warm themselves. Bear flexed his right hand toward the red glow, then curled the fingers back into a fist. He turned his hand over and flexed it several times more. Bear touched the four fingers to his thumb in succession, then reversed the action. He did this several more times before relaxing his open hand.

"Okay, Bill, I give up," Nathaniel said as he sat down on the log next to Bear. "What on earth are you doing?"

Stirred out of his trance by Nathaniel's sudden appearance, William Bear cupped his right hand with his left hand. He stared long into the embers before speaking. "Kind of odd, don't you think, Nate, these hands of ours?"

"I don't follow."

"They're wonderfully treacherous, don't you think?" With a wince of pain from his wound, Bear rubbed his hands together. "I guess I'm getting a little batty myself."

"No, go on," Nathaniel encouraged, staring down at the back of his own hands.

"I mean, and forgive me if I sound foolish, but, I'm remembering when I left home and held my wife's hands. This same hand of mine raised her palm to my lips and I kissed her open fingers. Most peculiar." Bear ebbed into a memory. "I like to carve, Nate. Pretty good too. Give me a penknife and a chunk of pinewood and I can make a toy for my boy. Made him a little dog. Carved a ship once. Even carved a rattle for him."

"Sounds like you have a gift."

"Oh, the toys were nice, nothing special. But I made them myself. With these hands." Bear lifted his head and looked vacantly over at Nathaniel. "And yesterday I shot at least five men with this hand. Killed one with my saber for sure, brought it right down across his neck." He stared back into the embers. "Strange things these hands." Bear reached toward the ground, picked up some dirt, and rubbed the dirt between his palms. He placed his hand on Nathaniel's knee. "Let me get you some coffee."

"Yeah, that'd be fine, Bill."

The light of this gray morning revealed the hands of all the men in the Company to be callused hands, fingernails split, fingers cramped and bent from holding paper cartridge and pulling metal trigger. Yet this new morning, these same hands tended to the ordinary. That hand yesterday pressed percussion cap, pulled musket trigger, and took a man's life. These hands killed. Slayers. Destroyers. They will again. Likely soon. Maybe even again later today. But yesterday's hand was not this morning's hand. For the hand that fed the fire a stick or poured a mug of coffee for a tired mate was today redeemed by these simple ministrations of the camp. These profane kindnesses were made sacred within the crucible of their grateful and awestruck souls.

The men comprehended what it was like to pay the price of living on both sides of fortune's coin. They knew what it meant to stand alone, scared, ashamed, and dirtied. They knew what it meant not to have given your fair share. They also knew now what it meant to be a man who had received far more grace, far more forgiveness than he deserved.

The men sat and sipped, grateful for the brief peace that had been conceded to them. They were blessed to linger beneath the tree's shadows, leaves which, with each breeze, trickled drops of water. Some took pencil to diary or, better, to paper. With those same trembling, tired, cramped hands they wrote home the good news that today they lived.

The men found time to write home. Nathaniel made time to write.

☉☉☉

My Dearest Alice,

We are so near home. But Gettysburg might just as well be Georgia. There is no chance of seeing you and our daughters. It is as if I can hear you and see you despite the miles between us and these times that interfere. Please forgive me for not having written sooner. It must be unbearable for all of you to have to wait to receive these letters we send.

Let the church know I am sending soon a letter to Harold Wentz for him to read during worship. It will tell about Joe and all their boys and how proud they can be of their service and sacrifice. All are optimistic that Lee is crushed and this dread ordeal soon will end. Lee's Army cannot last much longer. I also have listed a few items the men could use, should the church see fit to gather a collection. Although it will be hard to tell where we might be found in the next few weeks.

My dearest Alice, my letter to the church will say much that our friends and parishioners ought to hear, but, dearest, I must confess to you that there is so much I do not understand nor can say. I use to think I could describe and explain everything so well. Why are my words beginning to fail me of late? Father might smile when he hears this. Tell father I am beginning to understand what he meant shortly after mother died. And to think I was angry with him. Only now am I beginning to understand how his faith changed after mother's death. Could it be that faith is born more of suffering than piety? More by love than by even right belief?

But thank God, I still have you, and that General Lee has been kind enough to let you continue to have me (though, rest assured, my dear, this is more jest than reality—I have yet to come near harm— our good Colonel insists on keeping me safe and in the rear at all times). I miss our daughters so. They enjoy the gift of innocence. How I wish it could remain for them.

Please write as soon as you receive this letter. I long to hear of you and from you. I would love for you to just tell about one day, describe everything that you did, what the girls did, what they wore and said. That will be the greatest gift you can give. That will bring me home, if only by letter. Kisses to our daughters. Valentine, as ever, sends his fondest love.

Your loving husband,
N.

◎◎◎

Later that morning, Rupert found Nathaniel among the men of Company B collecting letters to post. Bear, balanced on a rickety box, caught Nathaniel's eye. Raising his unlit pipe, he pointed out Rupert cantering on his liver chestnut toward them. Nathaniel stuffed the men's letters into his haversack and turned to greet him.

"Morning, Alfred. What can we do for you?"

Rupert took off his hat and wiped his brow with the back of his sleeve. The sweat rolled down his face. "Morning, Nate." Rupert waved his hat toward Captain Bear. "Bill, how are you today? Heard you took one the other day."

"I'm here. Breathing, bloodied, and brave." He pocketed his pipe, the motion causing a vicious wince of pain. "It's nothing serious. You may report to Talley that I'm ready and so are my men."

"Might as well be. We're off in column within the hour. It's time to catch Lee before he slips away." Rupert settled his slouch hat back on his head. He rose in his stirrups. "We've got him, Bill. We've got him and he's hurt."

"So are we," Bear replied flatly.

"Yeah, but he's farther from home," Rupert continued earnestly. "And from all that we've heard and seen, they're hungry and running low on everything. We've bled them, hurt them bad."

Bear lifted himself from his box. Another flash of pain made his face wince. He gently pressed his hand against his upper arm. "The question, Rupert, isn't who's hurt most but who's hurt least?"

Rupert leaned forward in his saddle and patted the withers of his horse. "Actually, Nate, I'm here for you. Talley has a request. He'd like you to offer another prayer before the Regiment moves out. What he actually said was: '*We should enjoin services after all, it being the Sabbath.*' The man can be dreadfully formal at times." Rupert reached down and extended his hand toward Nathaniel. "You know, chaplain, I do believe you've almost got him converted to thinking you fellows belong here." Rupert leaned back in his saddle. "Keep it brief, though."

"It is Sunday, isn't it? I forgot. Second time that's happened." Nathaniel and Alfred shook hands warmly. "It would be an honor, of course. I'll follow directly. Did he say when?"

"As soon as the column is formed."

"What of Valentine?" Nathaniel asked the Adjutant. "Do you know if he is staying or coming with us?"

"Last I heard was that he'll follow when he can." Rupert's hands began gathering and tightening his leather reins. "Sorry, Nate. No time for good-byes. We're moving immediately."

"I understand. He'll figure things out," Nathaniel said. "I'll follow directly."

Bear put his good arm around Nathaniel's shoulders as Rupert wheeled and cantered away. "Throw in a prayer, Nate, for the good Lord to light a fire under Meade. I feel it in my bones, in my bones. I am convinced now is not the time for us to be cautious. I want it finished. I want to go home." He squeezed Nathaniel tighter. "Pray hard, 'cause he's got to throw prudence to the wind."

At the bugle sound and drum beat, the Regiment assembled. The men turned to face their chaplain. Nathaniel didn't know what to say. He felt that any word he might speak would be sacrilege, intrusive, that silence would be more fitting. They had aged much these few days. But, he concluded, there is comfort in tradition. Besides, he corrected himself, they are not his words anyway. He read from scripture and offered one stanza of the hymn, *Safely Through Another Week*, followed by an extemporaneous prayer of thanksgiving. Tradition did good service. More than a few of the men wept without regret or embarrassment. Tears creasing those dirty faces seemed the only fitting way to leave such a place.

Nathaniel refused the teamster's offer to ride in one of the supply wagons. He knew it would hurt, especially his sore and bruised hip, but he needed to walk with the Regiment. With each step south the tears of the men dried as the soldier's bravado gradually returned. The silence gave way to melancholy song. Soon enough, rightly enough, after miles enough, the bawdier songs crept in. Jesting returned, along with pranks. And the men began to complain about the mud and thirst and wet clothes and painful bunions. You know they're getting better when they start complaining. Laughter returned to the column, urged on by a strange anticipation that they just might be on the verge of bringing this terrible war to its knees. Before, they fought because of boast, pride, and principle—now hey fought to finish it, just to end this stinking, lousy business. They were sick of it. They were angry and tired and wished to be finished with it. They all, like Bear, wanted to go home and forget it. Erase it and get back to the harvest or shoeing horses. However proud they might be of their necessary service, only fools glory in being soldiers. So they marched on, confident that they could and would finish it. They walloped Lee on their ground. They would whip him on his. More so, they realized now Lee could be whipped. They, the Reserves, helped whip him. If they moved fast enough they just might whip him for good. The column's pace quickened, even without orders.

They marched past clumps of wounded Confederates, dozens of men unable to keep up with Lee's retreat. Most of these orphans were ignored by the Union infantry as they pressed on by to pursue their comrades. No longer threats, these ill, injured Rebels sat unguarded on the grass by the side of the turnpike. There was little to guard. Less to worry about. Weaponless. Often shoeless. Their clothes tattered and threadbare. Wreckage of the storm. These Confederates, not so much broken or beaten as they were worn out, simply stared back at the marching troops. They simply waited. They waited for somebody to claim them.

Only a few of the passing Union troops mocked them, tossing a boastful ridicule as they marched on by. The Rebs didn't bother to reply. These men knew that these taunts came from the greener soldiers, those clad in clean and bright blue uniforms, those who remained in safe reserve throughout the last week. The veterans, Nathaniel noticed, those men wearing uniforms faded and torn, would toss to the Rebels a piece of hardtack wrapped in wax paper. Several times he saw men from his Regiment break rank and offer sips of water from their own canteens. Let it be done, he prayed.

Near Falling Waters on the Potomac, the Rebels set up a defensive perimeter, making every sign that they intended to make a stand. Days before, the Union cavalry destroyed the bridge. Lee's desperate redoubt. The Confederate backsides were up against the swollen river. The Third Corps was marched double quick to Williamsport, where the Reserves were assigned to the position on the left of the main line of battle.

The mass of the Union army inexorably swelled up against this perimeter, building up the gravity of sheer mass for Meade to finally overwhelm and drown the weary secessionist troops. The men lay on arms waiting for orders. The men felt what Captain Bear felt. They too felt it in their bones. The omens were strong. They were eager, ready, and anxious to have done with it, to seize this moment and finish Lee. Get it done. Finish it, so they can go home. They waited for the orders to advance. They waited. And they waited a few more days.

On the 14th of July the advance against the perimeter finally began, only for Meade and his entire army to discover that the Rebels had abandoned the fortifications. The enemy had vanished. The collective heart of the Union Army sunk. They would not go home. Each man realized it would not be ended. It would continue. For on July 13th, screened behind Cavalry feint and skirmish, Lee's entire army had crossed the Potomac across the new bridge which the Union delay allowed the Confederate engineers time to construct.

Lee had gone home. The Reserves must follow him back to his familiar ground.

Bill Bear shook his head with raw disgust and gnawed on his pipe stem. "What happened to that prayer, preacher? My Daddy taught me never to follow a badger into his burrow. But we got to, Nate, we got to. We're going to stick our hands in and we're going to get bit bad. What was Meade thinking? Why didn't we act sooner?"

The Regiment marched down the steep declivity toward the hamlet of Berlin. Worn heels churned dust. The descent led toward the muddy flats along the river where the midges swarmed. Men swatted at gnats and mosquitoes as they crossed the canal with its stagnant water and then trod across the pontoon bridges stretched across the lazy, brown Potomac. The Army marched into the heights and trees on the opposite bank. The Regiment pursued Lee's escape.

July days were spent walking. Hot days were spent chasing, as Lee benefited from the mobility of the interior position. The Reserves marched across the crests and swells of the oceanic countryside that was Virginia. They marched across barren fields long played out, past deserted buildings. They walked across a battered and battled landscape. Through the weeks of July blending into August they marched day after day, their toes bleeding and soles wearing out. Men pressed one nostril to blow out the goo from the other. Hot, dusty days were spent on the march, the column contorting in every direction of the infernal compass. Despite the serpentine path, the Reserves invariably, relentlessly, headed south. They reached deeper into Lee's lair.

Hopes and enthusiasms sprung from Gettysburg's victory dimmed and dulled as the summer lengthened and as exhaustion and frustrations increased. The Virginian farms and villages had little to offer hungry men; they'd been foraged so many times earlier by both sides. The men asked aloud around the campfires whether or not Gettysburg was worth it. Desertions escalated.

Summer began with the valor of Gettysburg. The same summer ended in shame.

Five deserters had been captured and court-martialed. Five Pennsylvanian deserters from the 118th. These men were draftees, not volunteers. But Army law was Army law, even for draftees. It didn't matter how you got the uniform. Once you put it on, you got no choice. There was no you. There was only Army.

On the afternoon of August 29th, a cool Saturday, the entire Fifth Corps was ordered to stand at attention along the lip of a large plain. It reminded Nathaniel of drawings he had seen in his textbooks of a Greek Amphitheater. Before them a new tragedy unfolded. As Nathaniel approached the edge of the bowl, he saw below five graves freshly dug in the soft, green meadow.

A band entered center stage beating out the doleful rhythm of a funeral dirge. Next arrived the Provost Marshal leading fifty men selected from the First Division bearing reversed arms. Soon followed soldiers carrying a coffin, with the first deserter close behind. Then the other four coffins were carried to center stage, each in turn followed by the other four deserters. Each coffin was placed beside an open grave.

Nathaniel recognized three of his fellow chaplains accompanying the guilty deserters: a priest, a pastor, and a rabbi. He had worked with them before. He was not real familiar with them, but they'd talked at their monthly meetings. They had swapped ideas, advice, impressions. The last of the procession included an officer and a thirty man escort.

The deserters were escorted forward and forced to sit on the lid of their coffins. The five men struggled with their emotions as they bid good-bye to each other. They received their blindfolds. Squadrons of ten men faced each man to be executed.

It was a rapid: "Ready. Aim. Fire."

Joe Wentz dropped to his knees, convulsing. He had to be lifted to his feet and dragged along as the Regiment took its required turn filing past the executed deserters. Nathaniel made a point of reminding himself that he had better talk to Joe that night.

Three days later the Army crossed the Rappahannock in force and the Reserves were posted near Culpepper Courthouse. They began setting up the amenities of camp, which was a relief after having spent so many weeks engaged in unpredictable tentativeness. They began settling into camp, even looking forward to extended encampment. But orders arrived to resume the march. They returned pursuing Lee, once again giving up warm shelter, regular mail, and decent meals. They had no time for the coffee beans to be shelled, shucked, and boiled. It was back to gnawing on them. It was a return to the unpredictable.

The men, Nathaniel observed, were close to breaking. Among the ranks, there was more cursing, more drunkenness. Bounty men swaggered through camp. The morale had been worsened by the influx of the draftees into the volunteer Regiments. The newcomers were unwelcome by the veterans. "How can you trust these draftees who don't want to be here in the first place?" Nathaniel asked Talley, who stoically muttered that he had no choice in the matter. The Reserves experienced more fights than usual, sometimes over the declining number of whores. Sometimes men fought over a dry log for the fire. Sometimes they fought over nothing. Thievery, once rare, became frequent. Distrust grew. Harsher punishments were required. The guilty were assigned dirty duties. The guilty were lashed to wagon wheels, stripped and whipped. Heads were shaved and the felons forced to march about camp wearing signboards about their necks announcing their crimes. Often the Captains, even Bear and Coates, let the Sergeants take care of the problems in their own brutal manner.

Snakebites added to the unease. Water moccasins and copperheads. Some men were so exhausted, so ill, they simply fell behind in the march and were captured by Lee's patrols. More men deserted. All despised the weather. It was an ugly Virginia autumn—rainy days and cold nights. Always there was the march, Meade's meanderings. Always there was the lack of fires for warmth. Always there was the mud.

In his daily conversations with Talley, Nathaniel noted that a dangerous frustration was infecting the troops, boding ill for the coming winter months which surely promised to be all the more uncomfortable. He also noted how the bottle of whisky seemed to stay on Talley's desk rather than stored in the trunk. Even the hardiest soldiers began looking for excuses from duty. Valentine was sick and tired with the morning sick call and the whining. Valentine's orders to cancel sick call were overruled by Talley. But what should Valentine and his staff do when nearly 200 men report in sick? The newspapers trumpeted what the men spoke in whispers at mess, for they too doubted the competence of the men in charge.

Bear was among the most vocal. "I told you, Nate. I predicted it. He's too bloody cautious to command. He's an engineer, after all! God, help us, what can you expect from an engineering officer?"

Nathaniel raised his eyes. "Isn't Lee an engineer?"

Lee moved through his Virginia at will and the Union troops chased his tail or got bit by his teeth or occasionally were mauled by his claws. Stuart's Cavalry, mimicking the water moccasins, struck by stealth where it wished, capturing at times whole patrols, destroying telegraph line and railroads. Railway timbers got stacked for the bonfire. Red hot rails were bent at right angles in the heat of their own burning railroad ties. An Army requiring supplies by rails from the north needed these rails unmolested. Men without supplies become surlier men.

Near Brandy Station the Third Corps finally received orders and moved to form line of battle. Rumors raced that they had

Lee trapped. Terrible storms soaked them and chilled them all night as they huddled in the drenching gloom without benefit of shelter or fire. Nathaniel wrapped himself up in his ripped, rubber blanket. The two friends slept side-by-side underneath the ambulance wagon.

"Preacher, come quick," the voice yelled from behind the wagon. "It's terrible."

Valentine nudged Nathaniel.

The yell repeated: "Preacher, come quick."

Nathaniel supported himself on his elbow. "What's the matter, Isaac?"

"Please come. It's Joe. He's done somethin' awful."

Nathaniel threw off his blanket. Alice's latest letter fell into the mud. He grabbed his slouch hat and crawled out from under the wagon. He put his arm over Isaac's shoulder. "Now calm down. What's so awful?"

"He's done near killed himself."

"Who? What? Calm down, Isaac."

"Took his bayonet and tried to slice open his wrists. And we thought he was feelin' better."

"You mean Joe?"

"We thought he went off to take a crap." Isaac shook his head and repeated himself, muttering: "We thought he went to take a crap."

Nathaniel's heart sank. "Show me the way."

Isaac ran toward the picket lines as Nathaniel struggled to keep up with him, stumbling in the dark. When he arrived he saw two men restraining young Joe by the shoulders. Another man lay prone, using his weight to pin Joe's legs to the ground. Joe's forearms flailed, splattering the men with droplets of blood from the bleeding wrists. Another man, with a bandage draped over his shoulder, knelt beside Joe and struggled to catch one of the erratic and wild arms.

Nathaniel blurted out: "My God, Joe. Why?"

Joe's eyes flared at the sight of his pastor. "Not him! Not him!" he shrieked. With enormous strength and a wiriness fueled by panic, he wrested himself free of his three captors, kicking the man on the ground full force in the face with his heel. Blood gushed from the man's forehead. Joe lurched to his feet, standing hunch shouldered, heaving, salivating, feral. The men formed a half circle. They slowly approached him. Nathaniel reached out toward his neighbor's boy. "Let me help, Joe. Let me help."

Joe shrieked again, "Not him! Not him!" Suddenly, wildly, Joe spun about and plunged into the woods, careening past the confused pickets a hundred yards beyond. Joe dashed past them before they could react and attempt to tackle him. He plunged deeper into the woods. Joe disappeared.

Nathaniel didn't hesitate. He shouted over his shoulder, "Tell O'Rourke," as he swept under the low hanging branches of fir tree and entered the forest, following what he assumed to be Joe's course. As he too rushed through the pickets, he lowered his voice, alert to the likelihood of enemy pickets nearby, saying to them simply: "I'll be back."

The three men on picket stared at each other dumbfounded. They never even raised their Springfields to their shoulders. What were you supposed to do with men who rushed across the lines in the wrong direction in the middle of the night?

Relying upon his hearing more than sight, he tried his best to track Joe. A rustle, a snap, the muffled sound of a man panting. Anything. Yet all he heard was the wind swaying the branches above and his own noisy struggle to push through thicket and brambles. In the eerie dark he failed to see the slit of the ravine. His boot slipped at the edge of the bank. He tried to brace himself against the trunk of a nearby tree but missed and fell. He caught himself in time to twist and flop on his rump and slide down, squishing his boot deep into the swampy mud of a small, swollen creek. He sat there against the muddy bank, collecting himself. He half listened for Joe, half listening for Southern accents. He fully expected to hear shooting.

Where the devil am I? he asked himself. He checked to see if he had broken any bones or if there were bleeding anywhere. He had plenty of aches but no injuries. He leaned back against the ravine, his boot slowly sinking deeper into the mud and water. Going back without looking further for Joe was not even a question. The only questions were: how long to look for him? And where to look?

A cold wind turned the leaves over, announcing another miserable rain approaching. Nathaniel turned up the collar of his frock coat and pulled his hat snug on his head. He exhaled and studied the vapor of his own breath by hazy moonlight. Large drops of cold rain began to fall in a gradual rhythm. He looked up a the sky with annoyance. The intensity of the rain increased. Nathaniel slurped his boot from the mud, nearly pulling his foot out from the boot, and slid himself along the bank to position himself beneath the overhanging branches. The rain lasted for only a few minutes, but long enough to drench clothes already soaked. Still, he heard no sounds of Joe.

The other bank of the stream opened up onto a small grassy meadow, the last of the autumn wildflowers beginning to open to the light of coming dawn. Off to the far left he began to hear the muffled rifle fire of distant skirmish. It was like listening to a woodpecker. You knew it was somewhere nearby but you could never spot it. The shots, unlike the overlapping volleys of Brigade confronting Brigade, reported with a staccato beat. Soon the rumble of cannon fire mingled with the rifle pattern. He looked to see if somewhere beyond the shadows, hills, and trees he could spot the flashes from cannon mouth. The erratic rifle fire increased and soon the distant echoes blended into a steady rhythm. He had heard it before. It was the sound of a skirmish widening into a full blown battle. It was happening somewhere out there.

Nathaniel reached for his watch fob but discovered it was missing. He panicked until he remembered. He had left it behind. Back with his gear. Must be. He breathed heavily as he said aloud: "Boy, am I in trouble." Nathaniel wiped his eyes and peered across the meadow. He thought he saw a dark shadow of a structure. He wanted to yell for Joe but realized that would be foolish. Cupping his hand, he dipped his hand into the stream and raised the water to his lips. He drank, then stepped through the stream, and climbed up the other bank into the tall grass, pulling on roots and shrubs. A startled bluebird fluttered up from the meadow and landed on a tree branch and hid behind red leaves, from where it sang its clipped chitter and chirp. By the time he walked halfway across the meadow, he could plainly see the remnants of a burnt farmhouse. The thick base of a stone chimney still stood, the height of it collapsed into the charred timbers of what once must have been a pleasant home. The barn and the out-buildings still stood, spared of the fire, though years in disrepair.

Nate stumbled into the open door of the barn. The barn reeked of wet straw, urine, dung, and sweaty men.

A Federal soldier wearing a threadbare, light blue uniform stood leering with his hands on his hips. His teeth were yellow, gapped, and blackened. In a horse stall two soldiers held down a young Negro girl on a pile of straw. She looked to be no more than fifteen years old. She offered no struggle. She was silent, stony. Her dress was torn, portions of the gingham scattered, her small breasts exposed, her nipples a rich black. Her bottom half also was exposed, the torn dress bunched at her waist. The men held open her thin legs by her ankles. The standing Corporal fingered his bulging crotch, unbuttoning his blue trousers.

Her eyelids fluttered as her eyes darted to the dark stranger standing inside the doorway. The other three followed her eyes and saw Nathaniel standing there. The two Privates who held her arms and legs did not move. They knelt in old, crusty horse dung. One wore a checkered shirt, the other a blue blouse. Their muskets were stacked against the wall of the stall, near a rusted chain, their jackets and coats thrown bunched up into the corner. The Corporal finished unbuttoning his trousers before he turned toward Nathaniel. The girl's yellow eyes offered Nathaniel a faint flicker of pleading. Her closed mouth offered a brief whimper. One of the men released a hand and smacked her across her mouth. Fresh blood trickled from her lip and nose. Her eyes turned inward and vacant. She turned her head aside.

The Corporal began unfastening his holster belt. "Preacher, this ain't no business of yours. Git out, git out."

Nathaniel's heart pounded. He gulped at her nakedness and her helplessness.

The Corporal noticed his shaking hands.

Nathaniel strained to find voice. "You know I cannot do that, soldier." A tremor betrayed him. Nathaniel swallowed as he stepped forward. The planks of the floor creaked. He summoned from inside himself the tenor of command: "Let her go, I say. Listen to me, this is wrong. Let her go." He tried to be calm. "Don't do this."

"You're kidding me, right preacher?" he cackled, as dark liquid drooled from the corner of his mouth. The Corporal turned back toward the stall, dismissing Nathaniel. One of the kneeling men began to giggle. The naked girl shivered imperceptibly.

Nathaniel burst forward and shoved the Corporal, who stumbled against the broken door of the stall and fell into it. The other men jerked from the surprise of Nathaniel's lunge, but remained holding the girl by her limbs. The force and effect of his anger gave Nathaniel confidence. Quickly, he spotted and seized a broken pitchfork from the floor and threatened the three men. "I said, let her go!" The pitchfork shook in his hands.

The Corporal picked himself up, grinning wider, pushing himself up from his buddy's shoulder. His smile showed his yellow and blackened teeth. He spat tobacco juice, some of it splattering the girl's shivering leg. He smeared the splat of juice with the toe of his shoe. Then he casually unlatched the leather strap of the holster, pulled his revolver from its holster, and raised it. He pointed the cold blue barrel at Nathaniel's face. The pitchfork shook. The gun was only two feet away from Nathaniel's face. "You listen again, preacher. You have one choice: either leave or I will shoot you in the face. One choice. Make no mistake, I will put a bullet through your brain. It don't matter to me. Ain't no one to care."

"Oh, shoot him, Ned," suggested the soldier from the other side of the girl.

"Maybe he wants a try," the nearer soldier snickered. "He can poke the nigger wench after we're done."

"It's a simple choice, preacher." Ned's eyes glistened gleefully as he stared at him down along the dark blue barrel. "Your call."

Nathaniel gulped and looked down at the young girl. Her eyes no longer betrayed any terror. They were empty, hollow, detached, save the small tear that welled at the side of her left eye and rolled down her cheek. Her eyes offered him neither escape nor forgiveness. Her eyelids closed as she raised her face toward the loft.

Nathaniel's hesitation was broken by a painful crack as he was spared the decision. In the fray, he had failed to notice the fourth soldier standing at the open door of the barn. Stealing from behind, he clubbed the back of Nathaniel's head with an old wooden bucket. Nathaniel blacked out as he fell onto the filthy floor.

Chapter Fourteen

Crossing the Lines

Thou art a hiding place for me,
thou preservest me from trouble;
thou dost encompass me with deliverance
Psalm 32: 7

Dazed, his head throbbing, Nathaniel strained to reach for a peg to pull himself up from the barn floor. His fingers lacked strength and he could barely hold himself steady on his hands and knees. His pupils, rolling and unfocused, hurt as he tried to concentrate and look around. With a thick tongue, he swallowed a spasm of vomit. He pressed shut his eyelids. The blood on the back of his scalp had congealed to a sticky paste. Must have been a fourth, he guessed through a clouded and bruised brain. The collars of both his frock coat and muslin shirt were damp with blood. Kneeling, he reached back to inspect his head. His hand smeared the clot and reopened the wound. Blood trickled down his neck. He wiped his hand on the floor of the barn. His eyes, targeting a knot in a plank, gradually regained focus.

The deserters were gone. Rocking on all fours he looked up and noticed the naked body of the young girl. Once black and glistening, her body was now bruised and fetal. She laid curled in the corner of the stall, a broken lump of flesh and bone. Bits of straw and dung stuck to her skin.

Nathaniel staggered as he tried to stand, pressing his wet hand against the stall wall. He fell back onto his hands and knees. A panicked pulse of fear rushed his fingers toward his waistcoat. No chain. No watch. "Oh God," he said as he wobbled. But consciousness returned for a moment, dragging with it recollection. "Right. It's back at the wagon." Next he patted his coat pocket. His Bible was there. Not that they'd want it anyway. Last, he thumbed his waist and the hidden money belt. Still there. Why didn't they search me? Nathaniel's vision blurred again as he collapsed sideways onto the wet straw and mud of the planked floor.

Behind him came a vague sound of someone pushing the heavy barn door along its track and squeezing inside.

"We found you, thank God," the voice spoke, though hollow and distant as if the source were talking into an empty bucket. The voice shouted to those outside: "He's in here." Valentine hurried to kneel beside his friend and roll him over onto his back.

The Provost Sergeant and two Privates yanked the stable door wider as they entered. The flood of light stabbed Nathaniel's eyes.

Valentine looked around and stared the body of the girl. "What the hell?"

"Close, Valentine," Nathaniel seethed, rubbing his eyes. "As close as you get."

"We've been hunting you all night." Valentine studied the barn. He rose and entered the stall to check the girl's pulse. "My God," he said. He turned back to look at Nathaniel. "What happened here?"

The Provost Sergeant and the two Privates watched as the chaplain crawled across the filthy floor toward the dead girl curled in the horse stall. The tip of his fingers touched the heel of her foot. He crept closer. Nathaniel began covering her as best as he could with the pieces of her clothing within his reach. The rest of her he covered with straw. He began to sob. "I want them, Valentine. Deserters. Three, no, four of them. I want them."

"I know, Nate. I know." Valentine kicked a hardened piece of dung away from the girl's leg. He reached his arm around Nathaniel's waist.

"They were ours," said Nathaniel with a metallic tone of shame.

The Provost Sergeant pulled off his foraging cap and sent it spiraling against the stable door. He stormed outside. The other two soldiers removed their kepis and held them by the brim in front of them, as if waiting for their mother's permission. One of the men eventually walked over to where Nathaniel had been clubbed. He picked up Nathaniel's black hat and, after wiping off some of the blood against a wooden beam, tried to reshape it. Valentine used his own slouch hat to chase the flies from settling on Nathaniel's wound.

"Come on, Nate. Let's get back. We're not safe here." With his white handkerchief he wiped his friend's face.

"I want them, Valentine, I want them," Nathaniel hissed as Valentine helped him sit up against the wall of the stall.

The Provost Sergeant returned from scouting the outside. With one hand he slid the large barn door shut.

"Sir," one of the Privates asked Valentine, pointing the barrel of his Springfield at the mound of straw, gingham, and flesh. "What should we do with the her?"

The Sergeant, striding toward the broken door of the stall, answered. "Leave the lass be. If we bury her, her people will never know what became of her. Leave her." The Sergeant, after retrieving his cap, walked back to the barn door, and, through a crack at the jamb, again checked outside. "I hear plenty of movement around us. Far off but still movement. They're restless out there. Last night was only the beginning. We don't have time."

Valentine saw Nathaniel's pupils beginning to roll. "Let me dress that, Nate. It's pretty ugly. Here, sip some water first." Valentine held the canteen to Nathaniel's mouth. "Easy." Ounces of water dribbled down his throat. Pouring water from the canteen over his scalp, Valentine rinsed the wound. He compressed the bleeding with a piece of gingham cloth from the girl's dress and bandaged the wound. He pulled Nathaniel's hat down to secure the dressing in place. Nathaniel groaned as he pulled the brim tighter. "Try to eat a little too." Valentine unwrapped pieces of hardtack and pushed some of the crumbs into Nathaniel's mouth who tried to chew.

The instant they heard the squeal all five men turned to stone. A starling fluttered from the rafters. The Sergeant tensed. He lifted his head up. The squeal repeated itself, coming from the loft. The Sergeant waved a fast signal for one of the Privates to climb upstairs.

"A small pig?" one of the Privates guessed as he headed toward the ladder and passed the Sergeant.

"Go check," the Sergeant ordered.

They listened to the soldier's footsteps as he shuffled through the loft. Soon his face appeared at the trap door. "Take this, Frank," said the Private, lowering his musket stock end down.

His friend, standing at the base of the ladder, took the musket, and asked: "So George, did you find us supper?"

George clambered down the ladder with one hand on the rungs, his other arm holding onto something small. The object was obscured by the folds of his great coat.

"I don't think so, Frank." The Private, tenderly clutching the bundle in his arm, replied in a curious tone. "It's a baby."

"My God." Valentine exclaimed, jumping up, letting Nathaniel catch himself from falling over on his side. He quickly rinsed his hands from his canteen. Shaking the water from his hands, he rushed over to George who stood at the base of the ladder. Frank stepped aside. Valentine quickly examined the baby as it lay listless in George's arms. The infant, sensing the touch of Valentine's finger, tried to wiggle and reach with its head, pursing its lips. Instead of an angry, hungry baby's wail, the infant again squealed. "A little girl," he said, letting her weakly suck the end of his thumb.

Valentine surveyed the barn, his eyes darting from loft to stall. "She must have been hiding here when she saw them coming. Hid her baby. Dammit, mothers shouldn't die."

The words escaped the Sergeant's mouth before he could check himself: "No babies either."

Valentine chased the flies with his hand, then took the baby from George and cradled her in his arms. "I bet she hoped they would let her go afterwards. Poor little bugger." Valentine looked down at Nathaniel, noticing a hint of color returning to his pallid face.

The color came from rage. With a feral tone, Nathaniel growled bitterly: "I want them hanged. I want to kick the stool myself."

Valentine looked over his shoulder at the Sergeant. "Not much choice, eh?"

"Not much, sir."

"Let's get out of here." Valentine pointed towards the mound in the stall. "One of you, get some cloth."

The Provost Sergeant moved first. "I'll do it." The Sergeant bent over the young girl and ripped off a section of her dress. He covered the rest of her with more straw. He handed the fabric to Valentine and moved toward the barn door.

Frank, slinging his own musket over his shoulder, handed George's musket back to him, then slipped his hand under Nathaniel's arm to hoist him up. He kept his arm around Nathaniel to support him as the two of them followed the Sergeant. The Sergeant slid the door open wide enough for them to slip through. They straggled outside. The light stung Nathaniel's eyes. George followed, his musket at the ready. Valentine, last, carried the baby in his right arm, having wrapped her snug in the piece of her mother's dress, and slung his kit and canteen over his left shoulder. The Sergeant, posted by the door, hauled it shut. Three magpies, perched on the pulley track jutting out from the top ridge of the barn, squawked angrily and flapped off. They landed on the top of the chimney of the burnt farmhouse where they chattered angrily at the trespassers below.

Outside, with the sun filtering through the branches of ash and locust, they huddled together around the corner of the barn, away from the open meadow on the west side. Nathaniel signaled for another sip from Valentine's canteen.

Handing the canteen to Nathaniel, he asked: "Did you find Joe?"

"Nope." Nathaniel let the stale water slide down his dry throat.

"We didn't either."

"I had hoped to get out of this without hating anyone." With his finger, Nathaniel pulled a bit of the gingham cloth below the child's chin. "I want to strangle them."

"I know, Nate. I know."

The Sergeant emerged around the corner of the burnt farmhouse and waved his arm, signaling for them to follow him. The Sergeant disappeared behind a pine tree. Four more crows flew into the trees, their craw growing louder and bolder. The small band pushed after the Sergeant.

"Where are we, Valentine?" asked Nathaniel. "I got completely turned around last night."

"Where are we? We're lost. We were lucky to find you. We're all turned around." He looked toward the sun. "At least we know which way is east."

Hiding behind a large fir tree at the edge of the woods, the small band huddled to figure out their next step. Valentine cradled the child tightly against his chest as he searched his pockets. Nathaniel dampened the white handkerchief from George's canteen and tried to get the child to suck, but the child remained listless. Valentine studied Nathaniel's eyes. "You strong enough?" Nathaniel nodded and Valentine handed the baby girl over to him. His arms cradled her.

The two Privates kept silent as Valentine and the Sergeant argued. Neither knew exactly in which direction lay their escape. The Sergeant pointed toward the sound of distant batteries. Valentine pointed at the morning sun. The fog in Nathaniel's brain prevented him from tracking the entire argument but he did pick up on some of the names of the various towns that the two mentioned. Nobody paid attention to Nathaniel as he handed the child to Frank and pulled his Bible from his inside coat pocket. The pages were damp but legible. He opened the pages of his Bible to the Letter to Philemon. With clumsy fingers he found the page he wanted.

"Listen," Nathaniel interrupted. "Do you suppose we're anywhere close to Catalpa?" Nathaniel closed his Bible. "We may have an option yet. I refuse to let this baby die."

"What was that?" Valentine asked as he looked over at Nathaniel. "What's in Catalpa?"

"I believe we may find a friend there. If he hasn't fled. Or been killed. It shouldn't be too far away, if we are near where you two think we are. Look for a granary."

"How do you know?" quizzed the Sergeant, doubtful.

"Because I know, blast you," said Nathaniel as he pressed his throbbing forehead with his palm. He knew because he had been given more than a money belt from his benefactor on the hill that morning a year ago when, at the train station, he kissed his wife and children goodbye. There was that note. The note where written on the bottom he had read: *'You may find these Friends a blessing.'* A note with names and addresses. With the word 'Friends' capitalized. A note containing names of Friends he could trust. Friends of a Quaker friend. Before his train had reached Philadelphia, he had taken out the note, and, as best he could while seated in a jolting railway coach, transcribed the information into his pocket Bible along the margins of the Book of Philemon. He thought the allusion clever. "Listen," Nathaniel added, "I know people, I was given information. From people who were fighting this war long before you put on that uniform."

"Well, that convinces me," replied the Sergeant sarcastically.

"Shut up and listen for once."

The Privates stared open-mouthed at Nathaniel. The Sergeant drew his carbine close against his chest.

Valentine grasped Nathaniel by the arm. "Easy, Nate. We're the heroes, remember? Are you sure about this?"

Nathaniel answered with a shrug.

Valentine looked around at the other men. "What choice have we? This baby needs milk fast. She's nearly half past dead as it is." Valentine turned his back on Nathaniel. "What do you think, Sergeant Hunt?"

"I sure don't like sitting out in the open like this. I'd rather we keep on the move." Squatting, he drew with his finger a diagram of lines in the dirt and evergreen needles. "If I can recall the map right, Catalpa was due west of Brandy Station, north of Culpepper by several miles. A turnpike runs through it. Probably just a spit of a town." He scooped up and crushed a bunch of needles in his hand. "I'd rather be going north. But then we'd have to cross the Rappahannock somehow. Not many places to ford. At least places that ain't guarded. Heading west we could be walking into the thick of it. We'd be walking right up to Lee and say, 'howdy,' and then get invited to take a little trip to Andersonville."

"Aren't we in the thick of it now, Hunt?"

Sergeant Hunt threw the needles to the ground. He stood up and slung his rifle. "All right, sir. I'm agreed." He glanced over at Nathaniel. "I guess we can hope God's on our side, right Rev'rend?"

Nathaniel looked up, embarrassed, and met his businesslike eyes. "I'm sorry, Sergeant," Nathaniel said. "I'm sorry for a whole lot lately."

"Forget it."

Valentine settled the issue. "West it is."

Frank handed the baby back to Nathaniel. She tried to arch her back, but lacked the strength.

Sergeant Hunt grabbed Nathaniel by the arm. "They'll get theirs soon enough, Rev'rend."

"God can have them after I'm first done with them." His tone chilled even the Sergeant.

Four times this small band, trying to keep the afternoon sun in their faces, eluded Confederate patrols. With the sun nearly set, they finally stumbled onto a wide dirt road.

The Sergeant sniffed. "Gotta' be the turnpike I saw on the map. But the question is: where's the town? Are we above Catalpa or below it? Do we turn left or right? South or north?" The Sergeant glanced over at Nathaniel. "What's your call, preacher? We're following your lead."

The question went unanswered as the approaching hoof beats of hundreds of horses forced them to hide themselves in the shrubs and underbrush, camouflaging themselves among thornberry, viburnum, spicebush, and yew. From their left, a Cavalry Regiment galloped along the turnpike over the crest of the hill and down into the valley towards them. Over two hundred troopers rode swiftly by, heading north, led by a grandiose, black bearded General in hip boots who sported a plumed hat and billowing cape.

After the horse artillery careened by, led by a young officer who similarly wore a plumed hat, the Sergeant whistled. "Never thought I'd see him up close. Never wanted to."

Valentine teased the baby's feet. "Not good for us."

With hoof beat, leather slap, and clang of sword, Stuart's Cavalry and light artillery galloped in haste over the next rise.

The Sergeant looked back at Nathaniel. Nathaniel smiled at the Sergeant squatting next to him and asked: "Left?"

The Sergeant's beard hid his smile. "Left. But let's stay off the road, okay?"

Nathaniel noticed how Valentine kept tickling the baby's feet. "You're getting to be a regular family man, aren't you?"

Valentine pursed his lips. "You just never know."

"You want to know what Alice told me once?"

"Not really, Nate."

"Going to tell you anyway because surprises happen fast these days. We've never talked about this. She told me you're a man who loves fiercely but is not very good at being loved."

Valentine dismissed what he said with a curt wave. "Spoken like a woman," was all he said in reply. Returning to play with the bottom of the baby's feet, Valentine found himself mimicking his father's brogue and singing a nursery rhyme sung to him a long time ago:

One for anger

Two for mirth

Three for a wedding

Four for a birth

Five for rich

Six for poor

Seven for a witch

I can tell you no more.

Staying off the road, they had to fight the undulating ground southward, struggling through dwarfish timber, shielding the infant from branch and thorn, skulking across a few clearings, dropping into dense ravines and climbing out of them, occasionally taking the chance of walking along the narrow cart tracks used by woodcutters. They followed one such cart path that seemed to run parallel to the turnpike toward the edge of the woods. At the Sergeant's signal, the back of his hand upraised, the band halted and listened. They all heard the steady sound of men splitting wood. The swish was followed by crack. They moved closer toward the edge of trees. The sound of logs being split grew louder. They heard the familiar clunk as the pieces fell onto a pile of split logs. Lantern lights shone through the dusk, the orange sun flickering behind the sway of branches. The rising cart track emptied into a level open field. The shapes of two silos and several storage bins loomed near a large building. An unlit lantern had been placed on a stump. They saw two dark woodcutters swinging their axes. A broken, wheel-less wagon lay on its side in the shadows. Across the dirt road sat a large house, surrounded on two sides by a pillared porch, kitchen lights shining. Woods rose up swiftly behind the house.

"Looks like a granary to me, Nate. What do you think?"

"Worth a try." Nathaniel, holding the baby tighter against his chest, took a few steps into the clearing, then turned around. "You stay here. I'm the only one dressed the part today." He skirted the edge of the wood, making a circuit so as to approach the woodcutters by the roadway from the north.

Two inky black-skinned men, their muslin shirts tight against broad chests, straightened up as soon as they spotted the man dressed in black approaching them carrying a small bundle. The dusk gradually drifted into darkness.

The four soldiers watched as the two woodcutters balanced their axes in their hands and faced the stranger. One man was a few inches less in height than Nathaniel but the other was taller by at least half a foot. The Sergeant leaned his shoulder against a tree and aimed his Sharps at the taller of the woodcutters. None could hear the conversation but they all watched as the two woodcutters lit and picked up the lantern from the stump, signaled for Nathaniel to come with them, and escorted him across the lane, up the stone steps, and onto the wooden porch of the house. The Sergeant lowered his carbine. Without a word the Sergeant stole quietly toward the barn. The others followed him, each crossing the field toward the stump. The four huddled together, blending their forms behind the pile of wood.

The smaller of the two woodcutters lifted the lantern high. His face shone like coal. In his other hand he still held his at ax chest level. The tall woodcutter knocked on the door. Hearing a muffled sound, he immediately entered the house. The smaller man remained silent on the porch, standing slightly behind Nathaniel. After several minutes, the tall woodcutter opened the door and stepped aside to reveal a short, balding white man.

"Excuse me for the intrusion," Nathaniel apologized. "I'm looking for a man who operates a granary in these parts. I believe his name is Teiresias Young. Would you know of him?" Nathaniel offered his hand to the bald man standing in the doorway. The shorter of the two woodcutters remained standing behind Nathaniel, still holding the lantern high. The Sergeant flipped up the rear site and cocked the hammer to first notch, aiming his deadly carbine over the stump at his first target. The smaller of the two woodcutters periodically turned his head from side to side. The larger of the two woodcutters shifted behind the bald man in the doorway. Both woodcutters still clutched their axes.

"Who be askin'?" replied the bald man, ignoring Nathaniel's outstretched hand.

"My name is McKenna. Pastor Nathaniel McKenna. I am searching for Mr. Young so I can bring greetings from a friend of his. From one of my colleagues back in Pennsylvania. The village of Penningtonville." He stressed the name of his village.

"You're a little out of your parish, I believe, preacher."

"Been that way for a while." Nathaniel shifted the baby in his arms. "Thought I'd take up circuit riding. Someone told me, though, that the railroad is a much more comfortable way to travel these days. Reliable too. That is, if I could find a station nearby. At least, that is what my friend tells me. I suppose you can usually trust a Quaker."

The bald man offered no response. No blink, no wrinkling of the forehead.

Nathaniel continued: "And it seems I've taken up maternity as well." Nathaniel offered the bald man the child. "Your help, sir, that is, should you know this Mr. Young, would be greatly appreciated." Nathaniel began unwrapping the child's face, exposing the chocolate colored skin of her forehead and her half-closed eyes. Nathaniel lowered his voice. "Please, this child is not well. For God's sake, she needs milk."

The bald man stepped forward and pulled the gingham cloth down farther to reveal the whole of the child's face. He raised the child's limp arm.

"She's very weak," Nathaniel added.

"Her mamma?"

Nathaniel, fighting exhaustion and emotion, strained to hold back the surprising and sudden loosening of tears. "I'm afraid, we, that is, I," he gulped, "I was unable to help her."

The bald man cocked his head, studied Nathaniel's face, then turned around. "Abraham, please take this child to Rachel." Abraham, the tall woodcutter, walked past the man and leaned his ax against the siding of the house.

Valentine heard the Sergeant breathe a sigh of relief as he tilted the barrel of the carbine up slightly.

The bald man took the baby from Nathaniel's arms and placed her gingerly in Abraham's. The woodcutter's huge hands and thick arms received the tiny girl-child. Without a word he stepped off the porch and trotted around the corner of the house toward the small creek that ran south of the house. The creek trickled across the dirt turnpike and streamed down into the darkened, tree-filled gully that dropped off behind the barn.

The bald man put his hand on Nathaniel's shoulder. "Don't you fret. Rachel will know wha' to do with this littl' honey. Now, pastor, let's git off'n the porch." He beckoned Nathaniel inside.

"Thank you, but I'm afraid I'm about to inconvenience you further. I'm not alone. I'm traveling with several others." Nathaniel pointed vaguely toward the woods. "We seem to have lost our Regiment."

"Tendin' to other errands, 'vidently."

"Yes, well, I'm not sure if our Colonel is looking for us but we certainly have been looking for him." Nathaniel removed his hat, exposing the red stained gingham bandage. "I will understand if you cannot help. We understand the risk. It is enough that the infant is in safe hands."

"An' so are you. It's all a risk. Assume that we are friends." Young extended his hand to Nathaniel. "I'm Teiresias Young." As they shook hands, Young's left hand grasped Nathaniel's arm firmly. "Let'us git your friends inside." Young began chuckling. "I believe your four friends no longer are'n the woods." He pointed toward the stump. As Valentine and the three soldiers looked at each other, a large man, jet black and glistening, dressed in coveralls, emerged from the shadows of the building to their left. In his hands he held a large sickle.

Young pulled Nathaniel by the shoulder toward the entranceway. "This road has seen too much un-friendly 'tivity these recen' days. Come'n inside," he said with urgency. "I can' affor' to have my neighbors notice I'm entertainin' vis'tors again. Git inside all of you. Hush an' hurry now." Young stepped aside for him.

The large man with the sickle escorted the four men to the porch steps. The smaller woodcutter, still holding ax and lantern, moved away after they entered the open door.

Over a hasty but welcome meal of cornbread and a mouthful of dried beef washed down by chicory coffee, the men listened to Young as he crossed his arms on the oak kitchen table and leaned toward Nathaniel. "I know ya'll want to get back to your unit as soon as possible. But whoa now, 'cause it jes' ain't gonna' happen. Not now at least. The grapevine telegraph tells me ya'll gotta' stay here a'while. Nobody knows where any of these Armies are located these days; the lines are all mess up. Gotta' wait and see."

Abraham entered the kitchen and joined the men, sitting in the chair next to the stove. Nathaniel found himself staring at Abraham. Most of the colored folk he had seen, especially during these months in Virginia, had been like the young girl back at the barn, light skinned, almost the color of a river following heavy rains. These men were pitch black. They disturbed him.

Abraham waited until Young asked him if he'd like a cup of coffee. Abraham selected a cup from the cupboard. He presented the cup which Young filled. Young shook the coffee pot at him. "Abraham here is well 'quainted with guidin' contraband north. Trust a Gullah. Trust a Gullah," Young repeated. "He informs me now is not the time. You must trust him. He knows his work."

Young drained his own cup of coffee. "Part of your Army used'ta be camped right here. Took'n my las' hen too. That was two days ago, but, as far as Abraham can tell, they're already in the 'cinity of Catlett's Station. If ya'll keep retreatin' any more, your Army will end up fightin' in the streets of Washington."

The Provost Sergeant cleared his throat.

Young ignored him. "Ya' also got Stuart all over the map with his trooper boys. He rode through not too long ago. Raised up quite a dustin'." Young smiled. "He decided to pay me a visit along the way jes' a few hours ago. No more chickens lef' though."

Valentine interrupted. "We saw him too. Well, got a glimpse of him. We noticed that his artillery was with him too. That means more than reconnaissance."

"His men confis'cated my las' bushel of corn. Your war has cleaned me out. Lots of clean teeth these days." He banged his cup on the wooden table. "Listen boys, it's safer here. Wherever ya' started out, you're now far behind the lines." He traced the cup's lip with his finger. "Go north and you'd only run into Bobby Lee and the 'ntire Army of Northern Virginny."

Before Nathaniel could reply, the smaller woodcutter rushed from the front room. He braked himself at the kitchen door. Abraham jumped up from his chair and approached him. He bent his ear down to listen. Abraham immediately turned toward the men in the room. The single spoken word, "Secesh," ignited Young into motion. Young signaled to Abraham, who in turn signaled Nathaniel and the four soldiers to follow him out the back door of the kitchen. They did what they were told. The smaller woodcutter quickly began clearing the table. After scanning the room to make sure the men had collected all their belongings leaving no trace behind, Young followed. Noticing the dirt, Young snapped his fingers at the smaller woodcutter: "Silas, the floor!" Silas rushed from the sink and grabbed the broom leaning against a stack of firewood.

A silent Abraham hurried them outside to the entrance of a root cellar. With both hands he pulled open both slanted doors. Bending, he led them down into the damp and dark of the earthen cellar. He reached toward a mildewed pantry, tilting it toward himself. Rocking and walking the pantry away from the wall, he revealed a three foot hole that opened into another, darker section of the dirt cellar. Abraham urgently waved the men into the pitch black room. Young, standing on the steps, told them: "There's a candle in there, but light it only if ya'll must. If I git the chance I'll try to git ya'll some water."

First to step into the hole was Valentine, swinging his hands to clear the cobwebs from his face. The two Privates climbed in after him. The Sergeant handed their muskets to them. He balked at entering the hole.

Nathaniel pressed him from behind. "Do what they say."

The Sergeant gulped, cursed, then he too climbed into the cramped space.

Nathaniel entered last, sweeping his hand in the air, muttering: "I hate spiders." Abraham repositioned the pantry and sealed the entrance. The cellar doors banged shut as he exited.

Valentine held his hand up in front of his face. He could not see it. He could not see anything. "Damn," he said. "Where's that candle. Can't see any of you." He reached out and touched someone's arm. "Hey, Nate,' he quizzed from the back of the dank hole, "do you remember what Professor Fryling use to repeat in class? That you never see light. You can only see by the light."

"When were you paying attention?" Nathaniel joked.

Valentine wiggled his fingers in front of his face. There was no light to make the eyes see. They could only feel around and make some sense of their hiding place. The soldiers tried to find room for their muskets and the rest of their gear without poking each other. In the darkness Valentine started to chuckle. "You know, Nate, I have got to stop rescuing you."

Nathaniel began laughing also, overwhelmed with sheer exhaustion. "I'm so glad I listened to you last year. What was that you promised me if I'd join up with Regiment? Glory and adventure?" Nathaniel's belly laughter made it difficult for him to speak. "You, you, never..." he laughed, "...said anything about root cellars." The two cracked up and doubled over, trying to muzzle their mouths with their hats.

Frank and George crept farther into the corner, trying to keep to themselves, convinced that the Surgeon and chaplain had turned absolute lunatics. The Sergeant began breathing heavily.

Valentine sensed Hunt's escalating panic. "Calm down, Hunt. It'll be okay," said Valentine with a reassuring pat on the

Sergeant's shoulders. "Just easy breaths. Nice and easy. Easy breaths. Just like your wife giving birth. Easy breaths, slow breaths."

"Doc," Frank asked from the corner. "Do you think the little one will make it?"

"Beyond me," Valentine frowned. "I'm just a cutter."

Nathaniel snorted and swallowed. "She better."

The Sergeant leaned his face against the back of the pantry, mumbling: "Might be better off if she didn't." He pressed his cheek against the pinewood, trying to breathe through the small space between pantry and cellar wall.

Suddenly the Sergeant swung his arm backwards, hitting Nathaniel's shoulder, "Shut up. Listen," he demanded.

Immediately they turned silent. The hazy sounds of a great commotion outside approached, the clamor getting louder. It was the sound of men outside. Lots of men.

A voice, thick with southern drawl, hollered out: "Yaw'll now, takes'a look-see. Ya'll, check out that roo' cellar. Meebe' somethin' tastie."

They heard what sounded like Young's voice: "Check if you hafta'. Ain' nuthin'. All ya' soldier boys already done picked me clean."

The cellar's pine doors were yanked open and a man stepped down inside with tentative footsteps. He shuffled around. The glow of a candle shone from around the edge of the pantry leaking through the seams. Nathaniel's eyes adjusted as he noticed the Sergeant slowly reaching for the smooth trigger of his Sharps.

"Naw, sir. Shelves bare," the man on the other side of the pantry shouted over his shoulder to the fellows outside. "Shit," he swore.

They heard the soldier explore each corner of the root cellar, shuffling and sweeping the corners with his shoes. They heard him wipe his hand along each of the mildewed shelves. "Lordie, dammit all! 'Tain't nuthin' t'et." the man cursed, kicking the pantry. Then he took the candle light outside with him, again leaving the five men to the pitch black of their hiding place. The doors of the root cellar were thrown shut.

Two and half days later, the five men emerged from the hole, damp and stinking from each other's urine and sweat. They emerged staggering, helped by Young and Abraham. The sunlight stunned their eyes. Their muscles were stiff and cramped. Each suffered a terrible headache. They emerged only after Abraham had declared it safe and had come for them. Only after he had observed the last of the Confederate Division retreating south toward Culpepper. Only after he saw the Union skirmishers heading across the rolling hills in their direction.

Trembling, aching, thirsty, the five men crawled up the wooden cellar steps, shielding their eyes from the brutal sunlight.

Chapter Fifteen

Revolvers and Redemption

If thou wouldst view fair Melrose aright,
Go visit it by the pale moonlight;
For the gay beams of lightsome day
Gild but to flout the ruins gray.
"The Lay of the Last Minstrel," Sir Walter Scott

Chaplain McKenna, please unbutton your coat."
Nathaniel hesitated.

Talley's request razored into a direct order. "Dammit, I said:
'unbutton your coat.'"

"Colonel, I don't see where you have the right to…"

"I have every right when it concerns my Regiment," he
exploded. "Are you a member of this Regiment?" he pressed.
"Yes? I have the authority. So either unbutton or I will have the
Provost Sergeant strip you himself. He's almost as fed up with
you as I am. Him or me? Who's it to be?"

With his jaw locked tight, his lips pressed tighter, Nathaniel
began to unbutton the double breasted buttons of his black
frock coat. He unbuttoned it, then folded his arms across his
chest.

"You tax me, chaplain. You tax me," Talley said with
exasperation. "Chaplain, don't be coy with me. I have neither

the time nor patience for school-boy games. You know exactly what I am after. Remove your coat."

Nathaniel yanked his coat off and tossed it over the folding chair, the sleeves inside out. "Is this want you want to know, Colonel Talley?"

Talley verified what he had hoped was merely mess rumor. He saw the black leather belt buckled over the waistcoat, the holster and revolver braced against his right hip.

"Satisfied?"

Talley dropped down into the chair behind his desk and rested his elbows on the desk top. His folding chair wobbled. "No, sir, I am not satisfied. And mind your tone. I do not appreciate your insolence. Chaplaincy aside, you are under my command. I command here, not the church, not God, not you." Talley shook his head in disgust. "This does not become you, chaplain." He leaned back. "Perhaps I should be grateful you haven't taken up the sword as well." Talley played with the tin cup on his desk, rolling its base in circles. "I trust this is not on loan from our Surgeon friend. He ought to know better than that. For I know quite well he never carries his sidearm even though I've insisted that he should. He should. You should not."

"No, sir. O'Rourke has nothing to do with this. I purchased it on my own. From my own funds." A smirk creased across his face. "Revolvers are plentiful to come by these days."

"Too easy, I should say. I shall have a talk with the sutler later. As for now, you tell me what am I going to do with you? I will not have my chaplain armed. Do you understand me? Have you forgotten our first conversation?"

Nathaniel remained silent.

"I asked you a question: have you forgotten our first conversation? I thought I made it rather plain that first day that you were to remain a non-combatant."

"I remember. But circumstances have changed, do you not agree?"

"Don't be clever with me. I haven't the time to banter with you. I talk, you listen. And when I ask a question, you answer. Damn you both. Damn me too. I've let the two of you do what you've wanted for too long. Free-booters, both of you." Talley slammed the cup down with such force it bounced off the table. "For as smart as you are, you can be a mighty stupid man. You miss my point. My point is this: I won't let you do this to the Regiment. Nor to yourself." He paused, reaching to pick up the tin cup. "Your friends won't either."

"Valentine?" Nathaniel's lips tightened. He stepped toward Talley's desk. "Has he been talking to you?"

"No, he hasn't. Thank you for exonerating him from any complicity in this matter. And, again, mind your tone. No, he's been quite silent in this matter, raising my suspicions because of it. But you do have other friends. Those who better appreciate their duty. Bear. Coates. Rupert here. Dammit, man, you've not hidden it well. You should know by now that there are few secrets among us. You should also note how they share my sentiments." Talley shoved his chair back as he stood, retrieved his cup, and walked over to his footlocker. He unlatched it, swung open the lid. He removed a bottle halfway filled with brown liquid. He returned to his desk, pulled the cork, and poured several fingers of the whisky into his tin cup. He gestured the bottle to Nathaniel.

Nathaniel held up the palm of his hand and shook his head.

"Of course not." Talley said with private relief, setting the bottle on his desk. With the cup he pointed at the folding chair. "Oh, sit down, chaplain."

At first he wanted to refuse, but thought better of it. Time to be a man. Time to eat crow and do what he was told.

"Nathaniel, don't you see what this communicates to the men?" Talley finally said. "Oh, I've heard the tales of other chaplains taking up rifle and rallying the troops. In ninety-nine per cent of the cases, it's all whitewash and hogwash from the newspapers back home. Don't you understand, Nathaniel? We need someone not to give in. We need at least one of us." Talley sipped again and leaned back. "What I am most is, is disappointed. You should know us better by now. Do you really believe we enjoy these accursed things?" He pointed to his own revolver hanging on a post near his cot. "Dear God, I look forward to the day when I will never have to carry a weapon again. I am so stinking tired of all this killing. Stinking tired of my nose rubbed in this filth." Talley leaned forward on his elbows. "So I surely will not have my chaplain carrying any weapon. I need you not to. Come now, don't you see?"

"I don't see the harm." It's just that, well, I won't be caught without so few options again. I hate getting caught in corners."

"From the reports I've read, a firearm would not have made much difference."

"We don't really know, now do we?" Nathaniel swept his hair back with both hands, adding: "Nor will we."

Nathaniel met Talley's probing stare for a moment, then blinked and looked straight down at his black boots. He pulled on his mustache. He placed his hands in his lap. Talley leaned back in his chair. "What I do know is that you are back among us now. My Surgeon is returned along with three of my best men. From all accounts, you men did well. Exemplary under extraordinary circumstances." Talley pushed himself up from his desk and walked to the side of his desk, his head nearly bumping the slanted timber ceiling of the hut. "Where you erred, chaplain, was in crossing our picket lines in the first place."

"I had no choice, Colonel. Joe, you see…"

"Yes, yes, you did, chaplain," Talley reprimanded, cutting him off. "It is always a matter of choice. In this case, you chose wrong. Dead wrong." Talley reached for a paper on his desk. "So we move on. We move on." He handed it to Nathaniel. "I have a task, chaplain, more in your line of work than taking on rapists and Stuart's Cavalry." He balanced himself against his desk. "Read it."

While Nathaniel read the letter, Talley continued talking: "Since our arrival here at Bristow Station we have been frequented by a rather persistent and annoying local. And since it appears as if we will make this our winter quarters, I want this matter settled. Brigade, in its infinite wisdom, has referred her to me. I, in my infinite wisdom, refer her to you. McCandless agrees that you are the perfect candidate. You take care of this and then we can talk about that furlough."

"Colonel, with my regular duties, I don't see how I can take on any more."

"I'm confident that you will find time. We've got plenty of time now, it seems. It promises to be a rather lazy several months. Except for that fox Mosby, the war in our neck of the woods is pretty quiet."

"Mosby's proved noisy enough for us in the past."

"True, but with our new replacements and new Regiments arriving, we're beginning to crowd him out. More hounds for the hunt."

"The bigger the pack, the more tails to chase."

Talley tapped the letter. "Read."

A puzzled look spread across his face as he read on. From a table behind him, Talley turned and picked up a pile of letters. "I have about a dozen more just like them." He tossed the letters across his desk. "Actually, I rather admire this woman. But neither I nor Brigade has time for this matter, which means that you do. So settle it quickly and let's get back to our duties. Don't ask me how, but her father seems to pull some powerful influence in Washington. Which is pretty odd, I daresay, for one of the enemy."

"I'm not exactly sure what I can do."

"For a start, you can borrow Rupert's horse. I will see that he will be glad to consent. I will also promise on your behalf that you will return it. You will, won't you? He doesn't like the way you lose his horses."

"It's an unpredictable war, sir.'

"That it is. Second, she and this father of hers are Presbyterian so that should account for something. I'm sure you'll do your best. You have so far, Nathaniel. Until recently. Just don't let yourself get caught in any more of those corners. Use your wits, man, not this," he said as reached over and tapped the holster of Nathaniel's revolver with his tin cup. "Don't you realize by now, Nathaniel, how much I despise these things?"

As Nathaniel pushed the door to leave the hut, Talley called after him: "And chaplain, I expect the holster to be removed. That is an order."

After he returned to his tent, Nathaniel unbuckled and removed the gun belt. He unlatched his footlocker and laid the weapon inside on top of a bloodstained piece of gingham cloth. Outside someone yelled for a bucket of water to be brought over. A spasm of guilt tightened across his chest. His head still ached. The stink of straw, manure, and blood returned. Before he closed the lid he removed the Colt from its holster, checked the chamber, made sure the hammer rested between two live cylinders, then pressed tallow over the top of the caps, Cavalry style. Picking up his overcoat from his cot, he slid the bulky revolver into the inside right pocket, wooden grip first. Then, closing the lid over the holster, he draped his coat over the back of his chair.

The next morning Nathaniel pretended to sleep while Valentine woke and left for duties, then he rolled out his cot, ignored shaving, dressed, buttoned, and straightened his waistcoat. After coffee and bacon, he pulled on his overcoat, patting the heavy weight in the inside pocket.

Valentine, having finished sick call, entered in time to see his friend pulling the straps of his haversack over his right shoulder. He tossed his operating case onto his cot. "Off to Greenwich?"

"Soon as I pick up Rupert's horse."

"Is Talley sending any escort with you?"

"Hardly need it. Just some pest of a girl and her father. It's only a few miles up Broad Run. I'm looking forward to getting out of here. Looking forward to riding alone."

"You're getting to be your own best friend these days, Nate."

"Yeah, well, sometimes that's how it is." Nathaniel grabbed his hat by its crown and slapped it on his head. "Time to humor the locals. Might be back by supper." Without a wave he threw open the tent flap and exited.

Valentine scanned the tent and grimaced. Then he opened the lid and checked Nathaniel's footlocker. "Damn him."

The solitary ride was cold but bracing. Deciding to button his coat, he transferred the Colt to an outside pocket. He picked up the road at the rebuilt bridge north of Bristow Station. From there the road slanted northwest. The road, no more than a horse path, muddy and churned, ran on the high side, parallel to the winding and twisting Broad Run. The stream, replenished by the recent rains, flowed steady and deep. He spotted clusters of birch trees among the woods on the lower, wetter side of Broad Run. An occasional shack, long abandoned, sat tucked among the trees on the opposite bank. The shacks were more lean-to than anything else. He passed several deserted farmhouses, one burnt entirely to the ground. Its stone chimney stood erect over the ruins of the foundations. At that farm the winding Broad Run widened out and turned shallow, revealing stones and shoals. Farther on he entered another wood where Broad Run, bending and turning, dropped down, the banks steeper. Rupert's horse trotted up a short incline where the path spilt him onto a wider, rutted road. To his right a stone bridge led northeast over the Run. "Probably the last original bridge still standing in Virginia," he said grumpily into the ear of his borrowed horse. He pulled the reins to the left and the horse trod up a steep grade. Reaching the top of the hill, he noticed how the country opened up into farm land spread out among wooded lots. The fields, uncultivated for years, were weed and scrub. There were few fence rails left. Even the long stone walls had been dismantled in sections. "At least it used to be farmland," he said to himself.

In the distance, in the center of a gentle valley, he spied a grove of large, spreading trees. Among the trees appeared buildings. Rupert told him to look for the first church down this pike toward Greenwich. That's where he'd find them. "Still don't know what I'm supposed to do once I get there," he complained to the horse, scratching its ear. "Well, let's get this nonsense over with. I wonder how many times I'll have to tell them there's nothing we can do. They're hardly the only ones having a hard time."

The children stopped playing and retreated in timid silence at the black garbed stranger on horseback. Five of the younger children ran to hide behind tombstones or tree trunks. He rode across the turnpike onto the lawn that stretched between the roadway and the church. Or at least what once had been a church. The front steps led to rubble. The brick walls on three sides had collapsed toward the center of what used to be the sanctuary. The fourth wall, blackened and scorched, still stood only because it was buttressed by a small stone building.

Nathaniel gathered up the reins and leaned forward across the pommel. Off to the left of the ruins of the church, next to a cemetery marked by several fresh small graves, stood a large brick building, two storied, with a white cupola at the center of its sloped, slate roof.

Dozens of children stared at him from their hiding places. Gradually, seeing him remaining seated on his horse, they emerged. Children? He could not remember the last time he saw children. None of them was older than ten, he guessed. He tried counting them. Seven small girls in torn and tattered frocks. One little girl, no older than his daughter Penelope, wrapped herself up in an old shawl. He counted five boys in matching short pants and checkered shirts. Two of the boys wore short jackets. None, despite the chill, wore stockings let alone shoes.

Before he could dismount, a tall, lanky man threw open the front door of the brick building and strode toward him. He was elderly, gray-haired, thin, and, judging by his gait, still vigorous. His face betrayed gray stubble. He wore a silk vest, but his top coat showed signs of years of repair. His trousers lacked crease, the knees worn threadbare, the cuffs thoroughly frayed. His wooden cane was more than affectation, for the initial fierce stride began to reveal a pronounced limp as he neared Nathaniel. The man raised the tip of his cane at Nathaniel. The movement of his arms lifted open his unbuttoned frock coat. Nathaniel immediately noticed the polished handle of a large horse pistol tucked into his belt. The children instinctively huddled together.

Nathaniel sat up straight in the saddle. He slid his right hand down and hooked his thumb in his coat pocket. And this is a man with influence in Washington, he muttered under his breath with an increased agitation.

The elderly man pointed the tip of his cane at him. "What is your business here?" The elderly man's demand was cool, flat, controlled, spoken with a tenor of authority. A magistrate's tone. Or a preacher's.

Nathaniel began to dismount.

"Remain in your saddle," the elderly man commanded as one accustomed to being obeyed.

Nathaniel swung back up on his saddle. He leaned forward again, his hands pressed on the pommel. "Are you the Reverend Dr. Benjamin Atkinson?" he asked with an authority of his own.

"Who is asking?"

Nathaniel was in no mood for this. But orders were orders. "Listen, I've been sent here by my Colonel. You don't want me here, that's fine. I'd just as rather ride back. But if you really need to know," he said plainly, "my name is Nathaniel McKenna, currently serving as chaplain of the 30th Regiment, First Pennsylvania Reserves." The saddle creaked as Nathaniel shifted. "I used to serve as pastor at the Penningtonville Presbyterian Church, Presbytery of Northumberland. It seems we share a similar calling."

The elderly man pounded the tip of his cane into the ground. "That we certainly do not share, pastor, ever since your side of the denomination proved itself apostate."

"That was a long time ago, another time," Nathaniel answered wearily. "So, it is Doctor Atkinson I am addressing."

"And I thank you and your Army for leaving me this church to serve," he replied bitterly, pointing his cane at the ruins to his left. "We dedicated it in 1858. Your people burnt it a year ago."

Months ago Nathaniel would have been offended, defensive even. But no longer. Yes, they were his people who did this. So this is the result of our piety, Nathaniel reflected. Dead raped girls and burnt down churches. Suddenly he imagined what it would be like if this were Penningtonville and he were this man. He'd be angry too. What if these children were his own daughters? God help us, he thought. Unthinking, he rubbed his eyes and looked again at the burnt sanctuary. "It must have been a beautiful sanctuary, pastor," he said. "I'm sorry for your loss. Please, may we speak?"

"What you may do is leave."

Nathaniel rubbed his thigh in frustration. "Fine by me, Doctor, I do not want to be here either. I am simply under orders to follow up on your requests. If you don't want to talk to me, that's your choice."

"I have made no requests. No requests of you people at all. No, we may not speak. I repeat, 'what you may do is leave.'" Doctor Atkinson started to turn away, then stopped when he heard his daughter's voice calling from the doorway of the brick building.

"Father, let him get down." A young woman descended the stone steps. "He's here because of me." The children, as soon as they heard the young woman's voice, flocked toward her, clutching at her green dress, the littlest ones hiding behind its thick folds. Gently shooing the little ones into the care of two other women who had been hiding behind her in the shadow of the doorway, she walked toward her father and stood beside him. Her eyes shimmered with a rich cobalt blue luster. Her white shawl covered her shoulders. Bereft of bonnet or scarf, her raven hair fell loose across her shawl.

Nathaniel dismounted and held the bridle. The harsh smell of roasted acorns floated from the house.

She offered the hint of a curtsey. "Welcome. I am Miss Atkinson, and I at least am very pleased that your Army is finally taking this matter seriously."

"Nathaniel McKenna, at your service, Miss. Though, I must admit, it remains to be seen what the matter is that requires our attention, serious or otherwise."

"Chaplain, we are neither begging nor pleading." She took her father's arm in hers. "Yes, father, I sought their help without your permission. For the last weeks I have sent letters and once visited their headquarters. Forgive me, father, but I even posted several letters to your old friend, Doctor Gurley."

Doctor Atkinson tried to pull his arm away, turning his back to them. "Do not speak his contemptible name to me."

She clung onto his arm, refusing to let him go. Nathaniel decided now was not the right time to speak of his own father or of Gurley.

"Obviously," Miss Atkinson concluded, gesturing toward Nathaniel, "my perseverance did some good. They didn't send troops, they sent him."

"You did so, Ellen, without my permission." Doctor Atkinson exclaimed over his shoulder. "Unforgivable."

"Your permission? Father, you would never have given it. And I will look to the Lord for forgiveness rather than you if I have to. We are at the point well past pride. This war is past all pride."

"That's for certain," added Nathaniel without thinking.

Doctor Atkinson detached himself from his daughter's plaintive touch. "I will have none of this and I will have none of you," he pronounced, stalking toward the ruins of his church.

Miss Atkinson turned to Nathaniel. "I apologize, Pastor McKenna. These months have been hard. Please, I ask your indulgence. Two of my brothers were killed over a year ago. We've not heard any word from the third. Father cannot take much more. I tell you this not for your pity but so you may appreciate our circumstances. We are little different from any of our neighbors. We are all well past pity. I tell you this so you also may appreciate the work my father has done this last year despite his grief. Let me show you." One of the older boys came forward at her signal and took his horse's reins. Boldly, confidently, she slipped her arm under Nathaniel's and escorted him toward the brick building. With her free, graceful hand, her fingers long and slim, she beckoned the children over, "Come here, Elsie. Johnny, come over here. You too, Margaret." Nathaniel noticed her cracked fingernails. The children timidly approached Nathaniel. They peeked at him from behind her dress. The women remained in the shadows of the doorway.

Nathaniel knelt and peered around the folds of Ellen's dress. "Are you Margaret," he asked? A little girl, her golden hair pulled back in a long pony tail, bit her lip and blushed. Nathaniel began instinctively to reach out and touch her cheek but instead lowered his hand to his waistcoat. "My little girl back home is also named Margaret. We love the name Margaret. It's a very special name. I bet now she's almost three inches taller than you." He reached into his waistcoat pocket and removed his watch. He pressed open the lid.

Ellen gazed down on them both, her heart pounding.

"Would you like to see her? She gave me this picture of her and her sister before I left my home." He held the lid so the little girl can see the painting inside. She blushed deeper. "She smiles just like you."

Margaret pointed chubby fingers at the painting.

"Oh, that's my other daughter. Her name is Penelope."

"Babynelope," Margaret mouthed in sing-song.

"Penelope likes to listen to my watch. Would you like to listen?" Margaret bit her lip again and squirmed. Nathaniel reached around and held the watch up to her ear. A sweet smile magically appeared on her face as she heard the ticking of the watch. He swept a strand of her hair from her eyes. A smaller girl, standing behind Margaret stretched up to grab the watch. Her hair was ginger, her limbs as thin as spindles. "Everybody gets a turn," Nathaniel promised. "I'll hold it for you. Are you Elsie?" Clustering around Nathaniel, each child listened. Each child wiggled and beamed.

Ellen Atkinson touched his shoulder. "These children are only a third of our family. The others are much younger. Come with me and see."

Nathaniel followed her inside the brick building. Margaret, Elsie, and the others, like chicks, trailed.

"Once upon a time this was my father's Academy. The Greenwich Academy. In better days he was quite the scholar. Father retired from teaching seminary at Richmond to start this school and church. Obviously, there are no students now. This is our congregation now." She pointed at the two young women standing together in the corner of the hallway. Neither appeared to Nathaniel to be older than sixteen years old, both were pregnant. One, trembling, hid behind the other. "It's all right. He's not going to hurt you," Ellen said to them reassuringly. "You can trust him. He's a pastor." Ellen tightened her hold on Nathaniel as she guided him down the hallway. "Last year they just started arriving. They didn't have any where else to go. The word got out, I suppose. Father, of course, took them all in. A few come from the towns around here, but most are the poor folk who lived along the rivers or in the hills. Despite their age, most are widows. Or will be." She opened the door to what once was a classroom. The broken windows had been covered over with wax paper and scraps of cloth. Several young women lay on bedrolls on the floor nursing their babies. Ellen closed the door gently. "Most have no family left. Some can't go back to their families. Too many found themselves disgraced. The work of your soldiers. That's why they're here. No one else would take them in, not even their kinfolk. I don't believe I have to explain myself further, do I pastor?"

"No," Nathaniel said.

Ellen's deep blue eyes stared at him. "Except for what we can scavenge, and except for one other source, there is precious little food left for these children. This winter promises to be terribly cold." She turned aside. "Do you understand now why I have pleaded for assistance from your Army? Why I have begged for help from my father's old friends? For any act of Christian charity? My father and I cannot do anything about this horrible war of yours, but we can do something about these babies. Your commanders told me that this is none of their concern. Well, you tell me then, Chaplain McKenna, whose concern should it be?"

Before Nathaniel rode off to return to his Regiment, he told Miss Ellen Atkinson that he was not sure what he could do but he did promise that he would return to the Academy and let her know. He did. He returned the very next day with two sacks of flour and one sack of onions balanced across the pommel of Rupert's horse. He returned in three days with a mule, the lead line tied to his halter. The mule carried a bolt of cloth, a small bag of turnips, some salt pork, along with hardtack and coffee donated by the men of the Regiment, plus several sacks of beans.

Over the next month the buttoned pouches of his hidden money belt grew slimmer. Quartermaster Waggoner also reported to Talley how surprised he was at how hungry the men in the Regiment had become these recent weeks.

☉☉☉

My Darling Nathan,

We are so glad you wrote. It has been too long since we heard from you. We were so desperately worried. Our dear Margaret was convinced that you would write soon and she kept promising me that you weren't able to write because her Daddy had to take care of President Lincoln. She tries to read the newspapers and can't understand why they never mention your name. I am very glad it doesn't.

You would be so proud of your daughters. Penelope has begun remembering her alphabet already and Margaret has a talent with words. She wrote her own note to you, which I've included. I do pray our letters reach you safely, along with the package we sent for you and our dear Valentine.

Harold and Edith wanted me to be sure to tell you that it meant everything what you wrote in your letter about Joe. Their hearts are horribly broken but at least they find comfort in that Joe sacrificed himself saving those wounded men. He must have been so brave to have done what you described. Their prayers are with you.

We had been hoping and praying that your Colonel would allow that furlough you had spoken of several months ago as a possibility. Our second Christmas without you, my beloved, seems more than we can bear...

◉◉◉

One frosty morning, two days before Christmas, while driving a borrowed ambulance, Nathaniel pulled the reins and turned the mules onto the lawn of the Greenwich Academy. Ellen dashed out, her raven hair tousled by the gusty winter wind. Her father followed ten paces behind, limping more than usual. Dozens of children and women watched from the windows.

Nathaniel leapt down from the seat. "Can you or your father come with me?" he called out excitedly. "We have a chance for receiving aid from the Christian Commission. We have to travel to Manassas Junction. They have plenty of blankets and potatoes, even fruit. It took some persuasion, but my contacts said they are willing to cooperate. But the officials there need to meet with one of you. They need an interview. This is a bit irregular for them, working with locals. The enemy. I think Gurley once again had something to do with it. I have a suspicion he asked someone else. I believe that person, who seems to have some influence, wrote a letter to them personally asking them to begin showing the rest of our nation what we will need to do in the years to come." Nathaniel grasped Ellen by both her shoulders. "This is important, Ellen, Doctor Atkinson. They can help you in your work here, not only now but after my Regiment leaves. You must know that is going to happen sometime. We've got a chance, a real chance, to set you up."

She embraced him tightly. A flustered Nathaniel didn't know whether to embrace her back or not.

Doctor Atkinson placed his hand on Nathaniel's forearm. "I surely am not going to let my daughter go off alone, pastor. I shall go instead."

"Well then, get in. Whomever. Dress warm, it'll be a cold ride." Nathaniel tightened his old overcoat around himself.

As she scurried inside the brick building, Ellen shouted back to them: "I'm going too." Before her father could disallow it, she returned, wrapped in a large horse blanket. She skipped to the ambulance.

Doctor Atkinson, slid his cane onto the bench, pulled himself up, then reached to assist his daughter. "Someday, my dear," he said to her, "you are going to listen to me, and on that day I will be a happy man. You're impulsive ways are going to be your ruin. And mine."

The negotiations at Manassas Junction took far longer than Nathaniel had hoped. Doctor Atkinson's tendency to lecture caused them to stay an extra hour and a half. He had promised Valentine he'd get the ambulance back before supper. His watch told him that that was unlikely to happen. But the delay still proved worthwhile. When he returns to camp and tells Valentine of their success, he knows he'll pretend to be cranky but he won't mind. He'll tell him it was Val's Christmas present to the Academy. Nathaniel peered with satisfaction over his shoulder at the bundles packed inside the ambulance and, despite the chill of wind, he felt warm inside. There were dozens of blankets. A barrel of apples. Medicines too. A barrel of shoes. A barrel of salt pork and dried beef and onions. They'll be set up for a good while. And better, they left with an agreement between the Commission and Doctor Atkinson. It was Ellen who impressed them. It's a start. A promise. For once, for once, it was something promising.

It already was dusk by the time they departed Manassas Junction. The December wind whipped stronger, crueler. Nathaniel turned up the collar to his overcoat. Father and daughter buried themselves beneath the horse blanket.

The single shot screeched before Nathaniel saw the figures of the four riders in front of them. Doctor Atkinson groaned. Ellen lacked voice to scream. Nathaniel dropped the reins and fumbled with his overcoat pocket. He shook out the revolver and aimed at the rider who was closing in on them from the right. With a rage spawned of fear and stubbornness, he cocked the hammer, pulled the trigger, and the wavering pistol jerked back with a roar. The rider fell, tumbling beneath his horse. Stunned, but only for a second, Nathaniel whirled the pistol toward his left, trying to cock the hammer again. This rider crossed the distance between them. Just as Nathaniel prepared to fire again, the rider slammed Nathaniel across the face with the cold barrel of his carbine. Nathaniel crumpled backwards against the back of the bench, stung but still conscious, conscious enough to hear one of the riders scowl: "Why'd you clobber him, Ned? Should've shot 'em right out."

"All in good time," he said with a spit of black juice. "Doesn' hurt to find out what we've got 'ere," the rider explained coolly.

As Nathaniel struggled to right himself up, he heard Ellen calling first to her father, then crying out his name: "Nathaniel, they've shot father." Doctor Atkinson lay slumped across his daughter's lap, blood leaking from his side, her green dress soaking up her father's blood.

One of the riders, bareheaded, his revolver trained on them, trotted his horse over to Ellen. He holstered his revolver and reached out, stroking her cheek with the back of his hand. She shoved his hand away, but he grabbed her by her black hair and yanked her toward his face. "Hey, boss, looks like we have a sweet treat tonight."

Nathaniel, though gauzy eyes, spotted his fallen revolver in the shadows of the floorboard. "Leave her alone!" he shouted as he lunged for his pistol.

A dozen shots erupted from the woods surrounding them. The rider farthest from them fell instantly. The man bearing the carbine, called Ned, was hit full square in the chest by several bullets just as he was about to shoot Nathaniel. His blood splattered Nathaniel. Another rider tumbled backwards onto the roadway. His panicked horse stomped his hoof into his face. The bareheaded rider clutched Ellen's hair and dragged Ellen half out of her seat before his grip relaxed and he too fell to the ground. Ellen and Nathaniel's alarm turned to astonishment as they peered into the darkness. A dozen riders emerged like ghosts from the trees. Three of these riders galloped off after the four rider-less horses. Ellen instantly began compressing her father's wound with a folded corner of the horse blanket.

A rider, his white horse cantering, approached Nathaniel's side of the ambulance.

With bright eyes and a broad smile highlighted by a trim mustache, the Confederate Major doffed his feathered hat and saluted the chaplain. He gave a command: "Burke, see if you can lend some assistance to the lady and her father."

Burke rode over and instantly dismounted, handing the reins of his horse to another trooper. "Give a hand here," Burke directed, and two other soldiers slid off their mounts. He offered his hands to Ellen, and she, holding them, jumped down. With Nathaniel's help from behind, they lifted Doctor Atkinson from the seat of the ambulance and placed him on the horse blanket spread out along the side of the dirt road. Doctor Atkinson groaned as they moved him.

"Good sign, Ma'am," Burke offered in an attempt to comfort Ellen as she knelt near her father's head.

"Providential timing," the Major said to Nathaniel.

"Yes, indeed," Nathaniel said, rubbing his bruised face. "We are grateful."

The Major paused, studying Nathaniel's face. The Major winked. "It is good to meet you again, Reverend. I never did thank you for your Morgan."

Nathaniel cocked his head in return, then bowed in recognition. "Actually, Captain Mosby, 'er, pardon me, I see you've been promoted. Yes, Major Mosby. But that particular horse belonged to our Regimental Adjutant."

"A good judge of horses."

"So the Adjutant still reminds me." Nathaniel glanced over toward Ellen, then back at Mosby. "If you'll excuse me…"

"Yes, of course."

Nathaniel scooted along the bench and jumped down. After he landed he looked over at the body of the man he killed. The man was contorted, broken, his blood glistening, seeping. Nathaniel looked at him without passion. His mind tried to convince him he should feel some remorse, until a wave of numb indifference cooled his skin. What he felt curious was his lack of emotion. He thought he might feel more anguish than this nonchalant distaste. "Well, I had hoped to get out of this without killing," he observed aloud. The soldier holding the reins of Burke's horse supposed he was talking to him. The partisan shrugged, then asked, "So why'd ya' shoot 'em?"

Nathaniel turned and knelt beside Ellen and put his arm around her. They watched as Burke fingered the wound. Nathaniel motioned to Burke. "How is he?"

"Hurt bad but clean. He does need attention for sure. I don't smell any internal damage, but I can't be sure. He requires more than I can give."

Mosby had walked around the ambulance to face them. "Ellen, my regrets. I do wish we could have arrived sooner.

Fortune and chance favored us tonight, but not soon enough, I fear."

Ellen rose, supporting herself on Nathaniel's arm. "We are grateful, John. As always. If you hadn't arrived when you did..." She was unable to finish, pressing her face into Nathaniel's chest. Nathaniel looked at both of them and marveled at their familiarity.

Nathaniel, still holding Ellen, spoke: "Major, if I can offer a proposal. Our Regimental hospital is not far from here. Our Surgeon, my very best friend, can treat Doctor Atkinson. I'm sure he will."

Ellen pushed herself from Nathaniel and reached out toward Mosby. "Oh, please, John, do what he says."

Burke, tending to a moaning Dr. Atkinson, spoke one word: "Major."

Nathaniel put his arm around Ellen's shoulders again. He began talking faster. "Ellen, listen. Pull yourself together because you need to listen. My friend will take excellent care of your father. He's the kind of man you can depend on. Just tell him, Ellen, that I sent you to him. That'll be enough." His eyes looked into Mosby's. "Major Mosby, if you would let some of your men assist her in driving the ambulance in that direction, at least as far as you can."

"Are you not capable, Reverend?"

"I, I am," Nathaniel stammered. "But am I not your prisoner?"

Mosby waved his hat with a flourish. "Nonsense. We have plenty enough of our own preachers. Too many, in fact." He took a step closer and whispered into his ear: "Reverend, do you think we have not been aware of the recent activities at the Academy? One act of charity deserves another."

Burke reminded again: "Major."

Mosby and Nathaniel shook hands. Nathaniel signaled Burke. "Quickly now, if we could just lift Doctor Atkinson into the ambulance—there should be room on the blankets inside— we could be there within the half hour."

Mosby nodded his approval. His men followed Burke's instructions and lifted Doctor Atkinson by the corners of the blanket. Mosby extended his palm to Ellen and escorted her to the wagon. Before he lifted her onto the bench, he reached down into the floorboard. He picked up the Colt revolver, examined it, lowered the hammer, flipped it to catch it by the barrel, and, frowning, offered Nathaniel its wooden grip. "Yours, I believe." With a flash of a wink, he added: "As much as we'd like to offer escort, I trust you will appreciate how that would prove inconvenient."

Chapter Sixteen

Valentine's Day

"No more at dawning morn I rise,
And sun myself in Ellen's eyes,
Drive the fleet deer the forests through,
And homeward wend with evening's dew;
A blithesome welcome blithely meet,
And lay my trophies at her feet,
While fled the even on wing of glee, —
This life is lost to love and me!"
"The Lady of the Lake," Sir Walter Scott

She's infuriating! She's a plague! She's impossible! Damn you for ever bringing her here!"

"Ah, Ellen's visiting again." Nathaniel let the candle flame re-ignite the spent wooden match. He held the small blaze over his pipe bowl. Inhaling, he drew several puffs, pulling the fire into the bowl.

"I am going to banish her from my hospital. It is my hospital! I don't care if that's her father. I am going to ban her forever. And it's your fault, Nate. Your fault. He's a civilian. He shouldn't still be taking up a bed anyway. There are rules. I hope you appreciate that I'm bending regulations for you."

"So what did she do this time?"

"It's not so much what she does," Valentine ranted. "It is who she is. Did you ever get attacked by a mockingbird. She's just like that. Petite, beguiling, trilling. She'll seduce you with her song. But watch out, 'cause she comes swooping down out of nowhere and attacks you. She's infuriating. Demanding this. Demanding that. Trying to tell me how to treat him. Last week she brought in some nasty looking syrup she wanted him to drink. Today she actually brought in a chunk of tree moss to dress one of my patient's wounds. My patient! Damn that woman! And damn you too for bringing her here."

"She does have a way of getting to you, doesn't she?" Nathaniel settled back into his folding chair, rested his feet on Valentine's cot, and deliberately blew several smoke-rings. "Reminds me a little of Alice."

"Alice? Alice?" he shouted back, offended by the comparison. "How can you say that? Alice is a saint, an angel. Why did I ever let you steal her from me! This woman? This woman is a hound of hell. The devil's own mistress." Valentine collapsed on his cot, pulled out the bottle of bourbon from under his pillow, and enjoyed a long, burning, soothing drink. He slammed the cork back into the bottle. "Damn, she's beautiful."

"You, my sad, impulsive friend, have met your match. About time, too."

"Oh, shut up," Valentine said, twisting again the cork from the bottle and swigging another mouthful. "I'm lost, Nate. What's happened to me? And I can't do a blessed thing about it. She's got me. God, I love women." He wiggled the bottle at Nathaniel. "How do you married fellows stand it?"

"It has its rewards." He tapped his pipe on the edge of the cot.

"That's if you get the chance. I don't stand a chance. With any other woman, I would be cock of the roost—Alice excepting, of course."

"Of course."

Valentine locked his hands behind his head as he collapsed onto his pillow. "I walk into a room and they are there for the taking." Valentine closed his eyes and slipped into a memory. "I love the way they smell. I love the way your arms fit just right around their ready waists. There's nothing finer in the world, my friend, then having one of them in your arms when you dance. The smooth, intoxicating touch of satin and lace." His eyes widened as he looked over at Nathaniel and grabbed the toe of his boot. "Oh, Lord, I love women. But damn her, she's turned me off from all the rest of them. She has ruined me." He raised his head up from the pillow. "It is not as if I chose this, you know?"

"Sorry, brother. I'm not sure if you ever do choose. I just never thought I'd see the day you'd succumb to the curse. Come on now, it's only been a couple of weeks. You have disappointed all of us. We had such great hopes for our rakish O'Rourke."

"It is a curse. Damn straight. I am cursed and Ellen is my curse. Damn her. What I really despise is what a simpering, pathetic dolt I've become." Valentine pulled the sweat stained pillow from behind his head and flopped it on his chest. He folded his hands on top of the pillow. "At least her father is going home in a few days and I won't have to see her again. I think I can handle that. Let's send her away from here." He stared at the fold of the tent and at the way the candlelight haloed upon the fabric. "What I cannot handle is sitting next to her while she cares for her father. What I cannot stand is the way her breath touches my neck."

"Never took you for the romantic, Val. Can't escape it, can you? You're an authentic Irish poet."

"It's not poetry, its fact. Cruel fact. As me darlin' father would say, 'pog mo thoin.' The world can 'kiss my ass.' Whoever labeled the Irish 'romantic' was a goddamn liar. Bastards all. What we are, my Scottish friend, are sots and victims. We're the stinking realists in this stinking world. What's cruel is standing near her, smelling her, knowing I'll never get the chance."

Nathaniel exhaled a long stream of smoke, "She's told you about her fiancé then?"

"Yup."

◎◎◎

By the time Nathaniel arrived at the hospital, the mules already had been hitched to the ambulance. Valentine spotted Nathaniel approaching, "About time you showed up. I'm sending Chilson along instead. He'll drive the team and make sure the old fellow remains comfortable."

"Sorry. Got lost reading a letter." Nathaniel pointed to the ambulance. "Why don't you go with me? Be a nice afternoon for us."

"I, um, ah..." Valentine fumbled, not finishing or even finding the words for even a lame excuse.

"I understand. You coward. I'll give her your regards," Nathaniel lied, tossing his folded overcoat up onto the bench. It fell heavily on the wooden bench.

Hearing the thud, Valentine quizzed him: "Didn't sound like your Bible to me."

Nathaniel ignored him. He pulled on the end of his mustache. "Remind me to tell Chilson to stop by the sutler on our way out. I have some potatoes to pick up for her."

"Just don't linger, okay Nate? I don't want to push him. It's a hard enough ride as it is. Blast the good Colonel, the man really should stay another week. I'm worried about his lungs."

"For all our sakes, he'll be better out of here. You know it's time," Nathaniel said, putting his arm around Valentine's shoulder. "He'll be fine, you know that. After all, he has a very competent nurse."

"Annoyingly competent."

Chilson emerged from the hospital tent and held open one of the flaps. Two of the musicians emerged carting the litter that bore Dr. Atkinson. Nathaniel stepped up into the ambulance. As they prepared to hand the litter up to him, Dr. Atkinson noticed Valentine off to the side and caught his attention. "Doctor O'Rourke," he thinly called out, his breathing threaded.

Valentine hesitated before approaching him.

"Please thank your Colonel for the hospitality and skill of your staff." Offering a slight salute with his left hand, Atkinson continued: "As it will be unlikely we will meet again, I wish you well. You and Nathaniel have been most kind."

Valentine tapped the edge of the litter. "Chilson here will see that you are settled in once you arrive. Please, sir, for once, listen to what he suggests. It will take time, sir. There is yet much to heal." Without waiting for a reply, Valentine instructed the musicians. "Shift it, boys, hurry, slide him in."

Before Chilson climbed up to the ambulance bench, Valentine pulled him aside by the elbow and handed him a large canvas bag. "While you are there, you might as well see if any of the children require any attention. Check them out as best you can. If you happen to forget to return with the bag, it won't appear on any reports."

Chilson opened the bag and rummaged through its contents. Lint and bandages. Epsom salts. Bromine. A box of opium pills. Quinine. A variety of small, familiar vials: liquor of ammonia, iodine, tincture of iron, nitric acid, sodium chloride of soda, ipecac. At the bottom of the bag Chilson discovered his own checkerboard set. He was wondering what happened to it. He had left it out last night for one the patients. He should not have left it out.

Valentine, eyeing Chilson, patted him on his shoulder. "That's a good fellow. You won't miss it, now will you? It is not as if I give you much time for games, now do I?"

"S'pose not," Chilson conceded.

O'Rourke tapped the walnut handle of the bag. "Do make sure she knows exactly how she should use these medicines. I want them used properly. Write the directions down if you have to. Tell her she can keep her damn moss."

Nathaniel wrapped his overcoat tightly around himself as Chilson held the reins to the mules and, with a slap on their rumps, headed the ambulance along the frost and pools of thin ice formed in the hard ruts and hoof prints of the path. The wheels creaked and the leather harnesses slapped. The twigs of the branches hanging over Broad Run glistened, encased in sheaths of ice. The front wheel of the ambulance wheel hit a rock and the ambulance lurched. Doctor Atkinson, silent up to this point, grunted as if someone had punched him in the gut.

Nathaniel swung around. "We'll be there soon, less than an hour. Hold on, sir."

The mules trudged up the short incline, turned left at the stone bridge, then clopped down into the valley toward the grove of trees. Two dozen women, most wrapped in shawls and comforters, and triple that number of children, waited in a welcoming group as the ambulance pulled past the ruins of the church toward the brick building. Nathaniel noticed several new faces among the women. Nathaniel nudged Chilson. "As close to the stone steps as you can. They've readied a room for him."

"No problem, chaplain," Chilson replied.

Ellen, wearing a burgundy dress, emerged from the crowd. "Hello, Nathaniel." She looked at Chilson sitting next to him. A shadow of disappointment darkened her cobalt blue eyes, but they quickly brightened. "And Dr. Chilson, is it? So glad to see you again. We'll take him to my bedroom for now, please." Then she skipped to the rear of the ambulance. "We are all here, father. We missed you so." She walked alongside the litter holding her father's hand as Chilson and Nathaniel carried him up the stone steps.

Before they passed through the doorway, Doctor Atkinson pushed up on his stronger arm, and, detaching himself from his daughter's hand, waved to his parish. Emotions surged, preventing him from saying anything.

Nathaniel noticed Atkinson's eyes beginning to tear. Experience had taught him how the old especially cry quickly with this kind of affliction. "You're home, pastor. But I insist that you rest before delivering any sermons. And no baptisms at least until tomorrow."

Doctor Atkinson smiled in weak assent as they carried him into the makeshift infirmary and transferred him onto a straw mattress. Chilson and Nathaniel exited, leaving Ellen alone with him. She stroked his hair, held his hand, kissed his forehead, tightened the blankets around him, making him as comfortable as only a devoted daughter could.

Twenty minutes later Ellen joined Nathaniel in the hallway. See touched Chilson's hand. "He asked if you would assist him."

Chilson opened the oak door and entered the small room.

Nathaniel stood near Ellen. "How well is he?" Nathaniel asked. "It was bumpier than I would have liked for him."

"If what you mean by 'well' is, is he cranky, obstinate, and annoyed that he cannot start preaching again immediately? Yes, I would say he is well." Ellen slid her arm into his. "Thanks to you." Her face reached up as she lightly kissed him on the cheek. "You've been wonderful these weeks."

"Please don't say that. Nothing wonderful about it."

They strolled silently down the hallway to the end of the old schoolhouse, where Ellen stopped at another oak door.

"May we talk?" She pulled open the door. "This once served as my father's study. And his bedroom. I use it now." They entered. Ellen left the door ajar. A feeble fire glowed orange in the stone fireplace. They sat on the worn settee which was angled toward the fireplace. He lifted the heavy object in his coat's right hand pocket into the space between his leg and the armrest.

"I can offer you a little tea," she said.

"No, thanks. I'm fine. Quite fine." Nathaniel held his palms out to the fireplace. "The fire is welcome though." Several tiny snickers filtered from the open doorway. Nathaniel turned and noticed little Margaret and ginger haired Elsie peeking from behind the edge of the door. "We seem to have been followed," Nathaniel said to Ellen

Ellen swung around. "What are the boys up to, Margaret?" Ellen asked.

Margaret giggled. "Playin' checkers," she squealed in a sing-song. She rocked back and forth at the door.

"Oh, my, what could you want?" Nathaniel teased. "Come on in, girls. I bet I know what you want. Come on in."

The girls pranced to the corner of the settee without waiting for Ellen's nod of approval. Elsie climbed up on Nathaniel's lap. He instinctively stroked her hair. Her hair seemed thicker than when he first met her. Nathaniel suddenly reached into his pocket to double-check that the hammer of the revolver was secured. Elsie began pulling on his silver watch chain. Nathaniel shook his head and looked over at Ellen. "What is it with you Southern girls?"

"We learn to flirt early," Ellen laughed sprightly. "Why do you think we always get what we want?"

Nathaniel retrieved his watch from Elsie, opened the lid, and held it to her ear. She held her breath, intent on listening to the tick-tocking. Margaret, clutching his knee, squeaked: "My turn, my turn." Gathering the fob and chain in hand, he held the watch to Margaret's ear, cupping his hand over her tiny ear. Her grey eyes widened. Then as suddenly as the girls pranced into the room, Margaret squealed and dashed out. Elsie touched Nathaniel's mustache with her chubby fingers before she slid off his lap and chased after her friend.

Ellen extended her hand and opened her palm. "May I see too?"

Nathaniel placed his open watch onto her palm. She held the painting in front of her face. "They are beautiful, Nathaniel." Her voice lingered. "I had always hoped for my own family." She waved her other hand in the air, her long fingers swirling. "Of course, this family is not quite what I had imagined." She gently folded the watch lid shut and handed it back to Nathaniel, who slid it back into his pocket. Their hands touched.

"All our lives have been changed, Ellen. How could any of us have planned on this?"

Together they stared at the small fire as the flames wavered and danced in the fireplace. Nathaniel sensed that Ellen was trying to decide whether or not to say something. He waited. He smoothed the ends of his mustache with both hands, his fingers twisting the ends to a point.

"Nathaniel," she finally began. "We've become good friends since that day you rode up. I haven't had many friends with whom I could talk." She folded her hands in her lap. "We need to talk. I suspect you know that we need to clear the air." Her voice faltered. She looked away from Nathaniel toward the fire. "For once I would like to talk about something other than this place or my father." Ellen turned her eyes back toward Nathaniel, arresting him. Her eyes glowed bright as the blue sky. "Tell me about Valentine. I know how close you are. I need to know about Valentine." Her hand touched the back of his. "Nathaniel, why does he dislike me so? He can be so rude. He can be so coarse with me. Or else he ignores me. Whenever I would arrive to visit father, he would leave the ward. When I try to talk to him he barely looks at me." Her hands folded over Nathaniel's hands. She looked into his eyes before shifting her eyes down to look at his mouth. "Why does he hate me?"

Nathaniel breathed a deep breath, removing his hands from under hers, and, placed them on top of her hands. "Dislike you, Ellen? Hate you? You mean he's never told you?" Nathaniel tightened his grip on her hands. "That fool. What an idiot. Both of you." He lifted her hands. "Ellen, haven't you guessed it? Ellen, I would have thought you would have guessed, or are you as foolish as he is? Blast him, he leaves it for me to speak for him. You two amaze me. If you only knew how many nights back at our tent he's spent talking to me about you. He never stops talking about you. Someone smart once told me he's very good at loving but very bad at being loved."

She leaned toward him and kissed him again on the cheek. "There's lots of foolishness going around these days."

When Nathaniel left, he carried in his pocket a brief letter to Valentine from Ellen. The letter explained that there were several children at the Academy she was particularly worried about. She'd appreciate it if he would find time to visit them and examine them personally.

Valentine found the time, but only after Nathaniel bribed him with a bottle of bourbon, along with the threat of telling Alice on him. Valentine finally relented, only after first extracting from Nathaniel his promise that he would put away that gun.

Val found the time Sunday. He found the time the next Sunday. Sunday afternoons transformed the Academy into a regular clinic. Ellen eventually convinced some of the young women to let Doctor O'Rourke examine them. Doctoring others forced them to work side-by-side. They began to enjoy working side-by-side. They enjoyed the tease. And the danger.

One Sunday afternoon, after tucking a blanket around a feverish child, Valentine was startled when Ellen slipped her arm through his and pulled him outside. She skipped toward a buckboard. "Come with me. Step up," she commanded, talking too fast to give him the chance to object. "I presume you can handle the reins. You and I are going to escape. Nathaniel, bless him, is keeping father busy."

An hour later, Valentine and Ellen stopped the rig in the middle of the stone bridge to rest the skinny and tired horse. They watched a full Broad Run flow below. Valentine straightened the blanket to keep her warm. He removed his hat and reached around her shoulders with it. "All right, Ellen. Enough of this game. Tell me about your fiancé."

Ellen snuggled into him: "Laurence?"

"Yes, Laurence. Stop being distracting. I know his name. I've heard a little about him. How can I not? Your father reminds me of him every time I visit here. But I haven't yet heard you talk about him. I want to hear you talk about him."

"Why now? Here? I don't really want to. I want to be here. I want to be with you. I don't want to have to think about what is back there." A red-wing black bird swooped from the other side of the stream to land on the branch of a nearby linden. The bird cocked its head at the two of them.

"And I don't want to be used this way." Valentine studied the flowing water below. He removed his arm from her shoulders and placed his hat back on his head. Along the banks, the ash and willow were beginning to leaf out, the brown shrubs greening. "Yes, Ellen, now," he said flatly. "I need to hear you talk about him now. We've avoided it for too long."

"All right. If you insist. But you first," she teased breezily, tickling his ear. "What has father told you?"

"Stop it, Ellen. Stop it, dammit. For the first time in my life with a woman I am trying to be serious. This is unknown territory. Help me here." He took her hand in his. She toyed with edge of the blanket.

"Fine, we'll do it your way," he said. "At last report, he still rides with Stuart's horse artillery. A Captain."

"A Major, actually," she corrected. "His most recent letter told me of his promotion." Ellen smoothed the blanket against her lap. "They are Laurence's horse artillery now. His command for almost a year now. Ever since Pelham was killed in that foolish charge. So unnecessary. But I haven't heard from Laurence for months."

"Hell, we did. We heard from him, well, sort of. Must have been him. That was about four months ago around Catalpa. Stuart almost rode right over us. Your boy must have ridden right by where we were hidden. If I had known then I might have borrowed my Sergeant's carbine and risked a shot."

"Well, now, that would have solved our problem," Ellen said cynically.

"Or maybe Nathaniel could have given it a try. He seems handy at wanting to protect you these days."

"I don't need protecting. Nor do I cry easily anymore. I'm not one of your Southern Belles, if you haven't noticed."

"I've noticed."

"Besides, if something had happened that night when father was shot, maybe I'd understand a little bit better what most of my young women have to deal with everyday."

"That's a charming thing for you to say. I'm glad Nate was there. I'm glad he did what he did. And I'm glad you had your other friends protecting you, whether you want to be protected or not." Valentine studied her face. "So is this Mosby character a friend of Laurence's?"

"No, he's my friend. A very dear friend. John and I go way back."

"Ah, another victim."

"Would you stop it."

"Fine, we're following your rules. Let's get back to Laurence. Yes, I know a little. From your father. A graduate of The Citadel, I hear." Valentine's voice turned sardonic. "Blue blooded, of course."

She ignored his tone. "That actually was where we first met. After mother's death, father and I traveled to Charleston visiting friends. Several of the professors were classmates of father's. There was a ball, of course. There were always balls. What do you want me to say? Yes, we fell in love. We courted, mostly by correspondence. Laurence was among the first to enlist. He wears a uniform well. Laurence is a very honorable man.

"Unlike me."

"Stop that. Valentine. You're rude. You're brash. You're an absolutely astounding irritation. But you also are one of the most honorable men I've met."

"If I were honorable do you think I would be in this buckboard with you?" The horse suddenly twitched his hindquarters and jerked the rig. Loosening his grip on the reins, Valentine let them slide through his hands, giving the horse sufficient slack, until he slowly pulled them tighter settling the horse.

Ellen again smoothed the edges of the blanket, her hand lightly caressing his thigh. "Maybe I'm relying on you to be honorable."

He pushed her hand away. "Dammit, why are you doing this?

"Because I can. Because I want to."

"Do you love him?" Valentine bluntly asked.

"Do I love him?" she echoed. "Do I love him? It was all so romantic. My father approves of him, thinks him the ideal prospect for me." Ellen breathed a small laugh. "Mrs. Laurence Rush Dickson. How does that sound?"

"No doubt a more fitting name than 'Mrs. O'Rourke.' Your father thinks my blood a little too green and my profession not much better than being a street corner barber."

Ellen wheeled around to glare at Valentine. "You don't know my father very well if you think that. Yes, Laurence comes from a fine family. His mother is a direct relation of your Benjamin Rush. That's something you as a Pennsylvanian should appreciate. Wasn't he Washington's personal physician? Wasn't he?"

"I've heard the name," said Valentine, immediately accompanied by the *conk-a-reeeee* song of the red-wing blackbird.

Ellen tensed, her voice cold. "Why must you compare yourself? Yes, his people are quite prominent. The Dicksons of Greenville, South Carolina. They own a beautiful plantation outside Greenville. Or did own. Who knows by now?" Ellen turned spiteful. "They own plenty of slaves." Valentine turned his head away from her. Ellen plunged into sulky silence for a long while, listening to the wind and the trickle of water. Shivering, she leaned against Valentine. Her cuddling began to melt away the sting of the cold words. He relaxed and wrapped both his arms around her.

"We really know how to hurt each other, don't we?" Valentine observed.

"I'm tired of the hurt. All I see and hear is hurt." Her voice softened, her body welcoming his warmth. "It was all so sentimental, especially the farewell ball at The Citadel. We in our gowns and they in their fine uniforms, gray and gold. Trousers with stripes of red." Ellen snuggled closer. "Seems silly now. Is silly."

"No, it wasn't. It isn't." Valentine countered. "It's the joy of being young. I was there too. Same thing with me in Philadelphia, except I wore blue and gold." Valentine kissed her on her palm. "I can't hate him. You may not believe me, but I'm really not angry, Ellen. Can't be. Can't let myself get angry anymore. I've seen too much hate and too much hurt. There's no room left for any of it anymore. I'm not even jealous, even though you want me to be. I can't be. I don't have the right."

Ellen and Valentine watched the dusking sky. The crisp layer of cold turquoise, splashed with distant white wisps, ringed between the darkening hills and the reign of clouds above. The textured clouds in the west—creamy, swirling, rippled—glowed from orange to red. The farther the clouds spread out away from the setting sun, the more they blended into a gray and drab smoothness. Together they watched the fading brilliance of the sunset.

"You loved him back then. We all were in love back then. The question now is, do you still love him?" Valentine asked, breathing his question into her ear, holding her against him more tightly.

Ellen pressed her head against his chest, "Would you stop asking me that."

"Do you love him?" Valentine persisted.

"What do you want me to say?" Ellen's eyes glowed. Her cheeks reddened. Her hand swept a strand of her raven hair from her cheek. Valentine drew her body toward his. Her face lifted toward his. With open, moist mouths they kissed. Both tightened their arms around each other, refusing to part.

◎◎◎

The dogwoods blossomed in green leaf and delicate flower. The shiny willow branches hung long and full, waving in the breezes of spring. Wildflowers decorated the meadows, disguising the scars of battle.

Once again Nathaniel distracted Ellen's father by debating whether or not the Westminster Standards needed to be revised while she and Valentine went for a ride. Before they returned, Valentine halted the buckboard on the hill overlooking the grove of trees and the Academy. He reached into his coat pocket and removed a small package of green tissue paper. "Ellen, this is for you."

She paled. "No gifts, Valentine. No gifts."

Baffled, he held it out to her. "No, this is for you," he repeated. "This isn't easy for me. I'm not often in this position. Nathaniel is far better the penitent." Valentine pushed the gift toward her. "From me."

"I know very well who it is from. How can I accept this?" She pushed his hand away. "Don't ruin today. It's been so pleasant."

"I thought I understood you, Ellen. Damn, I don't like this lack of control. Look," he demanded as he began unwrapping the tissue paper for her.

"I don't care whether you like it or not." Ellen turned her face away. "I don't want to look. I don't want to know what it is."

"I had my father post it to me from Philadelphia." He ripped back the last of the tissue paper. It was a gold necklace. At the end of the necklace dangled a single, delicate pearl.

Against her own wishes she admired the gift, then pulled her hands against her breasts. "Oh, damn you too, Valentine, why did you have to ruin everything? Why did you have to do this?"

Valentine held the gift out to her. "Because I love you, Ellen," he said in a frank tone. "I don't understand the problem. Because I love you, and because you love me."

"Don't say that, Valentine. Don't you say that." Ellen lowered her clenched hands and pushed his hands away, immediately covering her dry mouth with trembling hands. Her rapid breathing gradually calmed. "It is my own fault, Valentine. You're not to blame," she said precisely, as if another person were talking. "You are not to blame. I am. I let this go on too long." Her hands folded over his hands, which still clutched the necklace. "Valentine, if you really love me, you will respect my wishes. You want to do something good with that? Then sell it and buy some decent clothes for my children. I cannot accept this. I cannot bear enduring another memory."

"Oh, Ellen, you do this all the time. Would you please stop denying yourself good things when they come your way."

"I let this go on far too long. This is what I get for being selfish." She pushed the necklace away and twisted her body away from his. "We should never have kissed."

"What about my love for you?

"It isn't always about you, you know."

ⓞⓞⓞ

Orders from General Grant raced down to Corps. From Corps to Division. Division to Brigade. Brigade to Regiment. Tomorrow they would march. The Reserves began to break camp. Trunks were stored on wagons. Equipment sorted. Weapons cleaned and readied.

Nathaniel entered their tent and found Valentine on his knees packing his gear into his trunk.

"For the last time, Val, you have to come with me."

Valentine, ignoring him, grabbed a blanket and stuffed it inside the trunk.

"Enough sulking. You'll regret it if you don't."

"I'm guaranteed to regret it if I do," he scowled back.

"All I know is that you cannot leave it like this." Nathaniel sat on Valentine's cot. "My God, man, isn't she worth one more visit?"

Valentine slammed shut the lid of the trunk, startling Nathaniel. Nathaniel prepared himself for an assault of his friend's temper but was shocked to look over and see Valentine still kneeling, the elbow of his left arm anchored against the trunk lid, his face pressed into his hand.

On two borrowed horses, they rode the miles to the Academy in silence. Nathaniel waited outside playing with the children while Valentine gained Doctor Atkinson's permission to meet with Ellen in the parlor. He surprised him by permitting it.

"We are finally marching, Ellen. I am disobeying orders even being here. General Grant will not waste this spring. I couldn't leave without seeing you again to say good-bye." Valentine held both her hands in his, fondling the back of her tender hands. "I'm no puppy. No love struck school-boy. I am here to ask you a simple question before I leave, and I'll leave it at that."

Ellen, smothering a chilled swallow, sat next to him on the settee, her hands unresponsive.

"Ellen, I'd like you to have me."

She withdrew her hands from his, folding them onto her lap. "Valentine, I thought we settled that the other week. You know I cannot. You have my answer. No, I won't."

"Listen, I am not here to beg or plead. Neither of us have the time nor temperament for that juvenile nonsense. We are both grown up. And we both, whether you want to admit it or not, are not the kind of people willing to waste life when it comes our way." Valentine spoke calmly and frankly, with neither desperation nor eagerness in his voice. "You try to be the sweet pastor's daughter, but inside you there is passion and excitement and a burning. Ellen, we'd kill each other for sure, but we'd love it. Our problem is that we both like to be in control. Haven't we both learned by now that we aren't?"

She turned her head aside, not wanting him to meet her eyes, not wanting him to see her face. "What of love?" she scoffed. "What is love but keeping our promises? What is love but accepting the barriers that divide us?"

"Nathaniel and I have learnt that in the Army you flank them, breach them, or bridge them. That's what you do with barriers. In surgery, you cut them. You got choices. Yours was a girl's promise. I want the woman. Which, Ellen, is the real promise? I will always love you," he said. "Nothing can take that away, whatever you say or do. Regardless of what might happen to either of us. Listen to me: I know it's not about me. I'm not certain it's even about you. It is something else. It's not as if my love depends on yours. I thought I learned that lesson once before, but now I've learned it for real. That's it. And that's all. No temper. No resentment. I wanted you to hear what I had to say before I had to leave. Certain things need to be said before they can't be."

"I feared you might force me to choose," she whispered. "I guess I didn't trust you. I'm sorry for that. I feared you'd want to make me look at you and tell you that I love Laurence more than you. I'm glad you didn't come here to play that game. Because, you know, I wouldn't have answered you. It wouldn't be fair."

"It wouldn't be fair to him, you mean," observed Valentine, resigned to her sense of duty.

Ellen, with tears streaming down her cheeks, answered: "No, you idiot. It wouldn't be fair to you." With a swirl of satin, she rushed from the room.

Valentine got up from the settee. Tossing a small package wrapped in green tissue paper on the table, he left.

That night, in the dark of the tent, save for the glow of one squat flickering candle, with half of their gear readied and their kit packed, Valentine and Nathaniel rested on their cots. Valentine sipped and Nathaniel smoked.

"You're a lucky man, Nate."

"Sometimes."

"I someday would like what you have, Nate."

"Me too, my friend. I'd like to have what I have."

"How do you manage? Really? How can you stand it, thinking about someone you love with every breath you take?"

"I guess it is what keeps you breathing." Nathaniel then snuffed out the candle flame between his fingers and rubbed off the residue of hot wax.

Come morning, after Valentine had left to oversee sick call, Nathaniel folded and addressed his letter to Alice. He set his pen down next to the bottle of ink. They marched in two hours. He pulled on his heavy coat, left his tent, and, soaking in all the blustery busyness of camp life, dawdled toward Talley's cabin. Tipping his hat to the guard, he knocked on the door. Rupert opened it and invited Nathaniel inside. Talley was standing behind his desk. He and Lieutenant Colonels Stewart and Kauffman were surveying the map of Fauquier County spread out over his desk, the four corners held down by four cups. They glanced up at Nathaniel. Nathaniel walked up to them. Offering Talley a mischievous smirk, he lifted the Colt revolver by its wooden grip from his inside coat pocket and placed it onto the center of the map. "Here, Bill, please get rid of this for me. It's begun to feel too comfortable."

Chapter Seventeen

Flames and Forests

Ah! May the red rose live alway!
To smile upon earth and sky!
Why should the beautiful ever weep?
Why should the beautiful die?
Lending a charm to ev'ry ray
That falls on her cheeks of light,
Giving the zephyr kiss for kiss,
And nursing the dewdrop bright—
Ah! May the red rose live alway,
To smile upon earth and sky!
Why should the beautiful ever weep?
Why should the beautiful die?
"Ah! May the Red Rose Live Alway," Stephen Collins Foster

Seven days ago the Reserves showed scant remorse at giving up the comforts of their lazy winter headquarters at Bristow Station and marching south. None complained about leaving behind the cots, the fireplaces, the cosy and waterproof tents erected on platforms, the fresh spring water, and the regular supplies railroaded from the fat north without incidence or hindrance. Nary a bark nor bite from Mosby. The Regiment was eager, resolved, to march south, for each man knew this campaign meant the final push to Richmond. They could and

273

they would. Grant would see to it. Would it take a month before Richmond would fall and they all could go home? At worst, they hoped, it would take two months.

Their cranky Surgeon was gladdest of all to leave Bristow Station, not because of what lay ahead but because of what he was leaving behind.

Five days ago Captain Bear confided to Nathaniel how Colonel Talley personally petitioned General Crawford for permission for the Reserves to lead whatever advance would be required. Talley chaffed to help end this war before his Reserves mustered out of service this coming June. Their three years enlistment would be up and the Regiment disbanded. As far as Talley was concerned, he had less than two months to personally defeat Lee. He had less than two months to finish the job. He wanted it done. Talley knew they could do it. The Reserves basked in their Colonel's confidence.

This was their springtime. They had earned it. They were fresh. They were restored. They were drilled. They were well fed and well fed up. They had what Lee lacked. Months of resting and recuperating. Months of healing. Months of darning socks and breaking in new shoes. Months of drilling the new recruits and draftees. The supplies—oats, shoes, coal, fruit, munitions, medicines, uniforms—poured forth in abundance from the fields and factories up north and piled up behind them, the way a bend in the river clogs up the flow of hewn timber felled till it is suddenly dislodged and flows downstream to the mill. Yes, by God, the Regiment was honed and ready.

Three days ago their mood was far different from those disappointing, dark months after Gettysburg. For the badger would soon meet a meaner hound in Ulysses S. Grant.

Two days ago they thrilled at the sound of reveille resounding all along the line of encampment. The entire Army of the Potomac had rejoined, reassembled, the drumbeats repeating, reaching a crescendo upon the fields of Culpepper. It was tremendous and exhilarating. It was like the first intoxicating days. But far better than those first days. Then they were green, naive. Now they were weathered, tempered. They had earned their scars. They were ready.

Yesterday the Reserves spotted Grant himself as he witnessed them crest the hill, march down the curving sloping hills, and cross over the wide and lazy Rapidan at Germanna Ford. The pontoon bridge—canvas, wood, and rope—swayed and bounced beneath their methodical footsteps. Grant sat slumped in his saddle, round shouldered and rumpled, scratching his scraggy beard. Grant appeared shorter and dowdier than they thought he should.

Into the woods and thickets they had marched. Few would admit how intimidated they were by the ominous beauty of this encroaching wilderness. The wildflowers of spring blossomed in an array of bright colors. Patches of azaleas bloomed in petals of startling red and white. Wild roses bloomed a deep red. Leaves sprouted in bright jade, widening to the sun, opening toward the light. The flowers invited them deeper into this wilderness, even as the dark, thick, forest beyond the meadows and turnpikes disturbed them. Within the tangled forest, thick with decaying leaves, beyond the flowers, Lee's army lay entrenched, snug behind breastwork and timber.

The First Brigade ventured forward to Parker's Store. They were the bait. The First Reserves were deployed to the left of the line. A detail of twenty men, two from each company, reconnoitered up Plank Road through the woods, but they advanced too far, recklessly entering an open field. To an entrenched enemy they became quick and easy prey. A fusillade erupted from the opposite trees. Isaac fell first, his skull skimmed by minie ball. A brush fire seared him. Luckily, he and most of the others were dragged to safety as the detail retreated, then stampeded, with the enemy fierce on their heels. Hundreds from the Brigade were captured.

Then the fires ignited. At bivouac near the Lacy farm the Regiment watched the eerie glow ascending beyond the trees against the backdrop of sky.

That morning the Reserves were supposed to occupy a position in the center of line. At 8 AM the whole front assailed the enemy. But the Rebels held their ground. Again a reconnaissance. The enemy again was met in force. But battle was nearly impossible. Killing, however, was possible, as pockets of lost soldiers ran into other pockets of lost soldiers within these dense, smoky woods. The flames attacked everyone regardless of the color of their uniform. That morning the impossible yielded to the improbable. The improbable became normal.

They had absolutely no idea where they were. They were lost.

"Weren't we in the rear?" questioned Nathaniel aloud, his words punctuated by a solitary roar of distant cannon fire and an enfilade of musket fire. The fierce explosions were followed by the popping of erratic, independent fire.

"We were at the rear, now it sounds as if we're at the front," Valentine shouted back as he threw the lid of the pannier shut and secured it.

"Difficult getting bearings. Everything is crashing around us. All I see are trees and smoke." Nathaniel suddenly yelled in alarm. "And flame. Look!"

Valentine squinted into the direction Nathaniel pointed. "God help us," he exhaled. "Come on, the fire is moving our way, we've got to move the men." Valentine barked his orders to the Steward, orderlies, and wounded. "Pack up what we need. Forget the cots. Get the men in! Now!"

From the small clearing, the caravan of the two ambulances and their escort of walking wounded quickly lurched down the cart path to the right, away from the onrush of flames.

The fury of gunfire intensified to their left. Nathaniel cupped his ear and listened. It was all small arms fire. Few cannons had been heard since early afternoon. Artillery was useless here. Who knew where anybody was anyway? No coordination. A battle from tree trunk to tree trunk.

Somewhere, Nathaniel assumed, someone must know where the lines are. But all of the fighting they've listened to had been small bands raging against each other in the ravaging underbrush. Battle by sound. Moving from rifle pit to log breastwork to cart path to tall grass to tangles of branches. Accidental combat can become the cruelest, for it usually meant hand-to-hand. To their left the whirlwind of fire and the crack of musketry and crashing trees drew closer. It was near, very near. Man fought man inside a furnace with the iron trap thrown shut and latched. As much as they fought each other, they fought the incendiary panic of this smothering, licking, searing inferno.

"Christ!" cussed Valentine as one of the orderlies pointed at the flames blocking their way. The cart path had narrowed to the point where the branches clawed at the canvas tops and the

277

tree trunks pinched the wagons. The mules, blindfolded, smelled the danger and started bucking, kicking, wrestling against the livery. In this forest, on this path, the ambulances simply could not turn around. Even if they could, they would only be heading back into more fire and flame. The caravan was trapped on three sides.

Chaplain and the Surgeon instantly surveyed the number of the wounded packed up inside the wagons or collapsed in pain on the woodcutters' path. They shook their heads at each other, coolly aware of the decision they must make. They would make the decision together. Nathaniel tightened his jaw and said aloud first what had to be said, "Have to. No choice." Nathaniel yelled to the Steward driving the first wagon, "Unhitch the mules and let them go. Don't let them trample the men." He looked down at his dirty and worn boots and mumbled to himself: "Always comes to this. It always comes down to us walking our way out."

Isaac tried to crawl out the back of the ambulance. Unable to lower himself, he tumbled to the ground.

"Isaac, can you walk? You must walk. Crawl if you have to! If you can't you're going to get left behind," Nathaniel shouted into Isaac's bandaged face, trying to keep him alert. The opium had taken effect. He dragged Isaac to his feet. Isaac curled his blackened hands up against his chest.

Valentine hastily counted those who likely would die from their wounds anyway. If they could not walk they must be abandoned, left behind. Five of them, thank God, were unconscious and would stay that way. Two, however, were not.

Valentine led the band into the woods. Nathaniel dragged young Isaac, his feet struggling to catch up to the pace. As they plunged into the woods on their right, the two men who had been left behind in the ambulance wagon shrieked after them, begging with what conscious strength they had remaining. "You can't leave us. Please, chaplain, in the name of God! Save us!" One continued his hopeless begging while the other screamed venomous curses.

Nathaniel dragged Isaac farther into brambles already beaten down by the stampeding mules. "God forgive us. God forgive us." An accusing image of Mrs. Reynolds rocking in front of her fireplace, holding a letter in her lap, flashed through Nathaniel's mind. A branch bent forward by the man climbing through the brush in front of him slapped his cheek, stinging him back into focus. He didn't notice the blood trickling from his cheek.

"Faster, faster," Valentine urged. But fast was impossible through the thick timber and ragged underbrush. They moved too slowly, close enough to be able to hear the men's begging and cursing turn into screams of agony as the blazing branches about them crashed and the ambulances burned.

Everywhere they stepped the hazy odor of burning flesh mingled with soot. Dark, ugly smoke hung as heavy as syrup, soiling skin and soul. The thick haze gradually descended, enveloping them, choking them, stinging their eyes. They coughed and hacked. They tied bandages around their mouths and noses and pulled their caps and hats low. They moved faster through an area of the woods already burnt. Soot billowed up with every step, covering their shoes and cuffs. An assortment of cadavers still simmered. Bayonets and tin cups lay near what was left of the cadaver's hands as they had tried and failed to dig trenches and hide. Delicate smoke spiraled from smoldering embers. Smoke and ash. Ashes.

Nathaniel pulled Isaac's bandanna up from his mouth and tried to give him a drink from his canteen. A lost Valentine and an equally lost Nathaniel let the men rest before they again guided their own lost, injured, bleeding, crippled refugees through this wilderness. It didn't matter anymore that they were lost. All they had to do was flee.

"Let's go," Valeninte yelled at them. "No time!" He pointed to where the smoke hung highest. "That way." The strongest men pushed in front, using their muskets to clear what path they might. This small band of the desperate, each hunched over to avoid the hovering smoke, stumbled though the crush of thicket and bramble. Finally, breathing relief, they broke through a green hedgerow and tumbled into a clearing.

A Confederate Major, his face pale behind dirt and soot, stepped forward, his hand on his sword hilt. "Gentlemen, welcome." he drawled with a North Carolinian accent. "Major Gibson, at your service."

Dozens of British Enfields pointed at them from the shoulders and hips of similarly dirty men. Dozens of other soldiers dressed in gray, butternut, and grime sat cross-legged on the ground, their rifles resting across their laps, casually interested in this accidental capture.

"Oh shit," Nathaniel blurted.

O'Rourke rocked back on his heels and stared at him, bemused.

Within a half hour they found their small band herded into a crowded procession of a hundred other Federal prisoners tramping methodically down a dirt turnpike toward Guinney's Station. Isaac leaned against Nathaniel as they stumbled together, Isaac's blackened hands still curled up against his chest. Nathaniel reached into his waistcoat pocket and pulled out the last of the opium pills he had been saving. He placed the pill in Isaac's mouth and helped him swallow it by holding his canteen to his cracked and bleeding lips. Isaac welcomed the last of the water.

On the far side of Salem Church a large mass of soldiers in dark blue and light blue uniforms squatted down or reclined in the middle of a trampled field, the fight in them spent. Confederate soldiers idled about in small pockets guarding this herd of exhausted prisoners.

"Goddamn, what's that smell?" cried out one of the Privates.

Sniffing, Valentine knew what was coming.

As they were marched past Salem Church, Nathaniel nudged the Private. "That's what smells so foul." They didn't want to look but they couldn't help but look. It was a fetid pile of limbs beneath one of the church windows. A sow and her piglets rooted among them. One little piglet rested serene. Her snout rested on top of the soft tissue of a man's white arm.

Valentine wiped his brow with his handkerchief and held it over his nose, "Holy Mother of God, it's worse than Gettysburg."

O'Rourke and McKenna tried to keep their cluster of men compact. "To me, to me," Valentine kept calling out. Several were lost in the commotion however, having pushed too far forward or straggled too far behind.

The mob of prisoners parted around them until they there was no more room to press forward. "Stop here and let's rest for a second," Valentine announced, taking Isaac from Nathaniel's arms and lowering him to the ground. "Guess we've arrived," Valentine said. Valentine knelt besides Isaac and adjusted the bandage on his head. One of the musicians, a young fifer named John Moore, peered up at Nathaniel who remained standing, trying to scout the crowd of prisoners, searching for familiar faces. The musician tugged on Nathaniel's pant leg and asked: "Chaplain, what's next?"

Nathaniel didn't bother looking down as he answered the young man. "Wish I knew, Moore." Nathaniel wiped his bleeding cheek with his palm. He noticed a Confederate patrol approaching in their direction from the other side of the church. With a gulp of apprehension, he squatted down next to Moore. "We'll be just fine," he said. "At least there is no more walking, and, thank God, we're out of the fire," he reassured them, patting the young man on the back. "You did great, John. All of you did. That's all we can ask."

The musician sighed. "Never thought it could be this bad."

"Who did? Who of us did?" Nathaniel confessed as he sat down on the ground and stretched out his legs and swollen feet. "Looks like we're out of it for a while though. Finished for us."

"What's that?" asked the Steward, noticing a commotion among a cluster of prisoners a stone's throw from them.

Nathaniel stood up to look. "Something's up. See the Reb patrol. Looks like a half dozen of our boys are being rounded up for something." The Steward and he watched as the Confederate patrol led six men across the field, beyond sight. Mintues later, gunfire echoed from that direction. After about thirty minutes, dark smoke rose from behind the barren hill. After another fifteen minutes the selected men were returned, ashen faced. They blended into the crowd of blue prisoners. One of them sat near where Nathaniel, Valentine, and their pocket of men rested.

His buddy gestured toward him. "Willie, boy, what was 'dat all 'bout?"

"Don' want to talk about it, Joe," Willie said.

"Come on, soldier," a Sergeant urged. "We all heard the gunfire"

"Damn it all. 'Dey killed a bunch of niggers. Our boys. Blue-boys. White officer too. Right between 'de eyes. Niggers, well, they gut shot 'dem to make 'em squeal like stuck pigs. I don' want'a talk 'bout it no mo'."

"Spit it out, soldier. We need to know," said a Captain.

"'Dat's it. Shot 'dem and made us stack 'dem and burn 'dem with ker'sene. 'Dey Rebs didn't want to touch 'dem niggers. Damn, it all, I'm sure 'dey want'd us to see it."

"Willie, you jes' shut up now," instructed Joe. "As fer as yer concerned, you ain't never seen nothin'. Fer yer own health, fergit it. D'hear me? Fergit it ever happen'd. It never happen'd, b'Gawd."

The whole group around them shut up the moment they spotted a Confederate Steward heading in the direction of their section, him determining which prisoners were dead and which ones soon would die. Several armed guards followed the Rebel Steward, swarming over the dead and dying, looting the casualties. Other guards arrived, like vultures drawn to carrion, and they roughly selected men from the crowd of prisoners and searched them, looting not only whatever coins or food or tobacco they could find on them, but in many cases their shoes, belts, and other articles of clothing.

It's not piracy so much as necessity, Nathaniel strained to rationalize to himself, still hoping for a touch of humanity in the midst of all this. There hadn't been a decent pair of shoes on the feet of any of the Confederates he had met lately. From all the Rebel prisoners he'd seen these last months, there wasn't one matching uniform in the entire Rebel army. It's been an Army surviving by scavenging.

A young barefoot boy shuffled up to Isaac. The young Confederate lad looked vacantly at Nathaniel. Nathaniel implored with a shake of his head. He mouthed one word: "Don't."

Without a reply of either boastful taunt or glint of charity, without altering his weary expression, the young barefoot boy began to pull Isaac's shoes off, followed by removing Isaac's trousers. Isaac covered his face and tried to roll over, exposing his naked backside, his thin white legs drawn up toward his chest as he tried to hide himself. He groaned from the pain and whimpered from the shame. The young boy immediately put everything on, pulling the new trousers over his own tattered pair.

A tall and gaunt Rebel Captain, his long, oily hair hanging from his gray slouch hat, sauntered from around the corner of the Salem Church toward the mass of prisoners. He was followed by a Corporal and six Privates. The Corporal was a short but massive hulk of a man, his fat, thick neck supporting a huge head. A dirty eye-patch covered his right eye. The Captain cupped his hands to his mouth and announced to all the prisoners: "Officers to my left. Enlisted men and non-commissioned officers yonder to my right. Now, move, you sons of bitches!"

"Nate," Valentine whispered, "right now you listen to me. Don't you give me any of your crap. This time you consider yourself an officer. The men will be fine with the Steward." Valentine rapidly whispered instructions into the Steward's ear, who nodded with an academic resignation.

"You go, chaplain, you go." urged the Steward. "You can't help us anymore – you do what he says."

Valentine grabbed Nathaniel's arm and pulled him off to the left side, clustering among the handful of Union officers. As the Captain retired toward the church, the six Rebel soldiers approached the officers, the ugly brute of a Corporal with a neck as thick as a bull leading them. He poked Valentine in the chest with a stubby finger: "Yaw'l th' Surgeon?"

"What do you want cut off?"

The Corporal snarled as he snorted over his shoulder: "Don' touch this cute'n." He slapped his paw on Valentine's arm. "They wan' ya'. They's a fetchin' all th' Surgeons they can git. You've jest enlisted. They sen' us to tell ya' to git your sorry blue ass over'n there ta' th' church."

Valentine swept the man's fat hand off his arm then turned and reached to shake Nathaniel's hand. "Looks like I've just switched Armies. Ellen might appreciate the irony. Please try to explain it to my father."

Nathaniel pulled off his hat and shook his head. "I will if I get the chance myself. You be good, my friend."

"You too." Valentine looked into the sky. "It's been one hell of a walk."

The Corporal, fed up with being ignored, turned toward Nathaniel. "Nice boots, parson. Preacher don' needs no nice boots, do he? Too nice for a preacher, don' ya' thin', Bill?" He moved toward Nathaniel. "Yaw'l won' a be needin' them." The Corporal's one squinty eye fastened on Nathaniel's watch chain. His fat fingers fondled the blue cameo and he began to lift the watch from his waistcoat pocket. "Sho'nuf' there's'n a dandy prize. Look'e'ere."

"No!" exploded Nathaniel. The mass of prisoners turned to find where this defiant yell came from.

With a strength erupting from a churning bellyful of fury and festering frustration, he wrenched himself away from the massive Corporal, swinging his fists fiercely, savagely, catching the Corporal square in his flat face, sending him reeling. The Privates jumped at him. Nathaniel slugged two more, one with the full force of his forearm breaking a Rebel's nose, before they were able to tackle him and tumble with him onto the ground, rolling on top of him in a heap, finally pinning him to ground. He squirmed and kicked.

It took four men to subdue him. The Corporal knelt full square on his chest as two others knelt on his struggling arms. The fourth soldier tried to take off his boots. Nathaniel kicked him in the temple with the heel of his boot. The man flew sideways. Two other soldiers rushed up and grabbed his kicking legs as they wrestled his boots off his feet.

"Bastard preacher," the Corporal spat, spraying blood and tobacco juice into Nathaniel's face, wiping his bloody nose with the back of his gray sleeve.

Valentine, restrained by the other two soldiers, cheered Nathaniel: "Atta' boy, Nate! Knew you had it in you! They didn't count on that Scotch Presbyterian temper! Wilder than the Irish!"

"Shut up." A solder jabbed Valentine in the kidney with his fist, doubling him over with a painful wince.

A harsh, strident voice exploded from behind them as loud as the blast of a Napoleon cannon, stunning them all. "Leave that man be!"

"Goddamn, it's Old Baldy!" the Corporal swore to the others. The Rebels immediately released Nathaniel, struggled to attention, and saluted the officer who glowered down at them from his tall, snorting horse.

Nathaniel looked up from the ground at the sight of this man. The man was bent, harried looking, with a huge beak nose sticking out from his face. Nathaniel noticed his wooden leg stuck in the stirrup.

The Lieutenant General cocked his head to the side. "Are you Presbyterian, sir?"

"Ah-huh, I am." Nathaniel grunted, his seething breaths slackening. He wiped the spit, juice, and blood from his face with his handkerchief as he stood up. "Princeton Seminary, class of '53."

The Lieutenant General removed his campaign cap, exposing his sweaty, bald head. He rested his other hand on the pommel of his saddle. As he smiled broadly, he swept his campaign cap in a gallant arc. "I thank you, Reverend for the exhibition. This is first time in months I've been able to enjoy myself ever since Chancellorsville." The Lieutenant General lifted himself in his saddle, then offered a courteous bow. "In tribute to another rather feisty Presbyterian of my dear acquaintance, you may keep your watch, sir." The bald General pointed a long bony finger at the Corporal. "Do you hear me, Corporal?"

The Corporal, fuming, bowed his head and wiped his nose. "Yas'sir."

The Lieutenant General looked down at Nathaniel's stocking feet. "The boots, alas, shall be considered a prize of war."

The very instant the Lieutenant General returned his campaign cap to his bald head his face lost its smile and resumed its creased look of sorrow and age. "God's blessings,

Reverend," he said with a somber sincerity as he wheeled his horse.

The Rebel with the broken nose bent toward the Corporal. "Wha' Old Baldy mean?"

The Corporal spat. "Jackson, ya' ass. Jackson."

Chapter Eighteen

Welcome to Libby

I know a breast that once was light
Whose patient sufferings need my care,
I know a hearth that once was bright
But drooping hopes have nestled there.
Then while the tear drops rightly steal
From wounded hearts that I shall heal,
Though boon companions may ye be—
Oh, comrades, fill no glass for me.
"Oh, Comrades, Fill No Glass For Me," Foster

W elcome to your new parish," an effusively cheerful Commandant Turner greeted a dusty, sweaty, and exhausted Nathaniel. His ears felt clogged, his hip hurt, his head stuffed. The Federal officers, most close to collapsing from the heat and miles, waited in the dirt lot in a long idle line for their turn at the clerk's table. Earlier that day, after they had arrived by train at the depot, the officers were marched through Richmond toward Libby Prison while the enlisted men were forced to march in a separate column toward Belle Isle.

Nathaniel worried about them, especially Isaac. They had heard the rumors. The enlisted men, rather than the officers, were likelier to be beaten. They would be robbed of what little they possessed. The enlisted men would be herded into a camp on an open field of the island, barricaded by fence, bayonet, brutality, and bullet. There would be no medical care. They would be left to fend for themselves, abandoned to survive as best they could. Officers rarely suffered such indignities. Libby Prison even boasted sinks and running water connected to the city pipes. Libby boasted a hospital. Libby afforded the luxury of a roof, even coal stoves. Of course, finding coal was another matter.

Nathaniel squinted toward the James River and the distant Belle Isle. "Isaac will not be as fortunate," he berated himself, ignoring Commandant Turner. "I should have stayed with him." With a grimace he looked down at his feet, now shod in shoes with torn soles and missing shoelaces. They were much too small for his feet, proved by the bleeding blisters.

Turner traced the movement of the chaplain's puffy eyes. "We shall see if we can find you a better pair of shoes," Turner chattered on, acting as if this were a cordial afternoon tea party. "We have several local pastors who offer their services as chaplains here, all volunteers tending to the men's spiritual needs. I shall look forward to introducing you to them. They will look forward to conversing with you, I have no doubt. You Reverends do help keep our community content. Though not all seek your services, do they? I was there when they hanged John Brown. Yes, I was. I was one of the cadets privileged to be present. Strange, as I recall. For such an avowedly religious man, he rejected all offers of spiritual solace. Then we stretched his scrawny neck. I suspect it was not his God whom he met." Commandant Turner whistled a light tune before continuing. "Yes, we like them docile. Whatever you should need by way of books or writing material, they, I am sure, will be happy to oblige you. A matter of professional courtesy. We haven't had the pleasure of welcoming many clergyman to our, 'um, to our facility."

"Paper, yes, that would be nice," Nathaniel finally replied, forcing himself to acknowledge Turner. "Very helpful."

Above Nathaniel loomed the imposing warehouse called Libby Prison. To his right, across 20th street, the wall tents of the guards sat in narrow rows. The gentle slope of the street led downward toward the canal, which was separated from the James River by a hardened tow path. The sign of the building's previous occupant, reflecting a more prosperous and kinder day, still hung at the near corner: 'Libby & Son, Ship Chandlers & Grocers.' Nathaniel was intrigued. While Turner chattered on, he mused pensively. What is the origin of 'chandler'? In his mind, he played the etymology game. Chandler. Chandelier. Chandlery. Candles. Yes, that's where it comes from, the Latin for candle: 'candela.' Candle sellers. Yes, of course.

The brick warehouse stood three stories on this side. Four stories must face the river, he guessed, given the degree of the road's gradient. The former Libby & Son warehouse, formed of three separate buildings built up against each other and connected inside, reached almost three times as long and twice as high as his sanctuary back home. Libby Prison itself, except for these several vacant lots, sat like a dowager tenement among a clutter of shoddy buildings.

He counted the iron bars on the open windows: seven vertical bars riveted onto the one middle horizontal bar. Nathaniel counted the windows: fifteen across the full length of the old warehouse, seven on the side. Several gaunt faces, half hidden in the shadows, gazed down from these windows at the newest batch of prisoners. Thank God, windows, he privately thanked. Nathaniel chilled at the prospect of being caged, confined, in a building bereft of windows. He knew he couldn't stand it if there were no windows. He'd suffocate. Couldn't stand being trapped in darkness again.

Commandant Turner continued talking despite Nathaniel's visible lack of interest. "We have been busy in recent days with you bluebirds, as one of our local newspapers has named you: 'our spring crop of Yankee blue birds'. The newspaper believes what happens here is of some interest to the citizens of Richmond. Just last month, to think, we were nearly empty. Ah, what ill timing. So sorry. Pity you men, now that your Grant has suspended all exchanges. Now that Mosby and McNeal seem quite active up north with their forays I suppose we shall soon be full again with new tenants. Unless of course we can thin you all out. We might possibly send some of you to Macon."

Nathaniel's belly wanted food, his feet ached for a chair, and his brain wanted this man to shut up. He didn't need to listen to a speech. "Forgive me, Major," he said as he stepped two paces toward the Commandant. It wasn't a wise move. Turner's Adjutant jumped at Nathaniel and pistol whipped him across the face. Nathaniel collapsed and grabbed his face, blood spurting from where the front sight of the LeMat revolver gouged him below the eye. His cheek felt fractured. The Adjutant stepped back grinning. It was rare day he got to hit a preacher.

It was Turner's turn to ignore the preacher who writhed on the ground at his feet. Turner signaled his Adjutant. "Dick, do take care of things here," he said before he strolled blithely back toward his office.

The Adjutant shouted the command calling the prisoners to attention. "M'name is Dick Turner," he crowed. "The

Commandant'n I may have the same las' names but we're very differen' men. He cares for you lik'n' your own pappy. I don' give a rat's ass about 'eny of you. I've been put on earth to make your lives a livin' hell." Dick Turner strutted in front of them. Turner reminded all the new prisoners of the Commandment's standing order. "You men – I tells this to you once. Anyone standin' at a window is li'ble to be shot. 'Eny clothes hung on the bars to dry will be confiscated. Any attemp' at sendin'messages by code will resul' in severe punishment. We don' give a tinker's damn between Generals, lowly Lieutenants, 'er fer that matter'n, preachers," he boasted with a smirk. "Ross, sign 'em in. 'Member, Erasmus, I wan' details."

As he spoke to his clerk, Eramus Ross, one of the guards swiftly raised his musket to his shoulder and fired a shot toward a face staring out from the top floor window.

"You clipped 'em real good," complimented another guard.

The man laughed. "Glory, like ducks on the wing."

◎◎◎

Two weeks later, with Nathaniel's cheek still swollen and blackened, O'Rourke finally arrived at Libby. He was driven to the front door in a fringed buggy, escorted by an elderly gentleman and, as rumors throughout the prison had it, a lovely young woman who was neither the elderly gentleman's daughter nor wife. Within the first hour of Valentine's arrival, Major Parkhill slapped Valentine across his cheek with his glove. Parkhill had taken offense at being compared to a certain portion of the human anatomy. Valentine had taken the greater offense at Parkhill's bloody rude attempt to confiscate a well earned flask of bourbon whisky presented to Valentine in Spotsylvania by a grateful Confederate colleague, indeed, the very same gentleman who chauffeured him to the prison. Parkhill slapped Valentine a second time. Valentine slugged Parkhill out cold. Valentine wound up in one of the condemned cells located in the middle cellar. Nathaniel's reunion with Valentine got postponed.

But postponed for only two days. Commandant Turner ordered an early release, canceling the full sentence of his punishment. The Surgeon's services at the prison hospital were required. With over 600 men sick and wounded throughout the prison, and only room enough for a quarter that number in the hospital, his skills once again were conscripted. Surgeon John Wilkins, medical officer in charge of the hospital, had heard from the clerk that a skilled Surgeon had arrived. Wilkins immediately requested that Turner put Valentine under his authority. O'Rourke would also be responsible to Doctor George Semple, one of the Confederate contract Surgeons from Portsmouth.

"With the exchange cartel ending, I am convinced the situation in the hospital will only worsen," Wilkins pleaded with an irritated Turner. "Mark my word," Wilkins warned, "there's only going to be more crowding. More wounded. More blood poison. More disease. More deaths. Do you want that on your record? We need his help. We need help anyone else can give."

"You surely know how to make an entrance," Nathaniel said when Valentine entered the room to a round of applause offered up by the prisoners. Valentine bowed to the room. "No doubt it's that lovely Irish charm of yours." The two men embraced. Valentine smelled of blood, mildew, and stale urine.

"He's a jackass of a Quartermaster," snarled Valentine. "Hell, it was his own fault. But I'll confess to you, Nate, I appreciated my little vacation downstairs in the cellar. The accommodations could have been better but at least it gave me two solitary, peaceful days. Well, except for the damn Carpenter hammering all morning. For the first time in weeks, I slept well. Hell, first time in weeks I had the chance to sleep. Slugging Parkhill was pure bonus. I refuse to let him make me a temperance man." Valentine scratched the stubble on his cheek. He threw his bag next to Nathaniel's feet and sat down on the floor. "To be honest, Nate, it made Dante's inferno seem like paradise. Worse than anything you preachers can conjure. Since Wilderness and then Spotsylvania, I never got more than three hours of rest. None of us got any rest." Valentine scootched his butt over and leaned against the stairwell. "It was the worst I've seen, Nate. The worst. I really can't talk about it."

Given the pain creased into his friend's face, Nathaniel didn't press. His friend's uniform was worse than he'd ever seen it. Blood had stained the front from him wiping his hands on it. "Well, welcome to Libby Val. This is not exactly how I imagined we'd arrive at Richmond," he chuckled awkwardly. "The wharf rats are tasty. You'll like them, especially with a touch of pepper. We'll feed you right." Nathaniel reached down and patted a thin Valentine on his stomach. "Looks like you could use a good meal. Besides acorns and goobers, what were they feeding you traitors in the Rebel army?"

"You should talk. I haven't seen you this skinny since your first year at University. 'Who is this stick?' I asked when I saw you arriving with all your mounds of baggage in tow." With a yawn, he stretched. "Alice will never recognize you."

"You learn quick to ignore the hunger. Though I must admit, I would die for a plate of Alice's fried brown trout."

Valentine reached out with his fingers and gently touched Nathaniel's cheek, still badly bruised, the scar mostly healed over. "And you want to tell me about this?"

"Not really. It's still tender. Well, I guess I wasn't respectful enough. They like you submissive here. Two things you need to know: stay away from the windows and don't try to escape. Any attempts and Turner—Commandant Turner that is— promises to blow this place up."

"What? Come on, you're joking."

"Honest. Remember back in February? The news accounts of Rose's escape? Dug a tunnel from the cellar beneath the hospital to the tobacco warehouse next door. Half of the hundred who escaped succeeded in making it to our lines. Made Turner look real bad. That man doesn't like looking bad. Thinks he should have been promoted to something a little more respectable than prison guard. So they had the rest of the prisoners fill in the tunnel. Then they stacked in the middle cellar casks of gunpowder. That's where you were—the cells for the condemned. But aren't we all now? Condemned that is. I seriously doubt Richmond approved it. Turner must imagine all five thousand of us would escape and rape their women and bash their children to death. Wouldn't look good on his record if that happened. War is such a lovely invention. Brings out our best. Honest, Val, we're sitting on a bloody mine. Any more attempts and he'll blow it. Of that I have no doubts. Kept things quiet here ever since."

"Hmmm…gunpowder, you say? Where again?"

"The middle cellar."

"Is that what all those barrels were? Was hoping they were beer. What's right below the hospital floor?"

"That's the rat cellar. East side of the building."

A sardonic and rueful grin creased Valentine's face.

"That Dick Turner is a sadistic little bastard," warned Nathaniel. "Both Turners are. But our prig of a Commandant does it to you smiling and only when it makes him look good. He's a glib prick. Now, Dick Turner? He enjoys it. That man's a rabid weasel. Men are known to go disappearing. That's the rumors. More than rumors. Since I've got more run of the place than most, I'm pretty sure it's true. Men disappear. I've seen that bugger kick a man out of his cot simply for not standing when he entered the room and then he cracked his skull with his boot. I tried to tell him that the man couldn't stand because he had a broken leg. I was lucky he didn't beat the crap out of me." Nathaniel reached into his waistcoat pocket and removed his pocket watch. He caressed the silver case between his palms, the cameo dangling.

"You don't let that tarnish do you? So, you've been able to keep it. Good for you, Nate." Valentine tugged on Nathaniel's sleeve. "Let me see them again."

Nathaniel pressed the catch.

"I bet your Margaret is looking more and more like Alice every day."

Nathaniel stared at the painting of his daughters for several minutes before handing the open watch to Valentine, who held the painting up to the setting sunlight dimly shining through the window behind them.

"Her last letter said Penelope was beginning to learn to read."

"You'll see them again." he promised, closing the watch and handing it back to Nathaniel.

"The torture of it is not knowing how they are doing. Not hearing from them. Not being able to tell them I'm all right. They must be terrified. Inconsolable. They probably haven't even heard we were captured. I cannot imagine how Alice is feeling. It's bad enough for me not having even one of her old letters to read, but for her not to know if I am dead or alive..." Do you think Talley would have written telling her I am among the missing? Do you think?"

"I don't know, Nate. I doubt he had the time. Maybe Rupert did."

"Yeah, but what would be worse: getting a letter telling her I'm missing or no information at all? God, I hate this. I hate being so cut off." Nathaniel pulled on his mustache. "There are times I cannot stand it."

"I've begun to know what you've been feeling."

With the closed watch held in his palm, Nathaniel flipped the chain and caught the light blue cameo on his forearm. Several officers shuffled near, stopped, and, like tourists visiting a zoo, stared at them. One of them carried a small box. The officers appeared as nervous as hens, afraid someone was about to jump out at them and steal their box. Nathaniel nodded affably toward them as they padded on. "Evening Roland. William. How's the leg today, Art?" He returned the precious timepiece to his pocket, then bent toward Valentine and said with quiet assurance: "Don't worry, Val, I'll be fine." His voice turned stronger. "We will be fine." His voice lowered again to a whisper. "It not you or me—it's them I'm worried about."

The officers sped up and shuffled toward a vacant corner, sat cross legged on the floor, and set up a chess board on the box.

"You use to be fairly good at chess, right Valentine?" said Nathaniel, nodding toward them. "You had some talent as I recall. You beat me once or twice. Well, just once."

"I could castle with the best of them, but Mother Mary, what a boring game. Takes too long."

"You got plenty of time now. You could get yourself into one of the tournaments. Chess is popular, though remembering which piece is which requires concentration. A button for a pawn, a cork for the Queen."

Valentine traced his finger between two planks that formed one of the stairway steps, scraping out the dirt with his fingernail. "I have a funny feeling I'm not going to have much time for games. I just came from the hospital. Wilkins promises to keep me occupied." He pointed at the chess players. "These fellows may get bored in this miserable place but I doubt you and I will have that luxury."

"I've got to rest," said Nathaniel. "Let me slide on down there." Nathaniel lowered himself to the floor and, with his back against the wall, stretched out his legs. "I am so glad you ended up here. Love it. We're packed into cattle cars and you arrive by fringed buggy. That's the trick I've discovered. You got to find a way. It's not what most people would call luck. It's not. I don't believe in luck. It's something else. Can't really explain it. It's why you always end up arriving in a buggy."

"Not always. Don't forget, that fancy carriage brought me to this damn stinking prison." Valentine shook his head. He picked dirt from under his fingernails. "No, Nate, I'll do what I have to. I'd grin and dance my way all the way to the gallows if

I had to. But you, you're the one with Alice. You're the one who didn't have join up. I joined up because I thought it would be a lark. Yeah, I do what I have to, but you, my foolish friend; you'll do what you don't have to."

"Some might think that. Yet, don't forget, that same carriage also brought you to these men who need you. Men who will require everything you have to give. And you know that. You, you old liar, just don't like admitting that you know that. Listen, you got to believe what I'm about to say. You got to clear out cobweb thinking." Nathaniel again gestured toward the three officers playing chess. "You got to get your mind around it or it will get you. You might not want to hear this, but the real villain in this place is spiritual. It's a spiritual battle here."

"Nothing spiritual about that Dick Turner. Or his thugs. Abandon all hope ye who enter here," quoted Valentine.

"Cute, so let me be your Virgil. Listen up. Most of these men have always been surrounded by wealth and power, men of prominence and privilege. Yet here they are. Caged. Humbled. They've lost everything." Nathaniel coughed and cleared his throat. "Look at Roland there. Eight weeks ago he was Major Seward. He was important. Now he's nothing. He pads around here scared and wounded, even if he's not bleeding. You and I, Val, we're used to it. They're not. Some of these men act as if they're still on the parade ground. Some manage. One General has proved quite adept at the harmonica. One Lieutenant saved his fiddle from confiscation when he got shipped in from Fort Pillow. Wait till you hear him play. Wait till you see the dances. Regular cotillions. Always is interesting to notice who leads."

Valentine rolled his eyes.

"And we have a Colonel, formerly a Professor of Rhetoric at Yale—'ah, there he is." Nathaniel pointed out a large man washing a pair of woolen socks in the sink. "He has proved most adept as cook for our mess. Great with rats. Brother, can he fillet them quick. Although now that you're here, we have an expert."

Valentine punched Nathaniel in the arm.

"Oh well, thought you might like a job." Nathaniel tilted against Valentine and pointed toward a Major seated in the corner. The Major buffed his brass buttons with a remnant of a tattered epaulet. "Though some find it difficult to be humble." Nathaniel inclined closer toward his friend. "I confess my own pride, which I fear has been a little swelled at times, has begun to mellow this last year. I don't think either of us are the same anymore. How can we be? You soak in this cask long enough and you sure get distilled."

"I'd rather soak right now in another kind of cask," Valentine sighed, then slapped his friend's knees. "Lighten up, Nate. You get too bloody serious at times. Stop preaching. Let's get back to that cask. Wish we could. Damn that Parkhill! He's going to make me sign the pledge."

"Oh, some of the guards might prove useful, especially those who hate Dick Turner. Semple is a decent sort, though unlikely to break rules even for you." Nathaniel stretched his arms. His attempt to breathe deep was interrupted by a hacking cough. After wiping his mouth with his sleeve, he locked the fingers of his two hands and brought his hands behind his head. He settled against the stairwell beam. "So tell me, what's going on out there? What did you hear? What of the men?"

"Nothing individually. Lost track of them all. All I saw were legs and arms. Never a face. But you'll like this, Nate—switching armies makes it easy to get news. Talley, it seems, took over for McCandless. McCandless got himself wounded. Not sure how bad. So Crawford pulled up Talley. Hell, all the Rebs know our plans before we do. Of course the next day, as I hear tell, the fool got himself captured by Ewell himself. We met Ewell, remember? He replaced General Jackson. That day you beat up the entire Rebel Army. You went wild."

Nathaniel coughed again, raising up a wad of phlegm as thick as a handful of oysters. "I remember. Wish I had my boots back. So, Talley will be heading here?"

"The man leads a charmed life, unlike us. The good Colonel got reprieved. Seems the next day Sheridan's Cavalry discovered the whole bunch of them being led away. Sheridan got to them before they boarded them up and shipped them here. Missed me however. I was still at that hellhole of a church. The one with all the pigs. So Talley got rescued and sent back to duty. Promoted, I hear tell, if Southern dispatches are accurate. Usually more accurate than our own."

"Glad for that. Glad for him. He'd hate it here." Nathaniel chuckled with a wince from the ache in his cheek, then coughed again, smothering it, attempting to keep the cough contained in his chest. "Not to mention, Bill would really hate being stuck with us two again."

◎◎◎

At Wilkins's intervention, Valentine and Nathaniel obtained permission from Commandant Turner for them to move their bedding one flight downstairs and two rooms over, to the large

302

room which earlier inmates had playfully labeled, as if it were a clubhouse, the Lower Gettysburg Room. Located a floor above the hospital ward, their new berth allowed both men direct access down a flight of wooden stairs to the room that would demand the majority of their daily attentions.

The three rooms on the first floor of the prison housed the Commandant's office, the dining room for the guards, and the hospital. The three cellars on the ground floors, accessible only from Canal Street, served as storage, a work space for the carpenter as well as the damp cells for dangerous prisoners, spies, slaves under sentence of death, and Surgeons who slug obnoxious Quartermasters.

Nathaniel appreciated the windows located along three sides of their new room. Every morning he got up and looked out the end windows and waited for the sun to rise above the nearby shed and warehouse. Streaks of cobalt sky swirled amidst sweeps of radiant orange. Red sky in the morning, sailors take warning; red sky at night, sailors delight. Looking out the window was worth the risk, although Nathaniel prudently stood several paces away.

The amusements, even in prison, were many. Such was the advantage of being imprisoned with a great number of learned men. Anything to lessen the boredom and indignities. Anything, as some men did, to keep you from walking up in despair and standing exposed at one of the windows inviting the shot. Which happened several times a week. The struggle of mind over circumstance. Some men idled the afternoon away whittling or carving messages in the walls. Valentine proved complicit in helping Nathaniel commit his own juvenile mischief, loaning him his penknife so Nathaniel could carve into the wall nearest their window his seminary class's unofficial motto: *non illegitimi carborundum.*

Debate clubs proved popular. So too cards and choruses. So too the bawdy humor. Owing to a copy of *Ye Book of Copperheads* circulating about the various rooms at Libby, the younger officers spent time with this new nonsense rhyme fad. Valentine himself, on occasion, mixed with the boys and enjoyed the lewd ones most. Many of the former teachers and professors turned field officers held classes in French, Latin, even drills in mathematics from artillery officers.

In every garden, however, even walled gardens, there always will be found a few serpents. While some men learned French or Latin or discussed the classics or played word games, other men gambled, cheated, and robbed. Some men of meaner spirit would, when the cards were laid on the barrel lid, claim with greedy delight his neighbor's only blanket.

Civilization required effort. The men did what men acquainted with death did; they tucked up the threat of the gunpowder mine and the disappearances into an alcove of their soul and left there those fears, undisturbed.

But Valentine was right. Neither of them got much chance to be bored. Over the next month, the arriving prisoners—the crop of Yankee bluebirds predicted by Richmond's newspapers—gradually filled the six warehouse rooms of Libby. Each room connected to the next by inner doors. Six rooms for housing over 2,000 prisoners-of-war. 2,000 Federal officers bunched together, sleeping on the planked floors in blankets, sharing the few indoor latrines, resting against the thick oak pillars. Nathaniel's parish ever increased. So too the number of Valentine's patients.

With each sunrise Nathaniel offered morning prayers near the eastern window in the Lower Gettysburg room. Evening prayers were offered facing each sunset in Milroy's Room. Many joined him, a success which began to infuriate the ministering Confederate chaplains whose services were either ignored or mocked.

Carefully, cautiously, mindful of the armed guards patrolling outside looking for a face to shoot at, Nathaniel squinted through these western windows each sunset. From there he could look toward the upstream length of the James River and adjoining canal, toward Castle Thunder, Mayo's Bridge and the Long Bridge, even, as the mist cleared, the Confederate Capitol building.

Far off in the middle of the James River, beyond Long Bridge, he could spot the thousands of tents flocking like sea gulls on the island rise that was Belle Isle. Every dusk he offered a prayer for Isaac and the other men suffering at that prison. At last count, as he learned from Semple, over 10,000 prisoners-of-war struggled to survive on Belle Isle. Every other week he petitioned Turner for permission to visit Belle Isle. Each time Turner rejected his request. Each time he tried, Dick Turner had him tossed into the cell off from the kitchen for a night. That was his breaking room. Bread and water for the lucky ones. The smoke from fireplace, oven, and stove suffocated those locked inside. That was where he punished the proud Colored Troopers who had been captured, until they would be either sent to the outskirts of the city in forced labor parties to build up the fortifications or else executed as runaway slaves. Nobody ever bothered to remove from the cell the tub filled with excrement and piss.

Chapter Nineteen

Letters from Prison

Soon, o'er the bright waves howled forth the gale
Fiercely the lightning flashed in our sail;
yet while our frail bark drove the sea,
Thine eyes, like lode stars, beam'd love me
Oh! heart awaken! wreck'd on lone shore,
Then art forsaken! Dream heart no more!
"Sleeping I Dream Love," Hewitt and Hewitt

"Welcome, Ma'am," Nathaniel said as he rose to greet her as soon as she bustled into the hospital ward. She was drenched in enough perfume to drown out the odor of the gangrenous limbs. In her basket, along with her usual bundle of intimate necessaries for the sick, she carried her familiar Bible. Why she still wore a hoop skirt, Nathaniel couldn't imagine. Though it did appear to him that she had long given up trying to constrict her ample self in any pretense of whalebone and corset. A orange fan dangled by a red ribbon from her wrist, half hidden by the wide pagoda sleeves of her faded purple silk dress. Her antique bonnet did its best to subdue her thick frolic of charcoal gray hair. "It always is a grand pleasure to see you."

"Are you well, pastor?" said Miss Van Lew.

"Better now, thank you. I'm steadier on my feet."

"He's lying through his teeth, Bet," intruded Valentine. "He only got out of bed because he knew you were coming."

"Young man, you are sweet but very foolish," she chided gently, tapping Nathaniel on his chest with her orange fan. "Your ague will only worsen if you ignore it."

Valentine slapped Nathaniel between his shoulder blades. "Maybe you'll listen to her. You sure enough ignore me. Third time this month. Damn bloody stubborn."

"What a fortunate time to visit, Miss Van Lew," Nathaniel said, ignoring Valentine. "What a happy coincidence. You arrived again just in time for our Bible study and prayers." With a gallant wave, he invited her to fold herself into her usual chair. "How fortunate. We would be honored, as usual, if you would join us," said Nathaniel, his comment punctuated by a smothered cough.

"That partly is why I am here, young man. Without the mended soul, what good is the healed body?" Miss Van Lew settled herself into where she customarily sat, as best as her hoopskirt allowed. Placing her rimless oval lenses on the bridge of her reddened nose, she followed the lesson along in her own Bible. A small, cherry table sat between her chair and Nathaniel's. "Before we begin, I must ask about our young Dacre," she asked of Nathaniel, spotting the thin young man on the other side of the hospital ward bandaging a patient's leg wound. "How is our Lieutenant this week?'

"Doctor Semple says he's a better orderly with one arm than most with two," answered Nathaniel. "It's the best way for any man to heal. Being busy. Otherwise he'd be upstairs moaning. Down here he's contributing. What could be better? Got to give O'Rourke credit. He treats them, then makes them work for him."

While O'Rourke searched for a new wound to sniff and fuss over, the chaplain began reading aloud to the men from his Bible. The Psalms had become of late his preferred choice. Occasionally he'd offer a few remarks and insights about their composition and meaning. More often, he let the Psalms speak for themselves. These months had taught him that the finer way to God is not by addition but by subtraction.

When it came time for prayers, both of them placed their Bibles on the cherry table. Nathaniel would rise and walk to the center of the ward, where he solicited from the patients their prayer requests and concerns. By this time, Valentine would be found in his chair at his desk sipping something from his cup, with a bemused look on his face. The simple service was concluded by the unison recitation of the Lord's Prayer. When Nathaniel returned to assist Miss Van Lew from her chair, she would haphazardly collect her spectacles, handkerchief, fan, and basket, invariably dropping a few items on the floor, along with retrieving her precious Bible from the table. Into her basket she stuffed them all. Nathaniel would then escort her from patient to patient, to whom she would offer kind words of spiritual comfort, and, often enough, small gifts of soap, toothpowder, or paper and pencil.

The suffering of the men always moved Miss Van Lew to tears, her compassion and tenderness softening even the callused hearts of the prison guards and officers. From her billowing sleeves she would pull yards of lace to wipe away her tears, often smearing the thick pink powder with which she blanketed her wrinkles.

To the Confederate Surgeons, Miss Van Lew was a godsend. For she was rich. Even with the Confederacy bankrupt and getting poorer, she remained a woman of wealth and property.

Other aristocrats were abandoning the Capitol City. Miss Van Lew refused to desert her mansion in Richmond. She refused to retreat to the safety of her plantation outside town. It was Valentine to whom the Confederate Surgeons turned when they needed him to suggest to her what supplies might be helpful. Somehow she never disappointed them, even if those items were no longer available through legal avenues. However scatterbrained, Miss Elizabeth Van Lew was very rich.

To Commandant Turner she brought into his prison a quaint distraction to his otherwise morbid, dreary, and mundane duty. Turner had assumed his martial skills would warrant receiving a more appropriate assignment at Headquarters—Headquarters in Richmond as opposed to an assignment on the field with Lee. But his jealous superiors kept thwarting his hopes. Meanwhile, she amused him, reminding him of his own great Aunt who use to host high tea parties with her cats as guests. She also could be useful, or at least profitable. At first Turner was reluctant to permit her visits. Miss Van Lew did have the reputation about town as a Union sympathizer. Among the locals she was popularly ridiculed as "Crazy Bet' This his clerk Erasmus Ross – oddly enough, her nephew—confessed to Turner with some embarrassment.

But his clerk finally persuaded him to allow her visits. Said her nephew: "After all, Commandant, I am her favorite. Why not let me persuade her to share her wealth where it could do us some good. For the welfare of the prisoners, of course." Turner appreciated his clerk's moral ingenuity as well as his sense of humor. The clerk added, "Besides, sir, I'll see that she brings you a few treats when she does visit."

Dick Turner scoffed at her visits, thought them coddling, but then, as Commandant Turner once observed to Erasmus, he suffered from a more linear view of reality. Besides, she never brought him her buttermilk biscuits or had her slaves deliver him by wheelbarrow a case of whisky.

None of the guards ever noticed that Nathaniel's Bible was identical to that carried by Miss Elizabeth Van Lew. A month ago she had been permitted to give it to him as special gift.

◎◎◎

When Nathaniel first was introduced to Miss Elizabeth Van Lew he was sitting beside a wounded Captain from Massachusetts. The Captain had been captured while leading his Company in the dawn assault at Cold Harbor. Nathaniel discovered his name from the slip of paper he had pinned to the inside of his jacket before the battle.

An odor of rotting meat floated up from the Captain's gangrenous wound. The Steward lifted the linen blanket which lightly covered the grotesque gash in the man's thigh, and folded it across the Captain's hips, partially exposing the helpless man's sagging testicles. Inside this mangle of blood, sinew, muscle, and rotting skin, Nathaniel imagined he saw motion. He blinked, then saw the maggots wriggling. "Good God," Nathaniel said with fascination.

Without bothering to open his eyes, the Captain whispered with an peculiar nonchalance: "When it is quiet at night you can hear them gnawing away at you."

The Steward looked up and wagged his head. "It's true. Listen for yourself."

Curious, he cupped his hand to his ear and leaned toward the thigh. Nathaniel heard the faint sound of chewing. "Fascinating," he said.

The Steward took a pair of tweezers from the pocket in his apron and reached to pluck the maggots from the wound.

"No, don't! Mother Mary, no!" Valentine shouted, racing over from another patient and restraining the Steward's hand. "Leave them be. I still want them buggers there." He peered down into the gash, his nose almost poking inside the wound. He turned, looked up, and winked at Nathaniel. "A cute little trick I discovered when I deserted at Spotsylvania. Those little buggers are wonderful. They'll eat the death. And to think we've been killing them off for years." Valentine gently covered the wound with the linen blanket. After pressing his palm on the Captain's forehead, he straightened up, stretched his back, then scolded the Steward. "You hear me? Leave them be. If the wound smells, they stay. I'll check this man myself after I finish with young Dacre." Saying this, Valentine returned to the patient he had been treating, a young Lieutenant.

The Lieutenant was more boy than man. His face exuded a boyish eagerness whose innocence masked the throbbing pain he was experiencing. The young Lieutenant was thin, slight of build. He hadn't yet enjoyed the pounds that either years or marriage add to a man. He was even leaner since O'Rourke, two weeks ago, had been forced to amputate his left arm at the shoulder joint. Disarticulation, he called it. When you lose the joint, you lose options. But it was a last desperate resort to cut away the poisoning. Lieutenant Dacre screamed and wept from the agony, then mercifully collapsed into unconsciousness halfway through the cutting. O'Rourke felt like a butcher slicing away at the sinews and sawing to sever the muscles of a pig's hind quarter. When you carve away a man's arm from his shoulder it takes far longer than two minutes, despite O'Rourke honing the blade as sharp as he could.

Pulling his worn pocket Bible from his pocket, Nathaniel prepared to read a few Psalms to the Captain. His fingers fumbled through the pages searching for an apt text. It was then he smelled the perfume. Heady perfume. Nathaniel sneezed.

A big bosomed woman dressed in an old-fashioned pink satin ball gown, the ribbons faded, stood beside Nathaniel, her matronly gray hair sticking out like straw from beneath her frayed bonnet. Behind her stood Doctor Semple. Wilkins stood at the end of the Captain's cot. O'Rourke stood beside Wilkins.

"Chaplain McKenna," Semple said. "I'd like to present to you and to Surgeon O'Rourke, one of our kind benefactors: Miss Elizabeth Van Lew."

It had been a long time since Nathaniel had been called upon to be polite and mannerly. "Pleased to meet you," Nathaniel mumbled, bowing awkwardly.

"Miss Van Lew," Semple continued, "has been a good friend of our lovely institution for several years now. When she heard of the presence of both a Yankee chaplain and Surgeon, she requested permission to meet both of you. Commandant Turner has seen fit to give her permission to visit our hospital as often as she is able. No doubt she will bring much relief to these men. Please extend to her every courtesy."

Nathaniel first looked over at Valentine who screwed up his face and pulled absentmindedly on his goatee. Nathaniel looked back at Semple. "Um, yes, indeed. It shall be our privilege. All help is most welcome."

Later, back in their space in the room, Valentine began complaining. "Wonderful! Just what we need. Did you see her outfit? I don't imagine she'll want to soil her gown with a little pus and blood. Goddamn. I don't need aristocratic tourists. Had that in Gettysburg. What are we, Bedlam? Let's pay for the privilege to see the freaks. What I could use is a few of those ladies from the Sanitary Commission. Those ladies don't mind a little dirty work." Valentine slapped Nathaniel with his hat, mocking him. "'It shall be our privilege.' Damn, Nate, you want her, you work with her. Just keep her away from me. What a doddering old nuisance!"

Nathaniel brooded, chewing on his mustache, yanking out a few strands of hair. His eyes looked up quizzically at Valentine. "Is her name familiar to you? Van Lew. It is to me. But where? I don't think I've ever met her. I'm sure I haven't."

"How many Richmond cotillions have you attended lately?"

"No, seriously. Her name is familiar, but I can't place it." Nathaniel lit the wick in the sardine can and pulled his Bible out from his coat pocket for his evening devotions. "It's really going to bother me." He toyed with the pages. Something nudged his memory. He flipped the pages of his worn Bible to the Epistle to Philemon. The writing was smeared, the pages worn, the print faded, but the five names were still legible. Nathaniel slapped the Bible against his thigh. He knew her name sounded familiar.

"What?" grumped Valentine.

"Nothing. Go to sleep."

He had to wait until her next visit. He waited until they were standing alone together. "I believe, Miss Van Lew," Nathaniel began, "that we have pleasure of several mutual acquaintances. Or should I say we have some mutual friends?"

"Really, Reverend?"

"Yes, I believe we do," he continued casually. "A Mr. Teiresias Young." He paused and studied her eyes for some reaction. "From Catalpa, Virginia."

It was if a match flared. Her clouded day-dreaming pupils suddenly turned crisp and focused. Her batting eyelids arched. The elderly woman searched his face with a dark, penetrating stare before responding. "Yes, Reverend, I do believe we do. An ecumenical Presbyterian. How rare." She began retying her bonnet ribbons under one of her chins. "I must leave now. We shall talk further of our friends. Next visit, I shall bring buttermilk biscuits."

During her tea with Commandant Turner that afternoon she mentioned how lamentable it was Chaplain McKenna had to strain his eyes reading such small print day after day ministering with such devotion. It just wouldn't do. "Would you be kind enough," she asked, "to allow me to present him with a more fitting testament to the true faith?"

Distracted by looking forward to tasting the liquid gift she had brought him, Turner barely listened.

"It would be," she explained further, "the very same edition I myself read daily for spiritual succor during these trying times. God's Word is best appreciated in the original King James Version."

Turner couldn't have cared less about which version it was.

The next week she arrived at the prison bearing a special gift for the Union chaplain. She could think of no worthier gift for no worthier cause than to present him with a finely bound illustrated edition of the Holy Scriptures. The patients, on the other hand, appreciated the biscuits.

That evening, with Valentine's body shielding him from magpie eyes, Nathaniel rolled the new Bible over in his hands. He turned the pages, searching through each familiar chapter, looking for something different, something unusual. Perhaps a code. Maybe some strange markings. He inspected carefully the covers and binding. Inside the thickly bound back cover, parallel to the binding, was a precise, thin sliver of an opening. Nathaniel slid his finger inside the almost invisible seam. His heart raced. The back cover formed a secret envelope. His fingertip touched what felt like paper. Nathaniel coaxed out from this pouch several tightly pressed pages of the *Richmond Sentinel*, as well as envelope containing a ten dollar US bill. A note was tucked in between the newspaper pages. In beautiful script the letter simply said: "From Ulysses."

Nathaniel reached for the tin box containing writing paper which had been provided him by one of the Richmond chaplains. He quickly scribbled a note and slid it into the secret pouch. He waited anxiously till her next visit.

Next week, as they sat together for Bible study and prayer, he placed his Bible on top of hers. When she left, the guards failed to notice it was his Bible she removed from the table and placed in her basket.

After mess that evening Nathaniel and Valentine visited the 'Stroughton Room' and approached the ranking Union officer at Libby, Brigadier General Nichols. "General, sir, may we have a few minutes," Nathaniel requested. "I have some more concerns I'd like to talk with you about upcoming worship services." The officers near General Nichols resumed their card game. "May we speak in confidence?"

"Is it really that important, chaplain?"

"Oh, I believe it might be."

316

"Is that also why you are here, O'Rourke?" the General questioned. "Are you also interested in matters of liturgy?"

"Certainly, General," Valentine gushed. "Can't get enough of 'that ol' rugged cross.' I'm damn near saved, I believe. Washed in the blood I am. The Lord's been working hard on me for my conversion."

"Yes, quite," Nichols replied.

The three of them walked toward the stairwell. Valentine scanned the room for prying ears. Nathaniel spoke softly. "Actually, sir, this isn't about services."

"I assumed as much. Despite allowing myself to get captured and ending up in this forsaken place, I am not an entire fool. What's on your minds?"

"We need to be cautious about this, sir. Very cautious. There are too many here I wouldn't trust with this information. Valentine and I see and hear things that most of you don't. Some here would sell their wife for a pot of stew. I include, I'm sorry to say, some of your own staff."

"I do not trust some of them either, which is why I keep them close to me. Go on, chaplain, to business."

"I cannot go into details. That might compromise things. What you should know is I have means of communicating outside the prison." The General raised his eyebrow. "What I mean is, and, I assure you that it is extremely reliable, that I can get word to Grant's Headquarters." The General rubbed his stubbled chin. "We have a contact, a courier if you will."

"Dangerous business, chaplain. Especially if you're being set up. Can you be sure this isn't some plot by Turner?"

"Dick Turner?"

"Commandant Turner or Dick Turner. They're two peas in a pod, equally contemptible," snarled Nichols.

"Neither has a clue. I'm sure."

"That could be true," observed Nichols. "I don't think either has the wit for it. More cruel than clever. I would be much more comfortable were you to tell me the details of this compact, however."

"That I can't. Well, I could, sir, but I'd rather not. You have to trust me, as much I have to trust. . .," Nathaniel caught himself, "...my guardian angel."

The General clucked his tongue. "Fair enough, McKenna," he concluded. "Though I am going to bring a few other of my officers in on this information. You do not have a choice in that, chaplain. We cannot do this alone. We require more ears and eyes. You cannot do this alone. We'll keep the circle small. My most trusted staff only, just in case." The General clapped his hands together, his decision made. "Well, let's run the mail. What have we got to lose?"

Valentine intervened: "Only our chaplain."

The General frowned. "Well, yes, there's that. You get caught, they likely will hang you. Turned collar aside. Do you understand?"

"General, if you remember: we came to you," said Nathaniel.

"Davey, come here," the General called out with a wave. A young Captain jogged over to them. General Nichols put his arm across the Captain's shoulders. "Vogan, you've just gotten religion."

"What, sir?"

"What are you? Methodist, Baptist?"

"Presbyterian, sir. My father's an Elder of our church back in Pittsburgh."

"Perfect," laughed the General. "How predestined."

"Actually, General," Nathaniel interjected, "too many confuse predestination with fatalism, when it really means…"

"Yes, quite," the General said, cutting him off. "Listen, Vogan, I want you to attend every Bible Study and worship from now on."

"I have attended some," Vogan protested apologetically, the situation reminding him of when his mother would ask him how often he went to church.

"Yes, quite. But for now I'd like you to be less interested in the condition of your soul than in doing your damnedest to confound the enemy. You're going to help run the mail here. The good Reverend here will be our postmaster. I'll pay the one cent myself if this works. God help me, our chaplain here says he can get information to Grant. So I want you to be my liaison. From now on you're my intelligence officer. You're the smartest I have. That bastard Turner watches me too close. No one is to know. Hear me? No one. You report to me directly. I want to know what information our Reverend is sending out. And you will take to the Reverend information I want sent out of here."

"I get it, sir. I promise to be devout from now on."

"Good man," said the General, who softened his voice and again wrapped his arm around Vogan. "Listen, Davey. I trust you more than the others here. I need you. There's a risk, one hell of a risk, but from now on, you're my chief of spies."

"You can count on me."

"I see that. You're cleverer than most of these. If it weren't for this damn mine of Turner's, Davey, we'd have you in charge of trying to escape. You'd be my Rose. Talk about clever. Over a hundred he tunneled out of here. Impressive."

"Actually, Nichols," said Valentine, scratching his chin. "Give us time, and I wouldn't be too worried about that mine. Nate here and I got an idea."

General Nichols studied O'Rourke's face. "What do you mean?"

"Trust us. Give us the summer. If you need him to become a hero and escape from here, we figure we might be able to manage it."

"The mine?"

"We know this place is nothing but a tinder box," Valentine said with a wink. "But trust us."

Vogan chimed in excitedly: "Dear Lord, if we could manage another escape, we'd keep a Regiment off the front lines. Maybe a Brigade. We can't let Turner think we've caved in."

Again the General studied O'Rourke's face. "Keep me informed, gentlemen. Until then we only run the mail. Grant needs to hear what we can tell him. We may be prisoners but we are still fighting this war. And O'Rourke, don't do anything stupid."

"Naw, not me, General. I'm a committed coward. I let my Godly friend take all the risks. His connections are better."

Guided by General Nichols and his circle of chosen officers, Nathaniel, with his free supply of paper and ink, courtesy of the Confederate clergy, secreted to Union headquarters, courtesy of Miss Elizabeth Van Lew and the power of the Holy Word, lists of prisoners, details about Rebel troop movements observed by arriving prisoners-of-war, plus reports from the spies to whom he ministered in their dank basement cells. He also wrote, and hoped that Grant would be kind enough to let them get there, letters to his Alice.

◎◎◎

My Dearest Alice,

I pray they let this letter reach you. If it does, you must promise that no one can know that I have written you. You must promise this. You cannot even tell our daughters or my father.

My darling wife, forgive me for my silence for so many months. I am well, except my heart aches for you and our daughters. Kiss them each a dozen times for me. Would that I could kiss you, my dearest love, a dozen times dozen.

Each minute I pray that you and our girls remain well and safe, indeed, happy. I repeat: I am well. I do not know what you were informed following the last campaign. But I am neither missing nor dead. Valentine and I are presently enjoying the hospitality of Richmond, that is all I should say. All is well and soon we shall be reunited. I remind you of your offer of a son.

Sadly, I cannot guarantee further letters, nor can I tell you how this has been secreted to you, but I give thanks for the chance to ease your heart.

It is enough today that I burn for you and miss you and our daughters with all my soul. Once again, my dearest, we are well.

Your loving husband,
N.

◎◎◎

Under armed escort, Nathaniel left the confines of Libby Prison for the first time since his arrival two months ago. The six soldiers ushered him down the path along the canal, past mule, boat, and small packet, to the far side of the building that bordered the vacant lot opposite Libby. He was brought to Castle Thunder, a drab and ugly squat of a building, which in another day served as a smaller warehouse for Richmond commerce. Now the commerce was war—in particular, it was the commerce of housing prisoners judged to be the more renegade and contemptible: Union spies, disloyal southerners, Colored Troopers.

"Of course I am, preacher," insisted the young man. "Guilty as sin. I faked my sympathies and 'nlisted in one of their Regiments a year ago. I ran information through the lines the whole time I served there. Nevah' shot a round. Promise. Don' like killin'. Too much of it goin' around. Made a lot of noise, though." The man jumped up from his stool. He scratched his chin. "Would like a shave 'fore they hang me. Think you could arrange it, preacher?"

"Not much time, I'm afraid."

"Well, I'm not. 'fraid that is. It was a good run though." The young man sat down on the stool, leaned toward Nathaniel, and cupped his hand to his mouth. "You sure you can 'member those drawin's?"

Nathaniel mirrored his actions, leaning forward and placing his hands over the young man's hands. The young man's hands felt cold. "I'll remember," he promised. "Rest assured, Henley, they'll find their way to the proper people."

"Good. Good." The young man jumped up again and paced between the wall and his stool. Grant needs to know about those fortifications. "Good. Good," he repeated. He sat down again. "You'll get them to him? Right?"

"Yes, trust me." Nathaniel again placed his hands over the young man's. "You've done well. They'll remember. They'll be grateful. Many will thank you, even if they never hear of your name. Their families back home will be grateful."

"That's'a somethin'. That helps. It do, it do." The man stretched his legs forward and rocked back on the stool. "What time is it, preacher?"

Nathaniel removed his watch from his inner pocket and opened it. "Soon, very soon. About fifteen minutes."

"I'm glad you're here. My momma is mighty deep religious. I ain't but that's okay. Never had a woman either. I'd 'preciate it if'n you could somehow get word to her. Her name is Janet. Janet Henley of Roanoke. We'en have a small place near Hollins. Dairy cows mostly. A few goats too. Doubt any are left, though. Tell her you were here with me. Please. You tell her that, will you? She'd like that." The young man abruptly hopped the stool forward and bent closer toward Nathaniel. "Where you from?"

"Princeton. Princeton, New Jersey, that is."

"Your momma misses you?"

"No. She died a year after I married. My father's still living. He's taking care of my parish in Pennsylvania right now. And taking care of my family."

"It's good to have fam'ly. You're married then? Tell me about her? What's her name?"

"Alice. Her name is Alice. What can I say? Well, she's a wonderful mother. She's beautiful too. Long auburn hair. In the light it turns almost a deep red."

"What color her eyes?"

"Hazel." Nathaniel warmed at the memory. "When she's excited or angry they shine a rich golden green. Sometimes when I stand at the kitchen door and look at her playing with our daughters in the back yard, it is as if she shimmers, even on cloudy days. When she smiles, her cheeks redden, and her smile fills her whole face."

"Wish'a I'd married."

Nathaniel didn't respond.

"Hey preacher, whatcha' your name anyhow?"

"McKenna. Nathaniel McKenna"

"Well, Nathaniel McKenna, I'd sho' 'preciate it if you would tell my momma that her son, Gregory, loved her. I reckon in time she'll 'cept why I had to do this. It'll help if you let her know that we prayed together 'fore they hanged me, even if you are a Yankee."

Footsteps thudded in the hallway outside. The heavy bolt was pulled back and the thick door hauled open. The officer bent over to enter the cell, his hand holding his sword sheath. "Time," was all the man said. The officer was not much older than the young spy.

The young man stood. His legs gave way slightly. Nathaniel reached for him. He smiled in embarrassment at his weakness. With his arm reaching around, Nathaniel pressed his hand against the young man's shoulders and moved him toward the doorway following behind the young officer. Commandant Gibbs stood in the hallway outside the cell door.

"Could the chapl'in come with me?" asked the young man. "I mean, all the way? Meebe' my last request?"

Gibbs nodded and waved permission. Nathaniel closed his eyes and shivered, but pressed his palm more firmly upon the young man's shoulders. He had seen a lot already, but not this.

Side by side they sat in the back of the wagon as they bumped to the Fair Grounds where the scaffold stood. Together they ascended the thirteen wooden steps. The young man counted aloud each one. Nathaniel placed his hands around the man's bound hands to quell the trembling, and they prayed together. Nathaniel lowered his eyes to a page of his pocket Bible and began reading as the noose was placed over the young man's neck and knotted snug. He looked up in time to see the young man looking directly back into his eyes. A sanguine curiosity burned in his young eyes as the lever was pulled.

Chapter Twenty

On Borrowed Time

Beautiful dreamer, wake unto me.
Starlight and dewdrops are waiting for thee;
Sounds of the rude world heard in the day,
Lull'd by the moonlight, have all pass'd away!
Beautiful dreamer, queen of my song,
List while I woo thee with soft melody;
Gone are the cares of life's busy throng.
Beautiful dreamer, awake unto me!
Beautiful dreamer, awake unto me!
"Beautiful Dreamer," Stephen Foster

*M*y Dearest Alice,
      *The kindest guards are those who have experienced what we
have. Most of our guards come from the Invalid Corps. Having been
wounded in the field of battle, most have no stomach for vengeance,
for bitterness. There is between us that bond of understanding,
compassion even, born of shared hardships. Trust a man with scars.*

*Those who have never been in the field nor faced musket fire nor
carried friends from the field are the thugs and ruffians, brutal—
especially the younger ones—they plunder the packages sent us from
the Sanitary Commission, or make us pay for the contents of our own
parcels. I thank God I have kept our girl's watch and your cameo safe
thus far. I would die without them.*

Our hopes rise and fall daily upon the rumors. Despite the rumors, I am certain that the ban on exchanges will continue. Grant will not budge, I am certain. The thought of not being able to put my arms around you or hold my daughters in my arms until this terrible ordeal is over, grieves me hourly, indeed, with every minute that passes. Yet I believe our government must hold to its pledge. No more exchanges. No more flags of truce. I do not expect to be home any time soon.

Some here in prison curse Grant and call themselves prisoners of our own President. What does it matter, they criticize, if the colored troops when captured are refused rights of exchange and are even executed or enslaved? But these men fail to understand. Maybe it is Grant who truly is the least harsh. Maybe he understands best: take away the fuel and the fire dwindles. All I can do is hope and take care of the men today. This Nathaniel today is not so quick with explanations or proclamations.

We have been overwhelmed as of late with prisoners from a place called Petersburg, many of whom arrive wounded. It angers me to the see the weak preyed upon by corrupt men. And I am helpless to prevent it, which may be the source of my greater anger. Fear not, my love. I may get angry but I am trying not hate.

It helps having no illusions. I am brutally aware of the capacity of man for causing such inhumanity—no false denials of the bestial within us. Yes, us becoming little gods ourselves clamoring and even killing for our piece of hardtack or portion of soup or the greater share of an onion.

I have seen one our own Colonels creep at night near the bunk of their feeble, dying Lieutenant and steal his blanket. And I have seen men share their own blankets, fostering civility and humanity as they pick lice off each other and listen to them crackle in the flames of our solitary stove. And I have seen the proud General turn lunatic, believing he is back home in Philadelphia dining at his mahogany table surrounded by wife and servants.

It is puzzling to see what adversity does to us—what it elicits—no, what it exposes. Does it alter us so much as reveal us? Yes, surely in some it alters—the fever or numbing shock addling brain and heart—but mostly, I daresay, adversity exposes our secret thoughts. It is one thing to be brave when the banner is unfurled and drumbeat sounds with the flourish of flags, when those many faces look at you to inspire them, their expectation forcing you to be what they require. But to face fear, silent fear, dark fear, lonely fear, with no one expecting anything of you, that is another matter. It is one thing to be brave when you're supposed to, it's another thing when no one cares.

You would be so proud of Valentine. All here admire his dedication. He does what must be done. His advantage is that he knows he must.

A thousand kisses.

Your loving husband,

N.

◎◎◎

The escape plans were laid. They only needed hatching. The new moon would occur the last day of the month. If they couldn't make it happen at that time, they'd have to delay it until the night before All-Hallow Eve. If. Plenty of 'ifs.' If they could coordinate the timing. If Van Lew's people could provide a diversion. If the winds were favorable for the sailing barge to make it up the canal. If no one detected the tunnel they had dug under the brick wall into the disused cook room. If they could pull the hinges of the exterior door without the sentinels on Canal Street hearing. The last time they did it as a trial run, the screeching of the rusty iron nearly betrayed them all. They needed more candle wax to rub down on the hinges. All those 'ifs.' If the sentinels could be caught by surprise. If they could slip silently into the canal and swim to the boat before being detected. Rose by land, Vogan by sea. And, last, if Turner wouldn't detonate the 200 pounds of gunpowder stacked in the middle cellar.

"Are you sure about this mine?" pressed Davey Vogan.

"Trust me," answered Nathaniel with a mischievous grin.

"You wouldn't want to go into a few details about this, would you? Just to make me and General Nichols happy?" probed Vogan.

"It's safer if you simply trust us."

"I do, Nate, you should know that by now. But I can't vouch for everyone. If word got out what we were planning, our own boys would shut us down. They know Turner isn't bluffing. They'd have a protest meeting, and if they couldn't convince us, I guarantee you someone would rat us out. Play the Judas. I wouldn't blame 'em. If I didn't trust you, I wouldn't run the risk either. This is one tricky leap of faith."

"They all are," replied Nathaniel pensively.

The muggy mosquito ridden Richmond summer had yielded to a dull September. Only when dozens of prisoners came down with some kind of mysterious contagion was there any distraction to the routine. By the second week of September every cot in the hospital was filled. There were so many men sick that some were forced to be bedded and treated on the floor. Even Vogan took ill. Semple was dumbfounded. So too Valentine. Broken bones or gangrene was plainer to diagnose and treat. Wilkens could have helped, but he already had been ordered to supervise the new prisoner-of-war camps set up outside Richmond. Both Doctors feared some perilous epidemic. Semple suggested the malady might originate from the fleas, ticks, or mosquitoes. Valentine suspected vapors from their close confinement. Plans were made for quarantine lest the contagion spread further. The sick men alternated between feeling feverish and chilled. Their hoarse coughing occurred in jagged waves. The doctors tried a variety of remedies, including Valentine's own secret black liquid mixture. Most gagged as they drank it, but drink it they did. But little improvement was shown in their condition.

The last night in September did provide Libby an hour of excitement. A crazed horse galloped down the hill along 20th Street. A slave chased after the runaway horse, yelling for help. The horse was hitched to a dray wagon in which two buckets of roofing pitch had ignited. Before reaching Carey Street, the wagon bounced over a mound of boulders and crashed through the tents of the prison guards, where two soldiers suffered broken arms. The wagon nearly overturned, the buckets falling out, sloshing out their contents, and rolling through camp. A Sergeant, fed up with the confusion, simply shot the horse. Soldiers rushed to kick dirt on the small fires ignited by the burning pitch. The slave was struck by several rifle butts despite him begging that it was an accident and he was real sorry. The Union prisoners who dared to gather at the barred windows to watch the fun hooted and cheered. The sentinels dashed from around the corners of the building. Hearing the prisoners shouting from the windows, they automatically raised their muskets and fired a barrage. The muzzle blasts illuminated the deep night for a bright instant. The prisoners ducked away in time, only to return and jeer the

Rebels even louder, tempting another volley, which the Rebels soon obliged.

When Semple arrived the next morning and opened the door to the hospital, he was shocked to discover the hospital was nearly empty. There were only a half dozen patients left, including young Tom Dacre still recovering from a relapse from his surgery, and, in an adjacent bed, Roland Seward half crazed from a concussion occasioned by Dick Turner's boot. One Union Major lay mortally unconscious off in the corner on what had become termed by Valentine as the dying bed, his breathing shallow, his lips bubbling blood. The bed sheets hung to the floor, soon to be drawn up to drape the corpse.

"Where'd they go?" asked an incredulous Semple.

"Damnedest thing. Like a miracle cure it was," said O'Rourke shaking his head and scratching his goatee. "I'll have to credit our chaplain here. More prayer than medicine it was."

"The devil took them all to hell, all go down to hell, down to hell!" screamed Seward, his ranting incessant, his mind as fractured as his skull. "And he descended into hell...descended into hell!"

"I'll try to calm him down," volunteered Nathaniel.

Seward shrieked another high pitch scream as the hospital door was pushed open. Commandant Turner entered, followed by a squad of armed guards. Dick Turner soon followed.

"How many missing, Dick?" asked the Commandant.

"Near as we can tell, 'bout three doz'n. Judgin' by Erasmus's count. Vogan included. Nichols refused to admit anythin'."

"Which brings us here," said Commandant Turner. "Sick call, 'twas it? You had a full ward yesterday, Doctor Semple. What has happened to your patients?"

Semple shrugged and put his fists on his hips. "I just arrived."

"I wan' answers," demanded Dick Turner, spinning toward Valentine, his tight face growing scarlet, "'er I'll see you in hell."

"They went to hell, I'm going hell, you're going to hell, we're all going to hell!" chanted Seward from the other side of the room. Jumping out of his bed, he raced frantically in his nightshirt over to the corner cot with the dying Major. Collapsing to the floor, he sprawled out next to the cot. "We're all damned," he screamed. In an instant he rolled under the cot and disappeared.

Dick Turner rushed over. With both hands he flipped the cot, tossing the dying man to the ground with a meaty thud. Beneath the bed, two floor planks had been pried up and stacked to one side of the hole. As the last man to lower himself into the cellar, Vogan had forgotten to shift them back into position.

"Yes sir—she drops right down into the rat cellar," said Dick Turner. "They musta' foun' a way out from there."

"Even the dead can be good soldiers," chuckled Valentine.

Commandant Turner breathed thinly and rapidly through his nostrils as he turned to one of his Sergeants and shook his finger at the hole. "Check it, man. Check it. See if they re-dug the tunnel. Find out how."

"Acts 5: 19, if you must know," smirked Nathaniel. "But the angel of the Lord by night opened the prison doors and brought them forth…"

"Very nice, Nate," Valentine complimented.

Dick Turner pulled his revolver dramatically from his black holster, slowly cocked the hammer with his thumb, and raised it and pointed it at Nathaniel' face. God, he hated this smug preacher. Nathaniel stared into both of its barrels, the octagonal and the smoothbore. It wasn't the first time he's had a pistol in his face. Would it be round ball or buckshot, he wondered.

"Dick, stop. Let him meditate instead on how he's just killed 2,000 men," said Commandant Turner calmly. "Blow it, blow it. Blow them all to hell." He tugged his Adjutant by the elbow and waved his hat toward Nathaniel. You've always admired his watch. He won't be needing it now." Turner smirked at his own wit. "He's no time left."

"I wouldn't advise it," warned Nathaniel. Worse men have tried."

"Leastways I hol' the revolver. Nine shots in this handsome piece." Said Dick Turner as he fondled the chamber. "'Nough for you two bastards and ever' patient in this room." Two of his guards rushed over and with vice like grips grabbed Nathaniel by his arms as Dick Turner approached him, slapped him across the face, and delicately pulled the pocket watch and blue cameo from his waistcoat pocket by its silver chain. No rock could have been more impenetrable or immoveable at that moment than Nathaniel's body.

"Clear out our men. Empty my office. Lock all doors," ordered Commandant Turner in a flat monotone. He pointed at Nathaniel and Valentine. "It's on your heads. I gave fair warning. Semple, please remove yourself from here." A guard steered Semple by his arm and pushed him toward the door. They left, and the door to the hospital was shut fast and locked. From every room of the prison there soon arose shouts of protest mixed with anguished appeals. The trapped prisoners pounded on the bars and floors with anything that would make noise.

"You want a drink?" O'Rourke asked, turning toward Lieutenant Dacre. "It's the only decent way a man should face his death. You're old enough aren't you?"

"I wouldn't mind a little sip, sir. If you're offering, that is."

"You'll get it back, Nate," said Valentine. "Of that I am certain."

"So am I," said Nathaniel with a stoic confidence. "So I am." Nathaniel strolled over to his Bible study chair and flung himself down into it. "Small consolation, but did Semple leave any of his tobacco here? Haven't had a smoke in weeks."

"I'll check." After filling two glasses with the last ounces of his bourbon, he went over to the desk, opened a drawer, found the leather tobacco pouch, and tossed it to his friend. "Feels like there's a little left."

The pounding and desperate shouts echoing from throughout each room of Libby prison grew louder, faster, furious. Those men who were scared and panicked became even more panicked and scared. The mean became meaner. The pious knelt and turned to prayer. The resolute accepted their fate with deeper resolution. These were the ones who would be damned if they were going to let the bastards gloat. Nichols tried his best to calm them all down.

Downstairs in the hospital, Valentine sat on the bottom edge of Dacre's cot while Nathaniel puffed smoke rings the size of biscuits.

Outside Libby prison, with the perimeter evacuated, Dick Turner himself asked permission to light the fuse. The Commandant handed him his own box of Lucifer Matches. Entering the middle cellar through the bulky door on the Canal Street side, he grinned maliciously, contentedly, as he struck the match and lit the white paper fuse. Five seconds an inch.

He ran outside, the heavy iron keys jangled in his other hand, and joined Turner and the cluster of forty soldiers standing at far boundary of the tents.

"I'd guess 'bout 30 more seconds," announced Dick Turner importantly, keeping his eye on the second hand of Nathaniel's pocket watch. "Ten. Five. Any secon' now." He lifted his greedy face up at Libby.

Nothing. Then came a muffled boom. It was more firecracker than detonation.

Inside the hospital, Dacre explained: "I left enough for effect. Couldn't disappoint them entirely. Besides, they might have checked the cask where the fuse connected."

"Smart. I told you, Valentine. He is a clever lad."

"Agile too. Can't imagine squirming down that old chimney like that. More squirrel than anything. With the eyes of a lynx."

"Well, sir, it were only difficult the first eight or nine times, but I got use to it after that. Couldn't have done it if I had both arms. Next to replacing the gunpowder with dirt, the hardest part was putting the bricks back in place each time so the Carpenter wouldn't get suspicious. Tough to do with one hand."

Their outburst of laughter erupted through the windows of the prison hospital. Their laughter echoed off the canal water. Buoyed by a relief mixed with joyous insult, soon the entire prison joined the laughter.

Dick Turner didn't bother unlocking the hospital door. He kicked it in.

"You really didn't think we were going to let you kill everyone here?" said Nathaniel, still seated and puffing his pipe.

"And I'd like to thank you," added Valentine with a twinge of his playful brogue. "You wouldn't believe how medically beneficial a potion black powder mixed with hot water can be. Teaspoon at a time. Effective against blood poisoning in wounds also. Not a bad seasoning on rotted mule meat either." He desperately wanted to wink at Dacre but that would have given him away.

It was eight men beating two. Both men were unconscious when Turner finally dragged them into the cell off from the kitchen. If he couldn't break these two, he was going to enjoy watching them die.

◎◎◎

They would have died had not one of the Confederate cooks secreted them plates of beans along with rags soaked in water slid on a piece of wood under the door. They would have died had not Semple needed Valentine's skill and pressed daily for his release. And had not the Confederate ministers sent a petition stating that their colleague had been punished enough for his sins. Though, each knew but refused it admit it, that they had more of an eye to pride than to justice. Clergy, however shameful their conduct, deserve some courtesy, if not for the man, then at least for the office.

After managing to survive a month in the kitchen cell, Nathaniel and Valentine staggered out from the darkness. Against Dick Turner's orders, Semple treated them both.

"You pressed your luck," Semple scolded them. "You're doubly lucky that the new Provost Marshall rejected our Commandant's demand for more gun powder. Between us, I doubt our Army has the powder to spare. All of them up at the

Capitol Building are convinced Turner's a madman anyway. There should be more honor in this dirty business. Even Jeff Davis believes it will be cheaper and safer to start emptying out Libby. The rate things are going, no one will be left behind in Richmond."

"We were banking on that," croaked Nathaniel through cracked lips and sore gums. "We may be idiots, but we're not complete fools."

"A few of your lads think that is exactly what you are, Reverend. Nichols's men call you heroes. Others thought you played pretty loose with their lives."

From the next cot, a drowsy Valentine started humming, then idly singing, his mind wandering seas of memory like a rudderless sailboat with loose sheets:

One for anger

Two for mirth

Three for a wedding...

◉◉◉

A week later, news of Lincoln's re-election spread like wildfire throughout Libby prison. Throughout Richmond, as the Monday the newspapers were distributed, the city cried out in collective agony. They had prayed for McClellan's victory and a chance for a truce. One guard, never before hurtful, pushed a one-legged prisoner out of his way with the butt of his musket. They did not like the news. This despised ape of a President would remain in office, a President who had vowed to continue this war. No chance now of negotiations.

Almost to a man, the prisoners-of-war voted for Lincoln. They lacked official ballots, but on Election Day a Major from

Ohio, formerly a magistrate in Cleveland, conducted a straw poll. Men lined up on each floor putting slips of paper in hats. Only a handful of officers, all from New Jersey, along with the lunatic Seward, voted for McClellan.

In Libby, it was Lincoln by a landslide, even though his election meant no truce for them either. No truce. No exchange. Lincoln's re-election meant they would be stuck at Libby. Yet they were willing. Old Abe had proved his mettle to them. They were willing to prove theirs to him. Once again.

"That's courage. They don't surprise me. To be willing to put up with this longer," Nathaniel said between gulps of thin tea from a cup brought to him by young Dacre. "What a price to pay, eh?"

Valentine, wiping clean his face and hands with a damp rag, said tiredly: "You would have voted for him too, if we hadn't been otherwise engaged."

"My ribs are still killing me. My lungs have more smoke in them than a chimney. I couldn't have lasted much longer," he grunted weakly, swallowing another gulp of water. "How come you and I end up every time in a dank hole together?"

"One way or another, we all end up in a hole."

Dacre couldn't hold back a quick laugh.

"Well, I believe it," yawned Nathaniel. "With Lincoln staying in office, victory is a matter of time." Even from the thick confines of their cell, they had heard the guns thundering leagues way. Each day the guns sounded closer than the previous. "It is a matter of time."

"Yes, Nate, but how much time? That's the question," he replied.

"Don't talk to me about time."

Later that evening, as the two men settled in for another restless night, Valentine tapped Nathaniel on the head with the copy of his newspaper. The guards had long ignored Doctor Semple's habit of bringing his newspapers into the hospital to give to O'Rourke. "Hey Nate, this you must hear."

"Leave me alone. It's cold." The dirty tarpaulin covering the window billowed and buffeted in the cold wind. Most of the wind whistled through tears in the fabric.

"No, you have to hear this, Nate. They're talking about you." He pushed the newspaper at him. "You're famous. Actually, you're infamous. I like it. My infamous friend."

Nathaniel stirred reluctantly. "What are you talking about?" Nathaniel rolled over, twisting himself up in his blanket, his eyes drifting over at Valentine, who reclined against the wall.

Valentine snapped and straightened the Richmond Sentinel and read the editorial with a tone of fatuous solemnity: "Yankees at Prayer—We learn that the Yankees confined at Libby Prison, among whom are one or two chaplains, are holding prayer meetings nearly every day. We should as soon expect the natives of the Feejee Island to unite in adoration of the Most High, but there is no limit to the presumption of an unadulterated Yankee. Can anybody imagine a more shameless proceeding than the offering of a prayer to God by a man who has willfully and wantonly violated the commandments of Jehovah?"

Nathaniel rolled back over, muttering: "I think when we get out of here you and I should check out these Feejee Islanders." He wrapped himself tighter in his blanket and tried to go back to sleep, resting his head on the Bible Van Lew had given him.

Valentine guffawed and hooted loudly. "Funniest thing I've read in years." Everybody in the room woke up and stared at

Valentine. Valentine laughed himself into hysterics, wiping the tears from his eyes with his dirty sleeve.

Several days later news arrived of the Confederate abandonment of Fort Sumter and the Union Army's occupation of Charleston. The surly mood of the guards turned as vindictive as Dick Turner's always had been. They began to beat the prisoners with batons.

⊚⊚⊚

My Dearest Alice,

My greatest pain these days comes from coping with your silence. We all suffer the absent voices of our loved ones. We receive so little news of home. I spend these long winter nights imagining my letters finding their way into your beautiful hands, then you set the letter down on your lap. It is as if I am with you already. May spring be warmer for us all.

How painful it must be for you not to write, not to be able to write me and tell me of what meal you cooked today and what childish joy Margaret and Penelope found in the day.

I fill the quieter moments of my days sometimes wandering from window to window trying to count the number of steeples in this city. There are so many tall steeple churches to be seen. Yet I most love our own small sanctuary in Penningtonville, even though it lacks a steeple. It has a bell and it has a pulpit. It has a Bible. That is enough. And to think that I spoke to you when we first married about my ambitions. I boasted how in ten years I would achieve a position at one of our steepled churches in Philadelphia or even Princeton. I confess, my love, I no longer need the grandeur of the fine church building so long as there is among the people the spirit to be the church. I have seen more of church here as we gather in the corner of our prison than in many of those stately steepled churches on market squares.

I am learning, my darling, to stop wasting God's time in my prayers asking why. Instead I only pray these days asking how.

Your loving husband,

N.

⊚⊚⊚

Grant's stranglehold on Richmond strangled them also.

With each spasm, Nathaniel clutched his dog-eared pocket Bible against his chest and the stabbing pain. This time the phlegm coughed up was clotted with blood. "Would you read it again?" Nathaniel managed to say.

While Valentine read aloud the text of Lincoln's second inauguration speech smuggled into the prison by Miss Van Lew, Nathaniel listened. As he listened he watched a tiny spider stretching its web across several of the iron bars in the window. Nathaniel had thought webs were always uniform. He'd never really examined one. Each strand formed a spoke fixed to each ring. But all were irregular. A pattern, yes, but each different. More geometric than circular. He'd never noticed before how different were each section of the web.

"...to care for him who shall have borne the battle and for his widow and his orphan, to do all which may achieve and cherish a just and lasting peace among ourselves and with all nations."

"And I thought I was a good preacher." Nathaniel joked lamely. "I wish I could preach that well. That's no speech. It's a sermon," he said, before he sipped some broth. The broth was lukewarm water with a spoon of grease mixed in. "By dread deeds…" His voice trailed off.

Valentine reached out and touched Nathaniel's arm. Nathaniel stirred.

"Don't worry. I will make it to see Alice and my babies, Val. I've got to. Things have to be said. It's not finished for either of us. We will get home. Besides, you old liar, there is one mother back home who needs to hear me say, 'I'm sorry,'"

"Only one?"

Another sip was followed by a long and hacking cough. Nathaniel's ribs ached. His joints throbbed. His hand instinctively reached into his waistcoat pocket for the missing pocket watch. "I miss her," Nathaniel muttered several times between the fever and chills. "Good Lord, I miss them." All the sad memories made him pause. "Sons shouldn't die. Babies shouldn't die. Mothers shouldn't die," he mumbled before he passed the cup to Valentine.

"We both have reason to get home. But mine no longer is West Chester," said O'Rourke as he poised the cup at his mouth. "When we get out of here," he said over the lip of the cup, turning his ear toward the distant sound of shelling. "I know exactly where I'm going. Since when was the home you love ever a place?" Nathaniel's steady breathing indicated that he had fallen asleep. "I refuse to let death win," he whispered under his breath. "But you, oldest friend, refuse to let hate win. Yes, your beautiful Alice was right about me."

Chapter Twenty-one

Angels Descending

So within a prison cell
We are waiting for the day
That shall come to open wide the iron door
And the hollow eyes grow bright
And the poor heart almost gay
And we think of seeing friends and home once more
"Tramp, Tramp, Tramp," George Root

The captives wondered how soon the flames would reach them. Only the most feverish slept, for they belonged to the comfort of oblivion. The rest of them waited. Simply waited. It had been a long night of waiting and watching. And listening. They had long ago embraced resignation as a necessary companion. It was easier if you just assumed you were going to die. They accepted that they were dead men. They just didn't know how they would die. Not if, but when and how. Some reached across the gap between their cots and held hands. A few of the sick sat up in their cots trying to breathe better. They clutched damp rags against their faces to filter out the smoke.

The most agitated in the room were the soldiers chosen to form the rear guard.

Before the Captain rode off, he had instructed the Sergeant to maintain order at all costs. Maintain order at all costs. Standard drill. The Sergeant looked blankly at his men as the Captain saluted them and galloped away intending to catch up with Commandant Turner. Rubbing the back of his thick neck, the Sergeant sighed when he inspected his threadbare command. Next he rubbed his temples, grumbling to himself: Ain't this the peach. And two years ago I rode with Stuart's Light Artillery. Hell of a war. And it all comes down to this. Damn near funny.

Three of his men could barely carry their muskets. The oldest of them had to be over seventy years old. The boy couldn't be older than twelve. Plus, the Captain left him the slackers and the whiners, the ones the Captain cared nothing for. The Sergeant shrugged. Standard drill? Did he really say that? Ain't nothin' standard today. Ain't nothin' standard no more.

None of his men moved. They never did take up their posts nor did he order them to. The Sergeant thought about it, even started giving the order, but he too found it pointless. He never finished the sentence. He just shrugged again and shouldered his musket, fingering the broken hammer. He and his men stood together on Cary Street. And they watched their beautiful city burn. The flames and worry finally urged them inside the prison.

Damn, the Sergeant swore to himself. What a dumb bastard I am. Should've gone with those boys when they said the hell with it and skedaddled away with the rest of the town. He pulled out his chew from his pocket and tore off a chunk with his last two molars.

With disgust he looked again at his at feeble command of six guards. They each realized they had nowhere else to go, themselves forlorn and forgotten, so they followed their Sergeant through the vacant rooms until they were drawn inexorably toward the companionship of the only room where people still were to be found. When they arrived at the open door of the hospital, their eyes asked direction from Doctor Semple, who alone among the Confederate medical staff remained. Semple calmly beckoned to them, welcoming them inside the hospital ward. "Make yourselves useful," was all he said.

Better to wait together than wait alone. The lanterns smoked from foul oil. The yellow light made the faces of the sick seem even sicker. The guards huddled near the stairs, nervously looking up and down the ward. The Sergeant sat down on the second step. Here was what his command had been chosen to guard, these remaining captives, these eighteen bed ridden prisoners, those too ill, too weak, too frail, too hopeless to have joined the hasty evacuation last week. Orphans. Orphans all of them. The Confederate Sergeant spat, missing the spittoon. So how come he had to be one of the chosen and left behind? Left behind to guard men who couldn't leave even if they wanted to. Some of them, bless them, weren't even aware of what they should want. Left behind to guard eighteen dying Yankees along with this Surgeon and preacher who, curse them, chose to remain behind with their dying men.

The guards stacked their muskets in the corner by the stairs and shifted around looking for something to do.

Nathaniel waved the Sergeant over to him. Earlier, smelling the danger, he had gathered up from the lower rooms, even from the Commandant's office, as many blankets, sheets, and large pieces of fabric he could find. "Here, Sergeant, if you and your men can find some way to attach them, let's cover the windows. I'm sure you'll find some nails downstairs in the carpenter's shop. I don't have the key."

"Right, preacher...," said the Sergeant, clucking his tongue. *So it comes to this? I'm taking orders from a preacher. Damn fool war.* The Sergeant signaled for two of his men to collect the nails and hammers. "Do what the man says," he said, tossing one of them a thick ring of keys. "Let's make it fast, Franklin, Hinson," he snapped. The soldiers stood there looking at him, arms at their sides, mouths open, slack-jawed. "Fast, you Georgia slackers!" With a jerk, the two Privates hustled from the room. The other soldiers teamed up and started piling up the blankets at the bottom of the windows. The Sergeant dragged a wooden chair to the wall.

"We should be safe," Semple assured the room in a soft monotone. "We are surrounded by vacant lots. We may suffer the smoke, but I doubt we need worry the flames."

A distant explosion belied his words. "Well, maybe not," Semple added with a wry smile. The blast thundered like a violent storm far off. Smaller explosions followed, each one growing fainter. The guards gathered at the windows and strained to see.

"By God," the Sergeant cussed through a mouthful of chew, staring out an eastern window. "It's the arsenal. Blast them! We're blowin' up our own munitions." Shaking his head, he turned toward Nathaniel, "It's all lost. It's all lost," he repeated. "Your troops must be close." Black juice dribbled into his beard.

Semple shook his head at Nathaniel, murmuring: "Who's the prisoner now?"

"Something is close, that's for sure," Nathaniel said. "I've got to see. Can't stand being closed up down here." Nathaniel slowly walked his way to the end of the room and pulled himself up by the railing onto the steps of the creaking wooden staircase. Halfway up he stopped and looked down at Valentine. Valentine, the pockets of his dirty and stained coat bulging, was seated at the edge of his wooden chair perched over a young man. The young man's dressing gown was wet from perspiration, his breathing labored. He wrung out a compress over the bucket of murky water next to the chair and soothed the young man's forehead. The wound in the young man's belly had stained through both dressing gown and bed sheet. Nathaniel looked down at his friend from the steps. "Take a rest, Val. He will be all right for now. Come on, don't you want to see?"

O'Rourke, intent on his patient, didn't bother looking up. His only answer was a dismissing wave of his dripping hand. Droplets splattered across the sheet.

Nathaniel continued up the two flights of steps. Reaching the upper 'Gettysburg Room,' as the prisoners had nicknamed this top section of the warehouse, he suddenly felt dizzy. He clung onto the worn banister and closed his eyes. The banister wobbled. Or was it his legs wobbling? Excitement had gotten the best of his own weakness. He blew through his mustache. He opened his eyes and stared into the empty room, the flickering glow from the fire outside exposing the old rags and worn pieces of uniforms piled up against the thick posts in the middle of the room. The room was littered with broken crates used as tables, upturned buckets, broken bottles, and clumps of mattress straw, the debris of hundreds of men confined for months, for years.

He steadied his head in his hands for a moment, swallowed a rising bile of nausea, blood, and phlegm, and then moved past the common sink toward the nearest barred window. Seven vertical bars, one horizontal bar. Smoke collected between the rafters of the low ceiling. Nathaniel pulled the lapel of his coat up over his mouth. His old frock coat: the buttons long gone, armpits torn out, collar frayed. With his other hand he gripped the coarse black iron bar and pressed his face against the bars to see. Waves of heat singed his face. He let go of the bar and removed his slouch hat to hold it in front of his face as a shield from the heat. Outside, the world burnt. Sounds of shouting could be barely discerned. The roar of the flame's fury whipped as buildings collapsed. A dragonfly hovered by his cheek before it darted farther inside the room.

Dibrell's Warehouse, one block away, had begun to blaze. Looking north across Cary Street, past the vacant lot, above the prison warehouse, the silhouette of Richmond spread out before him. What wasn't burning was smoldering. Gutters melted, stone work cracked, once handsome pillars turned to char, wrought iron railings imported from Northern foundries glowed red before they caked into pieces. The fire, like a fist, rose high, then crashed down. Fire like a thief crept its serpentine way wherever its greed would take it.

He staggered toward the south side of the room, tripping over an old boot, its sole torn out, and stood at a window to squint out the back of the warehouse prison across the canal and tow path along the James River. Across the river, Manchester was ablaze also. The water of the ever-flowing river reflected the mesmerizing flames of the burning ships, wavering, mirrored by the current. A double-masted packet, once used as a flag of truce ship in prisoner exchanges, had pitched over onto its side letting the river extinguish the fires. Only its bow and the top of the foremast, itself nearly touching the water, still burned. Farther away the *Patrick Henry* had been scuttled. Movement on the bridges pulled his eyes away from the dance of the flames reflected by the river. Dark figures raced against the backdrop of light along the bridges, some figures carrying torches. They were in haste to destroy it all. As a final gesture of defiance and despair these bridges were set to the torch. And the fox will gnaw off his own leg when caught in the teeth of metal trap. This was the desperation of the lost, destroying that which they cherished dearest to prevent its ruin at the hands of others who did not love what they loved. Destroying what you love. Smoke and ashes, smearing and smothering the clear sky, obscured the stars except for a single star close to the water's edge which shone brightly through the haze.

A deafening explosion thrusted Nathaniel from the barred window. A barge down river heaved a foot off the water with a burst of gunpowder and ball of flame. The hull thudded back into the river with a thick splash, extinguishing the fire in a cruel hiss. Sparks swirled in the wind, several whirling through the window and landing on Nathaniel's black frock coat and the plank flooring. With a hacking cough, Nathaniel swept the sparks off his coat and pressed the embers on the floor with the heel of his shoes. A last spark he extinguished by dragging it toward him with his toe.

Two figures walked deliberately, calmly, across the last remaining bridge. These figures poured fluid from cans, then pushed their torches onto the wood. They strolled. By the time they reached the Richmond shoreline, the wooden portion of the bridge was totally engulfed, billowing darkening smoke.

Within minutes the bridge heaved, creaked, twisted, and collapsed between its stone piers, surrendering itself to the water. The debris of sizzling wreckage and ruin floated downstream past Libby Prison. The river was choked with carcasses of horses, burnt timbers, broken oars, and fragments of ships and gunboats.

He was so very tired. His fingers gradually released their hold on the bars and he drifted to the floor, where he leaned his back against the wall beneath the window. There he slept, until a hand shook him by the shoulder. The familiar voice called out to him, "Wake up, Nate." Nathaniel found himself being lifted to the window. With his arm supporting him, Valentine said: "Come. See. It's time. Those are our troops. Can't you hear them? God, I do believe now it's finally done."

Nathaniel rubbed his eyes. Nathaniel peered out the window into a red morning smudged by smoke and soot. He silently asked: Done? I wonder. He reached his arm back around his friend's shoulders. Instead of inhaling a deep breath he coughed a bloody cough. Resting his temple against the side of Valentine's head, he chuckled softly. "I doubt it. Maybe. For some. It will be enough for me to hear their voices again." His face felt the wind beginning to rise. His hand reached for his watch. He frowned.

"Listen, Nate," said Valentine. "Why don't you go get something to eat? While you're at it, bring whatever you can scrounge back up to the men. Semple said there might be some acorns and lard for a mash. Grab the Sergeant. He's got the keys. We also could use some clean water if you can find any."

☺☺☺

The Sergeant found it odd that the kitchen door was already unlocked. As soon as the Sergeant pushed opened the door, Dick Turner turned and stared at them. The kitchen fireplace roared from the papers and ledgers he already had flung into the fire. Other ledgers he held in his arm. Feathery ashes fluttered about the kitchen. The surprise on his face squeezed into contempt when he saw Nathaniel standing behind the Sergeant. "Sergeant, hol' him!" ordered Turner.

The Sergeant scratched his head and looked back and forth between the two men, sizing them up. Then the Sergeant sat down at the kitchen table and pulled a chew.

"Looks like it's just you and me," said Nathaniel. "So, where's our good Commandant? Left you to answer for him?"

"He's halfway to Lee's headquarters," Dick Turner sneered. "Meebe' halfway to Cuba. He always said he wanted to visit Havana."

"Hmmp. And you didn't take off with him? I always thought you two made such a perfect pair," Nathaniel said, suppressing a cough.

"I dids my duty. He nevah' did his."

"And you did it very well," Nathaniel said as he removed his coat. "You know, I already have forgiven poor Seward. The man was scared. Poor Seward. Crazed and hurt because of you. I can't condemn the wounded ones. Which is why I can even forgive you, Dick," he said with a pity mixed with indignation. "But that doesn't mean I won't stop you. I may be weak but I got strength enough left in me. We will need these records for your trial. Besides," he added with a wry smile as he tugged on his torn and threadbare waistcoat, "you have something of mine."

"Sergeant!" cried Turner, throwing the ledgers at Nathaniel, who swatted them aside. Turner tugged at his LeMat revolver. Nathaniel lunged and grabbed his arm, forcing him backwards. The blast from the revolver burnt the side of his face. Turner wrenched the pistol away. Its walnut grip slammed into the Nathaniel's cheek. The spur of the trigger guard gouged open Nathaniel's old wound.

It only took one punch. Right in the stomach. Nathaniel's punch doubled up Turner. For satisfaction more than necessity, Nathaniel hammered him down on his shoulder-blade with his right fist. Turner crumpled to the floor which was littered with pieces of paper and ash. The Sergeant followed Nathaniel's eyes as Nathaniel peered over at the iron poker leaning against the stonework of the fireplace, but Nathaniel muttered to himself with a vague relief: "Enough. Too many dead sons." Instead, Nathaniel knelt down beside him, patted Turner down, and reclaimed what was his. In Turner's outside coat pocket he found a tin of quality chew which he tossed over to the Sergeant.

"Would you mind unbolting the cell, Sergeant?" said a panting Nathaniel.

"A right pleasure, preacher. Never did like the son of a bitch. Weren' no real soldier."

Nathaniel dragged Turner's body by his belt across the threshold of the cell, saying to the groggy man: "Trust me, I've been there. It'll be good for your soul."

The oak door creaked shut and the Sergeant slid tight the iron bolt.

In the darkness, a dazed Turner reached up and grabbed the edge of the tub to try to pull himself up, but the tub tipped over, spilling weeks of shit and piss.

◎◎◎

The men in the hospital room looked up as Nathaniel entered the room carrying a canvas sack of acorns and a wooden bowl filled with lard. Blood streaked his beaming face. Behind him trailed the Sergeant lugging two buckets of clean water.

"What the hell happened to you?" asked Valentine. Then he too grinned as soon as he spotted the blue cameo dangling on a silver chain from his friend's waistcoat pocket.

Author's Note

Nathaniel's journey probably started, as it likely did for many young boys, with a Christmas gift of <u>The Golden Book of The Civil War</u>, by the Editors of American Heritage, with an introduction by Bruce Catton. It would be impossible to number the times I, caught up in the illusion of the romance of war, sat in bed or at my desk imagining myself one of those tiny cartoon soldiers in those battlefield drawings (always a dashing officer, often one armed from a prior wound from a prior grand adventure—the empty sleeve nobly yet tragically pinned—always valiant and saving the day—and the ladies always swooned). That same young boy read as many books about the Civil War as he could scavenger at the Fanwood Public Library. Flash back with me to a family trip to Gettysburg in the early sixties and you'll find that same boy correcting the Park Ranger on his facts. There is a fine line between obnoxious and informed, or so my older brothers often reminded me by beating me up.

Then there were the Grandmas and their stories: Grandma Andrews taking me upstairs to the ancient attic to share with me my Great-grandfather Joseph's Civil War diary and sword; and Granny Young telling me tales of her Uncle Nappy (yes, there really was a Valentine, her uncle Napoleon Valentine) who rode with Sheridan as part of the Lincoln Cavalry. Granny was very proud that the Union's finest horsemen came from the Valentine homestead: Brooklyn, New York. Granny Young also told me the tales of the other side of her family, stories she heard from her Grandmother when she, the ill and aging Mary

Rebecca Rush Dickson, had to move north from Greenville, South Carolina, to sojourn among the Yankees. She kept her portrait of Robert E. Lee prominently displayed in her bedroom. Granny told me whenever she heard Sherman's name spoken, she, despite being a devout Christian, would mutter a few unkind words under her breath. All that remained from the Dickson plantation after the Yankees paid a call was a silver basket that her mother hid in the hollow of a tree, now to be found on my dining room table.

Nathaniel's Call is purely a fictional account of an authentic Civil War Regiment and its distinguished service during that terrible war. Though many of the characters are my invention to help spin this tale, many of the other characters you will meet in these pages are men and women of our actual history and heritage. Gurley, Semple, and Van Lew represent the civilians. Talley, Bear, Coates, Roberts, Rupert, Barber, Chapin, Chilson, Ressler, Waggoner, and Harvey were men enrolled upon the roster of the Thirtieth Regiment, First Reserves. I have endeavored to have written accurately about each one's rank and tour of service. McCandless, Stroughton, and that unnamed Colonel whom Nathaniel meets at the battle of Gettysburg wore the uniform of the Army of the Potomac. Ewell, Stuart, Parkhill, Turner, Turner, and Mosby were soldiers in the Southern cause. I hope and pray that their ghosts and their descendents will either appreciate or forgive my literary license and liberty at how I have presented their personalities and contributions.

Acknowledgments

I am indebted to the following source material for this novel:

- William Jennings Bryan, Editor in Chief, <u>The World's Famous Orations, Volumn IX</u>, Funk and Wagnalls, 1906
- William C. Davis and Bell I. Wiley, Editors, <u>The Civil War: The Compact Edition, Vicksburg to Appomattox</u>, Black Dog and Leventahl Publishers, 1994
- Horace Greely, <u>The American Conflict: A History of the Great Rebellion in the United States of America 1860-1865</u>, O. D. Case and Company, 1866
- David T. Hedrick and Gordon Barry Davis, Jr., Editors, <u>I'm Surrounded by Methodists...Diary of John H. W. Stuckenberg, Chaplain of the 145th Pennsylvania Volunteer Infantry</u>, Thomas Publications, 1995
- William B. Hesseltine, Edtior, <u>Civil War Prisons</u>, the Kent State University Press, 1997
- James Hoobler, <u>Cities Under the Gun</u>, Rutledge Hill Press, 1986
- Louis Le Grand, M.D., <u>The Military Hand-Book and Soldier's Manual of Information</u>, Beadle and Company, 1861
- Leon Litwak, <u>Been in the Storm So Long: The Aftermath of Slavery</u>, Alfred A. Knopf, Inc., 1979
- James M. McPherson, <u>Battle Cry of Freedom: The Civil War Era</u>, Oxford University Press, 1988

- N. Minnigh, <u>History of Company K. 1st (Inft.) Penn'a Reserves</u>, "Home Print" Publisher
- Elton Trueblood, <u>Abraham Lincoln: A Spiritual Biography</u>, Phoenix Press, 1986
- Alice Rains Trulock, <u>In the Hands of Providence: Joshua L. Chamberlain</u> and the American Civil War, the University of North Carolina Press, 1992
- http://www.magorman.com for material about Libby Prison and archival reprints from the *Richmond Sentinel* and the *Richmond Dispatch*

I also am greatly indebted to the following persons for their valuable assistance:

- The staff at the Medical Library of Geisinger Medical Center, in particular, Dr. Britain Roth (now retired) and Kathy Heilman, for their knowledge of Civil War era medicine
- Dr. David S. Franklin, Surgeon in Chief at Geisinger Health System, for his friendship and his expertise in amputations
- Dr. William Gibson, retired Surgeon, Geisinger Medical Center, for his medical advice as well as his general though skewed knowledge of what he insists on calling the 'War of Northern Aggression'
- The West Chester State College for use of their copy of Bate's *History of the Pennsylvania Volunteers*, 1869-1971

We salute also Chaplain Jeffrey Young (Colonel-Retired), a fellow classmate from Princeton Seminary. We thank him for confirming the special role of military Chaplains at wartime. Jeff finished his 30 years of military service in the Pentagon as the Personnel Director for the Army Chief of Chaplains. Jeff represents the best of love of God and love of country. For God and Country. We are grateful for service rendered by such inspiring men and women who "honor the sacred in each person." We thank them for their duty and devotion. Jeff himself wrote how "it is crucial that Chaplains help to sustain the spiritual resilience of our Army, that we have a sacred trust to care for America's sons and daughters in America's military; they are our most treasured resource."

Further expressions of appreciation must go to the congregations of the Penningtonville Presbyterian Church and the Grove Presbyterian Church for their support and patience. It has been an honor to serve as their pastor. They have shown me what being a pastor really means, as well as how to mature religion into faithfulness.

For every novel there are critics and editors. Despite their painful comments and recommendations, I could not have accomplished this good work without their insights. My heartfelt thanks go to Dr. Fred Jones for his medical corrections, my brothers Larry and Ricky Andrews, Roland Seward, George Humbert, Molly and John Chapman, Jim Walters, mentor David Vogan, Edward Nichols (he of the theological eye) and my daughter, Margaret Andrews (she of the vengeful red pen).

For this final draft I am truly indebted to Christina Schooley for her careful review of each page, and to Spring Taylor for serving as my electronic shepherd and guide.

It is with great pride that my son's artistic talents are on display as <u>Nathaniel's Call</u> book jacket.

Last, I thank my patient, charming, and lovely wife, Elaine, for being Nathaniel's Alice.

About the Author

Robert John Andrews has written columns for the Danville (PA) News since 1998, writing social commentary, historical pieces, and human interest columns with a spiritual twist. He currently is in his twenty-third year serving as the pastor of the Grove Presbyterian Church in Danville, Pennsylvania. His first parish, and the inspiration for the novel, was the Penningtonville Presbyterian Church, Atglen Pennsylvania, where he served after his graduation from Princeton Theological Seminary in 1978 until his relocation to the Grove Church in 1989.

Andrews' other writings can be found on his website: http://www.robertjohnandrews.com. He is the father of three grown children, Margaret, McKenna and Penelope, and resides in Danville with his wife Elaine.

The book jacket art is provided by graphic illustrator McKenna Andrews, whose other work can be found via: http://www.macink.deviantart.com.

CPSIA information can be obtained at www.ICGtesting.com
Printed in the USA
LVOW080306250412

279052LV00001B/78/P